PRAISE FOR EVER DUNDAS

"If you like your near future sci-fi dystopia delivered straight up, then HellSans *will pull you into a dark, brilliantly imagined world. We are lucky to have Ever Dundas' inimitable talent, HellSans' rage, love and sorrow is perfectly contained!"*

Jenni Fagan, bestselling author of *Luckenbooth*

"This terrific book; a dark and clever sci-fi social satire."

Joanne Harris, author of *Chocolat*

"Clever, terrifying, and full of love and rage – I'm deeply jealous."

Mat Osman, author of *The Ruins*

*"*HellSans *is speculative fiction at its best: political, fearless, smart, badass. And also with tons of horrific body horror and cruelty from just about everyone. To put it down is unthinkable, you care about everything and everyone all the time."*

Mariana Enriquez, author of International Booker shortlisted *The Dangers of Smoking in Bed*

"In my opinion, the best debut fiction by a Scottish author since 2012. Profoundly affecting, intellectually challenging and beautifully written. An instant classic of modern mythology."

Stuart Kelly for *The Scotsman* on *Goblin*

*"Terrific… *Goblin* brims throughout with reckless joy."*

Peter Ross for *The Guardian* on *Goblin*

"Enthralling... a captivating debut... Dundas presents us with an iconic protagonist: a powerful imaginative force who looks beyond the façade of 20th Century Britain."

Alastair Mabbott

Ever Dundas

HELLSANS

ANGRY
ROBOT

ANGRY ROBOT
An imprint of Watkins Media Ltd

Unit 11, Shepperton House
89 Shepperton Road
London N1 3DF
UK

angryrobotbooks.com
twitter.com/angryrobotbooks
Reading is Hell

An Angry Robot paperback original, 2022

Cover by Kate Cromwell
Edited by Simon Spanton and Travis Tynan
Set in Meridien and ~~HellSans~~ Helvetica

ISBN 978 1 91520 221 5
Ebook ISBN 978 1 91520 226 0

Printed and bound in the United Kingdom by TJ Books Ltd.

9 8 7 6 5 4 3 2 1

For Cherry Bee of the North
Cinnamon Curtis
all queer crips
and people with ME who have endured
decades of cruelty and neglect

with love and rage

"I ate civilisation. It poisoned me."
Aldous Huxley, Brave New World

"Man, you shall repent of the injuries you inflict."
Mary Shelley, Frankenstein

Note: The first two parts, "Jane" and "Icho", can be read in an order of the reader's choosing.

A sans-serif typeface is used on occasion; it is not HellSans and should not cause an allergic reaction.

HELLSANS

PART ONE OR TWO

ICHO

PROLOGUE

He hooked his hands under my armpits and pulled me up. Now that I was free, I thought to push him, knee him in the groin, elbow to the face, anything; but my limbs didn't obey, my legs collapsed. He caught me, as if he were saving me. His arm around my waist, he half-dragged me to the HSA quarters. We entered one of the rooms and he kicked the HSA body off the blood-spattered cot before laying me down in its place, my head resting in blood, brains, scraps of skull, scalp, and hair. I watched him walk away. The clear door slid into place and locked. I closed my eye but immediately saw the knife coming for me. I stared at the ceiling. All I could smell was blood and vomit. Rolling my head to the side, I stared at the dead HSA. I thought of clawing my way into their body, breaking off a bone and stabbing it into an artery. By the time he returned I'd be gone; taking myself out meant he wouldn't have access to Jaw's records. I knew Jaw would disapprove, but I lay there and thought about which bone to use.

CHAPTER 1

Tipsy, I walked down the stairs of Caddick's country mansion, Jaw hurrying in front of me, propelled by some kind of ridiculous urgency it wouldn't tell me about. I fell into the car, Jaw giving our destination.

"I honestly don't know what's wrong with you tonight. There's no need to whisk me away like I'm Cinderella, for bliss sake."

"It's now morning, and I need to show you something from the party."

"It can wait until we're back."

"It's urgent."

"Something from the party is urgent? I doubt that."

"Icho–"

"Jaw, just leave it. OK? I'm tired," I said, my head swimming. "I'll watch it when we're back at the lab."

"As soon as we're back."

I nodded and turned away, smiling as I thought about meeting Jane Ward, the feel of her hand in mine as she greeted me. I stared out the window, but it was all darkness as we moved through the acres of forest on Caddick's estate. I shifted focus and looked at my face reflected in the window. The normally silver scar slicing down my cheek had turned pink from alcohol-induced vasodilation. I looked at the rest of the scarring on my upper arm: angry vermillion. I was impressed Jane hadn't quizzed me on it; most people demanded to know what happened and why I hadn't had the scars treated. Tired of constant interrogation, I had a list of go-to replies: shark attack, tortured by Seraphs, cut myself shaving, chemical accident, self-harm, slipped in the shower, kidnapped by aliens, alligator wrestling – that usually left people speechless, uncomfortable, or pissed off when they realised I was messing with them; either way it ended the conversation on my terms.

I turned back to Jaw and flinched as I looked at it how Jane might have. Their velvety Inex skin came in an array of colours; I'd chosen a baby blue. I'd always loved Inex accessories, and I enjoyed dressing Jaw for different occasions. For the party I'd put it in a black sequinned jacket that swamped its slender eight-inch-tall frame. I'd chosen pink eye chips, silver star stickers spread across its cheek, a sparkling, star-patterned tiara topping it all off. Jaw sat inert, looking like some kind of odd doll, and I felt ashamed; a grown woman shouldn't be playing dress-up with their Inex.

"Everyone does it," said Jaw, its big round head turning, the pink eyes looking up at me, its spidery arm reaching out, laying a soft hand on mine.

"Jane doesn't," I said, thinking of Jane's grey-skinned Inex: no clothes, no accessories, permanent blue eye chips. "I saw the way she looked at you. She thinks I'm frivolous."

"You enjoy dressing me. You shouldn't change yourself to seek Jane's approval. And you don't need to; it was clear she liked you."

"Was it? Really?"

"Yes."

I turned back to the window, staring into the deep darkness of the forest as I thought of Jane. The trees soon gave way to an open bypass, only a handful of other cars on the roads at this late hour. I was tempted to detour to the city, thinking of the creature comforts of my apartment, but my lab was more convenient, allowing me to roll out of bed and get straight to work. Coming off the bypass, I watched warehouses and factories slide by. I passed those owned by The Company, with huge photos of an Inex and "**HELLING YOU BE THE BEST YOU**" emblazoned across them in bold HellSans. Because of the proximity to the ghetto, armed guards were stationed outside.

As we passed a couple of police car patrols, I was aware of Jaw in my periphery, climbing up the car window and onto the roof just above me. I glanced up as Jaw's tongue flicked out, snatching up a fly.

"You don't have to hunt," I said. "The car has snacks."

I fished a packet of Company Inex food out of the box in front of me, the car immediately adding it to my bill. Jaw crawled down from the ceiling, took the packet, and sat next to me. We arrived at my lab just as Jaw finished eating.

As I got out of the car and walked to the entrance of the warehouse, I thought about how lucky I was to have my dream job, in charge of a lab, with only an Ino, MedEx, and Jaw assisting, free to work how I pleased. There was only the occasional report to Caddick, but that was easy when Jaw did all my admin.

Jaw gained us entry and I walked through the cavernous warehouse, moonlight streaming in through one of the far corner windows. It should have been unnerving, but I always found the dark, isolated warehouse comforting. As I walked downstairs and into the basement lab my thoughts turned to Jane again and I frowned, remembering telling her that I'd named Jaw in her honour: "Jane Angelina Ward," I'd said. "Oh," she'd responded. "I see. How nice."

"Jesus," I said, entering the lab. "Jaw, you're right. I had far too much to drink – if you admire someone and want to meet them as an equal, don't act like a goddamn fan."

"That's the least of your worries," said Jaw. "You need to–"

"Oh God," I said, my head fuzzy, trying to remember how exactly it played out, how she'd reacted. "What else did I say?"

"It's all there for you to see. But I need to show you something else first. It's important."

"OK, OK, but give me a minute. I'm not feeling great."

"You drank too much."

"I know."

I walked through the lab to my office where I'd set up a camp bed. I'd pretty much abandoned my city apartment and spent twenty-four seven here; it was bliss: silence and work, work and silence. I enjoyed absolute focus and no human interaction – unless you counted the lab HSAs.

I dug out a t-shirt from my desk drawer. Unzipping my dress, I said, "Project my conversation with Jane."

"You said you'd watch what I need to show you."

"Jane first, OK?"

"Icho, we need to discuss–"

"I will. I just need to get changed, grab a coffee, and get my head straight. Project my conversation with Jane."

I threw my party clothes in the corner for the Ino to deal with later and pulled on the t-shirt. I glanced up at the projection as I stuck my head into the lab and summoned the Ino.

"Coffee!"

It had been waiting silently in the corner and I watched it unfurl and move towards the small kitchen just off the lab. The Ino was sixteen inches tall, grounded like early model Inexes, and all of them were boring as hell, only coming in dull colours and lacking accessories. Its face was more angular than the Inex and it had one personality. It was designed to barely exist, to complete chores quietly and without disruption. The Ino did so much so efficiently that I often forgot what it did.

I went back into the office, flopped on my bed, and stared at Jane's figure taking up the whole of the south wall.

"I fucked it up, didn't I?" I said, thinking about when I told her why Jaw was Jaw.

"You didn't," said Jaw. "I'm sure she was flattered."

"You think so? I'll dial it down a bit when I meet her for dinner. You need to be my inner censor, Jaw – keep me from making a fool of myself."

"It will help if you don't drink so much; you ignore me when you drink."

"I was nervous. It helped."

"But now it's seemingly worse."

I smiled. "Touché, Jaw. Touché."

"You need to watch a conversation with–"

"I will. Just let me see this first. Oh, God – what if *she* replays it? But why would she? But she could if she wanted to. Maybe meeting your heroes is just a really bad idea."

The Ino came in and handed me the coffee.

"Perfect," I said, wrapping my hands around the mug.

It disappeared back into the lab, and I sat with my back against the wall, legs tucked under me. I sipped the coffee and watched Jane closely after everything I said.

"It's good to meet you, Dr Smith."

We shook hands.

"And you. In fact, I'm a big fan of yours."

"Pause."

Jaw paused it and I leaned forward, smiling.

"She's checking me out, right? It's not just me, she's… Well, I guess it could be the HellSans dress, she's just taking in some bliss, but…"

I stared at her, paused as she was shifting her weight from one foot to the other, drink tipped slightly, head cocked, hooded eyes on me, lingering on the HellSans text winding round my dress. I wondered if she recognised the text, but her expression gave nothing away. I contemplated her, coiffed perfection as always; tailored black dress with small ruffs at the shoulders, bare muscular arms, her blonde hair pulled back in a tight bun. Her Inex stood next to her on the floor, its blue eyes fixed on me too.

"OK, resume."

"Is that right?"

"Yes, all you've done, setting up The Company, the success of the first Inex model. I even named Jaw after you."

I gestured to my Inex.

She looked uncertain, so I clarified: "Jane Angelina Ward."

"Oh, I see. How nice."

There was an awkward silence as we both sipped our drinks.

"I said to Jaw I wouldn't embarrass myself if I had a chance to meet you, but it seems I've blown that."

"Don't worry. I appreciate it, thank you."

"Pause," I said. "Her smile looks strained. I definitely put her off. Thank bliss I didn't buy her voice for you, Jaw."

I'd considered purchasing it, despite the expense, but the thought of Jane's voice emanating from Jaw made me uneasy. I chose a regular directory woman's voice instead, scrolling through accents and tones until I hit on one I liked.

I asked Jaw to continue.

"I've collected Inexes for years and I have a number of the early models on display back in my office. When I'm struggling with work I sometimes tinker with them."

"Tinker?"

"Yes, I mean, I did a couple of the Inex modules at uni, before specialising. I almost went in that direction, but now it's just a hobby; helps me relax."

"I'm glad the Inexes offer you some down time. How is your work coming along? Caddick tells me you're working on a cure for the HellSans Allergic."

"I, well…"

"You are, aren't you?"

"I don't–"

I looked panicked, checking nearby Inexes to see if they were focused on us. Jane laughed.

"Oh, don't worry."

She moved close to me and took one of my hands in hers.

"Pause," I said, and stared at her pressed up close to me, her hand on mine. I remembered her smell and how I was so tempted to put my arm around her.

"Resume."

"I know all about it."

She said this so quietly my Inex had barely picked it up.

"I really don't know what you–"

I was saved by a waiter offering hors d'oeuvres.

"Made with our finest farm meats."

He held out the tray to us and Jane let go of my hand.

"Farm?"

"Nothing but the best," Jane said, taking one and popping it in her mouth.

"I've never had farm meats before – actual living animals. It seems…"

"Never? Just taste it. There's a bloody earthiness you don't get with lab meat. All produced at the highest standards of welfare and hygiene, of course."

She picked one off the tray and held it at my mouth.

"Oh God, my face."

I opened my mouth and she placed it on my tongue, my lips brushing her fingers. She watched me as I chewed and swallowed.

"It's delicious. Though, I don't think I'd know the difference if I hadn't been told…"

The waiter held the tray at me expectantly, so I took another. Jane picked up two more and the waiter left us.

"You're good."

"Sorry?"

"Trustworthy. You're right not to talk about your work. But you should know, Caddick tells me everything."

"I know you're close. I really don't mean to offend you, but this isn't the place I can discuss it." I gestured to all the people and Inexes around us.

She smiled. "You're right not to, Ichorel. I was teasing. If you don't mind me asking, how old are you?"

"Twenty-four."

"You've achieved a lot for someone so young."

"Well, my Inex helps me be the best I can be."

Jane laughed. "You're a charmer, Ichorel." She looked over my shoulder and said, "James!"

She hugged a scruffy man dressed in black, giving him a kiss on the cheek.

"Icho, this is James." Jane put her arm around his shoulder, squeezing him to her. He looked awkward in her embrace, like he wasn't used to people touching him, but he smiled. "My best friend."

"Good to meet you," I said, shaking his hand. I tried to look him in the eye, but he stared down at our hands, then back at Jane.

"Icho has only just tried real meat. Can you believe that?"

"Don't listen to her," he said. "Lab meat is just as 'real', and it doesn't taste any different. It's all affectation; rich people and their luxuries. It's morbid, if you ask me."

"You just don't know quality."

I studied him, their voices drifting in and out of focus. He was nervy, dressed in ill-fitting faded black clothes, frayed at the edges. He was handsome, with sharp, alert eyes, but it was hard to see past his awkwardness; he seemed to writhe beneath his own skin, a constant sense of movement that leaked into the atmosphere around him, a contagious jitteriness. His black, unwashed hair kept falling into his face. I glanced at Jane, realising she'd been watching me watching him.

"I don't know why I let you persuade me to come," he said, looking around him. "I really need to be getting back to work."

"C'mon, man!" said Jane. I raised my eyebrows, surprised at the way she acted with him. "Relax. I know how hard you work."

"I don't like crowds, you know that."

"Just – grab another beer and go find that cute woman from HR."

James looked at her, surprised. "She's here?"

"Of course," said Jane, smiling smugly. "I invited her for you."

"You're a shit," said James and I choked on my drink.

"You OK?" said Jane.

"Yes, I'm just, it's strong–"

"No one talks to me like that, right?"

"Well…"

"We worked together. From the beginning. We've been through a lot. You don't forget that." She squeezed James's arm, smiling at him affectionately.

She looked past him and gestured. A waiter approached and Jane pried James's empty beer from his fingers and swapped it for two shot glasses.

"Down these and go find the HR woman. I want to hear all about it tomorrow."

The waiter was about to disappear into the crowd, but Jane raised a finger and they stopped, hovering. James downed the shots, placing them back on the tray. He took a third and downed that too. Jane smiled and shooed the waiter.

"Right?"

"Right." He was about to leave when he remembered me. "It was good to meet you, Icho."

"You too."

I watched him edge through the crowd, all hunched, dishevelled and completely out of place. I looked back at Jane, who was staring at me. I laughed, nervous.

"I'm sorry, I just–"

"An unlikely best friend, I know. I love him," Jane said, so emphatic it was as if she'd conjured the words in bold, underlined, italicised HellSans. "We've been through a lot together. When you get to where I am you don't know who to trust." She paused, staring at me. "But I can trust him. With anything."

"That's... well, beautiful, actually. That you have that."

Jane smiled. "It is. I'm lucky."

We fell into silence and I sipped my drink, trying to think of something to say when she said, "Right, I really must get over and talk to Kevin Mayor, if you'll excuse me, Dr Smith?"

"Of course, of course."

"It's been a pleasure. I'll have to have you over for dinner sometime with Caddick – I'd love to hear about your work. Are you free next week?"

"I – Yes, I should be."

"I'll be in touch."

She took a hold of me, her hands resting gently on my shoulders as she leaned in and kissed my cheek. She was gone before I could say anything else.

"Now the conversation I've been trying to get you to watch," said Jaw, jerking me out of my reverie.

"What? Oh, right. Just... Wait a second, will you?"

"Icho–"

"Just a second, Jaw."

I sat contemplating my encounter with Jane, thinking about meeting her for dinner, thrilled at the thought of seeing her again so soon.

Jaw broke in: "This is something you really need to hear."

"OK, OK, what is it?"

"At the party last night, you saw Caddick leave the room–"

I nodded, "Yeah, he likes his cigars."

"And you asked me to get him, when you were cornered by Steve and his colleagues after Jane left you; you told me to approach Caddick and say 'Steve Hendricks' and he'd understand and come rescue you."

"I knew it would make him laugh; he can't stand the insufferable bore either. So what? What's this got to do with anything?"

The projection resumed, showing the hallway outside the reception, as my Inex went to fetch Caddick from the balcony. I heard their voices first.

"It was mine, Caddick. It was mine and you took it away from me."

"Your skills are better utilised elsewhere."

"Don't give me that shit. I laid the groundwork and you just handed it over to that upstart bitch."

I couldn't hear Caddick's response – a group of people from the reception came out into the hall, talking and laughing.

"Who's Caddick speaking to?" I said as Jaw approached the balcony where Caddick and the other man stood, smoking cigars. All I could see was his back, until the man turned away from the view and faced Caddick.

"Dr West. What are they talking about?"

"You," said Jaw.

"Me?"

"I know she's on her own – just like I was, so there's no

one to corroborate. Just an Inex you'll have destroyed, back-ups erased. Everything's so goddamn easy for you, isn't it, Caddick? Well, let me tell you this: it will be just as easy to get rid of her."

Caddick sighed. "And why would I do that, West?"

"The Daedalus Project."

Caddick stiffened. He'd been completely relaxed until then, staring out across the grounds of his mansion. He turned to West, his voice hard. "What? What did you say?"

Dr West laughed and waved his cigar at him, ash scattering across Caddick's jacket. "Ha! See now, see; I have your attention now, don't I?"

"What do you know, West?"

"I know," he said, pausing to suck on his cigar, "that people are going to be appalled – you say one thing and do another. The Christian lobby – you'll lose their support in an instant. And you really can't afford that, can you, Caddick?"

"Are you threatening me?"

"Now you listen to me," he said, moving close to Caddick, his voice lowered, "You get rid of Dr Smith. I started that research and I'm going to finish it – I'm going to get my due. I have ambition, Prime Minister, *sir*," he said, spittle landing on Caddick's face, "and you think I'm just going to sit back while you fuck me over and let that bitch get all the glory. You go to the lab tomorrow and you get rid of her, just like you got rid of me. Or the whole goddamn country finds out what you've been up to. And don't think I haven't protected myself; don't think you can just–"

"What are you doing?"

The recording stopped and I stared at the blank wall of my office.

"Who was that? Why did you stop?"

"It was an Ino," said Jaw. "It ushered me back into the reception hall. That's when I spoke to you and told you to leave."

"I don't – I don't understand what this… I know I took over from West, but I thought it was his choice to move on."

"That's what Caddick implied in your first meeting."

Jaw projected it, Caddick sitting in his office telling me that:

"Dr West has started work on it, but this isn't his field of expertise and I need him on something else. You're the best, Icho."

"I don't want to step on anyone's toes."

"West? Don't worry about him. He'll be relieved to move on, believe me."

I looked at Jaw. "West wants me out. And he has something on Caddick – what was it he said?"

"The Daedalus Project."

"What is it? Why did Caddick react like that?"

"You don't look well."

I nodded, feeling cold and sweaty.

"You drank too much," said Jaw. "I warned you."

I rushed over to the toilet just off the office and leaned over it, retching. Nothing came, and I sat there for a few minutes, eyes closed, the nausea slowly subsiding. I stood up, unsteady, and leaned on the sink. I splashed cold water on my face and walked back through to the office, drying my face with a towel.

"I can't believe this is happening. I'm going to lose everything? Because of that weaselling bastard?"

Jaw nodded. "It's possible, but we don't know how Caddick will respond."

I sat down on my camp bed. "Replay the part where West says – where he talks about me being on my own…"

"I know she's on her own – just like I was, so there's no

one to corroborate. Just an Inex you'll have destroyed, back-ups erased. Everything's so–"

"Pause."

I shivered, genuinely unnerved as I stared at West's profile, his mouth open mid-sentence. I thought about the cavernous warehouse, the lab only populated by five HSAs, an Ino, MedEx, Jaw, and me. There was no feeling of comfort this time. I was keenly aware of how isolated I was.

"No," I said, shaking my head.

"Icho–"

"No, I won't let him." I stood and paced. "I won't let either of them. I'm not going to allow myself to be swept up in their fucking power games. Do they think I'd let all this go, after all my work, after all I've done?"

"We don't know what will come of this. We don't know Caddick's response."

"I'm vulnerable, Jaw."

"That is true. You are."

I stared at Jaw, uncertain, then sat down at my desk, head in hands. I sat like that for a few minutes, thinking it through. I looked up. "How were you able to share that with me?"

"It was a public event, I hadn't exceeded our distance limit, and if a privacy agreement had been made between Caddick and Dr West's Inexes, I wasn't party to it."

I nodded and thought about the conversation. "But I can't use it," I said. "If I shared it, it wouldn't make much sense to anyone. No one apart from Caddick, West, and Jane Ward know I'm doing this research. And who the hell knows what the Daedalus Project is? There's nothing there I can work with." I stared at Jaw. "What am I going to do?"

"We just need to make sure you're safe and the research isn't jeopardised."

"'Just'."

"We'll work something out."

I nodded, stood, rushed back to the toilet, and threw up.

I woke up to a blinding headache and fuzzy mouth. I asked my Inex to turn on the lights and dim them. I opened my eyes a little. "What time is it?"

"Twelve fourteen and eleven seconds."

"Shit!" I sat up. "Seriously?"

"I'm always serious."

"Why did you let me sleep in, for bliss sake?"

"We're not connected and you did not instruct me to wake you."

I stared at the ITG387 model and said, "You're right."

"Yes, I stated a fact."

"That you did. Get the Ino to bring me water. I feel awful."

"If we were connected, I could monitor your needs."

"It's just a hangover. I'll survive."

"I don't know if you'll survive," it said. "If we were connected, I could monitor you to ascertain if you consumed toxic levels."

I squinted at the Inex. "I'm not connecting."

"If you're hungover and dehydrated, your brain function will be impaired. I suggest a relaxed schedule for today."

"Don't alter my schedule. I'll be fine. I just need something to eat."

"We can reassess your schedule later this afternoon."

The Ino came in with water. I told it to make me some breakfast and I sat drinking the water as it left.

"I've only been awake a few minutes and I already miss Jaw."

"What is Jaw?"

"Nothing."

"Something cannot be nothing."

I stared at the Inex, then eyed the empty space in the cabinet where the ITG387 should be. I scanned over the other models. I'd have to stick with the ITG; the others didn't have all the capabilities I needed.

The Ino came in with toast and coffee. I got up and sat at my desk, cradling the coffee in my hands, sipping at it. The Inex crawled up and sat on the desk. I chewed my toast.

"*Jaw,*" I said internally.

There was silence, then, "*Icho – everything OK?*"

"*Yes, I'm fine. How's the journey? I hope you're safe.*"

"*I'm safe. The journey is going well, but slowly.*"

"*OK. Just be careful and let me know when you reach your destination.*"

"*I will.*"

I turned to the Inex and said, "Scan the news for anything on Jared Milligan."

"There was an interview with him on the news this morning, discussing the HSA right to vote."

"Fine. Project."

"Reliable sources state that Caddick is planning to propose legislation preventing HSAs from voting because they are of 'unsound mind'. We have the leader of the opposition, Jared Milligan, with us today – welcome, Jared."

Milligan's face filled the wall and I inspected him as he talked. His dull blue eyes looked slightly bloodshot, but that was the only sign of fatigue. His sandy brown hair shone under the studio lights; his white teeth were almost blinding. There was something enigmatic about him, something in his voice that commanded attention without the kind of histrionics engaged in by Caddick.

"Jared, it's been said by Jane Ward, and reiterated by Prime Minister Caddick, who often stands with Ward on issues pertaining to deviants, that you only care about HSAs because you know you have their vote."

"You know that's not true, Caroline. I campaigned tirelessly for HSA rights before taking up this post. We need to fund research into the allergy, and we need to find a cure. Depriving them of the vote will simply disenfranchise already alienated citizens, further fuelling discontent and Seraph terror."

"Speaking of Seraph terror, Caddick recently said if you were Prime Minister it would be catastrophic, given how soft you are on the Seraphs."

"Firstly, I unequivocally condemn Seraph terror tactics, but this doesn't preclude attempts to engage them in diplomatic discussions. I've been the subject of Seraph terrorist threats myself–"

"Because of your support for a cure?"

"That's right, but this doesn't mean–"

"How can you possibly engage with extremists, who not only threatened you, but who want to eradicate HellSans, who want to take away our bliss and destroy our way of life–"

"End it," I said, irritated.

I finished my coffee and walked through to the lab, stripping on the way and dumping my clothes on the floor for the Ino to pick up. I knew there were security cameras that one of Caddick's lackeys likely monitored, but I didn't care. I washed over one of the lab sinks.

"That's not a washing facility."

"It's a sink. If that's not a washing facility, I don't know what is."

"You require a shower."

"Who's gonna care? You? The Ino?"

"I care about your welfare, and this is not an ideal washing facility."

I rubbed soap under my arms and said, "I'm going home tonight. I'll shower then, OK?"

"It is not ideal."

"What setting are you on? You're a real bore, you know that?"

"I'm on Formal Assistant, the default setting for my model. I'm not programmed to be interesting."

"Obviously. Run through personalities."

"Good morning, Icho, I'm Senior Servant, and I'm happy to serve you. Good morning, Dr Smith, I'm Happy Worker and I can assist you in your tasks. Hey, doll, what's the plan? I'm Forever Friends and we're gonna have tons of fun. Greetings, Ichorel, I'm Deluxe Assistant, how would you like me to assist you today? Icho, welcome to another bliss-filled day! I'm Bliss Assistant and I'll do everything I can to help you be the best you."

"Let's go for Deluxe Assistant."

"Greetings, Ichorel. How would you like me to assist you today?"

I went through all the basics and told it I wasn't connecting.

"Understood, Ichorel."

"Call me Icho," I said, walking back through to the office.

"Of course, Icho," said the Inex, following. "Is there a name you would like to give me to make our interactions easier?"

"No."

"OK. But if you change your mind, I will take whichever name you decide on. In the meantime, I'll respond to 'ITG387', 'Deluxe', or 'Inex'. Is there a voice setting you'd prefer?"

"Gender-neutral is fine. Project the news."

The Inex projected the news onto the office wall.

"Throw it."

The office system took over the projection. I got dressed as I watched.

"Veronica Lambert, a representative of The Company, was on the *Becky Sutherland Show* today saying that The Company will not allow an Inex to report their owner to the police for 'thought crimes'…"

"Jesus," I said. "How is this even up for discussion?"

"It's healthy to debate things," said the Inex.

"I wasn't asking you."

"I thought you had decided to name me 'Jesus'."

I turned to the Inex, open-mouthed. I laughed. "Sure, why not? Jesus it is."

"Good. Our interactions will be easier now that I have a name."

I tuned back into the news.

"...Linda Connor, the girl who was murdered by her unblissed boyfriend was about to start university when she was brutally killed. Her family is campaigning for pre-act intervention..."

"'Pre-act intervention', come on!" I sighed and told Jesus to end the projection. "I don't think I can take the news today; it's stressing me out."

Jesus offered to guide me through a meditation, but I refused, drank the rest of my coffee, popped a SmileBrite pill, pulled on my lab coat and went through to the lab. I watched the Ino take the HSAs' lunch through to their quarters.

I did a couple of hours work before breaking for a late lunch in my office. As I ate, I asked Jesus to project the National Psychology and Sociology HSA Hub. Other than my own privately funded position, there'd been no funded medical research into HSA. Psych and soc have been the main disciplines investigating the allergy, psych dominating with its individualist episteme, positioning HSAs as deviants made sick by maladjustment to the demands of modern society, their sickness maintained by immurement in aberrant thought processes. Some studies suggested HSAs could be cured by engaging in an intensive programme of Cognitive Behavioural Therapy. In my own lab work, I found CBT and other coping mechanisms could sometimes assist deviants in their daily living, minimising some minor aspects of the allergy, but CBT wasn't a magic bullet for a biological illness.

Sociology research attracted less funding, which meant preliminary findings languished underexplored: most HSAs and Seraphs are women, a high proportion are Black women or women of colour, the majority from a poor socio-economic background with experience of trauma. One hypothesis is environmental factors and trauma trigger a genetic predisposition, which interested me, but lack of further research meant the hypothesis was just that. A group of sociologists posited that those from an affluent background might experience HellSans allergy at the same rate as others, but they were cushioned by their socio-economic position and may have the means to hide their ailments, with support from family. This was a controversial statement given it was illegal to harbour HSAs. There was a smattering of research on the unblissed but because of the stigma and the ease of hiding unbliss, there's been little beyond speculation. I skimmed through some of the recent discussions, but there wasn't anything that hadn't been hashed out before, including numerous pseudo-scientific papers specifically pathologising Seraphs, comparing them to serial killers and war criminals. I sighed and ended it.

Still feeling hungover and tired, I took a short nap, this time remembering to tell Jesus to wake me. When I woke, I checked in with Jaw – who was making good progress – before prepping for HSA04's review as I drank vitwater. I thought the nap would refresh me, but I was groggy. I asked the Ino to take Number Four through to the lab and to brew up some coffee. The prep tied up, I headed through.

"Morning, Dr Smith," said Four, smiling at me as he lay in the reclining chair.

"Morning, Kim. How are you feeling?"

"This guinea pig is just dandy, doctor. You're not looking too great, yourself."

I knew he was probably right – I hadn't looked in the mirror and hadn't thought about removing last night's make-up. "Late night," I said.

I told him about meeting Jane and realised my mistake too late – Jaw would have warned me, but Jaw wasn't here. I stared down at Jesus as Four launched into a monologue about Jane, The Company, Caddick, Inexes and surveillance: all conspiracy theory nonsense. I half-listened, shaking my head now and then, and thought how Four was at least part-right – he'd tried to get under my skin, asking me why I was on my own in the lab, not accepting that I'd requested it, that I preferred to work alone.

"Something happen to Jaw?"

"What?" I stared at Four, dazed. He pointed to Jesus. "Right, yes. Jaw's in for repair. Glitches."

Before he could resume his rant, I got started, asking the usual questions. The MedEx could give me all the stats, but I liked to talk it through with the HSAs, get their feedback on how they felt. Four had had no symptoms since I gave him the formula almost twenty-four hours before, his breathing and skin were fine, his wounds from the last allergic reaction were healing well.

"It's an affectation, you know," he said.

"What?"

"Your love for retro models." He stared at Jesus.

"Is it an affectation when I have no audience?"

"Do I not count, doctor?"

I frowned. "Of course, but do you care?"

Four shrugged.

"Any pain?"

Four shook his head. "In the ghetto we have no choice, you know."

"About what?"

"Inex models. We're stuck with what we can get our hands on. We're the ones who really need bio-monitoring, but it's tin cans or nothing at all."

I sighed. "Can we stay on track?"

"Sure, doc."

I went through a few more questions before getting Jesus to project one of The Company's slogans in HellSans. I asked Four to read it aloud.

"Forever and fucking always, helping you be the best arsehole you can be."

"Just read what it says on the wall, Kim."

"Forever and always," said Four, his tone sarcastic. "Helping you be the best you."

"How do you feel?"

"Dirty."

"Kim."

"Fine. I feel fine."

"No symptoms?"

"None. I'm cured."

"Not a cure. Temporary suppression of symptoms."

I asked him to read it a few more times. He rattled through it but stopped part way and stared at Jesus. I told him to keep his eyes on the projection, but he stayed fixed on Jesus and asked me if it was an ITG. Irritated, I confirmed it was and told him to stay focused.

"It thinks I'm human?"

"What?" I said, but as we locked eyes I knew exactly what he meant.

Inexes from model TRD upwards didn't recognise HSAs as human, allowing those models to harm HSAs – usually by means of a mild electric shock – if they posed a threat to humans or their Inexes.

My relationship with the lab HSAs was good. It made little sense for them to be difficult or turn on me; the lab was better than the ghetto or the streets, and there was the prospect of the cure they all desperately wanted, that alone making them compliant. Most of them were too sick to be otherwise. Four liked to push me, but mostly he just bored me with his conspiracy theories and his anti-Jane Ward monologues.

I stared at Four, trying to work out if he truly was a threat.

There hadn't been anything in our past relations that would have made me wary, and now we'd reached this far in the development of the formula it wouldn't make sense for him to turn on me. There was also no exit if he harmed me; he was trapped. It was more likely he was posturing, enjoying my discomfort. Still, I was glad I was bigger and stronger, and I tensed, ready for a possible altercation. He narrowed his eyes and smiled at me as I tried to work out how to diffuse things. Four was about to say something when Jesus spoke: "Caddick's here."

"What?" I said, not taking my eyes off Four. His smile faded.

"Caddick and Damon have entered the building."

"Shit," I said, both relieved and panicked.

I put my coffee down and backed away from Four. I looked round the lab, thinking things through. I told Four to get up and go back to his quarters, but he stayed in the chair, saying he wanted to meet Caddick. As I tried to persuade him, the door opened. We turned to see Caddick and Damon enter and walk down the stairs into the lab, their Inexes following, both grey like Jane's, no accessories, standard blue eye chips. I walked over to greet Caddick.

"Dr Smith," said Caddick, his arms wide, as if he were offering a hug to the whole lab. "A pleasure to see you again so soon. I hope you're not the worse for wear after the party?"

"I'm fine," I said. "It's good to see you again too."

We shook hands and he clasped mine in both of his. He looked me in the eyes and said, "Apologies for the unannounced visit, but after your encouraging words on your progress last night I had to come and see how things are going."

"They're going well, but I don't really have–"

He let go of my hand and swivelled. "And who is this?"

"HSA04," I said, pausing before saying, "Kim."

"A pleasure!" He glanced at Four, who mumbled a greeting as Caddick walked through the lab. He looked around then placed his hands on one of the tables. Eyes on Four, he said,

"And how are you feeling? You certainly look well. Or is it simply lack of exposure to your allergen?"

Four looked over at me and I gave him a warning stare, but I needn't have; all of his cockiness had vanished, cowed in Caddick's presence. He replied, too quiet for me to catch, looking down at his hands. Caddick told him to speak up. "I'm doing well," he said, looking over at Caddick, but struggling to hold eye contact.

Caddick came round from behind the table, and strode over to Four, who tensed. He placed his hands on each arm of the chair and leaned down, his face inches from Four's. Caddick's Inex moved smoothly up his leg and back, stopping on his shoulder. They both inspected Four's face as he pushed his head against the seat, trying to escape their gaze.

"Your skin looks very good, Number Four."

Four's mouth opened, but he didn't respond.

"Kim has some coping strategies he learned in the ghetto," I said.

"Those strategies seem to be doing a fine job – maybe we don't need you after all, Dr Smith."

"Well, I mean, it's not all... The work is going well, there's been an easing of some symptoms, but we're not entirely–"

Caddick raised his hand to me. He must have internally commanded his Inex, as it projected an Inex poster and slogan on the wall. Caddick pointed at it and asked Four to read it. Four glanced at me, uncertain, then turned to look at the poster. Caddick repeated his request and Four quietly read it.

"Keep going, until I tell you to stop. Keep your eyes on it." Caddick said.

Four complied as Caddick looked at him closely and Damon kept his eyes on me. I tried to interrupt, but Caddick shook his head. After what felt like an eternity of Four repeating the slogan, Caddick finally let him stop. He turned to me and requested MedEx stats.

"Caddick–"

"Now, Doctor."

I fetched the MedEx and it connected to Four. As it reeled off stats, Caddick listened, thoughtful.

"I think," said Caddick, pausing, "this is more than coping strategies. You're doing a lot better than you're giving yourself credit for, Dr Smith. Surely you should be proud of your work?"

"I am," I said, hot, hoping sweat wouldn't seep through my clothes.

"Why didn't you tell me about this last night," he said, straightening up and turning to me, his Inex shifting, settling down on his shoulder.

"Well, I knew it wasn't, that I wasn't fully... There's still more work to do, and it didn't seem the appropriate place to discuss it. Too many ears, too many Inexes."

"Aah, yes," he said, staring at me. "Too many ears, too many Inexes. It seems," he said, looking down at Jesus, "that I really ought to take a leaf out of your book."

"I'm sorry?"

He didn't respond and continued staring at Jesus. "Where's Jaw, Icho?"

"What?"

"Your Inex?"

"Right here," I said, gesturing to Jesus.

"Not your usual model." Caddick looked it over. "Seems more fitting for a ghetto dweller."

"She likes her retros," said Four.

"Jaw's in for repairs. I should get it back tomorrow."

"You can do better than that," said Caddick.

I stared at him, uncertain, as the Inex said, "I can assure you, I am operating well. But it would help if–"

"We don't need your input, Jesus," I said quickly, stopping it from telling him I wasn't connected.

"Jesus?" said Caddick.

Four laughed and I looked down at my hands, picking at the skin around my thumbnail. "It was just a joke," I said.

"Do you think this is a joke, Ichorel? Is that what you think of your job?"

I looked up at him. "No. Of course not."

"This," he said, pointing at Jesus, "isn't good enough."

"I have an affection for the older models. It's only for a day."

"I want you operating with the best tech when in this lab. You can do as you please in your own time, but that," he said, flicking his hand at Jesus, "doesn't belong in this lab."

"Of course." My head throbbed. "I'm sorry." I closed my eyes and rubbed my temples.

"Where did you take Jaw?"

"Holden's."

"I'll get Damon to contact them and speed up the repairs."

I protested, telling him there was no need, that it would be back with me by tomorrow, that my friend Charlotte worked there and had it in hand.

"Learn to accept assistance, Icho. Maybe it wasn't such a good idea having you out here on your own with no staff."

I stared at him, wondering how this could all be unravelling so quickly. "Of course," I said quietly. "I appreciate your help." I felt Four's eyes on me, but I couldn't look at him.

"Damon?"

"On it, sir."

As I watched Damon's Inex scale the lab wall in search of insects, I hoped Charlotte would understand and bluff for me. I felt nauseous, but I was sure I could handle this; Caddick didn't know anything, there was no reason for him not to trust me. I eyed Damon as Caddick wandered over to my office door and looked through the window.

"Sleep here last night?"

"Most nights. It's easier."

"It's not much of a journey into the city by car. Do you really find it such an inconvenience?"

"I like to get up and get straight to work. It suits me."

"Work-life balance, Icho," he said. "It's important."

"So Jaw keeps telling me. I'll spend more time at home."

He stared at me and asked if I'd come straight to the lab after the party. I nodded.

"But you went back into the city this morning?"

"What?"

"With Jaw. For repairs."

"Right," I said, feeling my stomach knotting up. "Yes, of course."

Caddick stared at me, and I looked away, glancing at Four, who looked tense. I walked over to Four, a welcome distraction, telling him I was finished with him and he could return to his quarters. He looked relieved and stood to go.

"Wait a moment," said Caddick. "I'd like to hear more from you, Number Four."

Four glanced at me, then back at Caddick and sank back into his chair as Damon leaned in and whispered something in Caddick's ear. Caddick and Damon both looked at me.

"Where did you send your Inex, Icho?"

"Holden's, I told you."

"There's no record," said Damon.

"That'll be Charlotte; she's doing it as a personal favour and just hasn't logged it. Honestly, it's fine. She'll have it back to me first thing tomorrow."

We stared at each other. I knew my face was flushed and I could feel sweat dribbling down my back. I saw Damon's Inex out of the corner of my eye, still climbing the wall. I focused on it, watching it stalk a spider.

"Ichorel, Ichorel," said Caddick in a quiet sing-song voice. I looked over at him. He was shaking his head as he repeated my name. He stopped, then said, "Where did you send Jaw?"

"Caddick, I really don't understand what–"

"Spare me," he said. Caddick glanced at his Inex and the next moment it had projected onto the lab wall – my Inex, Jaw, watching Dr West and Caddick. "One of the Inos at the reception reported suspicious behaviour."

I stared at the projection, the Ino telling Jaw to return to the party, the low hum of Dr West and Caddick's conversation in the background. The projection paused and he said to me, "You've done something rash, haven't you?"

Now I knew for certain that he knew, I was surprised to find I was relieved; I couldn't tolerate him toying with me.

"Don't you trust me, Ichorel? Do you really think I'd allow myself to be blackmailed by someone like West?"

"The Daedalus Project," I said, and he stiffened, just like he had when West mentioned it. "I'd never seen you react like that before. He really has something on you."

He ignored me. "Tell me where Jaw is."

I looked down, feeling sick, not sure how to handle this.

"You're distressed, Icho," said Jesus, "If we were connected I could–"

"We are connected," I said quickly.

"We are not–"

"Go silent."

Caddick eyed me, asking why we weren't connected. I insisted we were. "It's just a faulty old model."

"A model you saw fit to work with. On my time. My money."

"You're right," I said. "It was foolish of me."

"Why are you not connected, Icho? Are you still with Jaw?" He considered me, then said, "Jaw must be nearby if you're still connected. Am I right? Where is it, Icho?"

"I told you – repairs."

"Stop playing games, Icho. You won't win."

"What about you, Caddick?" I said, sick of the way he was treating me. "You owe me an explanation. I trusted you."

Caddick smiled. "I don't owe you anything." He shook his head. "I don't owe anyone anything."

"What was your plan? Even if West hadn't tried to blackmail you, what was your plan? I kidded myself I was here alone because I wanted to be, but it's what you wanted, wasn't it?"

"It was only a precaution, Icho. You'd done nothing to make me doubt you." Caddick sighed. "Until now."

"What's your plan, Caddick?"

"Where's your Inex, Ichorel?"

We stared at each other. I drummed my fingers against the workbench, finding comfort in the rhythm. I tried to stay focused on how to deal with Caddick, the best way forward, but all I could think was I'd made a terrible mistake and there was no way back. I thought of calling Jaw, telling it to return. I could apologise, say I'd panicked, I wasn't thinking straight. I focused on Caddick; his face had softened, he was smiling, a hint of warmth in his eyes, and I relaxed, thinking he'd understand if I called Jaw back now. It wasn't too late.

"Damon," he said, not taking his eyes off me. "Execute the HSAs, then sweep the area."

As Damon reached into his jacket, I stood, shocked, trying to make sense of what Caddick had just said. My eyes on Damon, I stepped forward, raising my hand in protest. "No– I– What are you–"

"Icho," said Caddick, sounding like an impatient parent.

"Are you serious?" I said, staring at the gun that was now in Damon's hand, held casually by his side. "This is… You can't… You need to just–"

"I'm cured," said Four, standing, eyes wide with fear. "I'm telling you, I'm cured. You need me."

Damon hesitated, eyes on Caddick, who looked thoughtful. I hovered next to Four.

"I need more time," I said, my voice steady, authoritative. "And I need Kim – losing Kim would set back the research."

There was silence as we all considered each other. Four visibly relaxed, but I knew he wouldn't be safe until he was back in his room. Caddick stood there, thinking. Damon watched him, fingering the gun at his side. Caddick glanced at Damon, nodded, and Damon raised the gun, shooting Four in the head before I could even move, blood spattering across me.

There was another shot as I crumpled, falling to my knees, my mouth open, but no noise coming out. I looked up and saw

Jesus had been shot, the Mnemosyne core destroyed. Blood dribbled down my face as I watched Damon walk through the slowly pooling blood on the lab floor, heading for the HSA quarters. I flinched as I heard four shots, short intervals between them. I leaned over, about to be sick, my hands pressed flat in front of me, but nothing came. I heard footsteps. I looked up and saw Damon, his gun held casually by his side, nothing in his face to show he'd just murdered five deviants.

"Dr Smith," said Caddick. "Tell me – where's your Inex?"

I pointed to the destroyed ITG387.

"Where's Jaw?"

"Repairs."

"Where's Jaw, Icho?"

I shook my head and stared at Four's body. I threw up. Shivering, breaking out in a cold sweat, I looked up at them, tears, snot, blood and vomit dribbling from my chin.

Caddick had his arm raised, examining a bloodstained cuff in disgust. He removed his jacket and tie and unbuttoned his shirt. I leaned over and spat on the floor before pushing myself upright. Shifting back, I rested against the side of a lab bench and stared up at Caddick as he removed his shirt. I imagined sliding a scalpel into his chest. I felt nauseous again and closed my eyes.

"Where's your Inex, Ichorel?"

I leaned my head back against the bench and rolled it from side to side as he told Damon to sweep the area. I heard Damon go up the stairs, and Caddick said, "You stink, doctor. You really stink."

I smiled and opened my eyes. He gestured to the Ino and it sucked up my vomit, leaving behind a pine fresh scent that mingled with the metallic smell of Four's blood. The Ino tried to clean up the blood but Caddick said, "Leave it. That's enough." The Ino returned to its corner of the lab.

Damon reappeared, walking down the stairs. "No sign, sir. She can't be connected."

On Caddick's command, Damon pulled me up by the arm and dumped me in a chair. I wiped my lab coat sleeve across my face and blew my nose on it, getting some snot on my hand. I flicked it into Damon's face as he leaned down to me. I laughed as he reeled back.

"Damon," said Caddick as Damon slapped me hard across the face, splitting my lip. I fell sideways, heading to the floor, but Caddick caught the chair and I jerked to a halt. He set me upright. I sucked on my bloody lip.

"Damon," Caddick repeated.

"Sir."

"Get it together."

Damon nodded, grabbed my arm and used Caddick's tie and his own to lash me to the chair.

"I'm telling you nothing," I said, slightly slurred as my tongue slipped around in the blood in my mouth. I laughed to myself.

"'Stupid' isn't the word I'd associate with you."

My head lolled as I said, "This isn't about me."

Caddick considered me and I smiled up at him, baring my bloodstained teeth.

"You're not cut out for this, Dr Smith."

"You," I said, "don't know me."

"Ichorel," he said, sitting in a chair Damon had brought, his Inex on the floor next to him. "I know everything about you." He leaned forward, his hands clasped, elbows resting on his thighs. "How do you think you got this job?" When I didn't respond, he said, "What's your back-up access code?"

I gave it, smiling. Caddick looked at me, bemused. "I thought you were telling me nothing."

I shrugged.

"That's your code?"

"What does it matter? The levels of security and bureaucracy in that place…" I was about to say it would take weeks, maybe months, but I trailed off as he smiled at me. Of course he could sidestep all of that, even with the notorious back-up facilities. His tendrils are everywhere.

He told Damon to use the code and we sat in silence for a few minutes, Caddick with his eyes fixed on me, trying to intimidate. I looked down at the floor, then quickly back at Caddick after my eyes fell on Four's body. I looked towards him, but focused past him, affecting composure.

"There's no data," Damon said.

Caddick turned to him, frowning. "That's impossible."

"There's only her childhood. Then it stops and there's a song on a loop."

"A song?"

"Something called 'Flytipping'."

I laughed and Caddick turned to me, "Is this all a joke to you, Icho?"

I smiled. Caddick told Damon to check the song wasn't hiding anything.

"They've already checked."

"Check again." Caddick turned back to me. "How did you erase the data?"

"I didn't."

"It's hidden behind the song?"

"No. It's not there. It never was."

I sang a few lines of "Flytipping" and Caddick listened, eyes narrowed.

"They checked," said Damon, "There's nothing there, sir."

Caddick nodded. "You had this planned all along."

"Since I was a teenager?" I cocked my head, raising an eyebrow.

He thought this over. "Then, why?"

"I don't believe in compulsory back-ups."

Caddick stared at me. I could see he was trying to work out if I was mocking him, I could see the rage in him, his jaw clenched.

"Damon, why was this not flagged?"

"She has no political affiliations, sir. She was being monitored by The Company because of her Inex hobby, but nothing was flagged by them."

"I underestimated you, Dr Smith," he said. "It seems, Damon, our focus is now exclusively on Jaw's whereabouts. Did you alter it?" he said, staring at me. "An Inex can't travel far without their owner. Or is it a package – is someone else involved?"

I didn't respond. The strange hyper-numbness of shock was starting to wear off, my lip throbbed, my tied wrists hurt. I suddenly felt so tired.

"Damon," said Caddick.

"Sir?"

"If you were Dr Smith, where would you send your Inex?"

I watched them hash it out, wondering how long it would take them to get there, hoping they'd investigate other possibilities first, giving Jaw more time. Damon suggested a contact from my university, but Caddick knew what a loner I was, that I didn't have anyone there I trusted. He floated the Seraphs but quickly dismissed it as too risky.

"She'd need someone with the power to take this on, to replicate the formula and disseminate it. And she'd need someone in the patent office, to lock it down." He paused and considered me. "It's either a connection at the patent office or it's Milligan. Or both."

I said nothing, hoping my face was impassive.

"How long has this been going on?" said Caddick. "Has he known all along? Or is this a rash response to what you overheard last night?"

A glob of blood mingled with sweat fell into my eye and I blinked furiously, but it didn't help. I jerked back when I felt Caddick's hands cup my face.

"Easy," he said.

His thumb pressed into my eye, rubbing the blood-sweat away. He pushed at my chin, cocking my head up, and poured water onto my face, making me jump with the shock of it.

He wiped the blood and water from my eyes. I looked up at
him and my stomach tightened as I was suddenly aware how
vulnerable I was. He kept hold of my chin as the water dripped
from my face.

"Damon," he said, letting go of me and walking over to him.
He leaned in close, whispering. Damon nodded and went to
the back of the lab with his Inex, clearly contacting someone. I
quickly called for Jaw as Caddick stared at me.

"Icho? Everything OK? You're–"

Jaw knew before I said anything; our connection was still
strong and it knew everything.

*"You could have a tail soon. I don't know what they're planning,
but be careful. They'll be looking for a lone Inex."*

"Maybe it wasn't planned," said Caddick.

"I need to go, Jaw. I'll check in soon."

"Was this a crisis of conscience, Ichorel? Or is this just all
about you – you want so desperately to play saviour? You
want the adulation, the awards that come with such a major
breakthrough."

"Are you psychoanalysing me?"

Damon approached Caddick and whispered in his ear. This
was all for show, to make me nervous, pushing me to give
something away; they could easily converse covertly via their
Inexes. Caddick nodded as he listened to Damon.

Stepping back from Caddick, Damon said, "Do you want me
to start on Dr Smith?"

"No," said Caddick, standing. "I want you to go."

"Sir?"

"It's with Milligan. Or it will be. I want you to intercept it.
If you're too late you need to extract it with minimal fall-out.
But I don't want to see you again until you have it. And get
someone on the patent office, just in case."

"Yes, sir."

Caddick kept his eyes on me the whole time he was
instructing Damon.

"*Jaw?*" I said internally.

"*Icho.*"

"*They're sending someone to intercept you when you reach Milligan. Be careful.*"

"*I will.*"

Caddick rummaged through various drawers and held up a scalpel. I was relieved, convinced I'd be able to cope better with the clean slice of a scalpel than anything blunt. As a child I was in an accident, my left arm shredded, part of my face sliced open; I remember the impact and standing up, feeling nothing, the shock numbing me. I only knew something was wrong as I walked towards my parents and saw the look of horror on their faces. It was on the way to hospital that the pain set in. I hoped for the same delay as I stared at Caddick and heard Damon walk up the stairs, exiting the lab. It was when the door clicked closed behind him that I truly understood I could die here. I thought I was going to pass out. I tried to will it. I said to Jaw, "*I might not make it out of here. Don't fail.*" I didn't give it a chance to respond. I couldn't deal with any inane platitudes, however much affection I had for Jaw.

"It's just you and me, Dr Smith."

"I won't tell you anything. You'll kill me anyway."

"I won't kill you, Icho. You're important to me."

Despite myself, I felt a wave of relief and let out a long breath, realising I'd been holding myself tight, my breath shallow and quick. I took a moment, getting my breathing back to normal. He was right – he couldn't kill me until he'd secured the formula. He needed me.

"But I can hurt you," he said, dragging his chair over and sitting in front of me. "Inex? Are all my meetings covered?"

"All covered as requested, sir."

The voice unnerved me: a kind, soft voice, which felt perverse in this situation. I was sure it was the voice of an actress – only the best and most expensive for Caddick – but I couldn't quite place it.

"Your Inex calls you 'sir'?" I said, rolling my eyes.

Ignoring me, Caddick reached into his jacket pocket and pulled out a Company snack packet. He handed it to his Inex and it sat next to him, eating, its blue eyes fixed on me.

"Shouldn't you be running the country, *sir*? I don't think torture is on the job description."

"There's nowhere else I'd rather be, Icho. But this doesn't have to drag out. Just tell me: where's Jaw? When did you send it?"

I spat, aiming for the floor but hitting my lap. Saliva-blood dribbled down my chin.

"Inex, check the building's surveillance."

There was a short pause, then it said, "Surveillance has been hacked. There's a glitch: three minutes past six this morning."

"How long have you been planning this, Icho?"

I didn't respond.

"An Inex on its own isn't going to get far. How did you do it? How did you get past its distance limit?"

I swayed my head gently, focussing on my breathing.

"Or is there someone else?" he said. "No, you don't have anyone you trust that much, and if you did, you'd transfer the data to their Inex. But you don't, do you, Icho? You're a loner. You don't have anyone who cares," he said, standing.

I thought of Jane Ward. I thought of her hand in mine, the way she'd teased me about my work. I thought of her invite to dinner. Then I wondered if she was in on this. Caddick told her everything, she'd said.

Caddick got down on his knees, slowly. He looked me over, taking his time, trying to unsettle me.

"You can't do this," I said. "Your Inex will report you."

"As you can see so far, it hasn't called for help."

"You've had it adjusted? That's illegal."

"For some."

"For everyone."

"You adjusted your own, Doctor."

"Did I?"

"Don't treat me like a fool, Icho."

"Was it Jane Ward?" I said. "She adjusted it?"

"Icho, Icho, I think we need to focus here. You can make this easier on yourself. Damon is already on his way to intercept Jaw. Where else would you send it but Milligan?" He leaned in, placing his left hand on my knee. "I know you're not cut out for this," he said, slipping the scalpel under my fingernail.

I was Jaw. Our right middle finger felt wrong, then it faded. We scanned to make sure all was well before arguing with ourselves.

Escaping torture by doubling is not effective. The further we get, the weaker the connection. We will become I and you will be back in a wounded body. I am focused on the mission; you are distracting–

I fell back into searing pain in my right hand–

Don't push me out. If I'm going back, it's a decision we make together.

I said this as I sank into our body like sinking into warm water, cushioned, comforted.

Please don't push me out.

I didn't push – the connection is weaker the further we go. We should not be we.

I can help get you to your destination.

I looked out at the city from Jaw's eyes. This caused a momentary glitch as the sight of the city and freedom worsened the anxiety of being trapped in the lab. I crashed back into my body for a second, the pain hitting me before I pulled back into Jaw, the force of this bringing Jaw to a halt.

I don't need your help – I am focused. You are distracting. I will not move until you leave.

I think I'm going to die there, Jaw.

He won't kill you if he doesn't have me, and he won't kill you if he does – he needs you to access my records.

He has Jane Ward.

You think he can use her to hack me.

It's possible. Just don't fail me.

You need to go back, or I will fail you; you are distracting from the mission.

I can coast. Doubled and silent. I can coast with you, Jaw.

You need to stay with your body, you need to know what your body is experiencing. It's too dangerous to be doubled – I felt your wounded finger as damage in my own. It is distracting and risky.

I can't take it, Jaw. I can't take it.

We can always take more than we think we can.

That's easy for you to say.

It is. I know you better than you know yourself… I will push you out and I will move on. I'll be careful, I'll complete the mission, and I will engineer a rescue plan.

I'm going to die in the lab, Jaw.

You will not die there. I will not be caught and you will not die – to complete the mission is our focus. You need to go–

I sucked in air, trying not to scream as pain coursed through my body. I looked down at my hand; he'd removed three fingernails. I closed my eyes and tried to focus on my breathing. Caddick was still burbling on, so I shifted my focus to his words, gritting my teeth.

"Cause and effect, doctor. You understand that, don't you? How would things have turned out if you hadn't stabbed me in the back? Our lab rats here would still be alive and you wouldn't be tied to this chair. You'd be running the most important lab in the country with your own staff, anything you needed. You'd be showered with praise, presented with awards."

"You're full of shit, Caddick."

"You would have gone down in history, Ichorel."

"Fuck you."

"Where's Jaw, Icho?"

He slapped me hard across the face, the sudden violence shocking me. I'd expected him to slowly work his way through all my fingernails. I sobbed, feeling panicked, unsure I could handle unpredictability; I needed some semblance of control. I choke-laughed, realising the utter perversity in thinking I had any kind of control.

"Something funny?"

I shook my head. I watched his Inex climb up his arm and perch on his shoulder. I tongued at the wound on my lip, where his ring had split it open.

"Where did you send it? There's nothing useful for miles. How did you sever the connection? Or did you extend it? Do you know how many years you'd get for that?"

I stared into the blue eyes of his Inex, thinking of Jaw.

"Can it reach the city? Can it get that far?"

I abruptly turned to Caddick and he looked expectant, thinking I was finally going to give him something, but instead I said, "I saw you with Jane. At the party."

He raised his eyebrows, waiting.

"You had your hand on her waist, sliding down until she pulled away. You want her and she rejected you."

Caddick was silent, staring down at his clasped hands, still holding the bloody scalpel, the blood drying on his fingers.

"The most powerful man in the country and she rejects you."

"You're really not in a position to be provoking me, Dr Smith."

"She was flirting with me, at the party. Her eyes all over my bliss-covered body." I smiled, winced, and tongued at my bleeding lip again. "I don't think you can give her what she wants, Prime Minister, *sir*."

He tried to keep the emotion from his face, but I saw the

muscles in his jaw tighten. He placed the scalpel down on the workbench next to him. He stared at it for a moment, stood, walked over to me and punched me in the face, the force of it sending me and the chair to the ground. He straddled me, my lab coat bunched in one hand, holding me up as his fist pounded into the side of my face over and over and–

I was back with Jaw and we were we when our left eye shut down. We adjusted our vision and got back on track, but our hand malfunctioned and we lost our grip on the wall. We scrambled to keep our hold, but fell into the arms of an HSA.

Shit, I'm sorry, Jaw. Shit.

The deviant pawed at us, inspecting. We gave them an electric shock and they dropped us as they crumpled. We quickly scaled the wall, reaching a ledge of safety, listening to the deviant curse. I pushed at Icho.

Wait! Jaw, please.

You're jeopardising the mission.

As our right leg malfunctioned, I relented.

I woke into pain and blacked out.

I woke, choking as water was poured on my face. The cold was both shock and relief. Dehydrated, I tried to drink it, but it gushed down my throat and nose and I panicked, shaking my head, writhing on the floor in an attempt to escape the torrent. It eased, turning to a trickle. I coughed, spitting out water, gulping in air. Hands gripped my shoulders and I was jerked upright. I breathed heavily, my heart pounding in my ears, and I looked up at Caddick, staring at him with my right eye, my left refusing to open. He was covered in blood, dripping water and sweat. I spat.

"You're clever," he said, sitting down next to me, "And observant. You knew exactly how to push me, Ichorel. I won't let it happen again."

He walked round behind me, and I tensed, waiting, but nothing came. I heard the door of my office, then silence. I sat for a few minutes, alert, listening. I don't know how long I waited, weary, my head drooping as I fell into unconsciousness.

I woke into forgetfulness and tried to move my arms. I looked down at my hands; my left wrist was bruised, cut, and swollen, the tie digging into it, my hand blue. It all came back to me. I didn't know how long I'd been out, didn't know what time it was, or even if it was the same day, and there was no Inex to tell me. I raised my head, my neck stiff, my whole body aching. Caddick was sitting there, staring at me.

"How do you feel?"

"Fuck you," I said, a husky whisper, my throat raw, my lips and cheeks throbbing as I spoke. I glared at him out of my good eye.

"I need you to connect." He nodded to the floor, and I looked down at one of the old models from my display. I shook my head.

"If you don't connect, I could go too far."

I laughed, but stopped abruptly because it hurt. "It would be my fault?" I said. "Of course."

He smiled. "Be sensible, Icho."

"You don't need an Inex," I said. "I can tell you myself – you need to untie this arm. I can't feel my hand."

He considered me for a few seconds, then stood and untied my wrist. It still felt as if it was lashed to the chair. I flexed my fingers, trying to rid myself of the pins and needles. I circled my shoulder a little and stretched. It was satisfying, but painful. Colour began to return to my hand. I'd been so busy working life back into my arm I hadn't noticed Caddick had pulled his chair up next to me and was opening a first aid kit. I tried to back away from him but hit the table behind me.

"Easy," he said. "I'm trying to help."

I grunted in disbelief.

"Give me your hand, Icho."

I held my arm to my stomach, but he gripped it, pulled it towards him and began cleaning my wrist. The feel of the cool wet cloth against my hot skin was enough to make me relent and his grip lessened. Once he'd cleaned it, he doused it with Ambrosia ointment and slowly bandaged it. He did this so gently and with such care I had trouble believing this was the man who'd slipped a scalpel under my nails, the man who'd punched me into unconsciousness.

"If you tell me what I want, I'll get the Inex to look after you, clean all your wounds, let you rest," he said, looking up at me.

He reached up and I flinched. He stroked my cheek and pushed my bloodied hair behind my ear. I knew what he was doing, yet all I wanted was to sink into this tenderness. My vision blurred, shifted, and–

Icho? I'm sorry.

Jaw?

I saw what Jaw saw: Damon, his hand pressing on us, reaching into his jacket with the other.

Mission fail.

Damon pulled out a knife and brought it down–

"Jaw!" I yelled as I jerked in the chair, slamming into the table behind me, expecting the knife, but nothing came, just Caddick's hands gripping my shoulders. I opened my eye and his face was inches from mine, his fetid breath making me nauseous.

"You've been connected," he said. "This whole time?"

I sobbed as he moved away from me and paced the lab.

"Damon has Jaw?" he said.

I tried to use my bandaged hand to untie my other wrist, but I couldn't get my fingers to work. I sat there, batting at the tie around my wrist, feeling dizzy and sick.

"Damon's Inex isn't responding," said Caddick's Inex.

Caddick walked over to me, got down on his knees and untied my wrist with such ease I thought he'd used some kind of magic.

"Looks like it will take a little longer for confirmation, Dr Smith."

He hooked his hands under my armpits and pulled me up. Now that I was free, I thought to push him, knee him in the groin, elbow to the face, anything; but my limbs didn't obey, my legs collapsed. He caught me, as if he was saving me. His arm around my waist, he half-dragged me to the HSA quarters. We entered one of the rooms and he kicked the HSA body off the blood-spattered cot before laying me down in its place, my head resting in blood, brains, scraps of skull, scalp, and hair. I watched him walk away. The clear door slid into place and locked. I closed my eye but immediately saw the knife coming for me. I stared at the ceiling. All I could smell was blood and vomit. Rolling my head to the side, I stared at the dead HSA. I thought of clawing my way into their body, breaking off a bone and stabbing it into an artery. By the time he returned I'd be gone; taking myself out meant he wouldn't have access to Jaw's records. I knew Jaw would disapprove, but I lay there and thought about which bone to use.

CHAPTER 2

I jerked awake and stared round the room, uncertain. I looked down at the body on the floor and remembered it all. I tried to sit up and flinched; everything hurt. My left eye was swollen shut and my face felt like one big bruise. I stood, slowly, wincing. I shuffled over to the door and looked out into the empty corridor. I didn't know how much time had passed, if Caddick was still here, if Damon was back. I turned and looked down at Number Three's body. I'd been exhausted before, only thinking of relief, but now my head had cleared. Sans Inex, Caddick thought I was locked in, but the door accepted eye-scan; he either didn't know, he'd forgotten, or he was still in the lab.

I wasn't sure if one eye would work, but the door slid open and I walked out. I moved stiffly along the corridor of the HSA quarters, listening for voices or movement. I reached the door and looked through the window into the lab. I could see the chair I'd been tied to. I shifted position, peering to the right, and saw Four's arm in a pool of blood, the rest of his body hidden behind the workbench. I looked over to my office door, but it was closed and dark. I scanned my one eye and walked into the lab. The stench of blood, sweat, and vomit mingled with the Ino's pine scent. Ignoring the body, I went straight to one of the work benches, stepping around the bodily fluids. I opened a drawer, wincing at the slight pressure as I pulled; my fingers were a dried-up bloody mess, throbbing with pain. I picked a scalpel out of the drawer. I doubted it would be much use against either Caddick or Damon, but it made me feel safe and would work better than a bone if I needed to use it on myself.

I went over to my office door and stood, listening. I stayed like that for several minutes, clutching the scalpel. I was angry with myself when I noticed my hand was shaking. I pushed the door hard, letting it slam loudly against the office wall in some kind of perverse protest at my own fear. The office light came on as the noise echoed through the lab and I stood, waiting, staring wide-eyed into the room. There was no one there and no one came rushing down the lab stairs behind me. Walking in, I grabbed a bag and an Inex repair kit. The kit was designed to go round your wrist, but my wrists were cut and swollen so I put it in the bag as I headed back into the lab.

I was still shaking as I clumsily rummaged through a first aid kit and threw sterilising liquid, Ambrosia ointment, painkillers, plasters, and bandages in the bag. I pulled open the drawer below, picking up two vials of the formula and an auto-injector, packing them too. Not looking, I stepped over Four's body and went over to where Caddick had left the inert Inex he'd tried to force me to connect to. As I shoved it in the bag, I realised I was sobbing.

My breathing was short and shallow, and I had to lean against a workbench to steady myself. I pawed at my face with my bloody hands, clearing the tears from my one good eye. I hiked the bag onto my shoulder and made my way over to the lab stairs, still shaking, my legs unsteady. Climbing the stairs only increased my panic and I had to stop and sit. I made myself take deeper, calmer breaths, all the while expecting the door above me to open, and Caddick to be standing there, looking down with that smug smile. I gripped the scalpel and held it in the direction of the door as if it would ward off danger.

My breathing more even, I stood and pulled myself up the stairs by the handrail, my wrists and fingers throbbing and bleeding. I clutched the door handle and stared out the window into darkness. I knew it was unlikely Caddick and Damon would be lurking in a dark corridor waiting to ambush me, and if they were returning, I'd likely see and hear them, their Inexes lighting the way. I shifted and looked down into my lab, at the blood staining the floor, Four's body, a destroyed Jesus. Turning back, I pushed the door open, walking into the darkness. I paused, allowing my eye to adjust. I'd walked through here so many times, not once feeling unease, but now the silence felt crushing, the darkness threatening, as if the horrors of the lab had leaked throughout the rest of the building. I made my way along the corridor and turned right instead of the usual left; now there was little chance of meeting Caddick or Damon as I headed for the back exit. I climbed the stairs up to the ground floor of the empty warehouse, eye-scanned, and pushed the back door open a crack; it was clear. I hurried out and edged my way along the building. I looked round the corner. No cars. No Caddick or Damon.

It was a clear evening, bitterly cold. I hugged my lab coat around me, shivering. I stayed hidden in semi-darkness, out of sight of the road, and pulled the Inex out of my bag. It was old, which meant I could be mistaken for a deviant or a retro teen, but it would draw more attention if I was without one. The Inex was so old I had to manually type in my chip code for it to connect, and while it didn't have the range of capabilities recent models had, it would allow me to buy supplies and get a car. The car was a risk – it would be traceable, but it was the only means of transport into the city. I'd have to ditch it somewhere central and walk the rest of the way.

"The rest of the way to where?" I said, looking out to the road, waiting for the connection to kick in.

I jumped when the Inex loudly said, "I can find any destination."

"Quieter voice."

"OK, Icho. How is this?"

"Much better. Deactivate GPS."

"I can serve you better if–"

"Just do it."

"Yes, Icho."

"What time is it?"

"One a.m. and forty-five seconds," it said. "Would you like to name me for–"

"We can do all that later. Order me a car."

"Yes, Icho."

After a few seconds, it said, "The car is on its way. It should take approximately twenty minutes."

"Right," I said, still staring at the road. "Get the car to meet me at the OCP warehouse."

The OCP was round the back of my lab, accessible by a different road, reducing the chance that Caddick or Damon would see me, but I was still jittery and sat crouched in darkness.

I started work on the Inex to make sure it didn't report me for doing anything illegal. I got out the repair kit, the light from the torch on the lid shining on the Inex, and slipped the needle into its neck, cutting off outer and inner communications with myself or anyone else. Fortunately, the procedure wasn't invasive; I plugged the kit's board into the Inex's side and altered its code. I'd altered various Inexes over the years, but I'd never worked on this model before. It had all been experimental, getting to know the Inexes an end in itself. Altering this Inex and Jaw were the only times I'd done it so I could do something explicitly illegal beyond the alteration itself.

It went smoother than expected, and after only a few minutes I unplugged the board and removed the needle. To test my work, I asked what it would do if I murdered the Prime Minister.

"I'm here to assist you, to help you be the best you."

"Would you report me to the police?"

"No."

"Good," I said, and packed up the kit.

Now that I was done, the next few minutes dragged out as I stared at the road, jumping at any sound.

"You're stressed," said the Inex. "You should engage in meditation while I monitor the road for you."

"I'm fine."

"You're not fine. You–"

When car headlights appeared on the driveway up to the building, I tensed.

"It's your car," said the Inex.

"You're sure?"

"Of course."

"OK."

The car pulled up to the entrance and I bounced up, running for it, ignoring my body as muscles protested. I fell into the car, the Inex following more gracefully.

"Destination?" the car asked.

I didn't reply.

"Destination?"

I didn't have a destination. There was nowhere to go.

"Just away," I said. "Away from here."

"A destination is required."

"City centre," the Inex replied for me.

The car headed back along the driveway. I turned and looked out the window, watching the OCP warehouse recede, a glimpse of the lab building just behind. I turned back round and sank into the seat, relieved. I was safe for now, but exhausted and in pain.

"We should take you to a hospital," said the Inex, pulling a packet of Company snacks from a selection in the door compartment, the car adding it to the charge.

"Destination: hospital," said the car. "The nearest is Saint Agatha's."

"No! No. We can't go to a hospital. Just take me to the city centre. I'll decide on a specific destination on the way."

"Confirmed," said the car. "Destination: city centre."

The Inex settled next to me, eating. I turned away from it and said, "Mirror, back left," to the car. I stared at my reflection. "Shit."

My nose and left eye were swollen, all deep reds and purples. There were two cuts in my lower lip, both lips swollen, smeared with blood. Tears, snot, and dried blood streaked my face. My hair was congealed with blood, my own and probably Four's.

I rummaged in my bag and took two painkillers, washing them down with vitwater in the car's refreshment selection. I pulled out the rest of the first aid and used one of the bandages to tie my hair back, cleaning my face with another, the sterilising liquid stinging the wounds. The Inex wasn't advanced enough to give me a full bio-report, but when my face was done, it helped me clean and bandage my fingers. I removed the lab coat, my once-white t-shirt underneath soaked through with blood. My blood-stained black trousers were at least less dramatic. I roughly cleaned the rest of the blood off my body, but I couldn't do anything about my clothes. I checked myself in the mirror again; I looked better with my hair scraped back and my face clean. I applied some Ambrosia ointment to help soothe and heal the wounds. By the time I was done, we were on the main motorway, other cars coming and going.

"I don't know where to go," I said, looking out the window.

"The hospital."

"No, for bliss sake – you'll confuse the car. We're not going to the hospital, I told you."

"OK, Icho."

"I have nowhere to go," I said, the reality of it sinking in. "Maybe we'll just drive round the city forever."

"That's not practical."

"No, not practical." I smiled at it, which hurt. "You old models are something else."

"I am model ITL042. We are something else in that we are not you and we are not other models."

"I'm glad you have a clear sense of self."

I stared at all the houses as we reached the suburbs, thinking about Jaw.

"Inex, give me news reports. Search for the name 'Milligan'."

"Visuals?"

"Audio is fine."

"...leader of the opposition, Jared Milligan. He's said to be doing well. He has a broken nose, severe bruising on his neck and will have trouble speaking for a few days. Other than that, he's lucky. Five people were shot today – three of them dead."

"Jesus," I said sitting up, wincing from the pain. Wrapped up in my own troubles, I hadn't thought about the fallout. It hadn't occurred to me that Damon would harm or kill anyone important, including Milligan.

"Is there any theory on who did this and what they wanted? Was it an assassination attempt?"

"We can only speculate at the moment, Claire. Obviously, the prime suspects are the Seraphs, but they haven't yet come forward to confirm or deny."

"Surely the Seraphs wouldn't target Milligan?"

"He's a known supporter of a cure for the HellSans allergy, Claire, and the Seraphs don't believe in a cure – they say society is sick, not them. They think HellSans should be eradicated."

Claire gasped, and I rolled my eyes. "Over-egging it, Claire."

"...extremists destroying our right to bliss. Surely the regular deviants can see the Seraphs aren't working in their favour."

"We can only hope so."

"Has Milligan made a statement about his attacker?"

"Nothing public yet, but we do know there's a witness who might be able to shed some light on what occurred. Our very own national treasure, Jane Ward, CEO of The Company, saw events unfold from her apartment window."

"Jane." I sat up, listening closely. I knew Caddick would have involved her, but I didn't know how.

"We don't know the details yet, as she's not speaking to reporters."

"But there's a recording of the crime?" said Claire.

"No, it seems Jane's Inex was attacked, the Mnemo core stolen."

"Aah," said Claire, deflated. "That's a real shame."

"Yeah, a real shame you can't get off on the footage, Claire," I said, thinking through what all this meant. Jane could have removed the Mnemo to keep the police from accessing footage in case it implicated Caddick. Or maybe it was all bullshit fed to the press.

"...the police will have submitted a warrant to the back-up facilities for both Jane and Milligan, and in the meantime, we hope to have Jane on the show later today to give us her eye-witness account."

"If her Inex was harmed, was Jane attacked too?" said Claire, sounding animated again.

"The police won't confirm, but we know Jane was checked over by a medic and MedEx. There are some eye-witness reports from the scene that she was covered in blood."

"Oh my! Her own?"

"We just don't know at this stage, Claire. But stay

tuned, folks – we'll give you every update as we get it.
Now over to Kevin who's talking with a student friend of
Milligan's – he's suggesting this is just all a stunt to–"

"Shut it off," I said.

I sat in silence for a while, looking over to the city lights in
the distance, my thoughts on Jane. As we hit the edge of the
city, I asked the car to take me as near to the Anthony Royal
Apartments as it could. My Inex warned me of the danger, but
I dismissed it, watching neon HellSans signs slip by in a blur.

CHAPTER 3

The Inex was right – it was dangerous. There was a large crowd of onlookers, press, several police cars, three ambulances, medics, and police coming and going at the Vedder hotel entrance. The Anthony Royal, Jane's apartment building, was cut off, police at the doorway.

I was about to get out of the car, but my payment and location would be traceable. I told it to drive on and it took me a couple of miles south. I got out, doubling back.

"We can't get near," said the Inex.

"I know," I said. "I just want to watch."

"Watch for what?"

"I don't know. Anything. Something."

"You can watch for anything or something anywhere in the city."

I ignored it. I was suddenly aware how hungry I was as I walked, my stomach growling at me. A group of teenagers, laughing and chattering, emerged from one of the basement clubs in a flurry, one of them shouldering me. She turned, about to say something, abuse or apology, but when she saw the mess I was, her face crinkled in disgust. I hurried on, past shops, bars, and clubs. Mannequins walked the length of a shop window and stopped in front of me, each pausing to let me look at the dress it wore, turning, posing, moving on, one after the other, but all I saw was my own bruised face and bloody clothes.

"I look awful."

"You do."

"Thanks, Inex."

"You're welcome."

I turned my back to the window, leaning against it, and eyed the people who passed. Some didn't even register me, but many stared, disgusted, some Inexes swivelling to look at me. With my messed-up face and old Inex model, I worried they'd think I was HSA.

"You need to relax," said the Inex. "You're breathing too fast."

"How can I relax? The Prime Minister is after me, I've nowhere to go, and everyone is recording me."

"Hyperventilating will not help the situation."

I laughed. "What am I going to do with you?"

"You can do many things with me. I am here to assist."

"Then assist. What do I do now? Where can I go?"

"Immediate priorities: Food and clothes. You can consider long-term plans once those are secured. Prime Minister Caddick may not yet know you are missing. It's best to make the purchases before he puts a trace on you. If he does know you're missing, you don't have a choice: you still need food and clothes."

"You're right," I said. "I need to get it together. And we both need to stop talking about this shit in public. Oblique or Internal only."

"OK," it said. "This is a good distance from Jane's apartment and the crime scene. You can buy what you need, clean up, change, and find somewhere to contemplate long-term plans."

"Right," I said, "Not so useless after all, you old tin can."

"I am useful for many things. I am an old model. I am not made of tin. The materials are–"

"I know, I know. Forget it."

"I can't forget."

Ignoring it, I said, "Do you have street access? Take me by the best route."

"I do. I can take you a circuitous route by side streets where you're unlikely to be noticed and recorded."

"Good. Lead the way."

"You're eating too fast," said the Inex.

Dismissing this, I stuffed the sandwich in my mouth, picking up chips in my other hand.

"You're eating too fast."

I shovelled the chips in and glared at the Inex. I washed them down with vitwater and said, "I'm starving."

"You're not starving. And if you were, I'd advise small portions eaten carefully."

I shoved more sandwich in my mouth and looked over at the café's muted projection on the opposite wall. It was the exterior of Jane's apartment building, the police still swarming, press vehicles everywhere.

"I advise leaving. Staying too long after a transaction is dangerous."

I nodded, finished off the chips, and picked up the remainder of the sandwich along with my shopping bags – I'd bought food, make-up, and a Halloween cop costume on my way to the café. I moved down some side streets, then ducked into a bar, my details immediately taken as soon as I crossed the threshold. I ordered a drink and headed to the toilets where I stripped, washed, and applied make-up in an attempt to disguise the bruising and minimise the childhood scar that slivered down my cheek. I cut off all my hair and slipped on the cop costume, hoping it would be enough to blend in at the chaotic scene by the hotel. The badge clearly looked fake, so I tossed it. I put on the police hat, pulling it low.

Staring at myself in the mirror I said, "Shit. This isn't going to convince anyone."

"The costume differs from a police uniform in eight significant ways, but people see what they expect. Your confidence is important – if you act like a police officer, you are a police officer. Environment and situation matters – take advantage of the chaos, and keep contact with people, especially police officers, to a minimum. If you heed this advice, I calculate that your chances of being caught are low."

"Confidence," I said, putting on shades and adjusting my posture.

I stared at myself for a minute before walking back into the bar. I grabbed and knocked back the whisky I'd ordered and left, my account debited, traceable. I took the long walk back.

Despite trying to affect confidence, I felt conspicuous and uncomfortable in the uniform – until I noticed no one was staring at me the way they had when I was a bloody mess. This buoyed me, and I held myself tall, walking in the middle of the pavement, taking up space. I reached a park near Jane's, found a nook in a corner near a tree and some bushes where I could hide my shopping, and headed across the road to the crime scene.

It had thinned out but was still hectic. I joined the rubberneckers, scanning the area. If Milligan or Jane were still on the scene, they'd likely be shielded from the public. I eyed the ambulance next to the hotel and ducked under the cordon.

"*Stay on the ground,*" I said internally. "*Stay inconspicuous. I don't want to have to explain why I'm using an old model.*"

I stopped a cop heading over to the hotel. "Just on the scene. What's the story?"

"It's an unholy mess," he said, distracted, staring over at the corralled protesters near the hotel. His Inex, just ahead of him, stopped and turned. My Inex moved behind me, out of its sightline.

"Five down," he said, looking up at the hotel. "Milligan was attacked – they're calling it an assassination attempt, but we're keeping that from the press for now. Jane Ward was involved too."

"Ward and Milligan – they're OK?"

He shrugged. "Seem to be. Not my area – you can speak to Dillon," he said, pointing. "He'll assign you."

"Thanks," I said, and headed over to Dillon. I checked behind me, making sure the cop and his Inex weren't watching, and swerved to the left, heading for the ambulance by the hotel. There was no sign of Milligan or Jane, just the medics packing up.

"Milligan and Ward?" I said to one of them.

"Gone," he said, glancing at me.

"Gone where?"

"Milligan's people took him, and Jane is back in her ivory tower." He gestured to the Anthony Royal.

I headed to the hotel and caught the lift to the crime scene. I wove between all the police officers and coroner staff, stepping over bodies and into Milligan's room. The bedcovers were half-strewn on the floor and amongst them was Jaw, a broken-up mess. I inspected it; the Mnemosyne core had been torn out.

"The Mnemo?" I said to the cop using her Inex to sweep for prints.

"No sign," she said, not looking up.

"You've swept the room?"

She looked over at me. "You Inex division?"

I nodded.

"Then do your job. I'm not everyone's fucking lackey."

She went back to focusing on the sweep, likely communicating internally with her Inex. I walked over to the window and looked out at Jane's building opposite, wondering which apartment was hers.

I turned back. "*Inex*," I said internally. "*Room scan for a Mnemo core.*"

"*Scanned. No Mnemosyne core.*"

I looked over to the surly cop. "Has anything been taken from the room?"

"Not yet. We've got to wait for Cameron to confirm."

"Who was first on scene?"

"Look," she said, looking up, "Dillon will give you the lowdown. Let me do my fucking job in peace." She considered me, eyes narrowing. "You a rookie?"

I nodded.

"Jesus," she said, shaking her head. "They put you on this? And what in the name of bliss is that piece of shit?" she said, looking down at my Inex.

"It's a temp – my Inex is in for repairs."

"They sent a rookie with a goddamn tin can to *this*?"

I shrugged, trying to look apologetic.

She huffed before saying, "Go speak to Dillon. I don't have time to babysit."

I nodded and she turned away, muttering to herself. I walked over to Jaw, knelt, and reached down, closing its eyes.

I left the hotel and returned to the park across from Jane's apartment. I sat on the bench near where I'd stashed my things.

"Damon must have the Mnemo core."

"Only the Inex owner can access the Mnemosyne core."

"I know," I said. "Caddick will hunt me down. I've nowhere to go. I won't be able to get near Milligan, not after this. There's no point in going to Jane; she'll be sympathetic to Caddick. My only other option is the ghetto, but the Seraphs will kill me at the merest mention of a cure. Even if I found any sympathetic HSAs, it would be too much of a risk and they wouldn't have the means to make the formula anyway. I could hide in the ghetto, but I'm clearly not HSA, and what good would hiding do? Hiding for what? Just to survive? Caddick will have access to everyone in my family, everyone I know, every place I've ever stayed. I can't approach anyone. I can't return anywhere. In a city full of Inexes, he'll find me eventually."

I stopped and looked up at Jane's apartment, visible between the trees. Sighing, I leaned over, clasping my hands, and looked down at the Inex next to my feet.

"Inex, I have nowhere to go."

"You're already somewhere."

I was about to shout at it, sick of the constant literal statements, but I stopped, feeling oddly comforted by what it had said. "You're the only thing I have."

"That is false. You have the clothes you're wearing and the shopping you hid in that bush."

I laid down on the bench and stared up at the night sky, listening as it itemised all the things I had.

CHAPTER 4

I woke at dawn, freezing, the park silent and eerie. As I sat up, my fingers, wrists, nose, and eye all throbbed. The cuts on my lips cracked open when I yawned.

I took two painkillers, smeared Ambrosia ointment on my hands and face, and applied more make-up to try and hide the bruising and my old scar. I ditched the police uniform and slipped into black trousers, shirt, jacket, shades, and a scarf that I pulled up over the lower half of my face to help avoid any Inex face reccing. If Caddick was tracking my transactions, he'd know what I was wearing, but it wasn't a cop uniform and it wasn't covered in blood, so I hoped I'd at least blend in.

I had breakfast, shivering from the cold, realising I should have bought more layers and a blanket if I was going to be sleeping outdoors. When I finished eating, I left the park and walked through the still-quiet streets, only a few cars here and there, Ino street cleaners, a handful of pedestrians. A woman was walking a dog: a rare sight. I stared at it as it pissed against a lamp post before sniffing at everything it passed, making its owner stop every few seconds. I couldn't see the point of the things – an Inex offered companionship and was at least useful.

I walked on and found a café a few streets away, where I risked a transaction. I walked across the street and waited in a shop doorway, my hands wrapped around my coffee cup, sipping, enjoying the warmth and the caffeine hit. I watched the café, glancing up and down the road. A couple of minutes later a car pulled up a few shops down, and a man got out, scanning the street. I jerked back as he looked in my direction. It wasn't Damon, but I was sure it was one of Caddick's men. I inched my way along the doorway and peered round. He was walking towards the café, Inex by his side.

"Time?"

"Six twenty-four a.m."

"It took around ten minutes for him to respond to my transaction."

He went into the coffee shop and I looked round at the car; there was no one else. I dumped the coffee in the doorway.

"Littering is against the–"

"I know," I said, relieved it couldn't report me, amused at the thought of Caddick getting to me because of a littering violation.

I ran across the road, pressed myself against the wall and looked in through the window. He was talking to the owner, the woman who'd served me. His Inex, now perched on his shoulder, projected my image onto the far wall.

"Get me out of here, Inex. Quickest route back to the park."

I followed it, and as we turned into the next street I saw another man in a suit looking up and down the road, scanning the few pedestrians.

"Shit," I said, backing away, turning and hurrying back to the street the café was on, only to see the first man walk out and look my way. He stopped and stared at me, both of us frozen in place. As he reached into his jacket I turned and ran back round the corner, almost falling over an Ino street cleaner. Staggering, I managed to stop myself from sprawling on the pavement. I was about to keep running, but I grabbed hold of the Ino, dragged it along to the corner and raised it over my shoulder, the wounds on my fingers cracking open with the weight of it. It flailed and protested, telling me I'd been reported. I tried to ignore it, listening for the man's footsteps, but I didn't need to – my Inex had calculated when he'd get to the corner, giving me an internal countdown.

I slammed the Ino into his face, blood gushing from his nose. As he fell back, I raised the Ino again, smashing it down on him just as he hit the ground. His Inex, fallen from his shoulder, was trying to right itself when I hit it with the Ino. Letting go, I crouched down and grabbed his gun, jumping as a dart flew right by my shoulder and clattered on the ground. I spun round and saw the second man running for me, firing. I grabbed the man on the pavement, hiking his body in front of me. The man running for me fired two darts into his colleague and in return I hit him in the thigh, my other shots just missing. He skidded to a halt and threw himself into a shop doorway.

The broken Ino was struggling on the ground, trying to get upright, informing me the police were on the way. The Inexes belonging to Caddick's men would have called it in too. I'd be surrounded.

"Inex, map the area and get me out of here now."

"The café," it said, and I ran back to the shop before I even knew why. "There's a door in their basement that leads you along a corridor to a shared storage space a block away, but as soon as you enter," it said as I neared the café, "you'll need to destroy the owner's Inex before it can report you, and shoot the owner with one of the tranquilisers." On the word "tranquilisers" I skidded into the café, grabbed a ceramic bowl of muffins and brought it slamming down onto the head of the owner's Inex, muffins scattering everywhere. I looked up, shot the shocked owner, and slammed the bowl onto the Inex again. "It's incapacitated," said my Inex. "Run." I glanced at the owner who was looking down at the dart, confused, before her eyes rolled back and she dropped. I ran into the back of the café and threw myself down the stairs, my Inex lighting the way through a small dark basement, leading me to a door at the back. It was padlocked.

"Shit. Who even uses padlocks anymore?" I said, propping my shades on top of my head and hunting round for something to break it.

"I'll get the keys," said my Inex. "I saw them on the owner's belt. But you'll need to come with me to the top of the stairs – that's our distance limit."

I ran back up the stairs, the Inex ahead of me. I hovered at the top, sweating, heart racing as I tried to catch my breath. I pulled the scarf down to help me breathe. The Inex seemed to take an eternity and I half-expected to see it appear with a cop carrying it. I heard it first, jangling the keys in its hand. I grabbed them and ran back down, Inex right behind me.

"The police have arrived," it said as it pointed out which key fit. I inserted it, opened the padlock and yanked the chain off, throwing it on the ground, pulling open the door.

"Shit," I said, as I heard voices upstairs.

It was a dead end. Just a cupboard full of bric a brac.

"This isn't an exit, Inex!" I pulled at all the junk, trying to get to the back of the cupboard, as if it might lead me to some kind of Narnia.

"Wrong door," said a voice, coming from the stairway.

I froze, and stared down at the floor, cursing my stupidity; I'd dropped the dart gun and now it was drowned in junk. I slowly turned and saw a boy standing halfway up the stairs. I couldn't see his Inex. He walked down the rest of the stairs and I stared at him, nervy, glancing up when I heard voices.

"A spook told the cops Caddick wants you." He looked me up and down. "Said you took out two other spooks. That true?"

I nodded.

"You a Seraph?"

I almost laughed, but just shook my head.

"Why's Caddick after you?"

"I have something he wants."

"You a spy?"

"Not exactly."

"I can help you escape." He went over to a shelf stacked with bags of coffee and pushed it aside. He unclipped something and part of the wall opened up, revealing a door with Inex and eye-scan entry. "It's my mum's shop, you know. You shot her."

"I'm sorry, I didn't–"

"She's going to be so pissed. I was in the alcove upstairs and watched your dumb Inex come up and get the keys. It didn't even see me."

"It's an old model. Not as sharp as the new ones."

"HSAs have old models."

"I'm not HSA."

"Your face is messed up."

"I was in a fight."

"They come off worse?"

"Not this time."

He nodded and turned to the door, eye-scanning. The door hissed open and he gestured inside. I hesitated.

"Well?"

I walked over, eyeing him, and said, "Why are you helping me?"

"Caddick's a wanker."

I laughed.

"I'm unblissed. When you're unblissed, spotting wankers is like a superpower. And he took my sister."

"What?"

"She's HSA. One of her friends reported her. She's in the ghetto."

"I'm sorry."

He shrugged and said, "You better go."

"Won't they come after me?"

He shook his head. "I'll tell them you ran back out when you saw the dead-end." He gestured to the cupboard I'd tried.

I walked in and held my hand out to him. He shook it and said, "If you need me to join your spy team, come get me."

"How old are you?"

"Twelve."

"I'm not a spy, kid."

"Whatever."

He gave a salute as the door slipped closed. I hurried along, my Inex lighting the way. As I jogged through the tunnel, I thought about the unblissed kid, his mum, his deviant sister, and started to feel sick as I grasped what this tunnel was likely used for. It seemed to go on for miles before it opened up into a low-ceilinged basement filled with boxes and junk. I was about to head up the basement stairs when I stopped and went over to the boxes, pushing aside cleaning products, old electrical equipment covered in dust, bags full of towels.

"You need to go," said my Inex as I pulled at the tape on one of the boxes, opening it up. I was relieved at first to see bubble-wrapped hairdryers, but I pulled them out and found guns underneath. I stared at them.

"You need to go. This is dangerous."

The kid put himself and his family in danger by helping me. He should have handed me over. If the police found this they'd be on death row for treason.

I pushed the hairdryers back into the box and closed it, dumping things back on top. In a daze, I walked slowly up the basement stairs as I put my shades on and pulled my scarf back up over my nose. The stairs led me straight into a kitchen where a man was making coffee, his back turned. I edged by him and emerged into a hair salon. I stared at everyone for a second, a couple of the hairdressers glancing my way before gawping at me.

"Can I hel–"

I ran for the door and out into the street, my Inex climbing through the salon window to avoid the door scan. It hopped onto my shoulder, and I kept running as it guided me through the busy concourse and quiet side-streets. I was relieved when we rounded a corner and were back at the park. I stood, staring at the park, catching my breath before heading in and collapsing on the bench near my stash.

"Idiot!" I said.

"It was foolish to think Caddick would only send one man."

"I thought he'd send a goddamn posse, but I didn't expect

him to be clever enough to spread them out in the surrounding streets. He had me locked in. All because of a coffee."

"It was risky, but now you know response time, general strategy, and that the police are involved."

"How involved do you think? What would Caddick tell them?"

"I don't know. It's likely he labelled you a Seraph or collaborator."

"Probably. Anything on the news?"

"Two brief items saying Chamber Street and surrounding area have been cordoned off due to terrorist activity."

"That's all? Nothing about me?"

"No."

"I thought he'd plaster my face everywhere. He must want to keep this low key for now. Anything on the kid or his family?"

"There's mention of his mother being injured in an altercation."

"OK. Keep an eye on the news for me – let me know if anything comes up."

The Inex helped me clean and re-bandage my fingers, the wounds weeping from using the Ino as a weapon. I lay down on the bench for a while, thinking, watching the overhanging tree branches swaying in the wind, the clouds slowly breaking apart, forming mesmerising swirls.

Sitting up, I caught sight of the Inex a few yards away, swallowing insects. I rummaged through my bag and got out some vitwater and a sandwich. Eating, I watched the Inex, thinking about when I was a kid and I went exploring the forest above our house with my best friend. We'd hiked as far as the Campbell waterfall and stopped to rest. It was a blazing hot day, and we'd fallen asleep in the sun, shocked awake by our parents; our Inexes had informed on us.

I resented my Inex for this, but it wasn't until they policed how we spoke, reporting to our parents every time we used a swearword, that I thought more seriously about the parent lock programme. I decided to learn more about them and tried adjusting mine, which of course got me pulled up not just by my parents, but by the Inex division of the police. This scared the hell of out of me but also made me more determined to understand them. I signed up for Inex modules at school and stayed on every day to work with Ms Stratton, taking them apart, dissecting the biological components, trying to put them back together, but usually messing it up. Stratton's class had to have a special license for this, and all our work was logged and reported so we couldn't do anything illegal. My name was on a permanent register – used both to vet new Company employees and keep an eye on potential hackers.

My parents didn't let me take up Inex work; they pushed me to follow them in medicine, my Inex obsession demoted to a hobby. But the Inex was still an inspiration; I promised myself I'd pursue medicine with the same tenacity as Jane Ward pursued her work. I'd had her picture on my wall since I was thirteen years old.

"You're wondering if I'm a threat."

"What?"

I was startled out of my thoughts and turned to my Inex who was sitting on the bench next to me, digesting its insects.

"You were thinking about when you were a child and your Inex betrayed you."

"Betrayed is a pretty strong word."

"That's what you felt."

"I was just a kid."

"It's what you feel now. You're wondering if I'll betray you."

"Not betray, for bliss sake. I think you might be vulnerable. If Caddick enlists Ward's help in this, I don't doubt she could have you hacked."

"You're right to be concerned. Because I am an old model, I don't have the kind of protection the latest models have. However, because I am old there are fewer vulnerabilities due to my limited programmes and reach. Hackers often find old models puzzling – they consider us, and the people who use us, worthless, so they don't bother to learn how to breach us."

"But Jane Ward."

"But Jane Ward," it said. "You have a skill in choosing enemies."

"I don't know if we are enemies. I don't know how close to Caddick she really is."

I stared at Jane's apartment building, which was still cordoned off.

"Speculating about Ward's involvement will not help. Your priority should be finding somewhere to hide."

"But there's nowhere. All accommodation needs an Inex ID. And I can't go to family or friends."

"It would be best if you went to Milligan."

"Oh, sure, like Caddick isn't going to have him watched, and as if I'm going to get anywhere near him after what happened in the hotel."

"I don't have another suggestion."

"I'll just rot away in this park."

"I advise against that."

I watched people come and go. An HSA caught my eye, begging just outside a clothes shop near the north entrance of the park. Most people ignored them, but a few Inexes surreptitiously slid their hands over the hand of the deviant's Inex, making a money transfer. I watched them for a few minutes. I got up and hiked my bag onto my shoulder.

"Where are you going?"

"*You know where I'm going,*" I said internally, walking through the park.

"*It's a bad idea. It's illegal.*"

"*You going to report me?*"

"*You know I can't do that. I can still advise you. This is dangerous.*"

"*It might not even work,*" I said. "*But at least it's something.* I can't sit in that goddamn park for eternity," I said out loud, a passing woman frowning at me.

"You need to be careful. You might not be on the news, but the police have your ID and will be face-reccing."

"My broken nose, messed up eye, hat, shades, and this scarf should be enough to throw off any face rec. And I have you to look out for me," I said, crossing the road, heading for the HSA beggar.

"I'll do my best," it said, *"but I need your cooperation and you are not very cooperative."*

I walked past the beggar, examining their Inex, but it was three models older than mine and badly busted up. I continued down the busy street and summoned my Inex to sit on my shoulder.

"You can keep an eye out for cops up there."

"This is a terrible idea, Icho."

"Do you have a better one?"

It was silent. I stopped at a shop window, pretending to be interested in the clothes, but really, I was eyeing another deviant beggar. Just as before, most people passed her by, ignoring her, some allowing their Inex a brief transaction. Some got their Inex to drop food in her lap. It was always individuals who gave money or food. Any groups of friends or work colleagues would abuse her, mostly swearing, laughing, some spitting, egging each other on. The HSA didn't react to the abuse. She said, "Bliss you," in response to money or food, wishing upon them what they already had, a reminder of the deviant's lack, eliciting pity.

After examining her Inex, I approached her, crouched down, and offered my hand. She looked at it, then up at my face, before hesitantly raising her hand. I took it in mine, shaking it firmly but briefly. I wiped the dirt and body fluids on my trousers, hoping she wouldn't notice. I figured she couldn't see too well, her eyes puffed up and red-raw, the rest of her face a mess of sores. It was hard to gauge her expression. I knelt down next to her.

"What's your name?"

"What do you want?"

"I have a proposition."

"No," she said, turning away from me.

"You don't know what it is."

"I know your type," she said. "Leave me alone. You can find what you want in the ghetto brothel."

"No." I shook my head. "That's not what I want."

She looked up at the people passing by, her Inex's hand stretched up, ready to receive a transaction.

"I want your Inex. Your ID."

"That's illegal," she said, turning to me.

I nodded.

"What's in it for me?"

"This Inex – a model up from yours and in better condition."

She leaned over and peered at it. "It's still shit."

"And money. Enough to keep you off the streets for a long time."

"What's your game?" she said, looking from me to my Inex and back again. I didn't respond. "What do you want with a deviant's ID, huh?"

"Keep it down," I said, eyeing the people passing by. "Just tell me: yes or no."

"You know Inex tech? You know how to false connect?"

"Yes or no?"

"What happens if I use your ID? Huh? What will that bring me?"

"Look, forget it," I said, sighing, standing up. "If you don't want my money, another deviant will." I walked off, and only a few yards down the street, I heard the HSA calling after me, "Hey! Hey, wait!"

I stopped and turned.

"Just… wait," she said, hurrying after me, her suppurating hand reaching out. "I'm Mary."

"You in, Mary?"

She looked at me and said, "I want food and enough money for a few days in one of the HSA hostels."

"I can give you more than a few days."

"Really?"

"Yes. But you can't use my ID straight away."

"I knew it." She pursed her cracked lips. "I fucking knew there'd be something."

"Just for a couple of days," I said, lying, knowing it would be longer.

"And what happens when I do?"

"A few questions, a night in a cell. Still better than being out here getting spat on. They'll probably reward you if you give them enough."

"And what exactly do I give them?"

"Enough. There's plenty of time to discuss that later."

"And what am I supposed to do until I can use your ID?"

"We'll deal with that. We just need somewhere private so we can work things out."

Her eyes narrowed and she said, "If the cops want you, what's to stop me from turning you in right now?"

I looked at her and said, "I'll say you're an accomplice. No one's going to believe a deviant."

She thought about that for a moment, then nodded and said, "Let's go then."

She turned and shuffled off down the street.

I caught up with her. "Where are we going?"

She ignored me and scratched at her face, flakes of dry skin floating off. It was repugnant, but I remained impassive in case her swollen eyes were on me. After months working in the lab with HSAs, I still wasn't immune to disgust.

"So what's your game, eh?" she said as we walked through a deserted side street. "You must be pretty desperate to want a deviant's ID."

"You don't need to know."

"You can false connect, so I'm guessing you work at The Company. An Inex engineer. Am I right?"

"No, you're not," I said. "You keep asking questions and the deal's off."

"Tetchy," she said and laughed.

"Where are we going?"

"Keep asking questions and the deal's off," she said in a whiny voice that collapsed into laughter, a rattling that turned into a cough. When she recovered she said, "Gideon's Hostel. It's a shithole, and Gideon charges too much, but it's better than being burnt alive by you lot."

I flinched. "I'm not like them."

She shook her head. "You're all the same."

The hostel was down an alley and had a peeling sign above the door that said "Gideon's" in a typeface I didn't recognise. The hostel proprietor was an HSA with extensive scarring, but little in the way of recent or open wounds; he must have found a way to manage his illness, or minimise exposure, which wasn't easy given how HellSans is internalised.

Gideon bantered with Mary while I hovered behind her. He eyed me now and then and got cranky when she said we'd pay later and I told him I wouldn't scan my ID. Mary worked her charm and persuaded him to let it pass.

"Fine. But I don't like the company you're keeping, Mary. We're a respectable establishment."

He looked at me, disgusted, like I was the suppurating, flaking deviant. "If there's an inspection..."

"You can just tell them it was a glitch, you old fart," she said, her Inex on the check-in desk, slipping its hand across the Ino's torso. "Stop making up trouble where there isn't any."

"Not yet, anyway," he said, staring at me.

Mary headed over to the lift, Gideon mumbling something I didn't catch as I followed her.

CHAPTER 5

The lift was broken, so we walked up five flights of stairs that smelled of vomit and shit. The ubiquitous Ino pine scent mingled in with it all, making the stench worse. The stairs were tacky, my shoes making a schlocking sound with every step I took. The stairway was dimly lit, giving the peeling pea-green walls a sicklier hue.

"Gideon's alright," said Mary. "He's just trying to keep things on the level. That's his selling point – he's not like the others."

I grunted. "This really is a shithole."

"Only if you're a pampered blisster."

"You said yourself it was a shithole," I said, as we reached the fifth floor and walked down the corridor to our room. "And you know nothing about me."

"You judge me on my appearance," she said, as her Inex opened the door with a wave of its hand. "I judge you on yours."

"Does my face look pampered to you?"

She laughed and shrugged as she walked into the room. I followed her, the door closing behind us. There was one small grimy window high up on the right wall. The room had the same pea-green walls as the stairway, the paint peeling away, but the light was brighter, the griminess stark. Two single beds took up most of the room. They had grey blankets and no pillows. Mary claimed one of the beds as I looked into the ensuite; a toilet and sink were squeezed in, with barely room to move. There was no shower.

"How many other places like this are there?"

"In this area? Four. I don't know every place across the city. I stick to these parts, but I've been to a couple in Lemmington."

"And they're worse than this?"

"Much worse."

I sat on the edge of the bed, finding that hard to imagine.

"The authorities tolerate these places?"

Mary shrugged. "We've had raids – or 'inspections', as they call them – but mostly they leave us alone." She stretched out on the bed and said, "So what's the plan?"

"I make the swap and I pay the arsehole downstairs."

"The payment will be traced."

"I'll be using yours."

"They'll trace the transfer."

I shook my head.

Mary whistled. "You're definitely ex-Company. That why you're on the run? You steal from them?"

"I'm not ex-Company, I told you."

"Yeah, uh-huh."

"The transaction will show," I said. "It just won't have details or be traceable. That's the best I can do. Ex-company would be more elegant in their hacking."

"Sure."

I sat on the floor, trying not think about the stains on it, and got out my Inex kit. It was a basic Inex toolkit, plus some items of my own that I'd added (technically illegal, but only if I was caught using them; on their own they were innocuous, even if Inex division police knew what they were).

"I know an ex-Company guy," said Mary. "Worked in Inex repair until he became HSA. He fixed this one for me when some arseholes tore its arm off. Raymond Palwick – you know him?"

"I told you – I'm not ex-Company. I need your Inex."

"Get over to the nice lady, Brian," said Mary.

"Brian?" I said as it came towards me.

"So? What's wrong with Brian?"

"Nothing," I said, slipping a pin into Brian's neck.

"What're you doing to him?"

"The pin cuts off communication so it can't report us while I work on them."

I slipped a pin into my Inex. I'd already altered it so it couldn't report me, but this made sure it couldn't communicate at all, either externally or with me, allowing me to work in peace.

"This better work," said Mary. "I'm losing begging time here."

"It'll work."

"If it doesn't, I want paid anyway."

"It'll work."

"How much money you got? If you worked for The Company you must be rich."

"I didn't. And Company employees aren't all rich."

"Rich to me."

I glanced over at her. "True," I said. "Look, Mary, I need to concentrate, so if you can let me get on with it."

"Someone's got a stick up their arse," she said, folding her arms.

I shook my head, thinking about slipping a pin into Mary's neck, and turned my attention back to the Inex. I sliced into its side and peeled back its synthskin. Some synthblood oozed up.

"That's disgusting."

I looked at her, raising an eyebrow, which hurt.

She looked back at me, defiant. "Yeah, yeah, I know – I'm no bloody oil painting, but that still gives me the boak."

"Don't watch, then."

"There's nothing else to do, is there?"

This was an invasive procedure, and wouldn't be easy, as the wrist toolkit only had the basics. Because they were part biological, Inexes bypassed all the problems robots had, the main ones being battery life and movement; they powered themselves on solar, insects, arachnids, small rodents, meal scraps, and The Company line of Inex snacks. Physiology was another major issue. There's an archive of early robotics experiments I remember watching during the Inex module in high school; we all laughed at robots falling down stairs, scoffing at their jerky movements. Then we moved onto Jane Ward's perfect marriage of biological components, including lab-grown musculature, and a 3D printed skeleton. It was a joy to watch the creation of one of the first Inexes in the lab – a timelapse of the muscles and tendons growing around the skeleton. It reminded me of an old horror from the late 1900s, a film I'd watched on a sleepover with friends when I was twelve. We laughed the whole way through, and I joined in even though I found it disturbing. It haunted me – the old attic room, all darkness and rats and rotten wood, the man emerging from the floor partially formed, glistening. His lover brought him men to feed off; he sucked the life out of them, his body regenerating, muscles re-forming. While my friends were laughing and making grossed-out noises, I was taut with empathy, focused on the pain of muscle and nerves exposed to the world's dirt and grime, no protection. Then he became Frank. A friend said he was hot, but I was disappointed by the fully formed man; what lay beneath was more interesting.

It was what lay beneath that fascinated me about Inexes. The bio components weren't only practical – they helped people bond to them. The early models had blue blood and didn't bleed easily. When later models came in, the blood was red and they bled when damaged. People reacted emotionally; they took better care of them, bonded with them. Further models included an organ similar to a heart, so that when you lay your ear against its chest you could hear its "heart" beat.

The blood and the beating heart were also a good way to keep people from opening them up as I was doing now, but I'd done this countless times with various models. I just had to improvise with the tools I had. Usually, any basic Inex repair or alteration could be done without being so invasive, but false connect wasn't supposed to be done at all and you had to get deep into the Inex. I peeled back muscle, revealing the matte silver skeleton.

"You sure it won't report you?"

"I already altered for that. And I told you, this pin silences it; it can't communicate."

"If you're not Company, how'd you learn all that?"

I looked up at her. "It's a hobby, since I was a kid."

"You were a sick kid."

"I was a curious kid."

"Curiosity killed the cat – isn't that what they used to say? When people kept those things for pets."

"Cats have nine lives."

"What?" said Mary, on the edge of her bed, leaning over me. "They regenerate? Is that possible?"

"No," I said, laughing. "It was another saying."

"People were stupid back then," said Mary. "How long will this take? It's making me sick."

"I told you, you don't have to watch."

She huffed, still leaning over me as I jammed the pry bar into the panel, trying to get it open. Designed for later models, it was giving me some grief.

"You're going to break it," she said, standing over me now and peering into the Inex.

"You're in my light," I said, and she shuffled round, sitting in front of me. "And I'm not going to break it – I'm doing the best I can with what I have."

"Didn't you get reported?"

"I told you–"

"I mean when you were a kid, when you were opening them up."

"So many times. I avoided a record when a Company employee stepped in and enrolled me on one of their courses – I guess they figured it was better to have me on side, where they could keep an eye on me. I was desperate to go into Inex tech at university, but my parents pushed me into medicine."

"And you let them?"

"It's complicated."

"What kind of doctor are you?"

"You ask a lot of questions. I can't do this with you hovering over me, Mary."

She was silent, lips pursed, then said, "Fine," and stood up, blocking my light again as I pushed the pry bar in harder. The panel snapped open and the tool slipped further into the Inex, blood spurting in my face.

"Shit!"

I quickly grabbed a hold of the vein I'd punctured as Mary said, "Told you so," and flopped onto the bed.

"Mary, this was – shit! Brian," I said to Mary's Inex, "Get over here."

It sat there, looking at Mary.

"Mary, tell it, I need it – I'm losing this one, c'mon!"

"Brian, go help Dr Whatever," said Mary, sounding like a petulant teenager.

It approached and I said, "Assess and repair. Quickly."

It scanned the Inex and took over from me, sealing the vein and coating the surrounding area in fast-healing ointment made specifically for Inexes (most Inex models stored a small supply for minor injuries).

"Well done, Brian," said Mary, doing an odd little victory dance on the bed.

"You," I said, "Stay there and shut up. You almost screwed up this whole thing."

"*I* did?" she said, puffing her chest, "*I* did? You've got some nerve, doctor."

I was about to argue with her, but instead I sighed and said, "Mary, I need quiet. I need to concentrate."

"I'm not stopping you, doc. I'm just sitting here, quiet as can be."

I ignored her and took hold of Brian, slicing into it as I had with mine. I expected Mary to protest, but she was silent. Brian had blue blood and no beating heart. Its panel was still difficult to get into, but I was careful and didn't cause any damage this time. Once I had them both opened up, I connected them to my Inex repair board and completed the false connect. When I finished, I briefly removed the pins to test them – Brian was now connected to me, and I had Mary's ID. I'd transferred most of my money, leaving Mary with a few hundred. I got her to confirm she was now connected to mine and had my ID, then inserted the pins again, disconnected the board, closed the panels and sealed them up, using what was left of their healing ointment to finish them off before removing the pins for good.

"How much money do I have?"

"You have four hundred pounds, Icho," said the Inex, addressing Mary.

"Four hundred? Are you kidding me?"

"I cannot kid."

"Four hundred," she said, her eyes glazing over. "Think what I can do with that – I can stay here for weeks, no begging, no bloody blisster abuse." She looked over at me, "Doc, you're a saviour."

I couldn't look at her. I'd done all this for me, and the amount I gave her meant little. If she knew how much I had in my account, she wouldn't be thankful at all. My money was now safe, under an HSA ID. As long as I kept a low profile and didn't end up in the ghetto, I wouldn't lose any of it. Mary hadn't seemed to notice her new Inex called her Icho; she just sat there talking about all the things she could buy.

"Not yet," I said, interrupting her fantasy shopping. "You can't use it. You can't go into shops, you can't go out at all."

"What the hell use is that, then?"

"You just need to be patient, Icho," I said.

"Icho? That your name?"

"You're Dr Ichorel Smith and you're wanted. You use that

ID, the police will come down on you within minutes, not to mention Caddick's lackeys. I've put a lock on it for a month to protect–"

"What the hell is the point in that? You've trapped me, haven't you? You've trapped me!"

"Mary–"

"I'll turn you in, that's what I'll do! You can't keep me–"

"Mary, for bliss sake! Just listen to me. I'll look after you–"

"Ha!"

"I will. Now I have your ID, I can go out, I'll get you supplies, all you need. You can stay here and rest and look after yourself – no exposure to HellSans, no abuse, no begging. I'll bring you all you need."

She looked at me, thinking this over. "Then what?"

"Then you can use it, a month from now. And when you do, use it quickly – they'll be on you and will most likely freeze the account. You can pre-order a supply of food, pay up Gideon for a few months. When the cops are done with you, you'll be set up, no worries."

She nodded, thinking. "No worries."

"No worries at all," I said, tying my scarf across the lower half of my face. "Where's the nearest supermarket that serves HSAs?"

"Xavier's on Johnston Place. I want Wurzels, Cherry Spirals, and Fizzy Lemons."

I laughed. "Anything, you know, nutritional?"

She frowned and scratched at a dry patch of skin on her cheek.

"I'll choose some things for you," I said.

"I want what I asked for."

"You'll get it – and more."

"Wurzels, Cherry Spirals, and Fizzy Lemons," she repeated.

"I'm on it."

I put my shades on, tightened my scarf, and went out to get supplies.

***

When I returned, I poured the shopping on the bed and Mary went through it all, like an excited kid, ripping open the pack of Fizzy Lemons and shoving two in her mouth. She clutched the packets of Wurzels and Cherry Spirals to her like they might disappear or I might snatch them back from her.

I'd bought myself a blanket so I wouldn't have to use any of the hostel bedding, and got new clothes so Caddick wouldn't know what I was wearing. I slipped on khaki trousers, a grey top, black jacket, and sturdy black boots.

"You can have these clothes if they fit," I said, handing her the black outfit I'd been wearing. "I've paid Gideon for you to stay here for a month and I've set up pre-paid food delivery for the month too, so you're all set up, Mary. You won't need to use the Inex at all in that time."

She looked at me, still clutching the packets of sweets. I waited for a thank you, but she just sat there, sucking on the Fizzy Lemons.

"Now, when the police question you, tell them I mentioned the name Dr Harold West, tell them it sounded like I was going to approach him for help."

She pushed the Fizzy Lemons into the side of her mouth and said, "Who's that then?"

"An old acquaintance."

"You putting him in the shit?"

"He's an arsehole. Let him entertain the police for a while."

Mary laughed. I rummaged through the things I'd poured on the bed and her laughter stopped. She looked ready to pounce on me.

"I'm just getting this," I said, holding the bleach. "I don't want any of your stuff, Mary."

I left her to her sweets and went into the bathroom to bleach my hair in the sink. It was awkward in such a cramped space and the water was barely more than a trickle. There was

no mirror, but Brian live-projected my image and helped me
bleach the parts I couldn't see or easily reach. It got into some
of my wounds, stinging like hell. I was impatient and rinsed it
off too soon, so it was more a coppery orange than blonde, but
it did what I needed, changing my image just enough.

Once my hair was done, I gathered all my things, wound
the black scarf round the lower half of my face, put on shades,
and donned a black hat, curls of orange hair sticking out of the
edges.

"You look like one of those privacy nuts," said Mary.

Mary told me the nearest HSA hostels. I didn't want her to
know which one I was going to, so I chose one randomly and
planned to stay one night – I'd head out to another HSAH at
the other side of the city the next day and I'd keep moving
around every few days. The security of being able to use an
Inex and have a roof over my head would allow me time to
figure out what to do.

I was about to thank Mary, but she was only helping
me because I helped her. She'd already lost interest in me,
rummaging through the sweets spread out on the bed. I left,
heading to a hostel a couple of miles away. When I got there I
flopped onto the bed, sighing with relief and exhaustion, and
fell asleep.

CHAPTER 6

I woke up late evening, groggy. I took some painkillers; my injuries were healing well with the Ambrosia ointment, and I could now see out of my left eye, but there was still an insistent, throbbing pain. After smearing the ointment on my wounds and rebandaging, I went out for a coffee and was thrown out of every café and bar I walked into. As soon as the entrance system took my details, staff or Inos would appear and turn me around with a "We don't serve deviants". The fifth place I walked into, I told them I had money, but they didn't care. By the seventh, I was looking for a fight, Brian telling me I was putting myself in danger.

"I just want a bloody coffee!"

"Is it worth getting arrested? The hostel proprietor will be able to tell you the HSA-friendly establishments."

Wired with fury, I headed back to the hostel. My rage dissipated as I walked, turning to an aching regret in the pit of my belly as I realised that in my rush to shed my identity, I hadn't thought through all the implications of a deviant ID. When I was back at the hostel, Brian went ahead of me and spoke to the hostel owner. The nearest cafe that served HSAs was four miles away. I was about to return to my room when the owner offered to sell me a coffee. He gave me a gritty, shitty-tasting brew for an extortionate amount and I didn't protest. I took it back to my room and slumped onto the bed.

"Brian, throw the news."

"I can't throw it," said Brian, "The hostel doesn't have its own system."

"Fine, project, whatever."

Every news channel was still reporting on the attempted assassination of Milligan, but none of them had anything new to say; it was all talking heads, speculating, rehashing. When they finished dissecting the attempt on Milligan on *Late Night with Chris Sterling* they moved on to Jane, who'd appeared on the *Rheya Gadon Show*.

"She looks so unwell," said Chris. "In case any of you missed the *Gadon Show*, here's a segment for you all to see for yourselves."

Jane's face filled the wall. She looked serious and tense.

"It looks like yesterday's events took their toll on you."

"I didn't sleep," said Jane. "That's all."

"Because you're sleeping with the enemy? Is that what's keeping you awake at night?"

"Excuse me?"

"There's something you're not telling us about last night's events."

"Is that right?"

Jane and Rheya stared at each other for a moment, Rheya waiting for more, but finally deciding to offer it up herself.

"You were in the hotel room with Milligan when he was attacked. The two of you are having an affair."

Jane laughed, looking genuinely amused, her body loosening.

"You find this funny?"

"Of course," said Jane, smiling. "It's absurd, but whatever keeps people entertained."

"It isn't true?" said Rheya.

"Me and Milligan? Come on!" said Jane, rolling her eyes.

"It's convenient there's no recordings of what happened last night."

"Are you serious?" said Jane, tense again, frowning, edging forward in her seat.

Rheya smiled sweetly.

"My Inex was attacked. That's why there's no recording. Same goes for Milligan."

"But there will be back-ups – have the police requisitioned them yet?"

"They're working on it."

"Are you worried about what they'll find?"

Jane huffed, shaking her head, and pushed a strand of hair behind her ear. One of her fingers was bandaged, the bandage bloody and peeling away. Rheya leaned forward, and said in mock-concern, "Were you injured last night? Were you attacked?"

"No, that's–" said Jane, glancing at her finger. "I tripped over something in my apartment, caught my nail."

"There are reports you were covered in blood."

"Inex synthblood; I found my Inex torn open. I was wearing white pyjamas – it looked more dramatic than it was."

I stared at Jane as they continued talking. The layers of foundation and powder couldn't disguise her sickly pallor and the dark circles around her eyes. Beads of sweat on her forehead glistened under the harsh studio lights.

"...description of the man to the police. I'm sure they'll catch him."

"Do you think it was a Seraph?"

"I really can't say."

"But it's likely, given Milligan's support for a cure."

"It's possible."

"Did they look like a deviant?"

"I couldn't tell."

Rheya looked frustrated at Jane's lack of engagement and refusal to speculate on Seraph involvement, Seraph terrorism being a topic Jane was renowned for discussing at length. Sweat slipped into the corner of Jane's eye and she wiped it away.

"Well!" said Rheya, smiling. "We're all very glad you're safe and sound, Jane, and we hope you get a good night's rest. Thank you for coming in to speak to us today."

It cut back to *Late Night with Chris Sterling*, the presenters discussing the interview.

"She looked *so* sick," said one of the inane presenters, mimicking Rheya's mock-concern.

"It must be stress," said Chris, nodding and furrowing his brow. "She's under a lot of pressure with the Ed Miller case and the Nathan Amos trial, and now to be caught up in an assassination attempt on Milligan, which exposed their affair. Her health is clearly precarious, and I honestly don't think she's fit to–"

"Stop," I said, and the projection ended. "I don't know how the hell she can tolerate that level of scrutiny, all the bullshit people make up. There's no way she's in a relationship with Milligan."

I lay on the bed, thinking over the interview, wondering if the strain she was under was from Caddick – was he pressuring her to hack my Mnemo? Was he angry with her for getting caught up in this? I took another sip of coffee, almost spat it out, and got up to pour the rest down the sink in the corner of the room. I dug out a sandwich I'd bought when I got Mary's supplies and sat eating it, trying to work out my next move, unable to get Jane's image out of my head.

"Brian, replay the interview. From when Jane says she didn't sleep."

"I didn't sleep," said Jane. "That's all."

"Pause," I said, and stared at her. Her skin was a grey-blue, dark circles under her eyes, sweat dribbling down the side of her face.

"Go to the part where the presenter asks about back-ups."

"But there will be back-ups – have the police requisitioned them yet?"
"They're working on it."

I watched Jane, realising she was shaking, only slightly, almost imperceptible.

"Are you worried about what they'll find? Were you injured last night? Were you attacked?"
"No, that's–" said Jane, glancing at her finger.

"Pause."
I looked at her badly bandaged finger. If an Ino had applied the bandage, it wouldn't be coming loose, and if fast-healing Ambrosia ointment had been used, the wound wouldn't still be bleeding.
"Close-up of her face," I said.
Jane's face filled the grimy, peeling wall.
"Background filter," I said, and the wall vanished, allowing me to see Jane's face clearly. "Close-up on her eyes."
Her eyes were bloodshot, her pupils dilated.

"Pull out, play on mute."

I watched Jane, my gaze focusing on her blotchy neck.

"Jane Ward is HSA," I said flatly, as if those words meant nothing, as if I was stating some innocuous fact.

I dropped what was left of my sandwich onto the bed and shifted forward, staring at her, still muted.

"Rheya is right," I said. "There is something Jane's not telling us about last night. Something triggered HellSans allergy." I stood and went over to the projection. "Shit, Brian, do you know what this means?"

"It means she's a deviant, her property and other assets will be requisitioned, and she will be sent to the ghetto."

"No," I said, shaking my head. "No, Brian. It means she *needs* me."

"Given her links with Caddick," said the Inex, "approaching Jane is a risk."

"But it's not," I said. "Not anymore. She would never want Caddick to know she's HSA." I stood, pacing, the silent projection continuing on the wall. "If I get to Jane, she can keep me safe. It'll be in her interest. She can set me up with a lab, she can get me access to Milligan. Jane Ward *needs* me," I said, grinning, looking at her on the wall.

"How will you get past the police?"

"I won't need to. All I need to do is let her see me. She knows I've been working on the cure. She knows she needs me. Tomorrow morning, when she comes out of her apartment, I'll be there."

I'd woken at 6.00 a.m., antsy, so I walked the four miles to the coffee shop that served deviants and was in the park near Jane's apartment just before eight, nursing the remains of my now cold coffee. I waited for an hour, staring at the main door of the apartment, pacing back and forth.

"Shit, where is she? Maybe she left by the back entrance."

I paced some more, then said, "Fuck it." I made my way out of the park and strode across the road to the apartment building, while Brian informed me it was dangerous. I pressed the buzzer, expecting an Ino, but a girl's face appeared on the screen.

"Use the scan pad, please."

"I'm here to see Jane Ward."

"Use the scan pad – we'll let her know you're here."

I said, "Tell her it's Icho," resulting in internal protests from Brian.

"Use the scan pad."

"But–" I said, hesitating. "OK, but my name, the name she knows me by is Icho."

This got even more protests from Brian, but it placed its hand on the pad as requested. I could see the girl's face scrunch up in disgust.

"HSAs aren't allowed in this building."

"I'm not–" I said, sighing. "OK, fine, but can you just tell her Icho is here."

"Your ID says you're Mary Moore."

"I know, I know that, but Jane knows me as Icho. If you let her know I'm here, she'll want to see me."

"HSAs are not allowed in this building."

"I'm not trying to– Just tell her. I don't need to come in. Tell her I'm here."

"I'll pass on your message, Mary–"

"Icho, it's *Icho*."

"–and I'm sure she'll get back to you."

"Jesus!"

I turned away and slammed the palm of my hand against the side of the building, kicking at the ground. I thought for a moment then pressed the buzzer again.

"Use the scan pad, please."

"Can you just tell me if she's still in the building?"

The girl was silent, then said, "HSAs are not allowed in this building. If you persist, I'll call the police."

"I only want to know if she's here."

"Please desist or I will call the police."

I stared at her image on the screen, all pursed lips and furrowed brow. I turned away so quickly I almost fell over Brian.

"Fuck!" I said, heading back over to the park. "What am I going to do?"

"That was extremely dangerous," said Brian. "If the girl contacts the police, your identity will be compromised."

My stomach tightened, knowing Brian was right. "I just need to get to her."

I was crossing the road back to the park when Brian said, "Jane Ward has just left the building."

"What?" I said, spinning round.

"Jane Ward has—"

I ran, dodging in-between pedestrians and their Inexes. I could see her; she'd come from round the back of the building and was about to get into a car, flanked by two police officers. I waved at her and she looked over at me briefly before getting in.

"Shit!" I said, grabbing at my scarf, pulling it from around my mouth, snatching the hat and shades off, dropping them on the pavement. I waved again and yelled "Jane!" as the car pulled away. I ran into the middle of the road, cars halting around me. She glanced back, but I couldn't tell if she'd recognised me.

I stood there, exposed, watching the car disappear, everyone staring at me, Inexes recording.

"Shit."

I ran back to the pavement and picked up my things just before an Ino street cleaner got to them. I put on the hat and shades, winding the scarf around my face again as I headed down a side street, escaping surveillance.

I leaned against the wall, my head tipped back, eyes closed. "Damnit!"

Between that very public display and telling the door girl I was called Icho, there was now a high risk of Caddick finding out I was trying to get to Jane. I had to hope the police officers' Inexes hadn't had a chance to face rec me when I'd pulled off my scarf.

"I warned you of the dangers," said Brian. "Repeatedly."

"I know," I said. "I know."

I doubled back to the park and sat there scanning Jane's apartment and surrounding area for anyone who looked like cops or Caddick's men, but no one stood out. I needed to get to Jane before Caddick realised what I was doing, before he realised she was HSA. I got up and headed for The Company.

The Company was on the other side of the city, and without access to a car it took me almost three hours to get there. In that time, I still hadn't figured out what I was going to do. I hovered opposite the building, watching people come and go at The Company main entrance.

"I don't recommend it," said Brian in response to a half-formed plan I'd only just started mulling over.

"I haven't even decided yet. It was just a thought."

"It's too risky."

"What else am I supposed to do?"

"Wait."

"I'm sick of waiting."

"You'll be trapped," it said.

"I only need to go into the main lobby – get her to come to me."

"They'll likely eye-scan you. The clock will be ticking."

"She'll protect me," I said, staring at the entrance.

"You don't know that."

On internal command, Brian crawled up and perched on my shoulder as I walked round to an alley near The Company.

"This will do," I said, plucking Brian from my shoulder and placing it behind some bins.

"I don't belong in the garbage."

"You're not in the garbage you're behind it, and I'm going past our distance limit, so you'll shut down; you won't be aware of your surroundings." I looked down at Brian. "I'll see you in a few minutes."

"Possible, but unlikely."

"Thanks for the faith," I said, walking away.

"I do not have capacity for faith," said Brian internally.

I lowered my scarf, pulling it snug around my neck, and removed my shades. I strode right into The Company and was immediately taken aside by a security guard who asked me where my Inex was. I explained it was in for repairs after an accident, I hadn't had time to get a replacement, and I had an important appointment with Jane Ward I didn't want to miss.

"Jane Ward has left."

"What?"

"She left at…" he trailed off and his Inex continued, "twelve thirty-five."

"I must have gotten mixed up – I was sure we were meeting here, and I don't have my Inex to correct me. It's funny how lost we are without them."

He eyed me. "What happened to your face?"

"Accident," I said. "My Inex is worse off. Can you–"

"That's an old scar," he said, drawing his finger down his cheek.

"I played with knives as a kid. Look, can you tell me–"

"No one has scars anymore. You should have that fixed."

"It's a badge of honour."

"Aaah," he said, nodding, relaxing. "Military?"

"Can you tell me where Jane's gone? I really don't want to keep her waiting."

"I can't give you that information, Miss–"

"Smith. Doctor Smith."

"I can't give out that information Miss Smith, but–"

"Doctor," I said. "Doctor Smith."

"–I'll speak to her PA. Give me a moment."

I took a seat, relieved he hadn't immediately eye-scanned me, but I was wary of all the Inexes and pulled my scarf up over my mouth again. The guard returned saying Jason didn't have a record of our appointment, but he'd be right down. I was relieved I didn't have to go up, but the guard hovered, asking questions about my military career. Fortunately, Jason saved me.

"It's so good to meet you Dr Smith," he said, taking my hand.

"And you," I said, pulling down my scarf.

"Jane mentioned you. Said I was to arrange a dinner with you... I – Are you...?" he said, staring at me with concern.

"I'm fine, honestly. Just an accident. It's healing well. Is Jane available?"

"I'm afraid you missed her – she's not been feeling well since the attack on Milligan so she's seeing her physician. I don't seem to have a record of your appointment, but there's been a bit of trouble with her Inexes, so it possibly fell through the cracks. Can I rearrange your meeting?"

"It's important I see her today," I said. "Do you know which hospital she was going to?"

"I really don't think she's in the best health for seeing anyone right now–"

"That's the main reason we were meeting: I think I can help her."

Jason considered me and said, "You've spoken with her about her health?"

"I have. I think I know what's wrong. I'm sure I can help."

"That's good. I've been so worried. She was meeting Dr Langham at the Gold Room bar. I've been trying to get in touch with her, but I've been getting an error – she's stubbornly using a MedEx and those things aren't good for much else. Can you tell her to get in touch with me if you see her? Caddick's been trying to get a hold of her too."

"Did you tell Caddick where she was?"

"I did. She's proud – always tries to cope with things on her own, but I think she needs Caddick right now, even if she doesn't know it."

"Right," I said. "Great. I'll see if I can catch her. Thank you, Jason."

"You're welcome, Dr Smith," he said, shaking my hand. "I hope you can help her."

"I'm sure I can." I turned to leave, telling Jason it had been good to meet him, then I quickly turned back and said, "Jason? If you see Caddick, please don't tell him you spoke to me."

He nodded, about to say something, but I headed through The Company doors, pulling my scarf up over my mouth, nauseous at the thought of Caddick.

"You made it back," said Brian as it climbed up my arm and sat on my shoulder. "But no Jane," it said, catching up on what it had missed during our disconnect. "You can't go to the bar," it said as I made my way there.

"I have to."

"Go back to her apartment and wait for her there."

I didn't respond.

"If you go to the bar, there's a high risk of Caddick seeing you."

"Just let it go, OK? I'm going to the bar."

The bar was forty minutes away, but I still hoped to get there before Caddick. When I arrived there was a cop car and one of Caddick's limos outside.

"Shit."

"I told you it's dangerous."

"Don't give me any grief," I said, pressed up against the wall, leaning slightly to look through the window of the bar. Caddick was talking to another man, the man's back to me. I could see Caddick clearly. I turned away.

"Your heart rate is up."

I was suddenly cold, breaking out in a sweat. My hands were shaking.

"You're having a panic attack."

"I'm fine," I said through clenched teeth.

"You're obviously–"

"Just… just give it a rest. You're making things worse. I can deal with this."

"Focus on your breathing. Count as you do so – it will focus you."

I nodded, back against the wall, knees slightly bent, hands on thighs, staring at the ground, counting and breathing.

"I'm OK," I said. "I'm OK."

I glanced back through the window to find they'd gone. I stood and edged my way over, peering in, searching. I heard their voices right next to me as they came out the door. I froze, then slowly turned my back to them. I tried to inch away, but I couldn't move.

"It's no trouble," I heard Caddick say. "We both want what's best for Jane, and the law is the law – if she's HSA, the ghetto is the best place for her."

"I'm glad you think I made the right decision, Prime Minister."

"Call me Dan. Please, after you."

"Thank you."

I heard car doors close, but still couldn't move. I was leaning against the bar window, a sweaty palm pressed up against it, trying to steady myself.

"You're suffering from PTSD," said Brian.

"No shit," I said. "Are they gone?"

"They're gone."

I nodded, concentrating on my breathing.

"You shouldn't be disappointed in yourself."

"What?"

"You're disappointed in yourself for reacting to Caddick this way, but it's natural. He tortured you."

"I'm not... I just... Jesus. Sometimes I'd just like time to figure things out for myself."

"I apologise. I'm trying to help."

"I know," I said, looking down at Brian and feeling bad, as if I'd hurt its feelings.

"We don't have feelings to hurt. You can discount that worry."

I stared at Brian for a moment, then laughed, my whole body shaking. I removed my shades, tears flowing down my cheeks, stinging my injured eye.

"It's good to expel the stress," said Brian.

I wasn't aware how tightly I'd been holding my body until it all unwound. I wiped at the tears with my sleeve. I looked down at Brian. It said, "I know," in response to my thoughts: I had to go to the ghetto. I had to get Jane out.

As I headed back to the hostel, still feeling sick and shaky, I tried to work out Caddick's move, if he would really let Jane moulder in the ghetto. They'd built up such a strong and public partnership, but there were cracks beneath the surface – I'd discovered that in the lab. It was possible, if she'd rejected him, that he wanted her out of the way. Maybe he had someone lined up to take her place. Either way, he'd never fraternise with a deviant.

"But it's *Jane Ward*," I said aloud. "I could be heading to the ghetto and he's already got her out. Maybe he's hunting me down to get the formula for her."

"If you go to the ghetto and she's not there, then you'll know he got her out. We can work out a new plan then."

"I really don't have much choice, do I?"

"Your options are limited."

"I'm walking into a nest of vipers."

"*It's true the Seraphs would not welcome Dr Ichorel Smith, but you are Mary Moore, HSA,*" it said internally. "*However, you made that problematic after revealing yourself to the door girl. She could report you.*"

I nodded. *"You'll alert me if anyone is tracing this ID."*

"Of course."

When I got to the hostel, I gathered up my things: a small backpack with the formula vials, auto-injector, a change of clothes and some food.

"How long will it take for me to walk to the ghetto?"

"Approximately five days."

"Right," I said, nodding.

I needed to stop off at an HSA-friendly supermarket to get more food and enough vitwater for the journey. Brian advised me to stay and rest for a few hours, my energy depleted after my reaction to Caddick, but I refused, wanting to get on. I pulled on the backpack and looked round the room to make sure I had everything.

"Let's go," I said, and Brian climbed up my arm, perching on my shoulder, its arm loosely around my neck. We set off for the ghetto.

CHAPTER 7

Brian was right. The walk to The Company, the fight-or-flight adrenalin surge when I saw Caddick, and the walk back to the hostel had worn me out. The first part of the journey was slow and difficult.

"You should have rested at the hostel."

"I need to get to Jane."

"Resting would have got you there sooner."

"You're probably right–"

"I'm always right."

"I'm not going to make it out of the city tonight anyway. I can rest in one of the other hostels. Are there any nearby?"

"Yes, but you'll have to go two miles off route."

"Fine. Lead the way."

As we headed to the hostel I kept going over Caddick's motivations, his options. Jane was a huge asset to excommunicate. Was he just humouring the doctor? Maybe he had someone waiting in the wings to replace her. Maybe it was revenge because she snubbed him – I had the still-bruised face to prove I'd hit a nerve with that observation.

"You've been over this. Speculating isn't going to help. You're in the dark."

"You're right. I need to focus."

The hostel was even more of a shithole than the others I'd stayed in; my room was barely more than a cupboard, the bed stank, and there wasn't a sink, toilet or shower. I flopped onto the bed and immediately fell asleep.

I woke confused and distressed, soaked in sweat. I'd had a nightmare about Caddick; I couldn't recall specifics but was left with a feeling of dread and the taste of blood in my mouth.

"What time is it?"

"One twenty-five a.m."

I got up and went out to look for the toilets, hoping the HSA residents would be asleep, but there were several in the hallway: two were fighting, shouting and shoving each other, one was passed out. Another approached me and said, "I can give you some bliss, baby."

"Get away from me. I'm not interested."

I pushed past, eyeing them, repulsed by their smell.

"Surly bitch," they said and spat at me.

I hurried down the corridor to the bathroom, hoping for privacy, but there wasn't a door. There were three stalls, and they didn't have doors either. It was filthy and the stench was overpowering. A couple were hunched on the floor, asleep, leaning against each other. I went into one of the stalls and squat-hovered over the toilet as I peed. One of the deviants I'd thought was asleep shuffled over to the stall and leered at me. I grimaced, telling them to fuck off. They kept watching, their Inex's eyes on me too.

"This is private," I said, staring at their Inex.

"Then close the door," said the deviant, laughing.

When I'd finished peeing, I pushed past them to the sink, but there wasn't any water and they laughed some more. I returned to my room, washed myself with anti-bacterial Ambrosia ointment, changed my clothes, and left.

"I'm never staying in another hostel again," I said to Brian as we walked through the outskirts of the city.

I made it to the posh part of the suburbs and fertilised someone's lobelias just as dawn was breaking. As I walked on and houses slowly came to life, I debated whether to remove the scarf; privacy nuts, who were a fixture in the city, were practically unheard of in suburbia. I watched kids tumble out of a nearby house, their parents waving them off, and knew I couldn't risk any face reccing. There was also the risk of being mistaken for a deviant with my retro Inex; if I was stopped and ID'd by police, that would only be confirmed. Technically, the police would give me exactly what I wanted – they'd take me straight to the ghetto, but I'd heard too many stories of police brutality from the HSA lab rats to think that was a good idea. There was also the risk they wouldn't only ID me, but face rec me, too. I kept the scarf on and tried to stick to the periphery of the 'burbs, Brian alerting me if it saw any police or anyone taking too much interest in me.

The first day walking to the ghetto was uneventful, the weather thankfully warm with a light breeze, but it was a slog. The endless manicured lawns and houses that all looked the same got tedious pretty quickly. I passed through a community called Bliss Valley and I couldn't think of anywhere less blissful. I'd take a shithole hostel over Bliss Valley sterility any day.

"No you wouldn't," said Brian.

"It's hyperbole. To show my disgust at the place."

"You were only thinking this, so for who's benefit was this hyperbole? Yourself?"

"Yeah, why not? Stop invading my thoughts."

"I thought you might benefit from conversation – you're bored."

"That I am, and I doubt your conversational skills will alleviate that. Just give me news reports – anything on Jane?"

There was a couple of seconds silence before Brian said, "Caddick was interviewed. He mentioned Jane."

I thought for a moment and decided against listening to it, worried his voice would provoke another panic attack.

"That's wise," said Brian. "I can summarise for you."

"Please."

"He discussed the assassination attempt on Milligan. There was a lot of anti-Seraph bluster despite there being no evidence implicating them. The interviewer asked about Jane's health – he said she's well but needs rest."

"So he's keeping it quiet. Anything else?"

"The doctor is dead."

"What?" I stopped and stared at Brian. "What did you say?"

"Jane's doctor is dead."

"What do you mean he's dead?"

"Suicide."

I shook my head. "Why? What happened?"

"He was exposed for sending newly diagnosed HSA patients to the ghetto and siphoning off their money. The money should have gone to ghetto upkeep. It's sparked a big debate about what happens to the money he stole. Many people don't want it to go to the ghetto because they think it's funding terrorism, but charities and NGO's are saying it's a scandal and the ghetto is in urgent need of medical supplies, clothes, and blankets as winter approaches. They're also debating Inex financial security, putting pressure on Jane Ward and The Company to make sure that kind of HSA exploitation can't happen in future. It's reignited discussion about whether we need physicians at all when we have sophisticated Inos, Inexes, and MedExes that won't fall prey to exploitation and greed. Veronica Lambert, spokesperson for The Company, insists that all Inos and Inexes are there in an assist capacity only – they do not replace people, but help us be the best we can be. She emphasised that in medicine we need the human touch. She stated stringent safeguards are the best route and The Company will consult with the medical and financial establishments to bring this about."

"It's not suicide," I said, shaking my head. "It's Caddick. The doctor was the only other person who knew about Jane's HSA status, the only other person who knew she'd been taken to the ghetto. What's Caddick's plan?"

"It's unclear what Caddick's motivation and plan is."

"What if she's not in the ghetto? What if Caddick has her? And all this is for nothing?"

I sat down on the curb, head in hands.

"You're not thinking clearly," said Brian. "I don't know what to respond to."

I laughed and stared at it. "I don't know what I'm doing, Brian. I should have stayed in the city. I should have tried to get to Milligan."

"Your original thinking was sound," it said. "It will be too difficult to get to Milligan after the assassination attempt and you would risk exposure. Getting to Jane because of her HSA status makes sense – you provide her with the formula and she can return to her former life. She can get you immediate access to Milligan, who's in her debt. Even if her allegiance lies with Caddick, you have power over her because you have the formula. It will be risky, but it's worth trying. It's unclear what Caddick's plans are – you shouldn't let him sidetrack you, but I will continue to scan the news for any relevant updates."

I stared at Brian, unsure how to respond.

"I'm doing what I'm supposed to do – assisting you. There's no need to thank me. Sentiment means nothing to me. But if it helps you bond with me, I can engage with it."

"How did humans ever manage without you?"

"They had difficulty being the best they could be."

"I bet they did. I really can't imagine what it was like."

"There's various books and films that can help you imagine if you'd like me to source them for you."

"No," I said, smiling. "It's fine." I stood up, resuming my walk. "Just keep me updated on any relevant news."

"I will."

"Is there anything on me?"

"No," said Brian after a short pause.

"Good."

"But you're worried?"

"I thought he'd have my face all over the news, all over hoardings. It actually frightens me that he hasn't done that."

"It's good – it gives you more freedom."

"It does," I said, but I still felt on edge. "I'd thought about heading him off... Going straight to the press – safety in the public eye."

"No," said Brian. "That wouldn't–"

"It would just make me vulnerable; I know. If Caddick didn't get to me, the Seraphs would take me out. But it's an option."

"A bad option."

"Still an option. And better than my final option."

"That is true, but it could amount to the same thing."

"That's very comforting, Brian, thanks."

"I don't want you to underestimate the risks."

I walked on for another few miles, blisters forming on my feet. I'd had a few looks from people, which made me twitchy, so I got Brian to lead me out of the neighbourhood to a nearby river, continuing my journey undisturbed. As night fell, I found a place to sleep in some bushes on the riverbank.

"Your period is due in approximately four hours."

Thrown, I stared at Brian. "What?"

"Your period is due in–"

"I heard you," I said. "Shit."

Jaw usually gave a more advanced warning. I didn't have anything with me, so I got a clean sock from my bag and stuffed it in my pants. I could wash it in the river in the morning and use the other sock until I found a shop. Legislation had recently gone through banning sanitary towels and tampons in a bid to save the environment, despite many other frivolous disposables escaping a ban. The only things available now were reusable pads and menstrual cups, but amidst everything that had happened, it hadn't occurred to me I might need them. Wrapped in the blanket, I settled myself in the bushes and fell asleep listening to the river.

I was woken at dawn by the noise of birds, something I wasn't used to, and despite the foliage providing some protection, I was damp from overnight rainfall. My period cramps were bad and my sock already sodden. I replaced it, stuffing the spare sock down my pants, and went down to the river and washed the blood-soaked sock. I hung it on my bag, hoping it would dry as I walked on. I stuck to the river for most of the day, until the thickening undergrowth made it impossible to walk along the bank. I made my way back into the suburbs, keeping to the outskirts, hoping to go unnoticed.

The next day I reached the edge of the 'burbs, which gave way to a small green belt of fields and farms. One of the farms was surrounded by a barbed wire fence and surveillance Inos. I could see cows grazing. I was curious, as I'd never seen one before, but I kept my distance, not wanting to be mistaken for an animal rights extremist. I also didn't want to stray too far from the river, given I needed to be able to wash my socks every day. As the sun was setting, I could see the housing estates about a mile away, and I retreated to the river, setting myself up for the night.

The next morning, I entered the estates. After the quiet of the 'burbs – the green belt birds, furtive rodents and creaking trees – the noise and bustle of the housing estate was unnerving. I watched people hurrying to work and school, kids on bikes and scooters – something you rarely saw in the city, most people travelling by car. I got caught up watching people, enjoying the human presence for a moment, but felt nervous when Inex eyes fell on me. I didn't dare pull my scarf up, but my shades and hat offered some protection.

I'd never been to this area before; I'd always taken the motorway by car to and from the city, far removed from the housing estates. The high-rises were all previous century, in varying states of decay. HellSans was everywhere. Corner shops and pubs were adorned with massive neon signs in HS, their windows decked in advertisements and special offers, drawing people in with a bliss hit. Street names in HS were all clean and clear, and almost all windows in the high-rises were plastered with HellSans – some showed political affiliations, others were posters of favourite sports teams or bands, and there were various Inex posters: **"HELPING YOU BE THE**

BEST YOU" – bold, capitalised bliss. Unlike the city, all the HS was free from the Seraphs' serifs.

I went into one of the corner shops and bought a menstrual cup, extra food, and vitwater. I didn't know if they served HSAs, but they didn't have a door ID system. I knew the shopkeeper and their Inex were watching me as Brian led me to everything I needed.

"New around here?" said the shopkeeper as their Ino glanced at my purchases, calculating the price.

"Passing through," I said.

When Brian made the payment via the Ino and Mary's HSA ID came up, nothing in the shopkeeper's expression changed, but his voice was harder when he said, "I wouldn't linger."

"Passing through," I repeated as Brian put my things in the bag.

"Good."

On the surface of it, there was nothing threatening about the exchange other than the usual HSA prejudice. The instruction not to linger could even have been to help me, but it made me tense. I felt like I had a huge X on my back.

"Brian, alternate route?"

"The woods above the estate are your best option – and should be safe for sleeping tonight."

"OK, lead the way," I said, staring at one of the street signs. I looked closer, realising red serifs had been scrubbed off; the paint had stained the white of the sign, leaving behind a pink shadow.

I hiked up the hill and had some lunch when I reached the top. I ditched my bloody sock, washed my hands in the anti-bacterial liquid I'd brought for my wounds, did the same with the cup, and inserted it before heading on.

I set up camp in the woods before nightfall and woke at dawn the next morning, freezing, wishing for a hot coffee. I got up, stretched, and jogged around, trying to get the stiffness out of my muscles and bring myself some warmth. I settled back down, huddled in the blanket, and ate breakfast as I listened to the news. There was nothing new on Jane or Caddick, but there was a short report on Jane's doctor, saying his HSA exploitation had gone on for years. They moved on to a segment on animals, featuring an interview with a renowned animal rights activist – he'd been in the news a lot, campaigning to have the farming of animals completely outlawed; but he was up against the elite, his efforts always stymied despite popular support. He was now pushing for legislation that would allow Inexes to be connected to animals.

"Non-human animals were sacrificed to bring about these things that we can't live without. It sounds barbaric to us now, but non-human animals were tortured in the early days of the development of the Inex. It's rarely mentioned in any of the textbooks, and Ward glosses over it in The Company guided tours. Now people like Caddick and Ward are blocking use of Inexes to help us communicate with non-human animals – citing cruelty as the reason, ironically. But we all know it's because it will give us irrevocable proof of their sentience, which would make any exploitation of non-human animals unthinkable, including the so-called 'ethical' farms that the rich are so fond of. If Caddick and Ward–"

"Jesus," I said, "How can this arsehole get so sentimental about animals when there's still so much human suffering? Let them hook up an Inex to a rat or whatever and we'll soon see all it thinks about is screwing other rats and eating. They have no more emotion than you do," I said, gesturing at Brian.

"There have been numerous studies showing that rats–"

"I don't want to hear it. Just pack my bag while I take a piss."

"OK. If you'd like to know more about non-human animal sentience–"

"I don't," I said, shedding the blanket, pulling down my

trousers, exposing my arse to the cold air as I crouched to pee. "Just pack, and scan for any other news on Jane and Caddick."

After peeing, I emptied and rinsed my cup, reinserted it, and got dressed. When I set off, I listened to Brian's summaries of news reports on Jane and Caddick – there was little of use; mainly rumours, gossip, and repeated soundbites. I walked on for several miles, keeping to the woods above the housing estate.

"How long until I reach the ghetto?"

"Approximately eight hours."

I stopped, took a drink of vitwater, and lay down for few minutes before continuing. In just over two hours, the housing estates below gave way to industry; factories and warehouses spread out for miles. Somewhere to the south was where the latest Inex model was manufactured, and north of that I could see the sprawling ghetto, much larger than I'd thought. I saw half a dozen police patrols between the ghetto and the factories. Each factory's complex was gated off, with the roads outside only designed for cars, not pedestrians, so I would immediately stand out. Getting picked up by police was too much of a risk, so I stayed in the woods until nightfall. I doubted they were looking for me; Caddick would have no reason to believe I would head for the ghetto, unless he thought I was foolhardy enough to think the Seraphs would welcome news of a cure. Maybe he had worked out every option I had and covered all of them, just to be sure. More likely it was because we were close to the ghetto and the police were scanning for rogue deviants – I'd heard about HSAs breaking into a factory to steal MedExes.

I sat down and had something to eat as I watched the patrols, soon realising they followed a pattern.

"Brian, watch the patrols for the next hour and map their routes."

If they followed the same routes, Brian could help me avoid them. I finished my food and waited impatiently for the sun to go down.

CHAPTER 8

In the twilight, I made my way down. Brian, having mapped the police patrol routes, led the way. I tried to stick to dark spots as best as I could, but all the factories were lit up, the brightness spilling out into the surrounding roads.

As I approached the ghetto, I knew something wasn't right. I could hear voices, like there was a street party, and dozens of cars went past, stopping on the side-roads closing in on the ghetto. I followed the cars, the voices getting louder, and as I turned into the road that led to the ghetto entrance, I saw row upon row of cars and groups of kids, likely in their mid-to-late teens. I'd heard that some rich kids went to the ghetto brothel, that they got off on the illness, but that was just a handful of kids, not this – there were hundreds here. As I watched them, I noticed they all had something in common: weapons. They carried baseball bats, hammers, knives. A few of them had guns tucked into the back of their trousers.

"Shit."

It was a raid. I'd seen coverage of them on the news, and I'd heard about them from my lab HSAs who told me how brutal they were. The news reports were always vague, with talking heads basically saying they deserved it for trying to destroy our bliss. The raids usually took place after a Seraph attack on the city, but there hadn't been anything recently.

"This couldn't be worse timing, Brian. Shit. I need to get in there. I need to warn them."

"You need to walk out into the open."

"What are you talking about? I'll be torn apart by fucking children."

"Pretend to be them – look. They're all dressed in muted colours. They all have scarves over their mouths."

"You're right."

"Pretend you're reconnaissance."

I thought this through, and Brian said, "I know you're afraid. Stepping out into that crowd isn't going to be easy, but you only need to believe in your cover. Believe you're one of them and have every right to be there."

"Just give me a moment."

"You'll need to hide me – none of them have Inexes."

"Ah," I said. "You're right."

I'd known something was off the whole time I'd been staring at them, but in my panic I hadn't realised what it was.

A few yards from me, a car door opened. A man in a navy suit stepped out, followed by a high-end Inex. A teenage boy broke away from one of the groups and came to meet him. They shook hands and stood talking only a couple of yards from me.

"Brian, can you hone-in?"

"*…As much chaos as possible,*" said Brian internally, picking up the man in blue. "*It just needs to look like kids getting their kicks. You know who you're looking for?*"

"*Jane Doe, block 366, bunk 89.*"

"*Your Inex has her image – make sure it matches before you kill her. Tell me the procedure.*"

"*Teams Alfa, Bravo, Charlie and Delta will be in place. I take her out, then they light the place up and Team Foxtrot bombs the council building.*"

"*Good. Inex – time?*"

"*Eleven twenty.*"

"*Just under forty minutes and you're in,*" he said, placing his hand on the boy's shoulder and leading him further up the street, out of earshot.

"What the fuck is going on?" I said. "You think Jane Doe is Jane? This is all for her?"

"Possible."

"Block 366, bunk 89... I need to get to her first," I said, taking my bag off my shoulder and opening it for Brian. "I'm going in."

"Hey!"

I turned to find a white rich kid with floppy blonde hair and a sword by his side.

"It's not time yet."

"I'm reconnaissance. Ask the chief," I said, cringing when I said "chief" and trying not to look at the kid's sword.

"The chief?"

"Yeah, that's what my crew call him," I said, Brian in my head telling me to stop trying to talk like I think teens talk. "We have another name for him too," I said, smiling, arching my eyebrow. "That government bastard has a real stick up his arse, huh? But we get a fun night out of it, so I'm in. Look, I need to go. I've got to check security at the main entrance."

The kid looked at me, swinging the sword.

"Where's your weapon?"

"I'm reconnaissance," I said, backing away. "Chosen for my ninja skills – don't need a weapon."

He seemed to buy this bullshit and said, "Good luck."

I smiled, saluted him, turned and ran.

"It's gonna be a massacre, Brian," I said, trying to get that sword out of my mind.

"I calculate–"

"I don't want your calculations."

I walked straight up to the main entrance, nervous, expecting it to be heaving with Seraphs, but there was just one man, half-asleep, his tin can Inex keeping lookout for him.

When it saw me it must have internally warned him, as his eyes snapped open and he stood up.

"There's hundreds of kids out there with swords, clubs and guns. You have to warn the Seraphs."

The guard looked at me, dazed.

"Midnight. They're moving in at midnight. We have thirty minutes at most."

"Twenty-five minutes and thirty-three seconds," said Brian from my bag.

"Twenty-five minutes and thirty-three seconds," I said, taking my bag from my shoulder and letting Brian out.

The guard stared at Brian, then out into the empty streets surrounding the ghetto. "I don't see anyone."

"You're all going to be slaughtered in less than half an hour – you need to let me in. Warn the Seraphs now."

"This how you get your kicks, causing panic and putting me in the shit?"

I hadn't properly thought this through. I'd counted on them believing me. I should have attempted to sneak in and get straight to Jane.

"Maybe you're a bomber, huh?"

"Look, you can scan me, scan my Inex, but we're running out of time."

"I don't have that kind of tech."

I sighed and told him to search me, but he frowned and crossed his arms. I got Brian to replay what we'd heard, but he didn't buy that either, accusing me and my friends of taking the piss.

"Look, you sonofa–" I stopped as Brian internally interrupted me with a suggestion I should have thought of. "Let me ask my Inex, then – I ask it a direct question, it can't lie, right? Brian, did I overhear plans to raid the ghetto tonight?"

"Yes, you did."

"Did I see hundreds of kids with weapons on the main road to the ghetto?"

"Yes, you did."

"Better to be safe, Steve." I flinched as a woman emerged from the shadows behind him. "Let her in."

"That's right, Steve," I said, scornful, but eyeing the woman, my heart racing. "Better be safe."

"Don't provoke him," said Brian.

"He's an arsehole."

I walked through the gate and the woman frisked me. She told Steve to take me to the Council Building and secure back-up teams for all entrances. I followed him, but turned and looked back at the woman and asked if she had any weapons. She nodded, raised a gun, and turned to look out onto the streets.

"She's gonna die, Brian," I said, catching up with Steve.

"Likely."

I told Steve we needed to go to block 366, but he ignored me. I continued to press him and was on the verge of bolting into one of the dark alleys when we were surrounded. I jerked back and turned, staring at the five silent women dressed in black. Seraphs. One of them nodded to Steve as another took hold of my arm. Steve smiled as they led me away.

"Did he tell you?" I said, turning to the woman gripping my arm. "Did he tell you there's a raid?" I assumed he'd internally communicated with them and I was sure he'd told them I was full of shit. "There's hundreds of kids out there with weapons. We've got–" I checked with Brian "–thirteen minutes and thirty-five seconds."

The woman was impassive; none of them responded.

"Look, I need to… Block 366. There's a specific target. Bunk 89. They're going to kill her."

"Aren't they going to kill us all?" said the woman up front, turning slightly, her tone making it clear she didn't believe anything I said.

"But she's a specific… We need to get her out of there."

There was no response as we continued up the path.

Desperate, I tried to writhe out of the woman's grip, but she yanked my arm behind my back and whispered in my ear, "Do you want me to break it?"

I froze. "Please. Just send someone to block 366, that's all I ask." She jerked my arm and I shut up.

"We have to get out of here – they're going to bomb this building."

I was in a room in the basement of the council building with three Seraphs. It was only later I realised how terrifying that was, but I was fixated on Jane; the danger hadn't fully sunk in.

Two of the Seraphs stood flanking the entrance, the lead Seraph sat opposite me. With a head gesture she called her Inex up on to the table and it walked across to mine, its hand out, after my ID. I internally OK'd it and the Inexes touched hands.

"Mary Moore," said the Seraph's Inex. "HSA for four years, six months and eight days."

The Seraph looked at me, examining my face and my hands. My old scars and current cuts and bruises were clearly not HellSans-allergy-related. "Looking good for a city-dwelling HSA," she said, leaning forward. "Those four years have been kind to you."

"We don't have time for this," I said. "The ghetto is going to be–"

"Ask your Inex," she said, "Ask if you're Mary Moore, HSA."

I eyed Brian and said, "Look, this doesn't–"

"Emergency call from S51," said the Seraph's Inex. She must have given internal assent as a panicked voice emanated from it. "Nine, we've got a raid on our hands. On a scale we haven't seen before. They're taking out Inexes so we can't communicate. There's hundreds of them, with guns and knives. They're burning the place to the ground–"

There was silence. Her Inex said, "Connection lost."

"Try again," said Nine.

"No connection."

"Contact all squad leaders," said Nine. "Code Four."

"See," I said.

Living up to the Seraph reputation, she didn't seem phased by confirmation of the raid other than a look of mild consternation. "Let's go," she said, standing, gesturing to the sentries at the door.

I got up to follow them and she raised her hand. "You stay."

"You can't leave me here."

"I think we can."

I reached out to Nine, but one of the sentries stepped in, blocking me. I backed off and said, "I need to get to Jane."

"Who's Jane?"

"Jane Doe," I said quickly. "Block 366, bunk 89. I heard them plan it. Whoever she is, she's important to the raiders – they want her dead and the confusion of the raid to cover it up."

"Why do we need you?"

"I know what she looks like – they projected her photo," I lied. "I can make sure it's her. If she's this important to the raiders, you'll want her, right?" I said, realising I was digging a hole for us both – if we found her alive, I'd be handing her straight over to the Seraphs.

"I can hel–" I said, but was cut off, Nine raising her hand to silence me. Her head was cocked slightly, internally conversing with her Inex.

"Twelve, go ahead and get our weapons," she said to the Seraph who stood between us. She ran out without a word.

"If you're responsible for any of this," Nine said, walking over to me, her face inches from mine. "I'll personally eviscerate you."

"I tried to *warn* you," I said.

"*Calm down*," said Brian internally.

"I won't fucking calm down," I said aloud, looking down at

Brian. I turned back to Nine. "You should have listened to me."

The Seraph only gave me a withering look and said, "Records tell me bunk 89 of 366 is Sarah Hamilton. What's so important about her?"

"I don't know," I said, confused. Even if Jane had used a pseudonym, they would have surely ID'd her. I looked down at Brian, thinking she must have false connected too. I thought about the man in blue, the government lackey, how he knew what block Jane was in. *"The ghetto have to register every new entrant with the government,"* said Brian internally. *"They likely guessed it was Jane."*

"But why the raid?" I said. *"Why not just send an assassin?"*

"Two birds with one stone." said Brian. *"The raid clearly serves a purp–"*

"Why are you here?" said Nine, interrupting our inner dialogue. "You're not HSA."

I was thinking of a response when an explosion shook the building. I cowered, pressing myself into the wall, as if it could offer me protection. Nine didn't even flinch, the only sign of emotion was the fury in her eyes.

"You," she said, grabbing at my shirt, bunching it in her fist, "piece of shit blisster–"

"I'm not a blisst–"

"You take her," she said to the other Seraph, pushing me towards her and letting go of my shirt. "Then meet up with Five's squad. If you find this Sarah alive get her to–" She stopped, eyed me, and said, "Safety. I want to question her. And don't let this bliss-shit out of your sight."

"I'm not a blisster," I said, as she ran up the stairs and the Seraph charged with looking after me shoved me up after her, Brian clinging to my shoulder.

Smoke filled the stairway the higher we got. Nine had vanished, and when we reached the top of the stairs we could hardly see anything for the smoke in the hall. I struggled to breathe and brought my scarf up over my mouth as if that would offer some relief. We looked down the hallway to the main entrance and saw it was in flames. The Seraph grabbed at my arm and pulled me in the opposite direction. I jumped when Twelve appeared suddenly and handed my Seraph several weapons, which she clipped onto various parts of her body with ease, still half-pulling me along the corridor. My eyes were watering, my breathing laboured as I staggered along with her. We burst out the back exit and I pulled the scarf down, gasping. Twelve ran down the back stairs, disappearing as we headed round the side of the council building towards the square. Most of the surrounding blocks were on fire, the main entrance of the council building was spewing smoke, deviants were running through the square, shouting. The Seraph surveyed this for a moment, then led me back round the side of the council building, weaving through all the dark walkways between the still untouched blocks.

"How far?"

The Seraph didn't respond. I followed, catching glimpses of fire and people running. We ran on for another few yards when the Seraph said, "Here," and pointed at a block.

"Are you sure?" I said, and she narrowed her eyes in response.

The block was on fire, but it was supposed to be one of the first targeted and should have already burned to the ground. Either this wasn't the right block or something – possibly my early warning – had delayed their plans.

We made our way to the entrance, but it was in flames. We went round the side and climbed through a window. Inside, we couldn't see much for the smoke. The Seraph placed a cloth over her mouth and disappeared ahead of me. I pulled my scarf up again and crouched low, coughing. I couldn't see her, but I continued down the main aisle of the block and she emerged out of the smoke, knocking into me. She signalled we were to leave, but I protested.

"Is she there?"

The Seraph nodded and headed on, but I needed to see for myself. I continued to the back of the block, barely able to breathe. I wasn't ready for it – the body or the blood. Jane had been shot in the chest and the head.

"*You need to leave,*" said Brian. "*You're suffering from smoke inhalation. This is dangerous.*"

I ignored Brian, staring at the body. I was nauseous, about to turn away, but instead I looked closer and saw it wasn't her. I lingered, staring, just to make sure.

"*You're right,*" said Brian. "*It isn't her. Now get out.*"

The Seraph emerged from the smoke and grabbed me by the arm, pulling me the length of the block. I half-walked, half-stumbled, falling, feeling the Seraph's strength as she dragged me. She pushed me up and out of the window and I lay on the ground coughing, spitting, breathing in the hot air as the flames engulfed all the blocks around us. The Seraph dragged me over to one of the dark walkways, away from the spotlight of the flames.

She took out a hip flask and offered it to me. I refused, thinking it was alcohol.

"Water," she said.

I snatched it and gulped, much to her annoyance, and she grabbed it back from me. She drank some herself, then took me by the arm and set off, likely taking me back to the council building to throw me in that room again before meeting her squad. I had to lose her; she believed Jane was dead, and I needed to continue my search, even if I didn't know how to find her in this chaos. I couldn't return to that room, and I couldn't risk another Seraph interrogation.

We kept to the darker walkways, but more and more blocks were alight, and it was harder to find safe passage. The Seraph's grip on me was loose, and she seemed distracted, likely communicating with other Seraphs via her Inex. She suddenly let go and ran ahead of me and I stood there, surprised and confused.

"Hide!" said Brian, snapping me out of it.

As I turned to run, I caught a glimpse of what had made the Seraph drop me; one bloody and flailing Seraph holding off three raiders. I heard three shots as I ran in the opposite direction, wanting to get as far away as possible before the Seraph noticed she'd lost me.

As I ran, Brian said, *"Mary has used her Inex."*

"What?" I said, not understanding at first. I stumbled and half-fell over a body. Righting myself, I stood, leaning up against an untouched block, catching my breath. "What did you say?"

"Mary has used her Inex."

"That's not possible. There's a lock on it."

"She used it."

"How? There's no way she could–"

"She has an ex-Company friend with Inex repair experience. She may have employed his services."

"Damnit, Mary," I said. "Why would she do that? I gave her everything she needed. Does Caddick have her?"

"The police."

"Same difference."

"She's been arrested for theft and false connection. It won't be long before they trace me."

"Shit."

"Do you want me to shut down?"

I heard gunshots behind me and jumped, spinning round. I couldn't see anything for the smoke and the flames. I turned back and ran through a main concourse between two rows of burning blocks. *"No,"* I said to Brian, running, directionless. *"They'll trace me to the ghetto and then what? It's mayhem here."*

"You're right, but I advise finding a replacement Inex within the next hour."

"Given the likelihood I'm going to be killed by Seraphs or raiders, that might not be much of a problem."

"You should acquire a weapon for self-defence."

I laughed. "I doubt that'd make much difference," I said aloud.

"*You underestimate yourself.*"

"*You know how I reacted in the lab.*"

"*You've improved since.*"

"*I appreciate the pep talk.*"

"*It's best you avoid confrontation, if possible, but I advise securing a weapon.*"

I watched Brian scan the dead bodies a few yards in front of us.

"That Seraph has a gun," it said, spotlighting her body.

"I don't know how to use it."

"I have access to basic instructions."

I approached the Seraph, took the gun from her hand, and searched her jacket for more ammunition. Brian told me how to load the shells, where the safety was, how to hold it. I was clumsy but managed.

"I'm not sure I–"

"It's better than nothing," said Brian.

I stood up and looked out into the square. I saw the Seraph I'd managed to shake, the bloody Seraph she'd rescued trailing behind her, struggling to stay upright.

"Shit."

In my confusion, I'd come right back around and had almost run into her. I watched her move through the square, elegant, hopping over obstacles with ease. Before I even registered them, she'd shot two raider kids in the head. She was casual, effortless – took them out within a second of each other without losing stride. It didn't feel real; their heads spurted, they fell. I looked down at the gun in my hand, then back up. Both Seraphs were gone. I stood there, dazed, not knowing what to do. I needed to find Jane but I didn't know where to look. I thought of walking through the whole ghetto, searching, shooting anyone who got in my way. I looked at the gun again.

"With current bio readings and noted inexperience I calculate

a high risk of you being killed," said Brian. "The weapon is for
self-defence only. I advise sticking to the shadows."

"And then what? Where am I going?"

"Find the Inex workstation and replace me. I've accessed
the ghetto map."

"I need to find Jane."

"We can search on the way. I should be able to identify her
within ten feet," said Brian. "Although, in these conditions it's
difficult."

I nodded. "OK. Let's go."

"This way." Brian walked into a darkened alley where the
blocks had almost burnt themselves out.

As I followed, I looked out into the main square and saw
an HSA being beaten by one of the raiders. I stopped, staring.

"*No, Icho.*"

"*No, what?*"

"*You can't shoot from here.*"

"*Then I won't,*" I said.

I strode out into the square.

"*Don't, Icho! Come back.*"

I ignored it.

"*I calculate–*"

"*I don't want to know,*" I said, trying to suppress my panic. "*I
don't want to know what you fucking calculate.*"

"*You'll get yourself killed. You need to find Jane, Icho.*"

I hesitated, hovering. Then I gripped the gun so tight it
hurt, and I walked straight for the raider kid, barely thinking,
just heading for the target, not sure what I'd do when I got
there. The kid glanced up at me, then stopped, letting go of the
bloody mess he'd made of the deviant. He grinned at me, his
teeth coated in blood.

"You want a piece of this scum?" he said, mistaking me for
a raider.

I was right in front of him and I raised the gun to his face,
pulled the trigger, and... nothing.

He blinked at me, surprised. I thought I could hear the sound his eyelids made; a frantic clicking, but it was me grappling with the safety, flicking it off as he moved towards me, reaching to grab the gun, throwing me off balance, a bang and we were both down. I fell onto the body of a dead deviant, feeling their bones crack beneath me, my ears ringing, sound muffled. The gun clattered between us and I made a grab for it, desperate, but there was no need – the bullet had missed the target but had gone through his cheek. He was clasping his face with both hands, choking on blood, making sickening noises. I picked up the gun, placed it at his forehead and pulled the trigger. Dropping it, I closed my eyes and crouched down, breathing heavily, trying not to be sick.

"*Violent action is not for you,*" said Brian.

I laughed.

"*You should keep to the shadows. That is the best course of action, given the circumstances.*"

I looked over at the teenager I'd killed as I picked up the gun and slid it into the waistband of my trousers. I crawled my way over to the HSA he'd been beating. Their face was a mess. I felt for a pulse: nothing.

"*You're right,*" I said, pulling myself upright.

I was going to get away from the square and follow Brian to the workstation when I looked up and saw a Seraph fighting one of the raider kids. I thought about whether I should help her, Brian protesting again, but just as I was going to approach them she kicked him in the face and he fell against the wall, hitting his head. He slumped. As she leaned down to him, I exhaled and scanned the area, about to head off when a group of raiders ran into the square. I crouched down amongst the bodies, pressing myself flat. I watched them as they ran off into an alley. I lay there, willing myself to get up, but I couldn't move. I wanted to stay there, safe amongst the bodies.

"You're not safe here, Icho," said Brian. "You need to get up."

I watched as Brian checked the area.

"It's clear. Get up, Icho."

"OK," I said. "OK."

I got up slowly, eyeing the nearby alleys. When I turned back to the council building, I was shocked to see the boy straddling the Seraph, stabbing her repeatedly. There was movement in my periphery, and I looked over to see someone approaching them, club in hand. I wasn't sure if they were deviant or raider, but as I found myself walking towards them, I could see they were shaking. It could have been shock, but it looked like HSA symptoms. The boy dropped the Seraph and grinned at the shaking deviant, who stopped and fell onto the steps, vomiting.

"*What are you doing?*" said Brian as I ran towards them, hopping over bodies.

"*I'm going to kill the boy.*"

"*Why? You need to hide.*"

"*They're going to kill that deviant.*"

"*They've killed a lot of deviants. You can't save the whole ghetto.*"

"*Stop telling me what to do.*"

"*I'm trying to keep you safe.*"

"*I know.*"

The boy was coming down the stairs as I fell to my knees in front of the HSA, trying to shelter them from him. I looked down at them and it was her, her face a mess, skin cracking open, but I could see it was her.

"Jane," I said, my voice breaking. I looked up at Brian as it came towards us. "Brian, it's–" I looked back down at her. "I've found you. Jane."

She looked up at me, confused.

"I can't believe it's you," I said.

"Elena?"

"No, I–"

I jumped as a nearby block collapsed, crashing in on itself. I kept my eyes on Jane, gripping her shoulders, as if that could stop her shaking, as if I could stop the attack through force of will. Tears of anger, frustration, and relief blurred my vision and I swiped at my eyes. I took a hold of her hand as Brian said, *"The boy."*

"Breathe steady," I said. "Just hold on..."

I let go of her and looked up at the blood-soaked boy, blocking Jane with my body. "She's one of us." In case he'd seen her face, I added, "One of those fucking deviants mutilated her. She's gone into shock."

I stared up at him, hoping he'd buy my lie, hoping he wouldn't notice it was HS allergy breaking up the skin on her face. As I looked at him, I realised he was clasping not a knife, but a huge shard of glass, his own blood dripping from it as he gripped it. He looked obscene; his adrenalin-fuelled, wide-eyed stare boring right into me, the rest of his face blood-spattered, his blonde hair dyed with it, his clothes soaked through.

"We'll fucking mutilate them." He grinned and stalked off. I stared after him, fumbling for the gun. I raised it, struggling to aim. Shaking, I shot him. I hit his shoulder and he jerked forward, half-turning, staring at me in surprise. I fired again, hitting him twice in the chest and he was down. I lost sight of him in a pile of bodies and the thick smoke pushing across the square. I turned back to Jane, who was on her side, violently shaking. I pulled her onto my lap. Her breathing was laboured.

"Jane. Stay with me," I said, as she shook, her skin breaking open, her face swelling. "Stay with me."

I scrambled to find the formula in my bag. "I have something to arrest the attack," I said, grasping it.

I pulled the formula vial out of its box and inserted it into the auto-injector. Her breathing was shallow. She tried to speak as I pushed it against her arm. It shouldn't have worked so suddenly, but she immediately stopped shaking. I felt relief as she stared up at me wide-eyed and said, "Icho."

"Yes–"

Her eyes rolled back, her body went limp.

"Jane?"

I felt for a pulse.

"Jane!"

I couldn't find a pulse in her wrist. I dropped her hand and pressed against her chest, listening for her heart, but there was nothing. Jane was dead.

HELLSANS

PART TWO OR ONE

JANE

PROLOGUE

"What time is it?" I said, looking up at the security guard.

"Lady," he said as I scanned the carpark, trying to remember how I got down here, where the exit was – all I could see was row upon row of identical cars. "I think you have bigger problems than needing to know the time."

I turned back to him and snapped, "Ask your Inex. Ask it!"

"OK, OK. Calm down." He glanced down at his Inex. It looked like an animated doll in the low light.

"Give us the time, Charlie."

"Sure, John," said his Inex in a cheap generic male voice. "It's ten twenty-six and seven seconds."

"Alright, lady?"

"Ten twenty-six," I said, staring into his Inex's round, blue eyes.

"Ten twenty-six… the Ino would be… removing this," I said, pulling at the dangling gel on my face. "Then my Inex would tell me… It would tell me it was time to take my SmileBrite." I looked up at the guard. "I take good care of myself."

"I bet."

"My Inex." I looked at it lying on the ground, its face in repose, its torso torn open. "My Inex helps me be the best I can be."

"And you can get a new one, don't you worry."

"It keeps me on schedule."

"Sometimes life throws us off. You'll be back on track in no time."

"In no time." I looked at the Inex heart I was holding in my right hand, the rhythm soothing me as it continued to beat.

"What's your name, lady?"

"Jane. Jane Ward."

"Jane War–" He laughed.

I looked up at him, impassive, and he sobered. He approached, crouched down, and peered at me.

"You're–" He frowned and turned to his Inex. "Charlie – face rec."

His Inex turned to me, its big eyes focused on my face. There was a long pause, the Ambrosia gel causing delay. "Confirmed," it said. "Jane Ward, CEO of The Company."

"Holy bliss," said the security guard, swaying back. He steadied himself and ran his hand through his hair, staring at me. "Jane? Ms Ward? It's going to be OK. Charlie, tell the police I have Jane Ward and she's in a pretty messed up way. Get them down here now."

"Yes, John."

"Ms Ward, help is on the way."

He put his hand on my shoulder and I gripped the Inex heart. A wire pulled loose. It stopped beating.

"It's too late," I said, looking at the mess of wire and blood dripping from my hand. "It's too late. My schedule is ruined."

CHAPTER 1

"Seven a.m. and one second, two, three, four, five…"

"Alright, Inex."

"…eight, nine…"

"Cut it out. I don't need to hear my life ticking away."

"Yes, Jane. You're dehydrated. The Ino is bringing vitwater."

"I drank too much last night…"

I opened my eyes and focused on the Inex's mouth as it said, "I informed you at nine fifteen and forty-three seconds that you were drinking too much."

"I know you did."

"Your sleep quality was poor, scoring only 42 points, worse than 76% of the population. You won't be operating at full capacity today."

"Don't lecture me about it, I can't bear it."

"I won't lecture you. I will help you get through the day in the most efficient way possible."

I lay on my side, contemplating the sleek grey Inex as it rested on the bedside table like an ornamental doll. Its large round head and big eyes gave it a puppy-dog innocence, always "happy to please" whatever personality setting it was on.

The Ino came through with my vitwater and placed it on the bedside table next to the Inex. The Ino was the same muted grey, but twice the height of my eight-inch Inex, with legs that could extend a few feet. Inos were often described as unsexy Inexes, so dull, so taken for granted that The Company had a hard time getting people excited about new models.

Ironically their selling point – to be in the background doing the chores you hate – was hurting them. I stared at it as it left the room, thinking that if all Inos suddenly broke down there'd be uproar.

I sat up and took a drink of my vitwater. "Project last night's reception."

The Inex projected onto the white wall opposite, starting from when I stepped out of the car. The Inex Con evening reception took place at Prime Minister Daniel Caddick's country residence every year, and I watched myself walk to the entrance.

"Throw it," I said to my Inex, and the house system took over the projection.

"Skip to Ichorel."

Icho filled the wall and I caught my breath, unsure if it was the effect of her beauty, the HellSans text adorning her figure-hugging dress, or – most likely – both. Despite this, I was still unnerved by the scarring.

"Pause."

Her brown hair was a mess of curls tumbling down to her shoulders, her brown eyes almost as dark as the heavy kohl she'd used, her lips bright red. I focused on the scar just below her right eye, slicing down her cheek, stopping at her jaw. It shimmered silver in the light, a slight hint of pink. Her dress was sleeveless, revealing more scarring on her shoulder and across her upper arm – larger, more severe than the neat sliver across her face. Scars were almost unheard of now that we had Ambrosia, but they were a badge of honour for military personnel, who shunned any cosmetic treatment. Many Seraphs were ex-military, and this, combined with Ambrosia-resistant HSA scars, meant scarring was mainly associated with deviants. Her blatant disregard for this made me uncomfortable.

"Resume."

Movement caught my eye and I focused on her Inex,

standing next to her on the floor. It was garish: blue skin, pink eye chips, stars glued to its face, a sequinned jacket, and a silver tiara on its head.

"It's good to meet you, Dr Smith."
We shook hands.
"And you. In fact, I'm a big fan of yours."
"Is that right?"
"Yes, all you've done, setting up The Company, the success of the first Inex model. I even named Jaw after you."
She pointed to her gaudy Inex.
I looked confused, so she clarified: "Jane Angelina Ward."
"Oh, I see. How nice."

"Jesus. Could I have been more condescending?"
"You found it embarrassing," said my Inex.
"A little."

"I said to Jaw I wouldn't embarrass myself if I had a chance to meet you, but it seems I've blown that."
"Don't worry. I appreciate it, thank you."

I told my Inex to move on to when I asked about her research.

"Caddick tells me you're working on a cure for the HellSans Allergic."
Icho looked uncomfortable.
"I, well…"
"You are, aren't you?"
"I don't–"
I laughed. "Oh, don't worry." I placed my hand on Icho's. "I know all about it."
"I really don't know what you–"

I watched Icho's face, an expression of panic. I found her discomfort amusing. She was saved by a waiter who offered us hors d'oeuvres and we briefly discussed farm meat before I returned to the subject of her work.

"You're good."
    "Sorry?"
    "Trustworthy. You're right not to talk about your work. But you should know, Caddick tells me everything."

The recording had been from an odd angle, my Inex on the ground, looking up at Icho and myself, but it shifted when I'd summoned it with an internal command and it crawled up onto my shoulder, all the time keeping its eyes on Icho, the recording moving up Icho's body, stopping directly in line with her face. She was flushed, uncertain.

"The Ino informs me your breakfast is ready," said my Inex.
"I haven't done my workout."
"I advise against a morning workout. You're not operati–"
"I know, I know." I waved my hand dismissively. "Pause," I said, staring at Icho's face, which filled the wall. "She was extremely nervous," I said, staring at her.
"You were asking difficult questions."
"Do you really think she's a fan? Or just flattering me?"
"You're still asking difficult questions."
"Those red lips and kohl eyes... it's a bit sloppy. Her Ino didn't do that make-up. Who does their own make-up?"
"Despite the Ino's usefulness, some people prefer to complete their own tasks."
"Go back to when I first meet her. I want a full view of her in the HellSans dress."
It complied and she filled the wall again. Her figure was larger than I'd usually like; her Inex really should have kept her in line with normative body weight. The sheer audacity of her – the self-applied make-up, the messy hair, her size, the

scarring – both unnerved and impressed me. It couldn't be that she didn't realise, as her Inex would make sure of that. It was more likely she didn't have time to care – Caddick had told me she was a workaholic. Despite her flaws, she was beautiful, and the HellSans dress added a bliss hit. I put my glass down and pushed my hand into my pants.

"You're masturbating?"

"Yes, Inex, I am."

"Masturbating is not on your schedule."

"Rearrange it."

"I don't–"

"Go silent."

I stared at Icho's HellSans dress, blissing out on fragments, words, letters. "Data," I said, rubbing my clit. "Capacity... technology... muscle... initial tests on rats revealed." My breathing heavier, I said, "Disease and... pain." I pushed back the bedcovers with my free hand and said, "Is wired into." I tilted my head back, closed my eyes, and pictured the word "synthskin". I moaned as I reduced the word to the sublime curve of the "s", a favourite HellSans letter. I lingered on it, gasping, eyelids flickering, catching glimpses of Icho, holding her image as I closed my eyes tight and came. I lay there, hand on my stomach, staring up at the ceiling, the Inex in my peripheral vision, climbing up the wall in search of insects. I watched it for a minute, my breath steadying. Sitting up, I stared at Icho's dress, realising what I'd missed when I met her.

"Close up on dress."

I read a couple of the sentence fragments as they curved round her body, nodding as I recalled writing it. The text was from my research paper on the development of the first Inex model.

"Very good, Icho," I said, smiling. I jumped out of bed, invigorated. "End it." Icho's image vanished. "You can speak now," I said to the Inex, above me on the ceiling. "Remind me to arrange dinner with Icho."

I'd suggested to her that we meet with Caddick but, "Three's a crowd," I said as I threw on my workout clothes and headed downstairs to my gym.

"This isn't wise," said the Inex, following me. "You're not operating at full capacity – you need breakfast. You should cancel your workout."

"I'm not asking your opinion."

"It isn't opinion. It's fact. You're not operating–"

"Yes, I know, at my full capacity. I'm working out anyway."

"You shouldn't–"

"I don't care."

I was about to head through to the gym when I turned into the kitchen, where the Ino had set out my breakfast on the island counter.

"OK. See?" I said, picking up a glass of green liquid. "Smoothie first. That should make you happy."

"I cannot be happy. You need time to ingest it before working out."

"Just keep me on time. I don't want any more advice."

The Inex followed me through the open-plan kitchen and sitting room, through the dining room and into the gym. I spent fifteen minutes on the runner, followed by crunches, cycling, weights, ending on tai-chi and five minutes of meditation.

"Inex? Stats."

"Weight: 9 stone 2 pounds, body fat: 15%, blood pressure: 110/70."

"Good."

"I advise skipping your lunchtime workout today."

"Fine," I said, jogging upstairs to have a shower.

I came down a few minutes later in my usual suit: black trousers, white blouse, black tailored jacket, and comfortable saddle shoes. The Ino had applied my make-up over a foundation of Ambrosia cream; I admired my smooth, glowing skin in the sitting room mirror as the Ino tied my hair into a ponytail.

The Ino packaged up my breakfast to go: a high-protein meal

of farm meat, egg, and seeds. I ate it in the car as I watched the news projected onto the screen in front of me.

"Reliable sources state that Caddick is planning to propose legislation preventing HSAs from voting because they are of 'unsound mind'. We have the leader of the opposition, Jared Milligan, with us today – welcome, Jared."

"Thank you for having me, Caroline."

"What do you think of this proposed legislation?"

"Firstly, I have to emphasise this is just a rumour – I haven't heard anything official. However, Caddick's party have repeatedly suggested HSAs are not fit to vote, but there's no proof, Caroline, that HSAs are of unsound mind. In fact, there's no research at all on the effect of HSA on people because the government refuses to fund it. Research is what we need, not knee-jerk legislation based on prejudice. If anything, I'd like to see legislation in place that allows the city-dwelling HSAs a right to vote – homeless HSAs have fallen through the system."

"Jared, it's been said by Jane Ward, and reiterated by Prime Minister Caddick, who often stands with Ward on issues pertaining to deviants, that you only care about HSAs because you know you have their vote."

"You know that's not true, Caroline."

"Of course it's true. That man makes me sick. End it, Inex. I can't tolerate his socialist bullshit."

"The Ed Miller segment is being aired half an hour early on the *Becky Sutherland Show*. Do you want to switch?"

I shook my head as the sentence "…who often stands with Ward on issues pertaining to deviants" played over in my head. "No, Jason can brief me. I want you to replay the fragment 'stands with Ward'. Loop it."

I took one more bite of my breakfast and put it aside unfinished, closing my eyes as I listened to Milligan's voice.

I envisioned every word in neon, bold, italicised HellSans, stripping them of meaning, pulling specific words to the foreground, floating on the bliss of the beautiful curve of the two "*S*"s in "***STANDS***", visualising my tongue tasting the sweet simplicity of the "*T*". I basked in the delight that is my own name, my irritation with Milligan transmuted into bliss.

"Stop." I opened my eyes, feeling cushioned and content. I looked out at the city, staring at the hoardings, most of them digital, flicking through several ads on a cycle, a number of them advertising the newest Inex models. The Seraphs had scrawled across one of the screens. It looked like random strokes until it scrolled round to the advert the graffiti was meant for – it was the latest Inex model: "ALWAYS AND FOREVER HELPING YOU BE THE BEST YOU", with added Seraph serifs. It immediately threw off my bliss, so I looked away, but my eyes fell on a retro paper hoarding – it was one of ours, advertising an old model we still sold, capitalising on the cool kids who bought into anything seemingly retro. Paper hoardings were on their way out; it was rare to find them without Seraph interference – sickening serifs and an angel logo, often in red, dripping spray paint like blood. I felt nauseous just looking at it. Internally, I told my Inex to send the image to advertising. "Get them to find a new way to reach the retro kids," I said out loud. "The bloody Seraphs are just making it backfire."

There was an HellSans Allergic beggar sitting beneath the hoarding, a scarf wrapped round most of their repulsive, broken-up face. The deviant had the very same Inex model, battered and dirty. My bliss was so off-kilter I had to close my eyes to get myself back together.

"Project scrolling schedule, Inex," I said. "I need to get my bliss back on track. This city seems to belong to the goddamn deviants."

"The city doesn't bel–"

"It feels like it does, Inex. Let me concentrate on my schedule."

The Inex projected my schedule onto the back of the seat in front of me and I soaked up the HellSans. When I finished, drifting on bliss, I said, "What is life without a schedule?"

"I've not had experience of unscheduled lives, but I know of them. Most HSAs have no schedule. Holidays can be without schedules, but yours are not."

"It was a rhetorical question."

The car arrived at The Company. An Ino opened the door and I stepped out and in, taking a lift up to the ninth floor. I walked through the open-plan office, a hubbub of activity, the atmosphere shifting as soon as I stepped out of the lift, people or their Inexes turning to watch me.

"Morning, Jane," said Jason, joining me as I walked to my office. "It seems last night was a success. I hope you enjoyed the party."

"I did."

I must have looked off-kilter, as he said, "Everything OK?"

"Between Milligan, Seraphs, and deviants littering the streets, I'd say no, everything isn't OK – everyone's intent on polluting my bliss. My files?"

"Already transferred. You have the Board's physical meeting at three p.m. – items all on the agenda and the room is prepped. Did you see the first part of the *Becky Sutherland Show*? I asked your Inex to remind you–"

"I didn't watch it."

"The second part will be on in fifteen – I'll come and brief you in a few minutes."

Settled in my office, I took a moment to stare at Caddick's campaign poster opposite, above the couch, in bold, capitalised HellSans: **"WE'RE IN THIS TOGETHER"**. There were various versions, this one consisting simply of the slogan with party details at the bottom. I read the words a few times and enjoyed a minute of bliss before I adjusted my chair and lay back, closing my eyes as the Inex internally went through what I needed to know from the day's files. When I finished, Jason came in with my morning coffee and sat on the couch.

"Veronica is nailing it, as always."

I nodded, pleased something was going well this morning. Veronica Lambert, head of public relations, was always a joy to watch.

"So," said Jason, "Becky talked about Ed Miller killing his girlfriend in a – and I quote – 'unblissed frenzy'."

I rolled my eyes.

"I know. Then she laid it on thick regarding pre-act intervention."

"Just what we need."

"But Veronica's hitting all the right notes: we're proud to be a democracy, the Inex is the backbone of society, The Company refuses to be the thought police, we value your freedom, and so on. In fact," Jason said, pausing, communicating internally with his Inex, "Veronica used the word 'freedom' eight times within the space of five minutes. The next part should have started already, if you want to watch it?"

I nodded and my Inex projected the *Becky Sutherland Show* onto the office wall, a wide shot of Becky and Veronica sitting opposite each other, their chairs angled slightly to face the viewers. Veronica was already in her stride.

"If we start policing thoughts, where do we draw the line? What effect does this have on our sense of self? Constantly monitoring, controlling, stifling. We'll be getting into off-kilter bliss territory, and people will no longer trust their forever friend – an Inex is there to assist you and help you be the best version of yourself. If we use the Inex against people, the fabric of our society will start to crack."

"You're not exactly impartial here, are you, Veronica? The Company needs people to trust their Inex."

"You're right, Becky, we do. Of course we're invested in people trusting their Inex. The Inex is the backbone of our society. But that's also why we have a keen sense of social responsibility – we're responsible to each and every customer and we take that very seriously, so we are, of course, going to act. One of the main ways forward is to de-stigmatise unbliss – catch people before they're so distressed they don't know how to cope anymore. The Company will be setting up an Unblissed Support Centre as well as donating a sizeable sum to victim-support organisations. This is how we can make a difference without losing our precious freedoms – we believe strongly in freedom, Becky, and we will never compromise on that."

"Well," said Becky, "Freedom – that's a good note to end on as we turn to viewer questions and comments. We've had quite a few anonymous unblissed get in touch insisting they're not psychopaths and can't be put in the same category as Ed Miller. One viewer commented, 'We don't murder people. We're misunderstood and often isolated because of our condition – there's a stigma attached, and we're being unfairly treated. You can't blame us for being scared we're going to be put in ghettos like the HSAs, when we're nothing like those deviants. We need compassion and understanding.' What do you make of this heartfelt plea for understanding, Veronica?"

"End it." Veronica and Becky vanished. Jason raised his eyebrows and I said, "The last thing I need is having to listen to unblissed whining and moral panic from the pre-act lobby. Get Jenni's team to compile a report on where the general public stand on this."

"They're already on it."

"Good. And schedule Veronica for dinner with me at Carter's on Friday."

"I'll do that."

Jason left and I went through the rest of my files, my Inex sending them back to Jason with various notes. Before lunch,

I had the VR Pressure Group meeting, all the while feeling the pain of a hangover headache. I was able to disguise this via my bliss-fresh avatar, signs that anything was amiss only evident in my curt answers when a question came my way. We were on VR Meeting Room Deluxe (VRMRD) – templates were available, but I'd had it modelled exactly on the Dick Jones room. In the early days, this was problematic when I'd forget it was VR and attempt to leave via the door, only to find myself, startled, back in my office.

This meeting was mainly focused on the Christian Coalition. Much to my eternal frustration, we had to baby the bastards because of their alliance with Caddick. All other pressure groups I openly disparaged, the media lapping it up, but the CC helped build Caddick and he needed their support.

The CC believe Inexes are abominations. They dislike the invasion of privacy, but have nothing in common with the privacy nuts – the CC regard their thoughts as private between them and God. No one can operate in society without an Inex, so they're forced to use the things they despise, resentment permanently simmering. A freak splinter group have gone "off grid", living without them. The rest, spurred on by CCs in prominent positions, try to stymie everything The Company does. Caddick has the task of trying to keep us both sweet.

My foul mood wasn't vastly different from when we had other PG meetings, but my hangover and this month's focus on the CC made me especially recalcitrant. Miles Cartwright started the meeting, but I had trouble focusing, zoning in and out. I took a sip of VR coffee, hoping the fake hit might be enough to keep me alert.

"The Police Chief is putting more pressure on the Inex division," said Cartwright, "cutting their funding by twenty per cent."

I purposefully knocked my coffee cup off the table and watched it fall. It disappeared when it hit the floor, reappearing on my saucer in front of me.

Cartwright stopped mid-sentence and everyone turned to look at me. Irritated, I waved at them to continue. Cartwright stuttered, trying to pick up where he'd left off. I had the sudden desire to smash everything in the room, to keep throwing cups to the floor, smash paintings against the walls over and over and over, as if, eventually, through sheer will, something would crack.

Instead, I interrupted Cartwright just as he'd regained his flow, and said, "Bett and Enriquez, work out a way forward and present to me on Thursday. Cartwright, keep me updated if there's anything urgent on the intractable CC arseholes. Ballard, strike 'intractable' and 'arseholes' from the minutes." I nodded, smiled my goodbye, and opened my eyes; I was back in my office and my own tired body. Jason came straight in.

"Finished early?"

"I left them to it."

"Anything I need to know?"

"No. Ballard will send over minutes."

"Right. Lunch? Jackson has your favourites on today."

I shook my head. "I need some fresh air. I'll go out."

At the back of my office was a small gym and ensuite. With my Inex protesting because I wasn't "functioning at full capacity", I did my workout, had a shower, and put on my usual uniform of wide-brimmed hat, shades, and silk scarf that partially covered the lower half of my face. It made me look like a privacy extremist, but I'd rather see disgusted stares than the fuss made when people realised who I was.

As I left, I glanced at the receptionist. I stopped and turned to look at her properly. She was pale, almost blue, with dark circles under her eyes. Her lips were dry and cracked. As I watched her hand a packet of The Company's Inex snacks to her Inex, I told mine to get Jason to find out what was wrong with her.

I walked through the busy streets, ignoring hostile glances, and entered Osman's, immediately greeted warmly by Claude. I had a private chef at The Company, but Osman's was a local favourite, and one of only ten establishments in the city serving meat, eggs, and dairy from farmed animals. It was club members only, which kept out animal rights activists. The moment I walked in I felt a strong urge to be alone, back in my office. I opted for takeaway, confusing Claude, as I'd normally send someone to pick up or get it delivered. It pained me to admit it, but my Inex was right – I shouldn't have done that workout. I was hungover, moody, tired, and my routines felt like a chore.

Back at The Company, I looked over at the reception girl again, watching sweat trickle down her white-blue skin. I detoured to Jason's office.

"You're back early."

I raised my Osman bag in answer and said, "What's wrong with the reception girl? She looks like a walking corpse."

"Ongoing health problem. It's being investigated."

"It's not HSA? Don't we have a health report?"

"Not yet. It's being investigated."

"How can they not know what it is? An Inex diagnoses health problems before they even happen. We can't have a half-dead girl on reception."

"Her Inex is in for repair and she's had some trouble with the rental company – the temp model they gave her can't diagnose."

"We're The Company, for bliss sake. We can provide her with one."

"It's not policy, but I can arrange it," he said, pausing. "She's not a girl."

"What?"

"She's twenty-two."

"I don't care how old she is, she'll scare the clients – get rid of her."

"I can't just–"

"You can just."

"You mean temporary leave while she–?"

"I mean get rid of her."

"Right. Of course."

I eyed the girl as I walked back into my office. I sat at my desk and the Inex laid out my lunch as I leaned back and closed my eyes.

"Jane!"

I jumped and opened my eyes. "Jesus, Jason."

"Sorry, I'm sorry. It's just, the court ruling on the Amos case has come early; it's all over the news, journalists are calling for a statement."

"I thought the ruling was tomorrow."

"I know, I know."

"Inex, throw the news."

"...for sharing private recordings of him and his then girlfriend, Elspeth Blackmore. Amos has treated the whole trial as a joke, enjoying the media attention, mocking his ex-girlfriend and showing no contrition. We all thought revenge porn had been consigned to the past because of stringent Inex legislation and robust built-in protocols, but this–"

I shifted my attention to the highlights in HellSans that scrolled below the newscaster:

"BREAKING NEWS: Nathan Amos, the first revenge porn criminal in fourteen years, receives three years in jail. He will be subject to a number of tech restrictions for up to a decade, including Inex model limits."

I tuned back in to the newscaster.

"While this is the first case of its kind in well over a decade, the question still arises: are our Inexes more at risk than we thought? Should we worry? What are Jane Ward and The Company doing to prevent these crimes?"

"OK," I said, "we can deal with this – we already have the drafted statements. Liaise with Veronica for the fine-tuning. You don't need to pass it by me; I trust her to get it right. And when that misogynist arsehole gets out of jail, get him on the payroll."

"What? Are you serious?"

"Of course I'm serious; we need him on side. We can work something out regarding his tech restrictions when it comes to it. And fire our current hacker arseholes."

"But you ca–"

"No, I don't mean it. Just schedule me a meeting with them – in person. They'll soon wish they'd been fired."

"Right, I'm on it." Jason was about to leave when he stopped and said, "Rory just reminded me, I talked to the advertising division about the retro posters you mentioned this morning. They've done market research and it seems the retro kids love the defaced posters and the 'sick' feeling they get when looking at them. It helps sales."

"Is that right?" I said. "I guess I'm out of touch."

"They've provided a report if you want to see it?"

"No, it's fine."

Jason left, and as I ate lunch, I continued watching reports on the Amos case. I had news and social media projected side by side, giving me a feel for how it was being received.

"What's next on my schedule?"

"VR meeting with Peter," said my Inex.

"Send him a reschedule – I want to watch how this unfolds."

"Yes, Jane. But I advise a short nap instead of watching the news."

"I'm fine."

"You're still not operating at full capacity – a short nap should help get you back on track."

"I'll get an early night tonight."

"I recommend–"

"Just leave it."

"Yes, Jane."

"Sometimes you're more trouble than you're worth."

"I'm not supposed to cause trouble. I'll run a self-diagnostic."

"Don't."

I continued watching the news as my Inex crawled up and sat on the desk. I looked at it, my eyes glazing. "I sometimes imagine life without you," I said. "I imagine life without your advice, your records, everything repeatable."

"You are ambivalent about my presence in your life, but you would not be the successful entrepreneur you are today if you had not invented me. While imagining things is healthy and productive, and is what led to my invention, I must point out that there are many drawbacks to life without me, and my records and playback are one of my main selling points."

"I'm making millions as people live their life on a loop, stuck in the past."

"That is one negative view of my capabilities – there are many ways in which my various features are put to good use. Society would be dysfunctional without me. I can provide you with the relevant statistics."

I leaned back in my chair and eyed the Inex. "No, just let me watch the news in peace."

"The news is rarely peaceful, but I will stop interacting with you until I am needed."

Jason returned and said, "Everything's sorted with Veronica. I saw you rescheduled your VRM with Peter – anything amiss?"

"No, I just want to see how this all unfolds. And Peter's an arse – I don't have the patience for him today."

Jason laughed.

"Do you like your Inex, Jason?"

"What? Sure. Of course. Why wouldn't I?"

"It never annoys you?"

"Ah, you know, it depends on the setting. The formal one yours is on wouldn't suit me."

"I like it," I said. "On the whole. I like the pushback."

"I prefer Rory to be more chatty, more relatable."

I'd overheard Jason interacting with Rory on a number of occasions and it bordered on nauseating. Rory's voice belonged to some quirky young actor, and it grated on me. I had free access to innumerable expensive voices, but I'd always kept my Inexes on the default gender-neutral setting.

"Is your Inex your friend, Jason?"

"I don't know if I'd call him… but I suppose…" He paused and looked thoughtful. "You know, he's actually more than a friend. A friend can fail you, but the Inex is always there for you no matter what."

I smiled up at him. "You should be on one of our ads."

He laughed and was about to leave when I stopped him. "Did you deal with the reception girl?"

"She's packing up now."

I nodded. "Good." I waved him away.

The afternoon creaked by as I watched the news (Veronica coming through for The Company, as always) and attended meetings (unintentionally intimidating people with my uncharacteristic hungover silence, which I made a note of for future use). Late afternoon, I fell asleep at my desk and my Inex didn't rouse me – "despite the inadequate position your body was in. You were getting much-needed deep sleep." After some stretches and a healthy snack, I was feeling better and made my way through files for the next day before winding up. On my way out I looked over at the reception desk. The girl was gone, replaced by a boy with good colour, clean hair, and the latest Inex model which didn't have any fussy accessories. I nodded at him as I passed. His teeth shone as he smiled.

As I stepped out into the street, an HSA beggar was sitting outside the building, polluting my bliss. I told my Inex to contact security and have him removed. "Then report security for the lapse. This building has a reputation to uphold."

On the journey home my Inex told me about a protest outside the Vedder hotel, right next to my apartment building.

"Who?"

"An HSA faction protesting Milligan's support for a cure, and–"

"Those nuts. Why are they at the hotel?"

"Milligan's staying there. But most of the protesters are animal rights activists – they're responding to a rumour that he eats farm meat."

"Oh God," I said, laughing. "Good luck dealing with them, Milligan."

"You'll need to be careful when you arrive that you aren't seen. They might turn on you. You can take the car down into the carpark and enter the apartment building from there."

Animal rights activists hated me. They all knew I spurned lab meat and wore real fur and leather. I also blocked access to Inex/animal research. One unfortunate side effect of using animals to test early Inex tech was the access to their inner lives. While there was some trouble with the Inex translating in a way we could grasp, there was no doubt this almost direct access to non-human animals' cognitive abilities and emotions would bring the kind of attention I did not want. I kept the data strictly confidential. I had no intention of alienating my friends and colleagues who enjoyed hunting and fishing and who were already under pressure. With the advent of affordable lab meat and dairy, industrial-scale farming had died out, but a dozen small farms operated across the country, their clients all rich, the restaurants they supplied all exclusive. If the activists got their hands on this data on animal emotions, attachments, memories, and dreams, all justifications of animal exploitation would be under massive strain. A whistleblower had leaked part of the findings, causing a mass outcry and a call for transparency. We easily smeared her (I hacked her Inex, found some exploitable aspect of her past, and threw a few rumours to the press) and used the animal rights fanatics own ethos against them, pointing out that any further investigation of animals using Inexes would be invasive and unethical. This caused infighting that's still ongoing, distracting them enough to reduce them to a manageable irritation. We harvested Inex information on the general population that revealed only 28% genuinely care about animal welfare; some were posturing as they followed the majority, and others gained a smug sense of altruism as they helped "save the environment". This data allowed us to manage our response to any animal rights campaigns, often successfully turning the general public against them. The most powerful means, of course, was to cite the Seraph terror as a more important, immediate concern, but generally all it took was to call the activists unblissed; no one protested anymore unless there was something wrong with them, and the blissed didn't want to be associated with degenerates.

I arrived home at seven, avoiding the protesters by entering the building via the underground carpark. I had an energy drink and used my gym until seven-thirty, followed by a session with my boxing instructor until eight-thirty. She stayed on and did tai-chi and meditation with me until nine. When she left, I took a shower, got into my white, tailored silk pyjamas, and sat down to a light meal prepared by the Ino. As I ate, I went over the next day's schedule before decamping to the beauty therapy room just off the gym. I scraped my damp hair back into a ponytail and lay down for the Ino to smear the Ambrosia anti-aging gel over my face. I enjoyed the tingling cool feel as the green-tinged gel settled on my skin. Returning to the sitting room, I sat in the window seat with my Inex, staring out across the city. The Ino brought my vitwater and retreated to its cupboard for the night. I sipped my drink and scanned the hotel opposite – all the windows had lace curtains, giving the occupants the illusion that no one could see in. There was a couple in bed watching a projection while their kid sat on the floor playing a game with their Inex. In another, a man walked back and forth, unpacking his suitcase. I glanced down at the street and saw some protesters with placards and banners spilling out onto the corner. The entrance to the hotel was just round the other side, on the main street, where they were sure to be causing massive disruption.

"You need to finish your vitwater. You're low on vitamin C."

"I'm drinking, can't you see?" I finished it. "Satisfied?"

"I'm satisfied you will soon be operating at full capacity."

"Good. I'm sick of hearing about it."

I leaned against the wall, tilting my head back, looking at the night sky. I glimpsed a flashing light out of the corner of my eye and looked over at the hotel window opposite. A lamp had been knocked over and was rolling on the floor, creating dramatic shadows across the room. Two men were locked in an embrace.

"Looks like someone's getting lucky tonight, Inex," I said, raising my empty glass.

I watched the men, one behind, with his arm around the other's waist, trying to lock an arm round his neck, but the other man pulled free, elbowing him in the face.

"Jesus!"

I stood, my hand pressed against the glass. The rolling lamp had slowed, making it easier to see what was happening.

"What's– Inex, give me visuals."

It climbed up the window, looking directly into the room, allowing me to see using its eyes, as if I was standing right outside the hotel window. The man who elbowed the other was crouching and had a hold of an Inex by its leg.

"Wait, is that–?"

"Jared Milligan, leader of the opposition," confirmed my Inex.

"Are you sure?"

"I'm sure."

"What the hell is this?"

There were three Inexes in the room; the one Milligan was

grasping, one inert on the floor, and another by the door that looked damaged.

"Why are there three Inexes? Is someone else in the room?"

"I cannot ascertain," said my Inex as I watched the man who'd been elbowed pull something out of his jacket, stagger over to Milligan and hit him across the head.

"Jesus! You've contacted the police, right?"

"Of course. It should be a quick response – there are police at the protest."

There was a flash and the Inex at the other side of the room was thrown backwards.

"Holy sh– He just shot an Inex."

The man pulled Milligan up by the hair and dumped him on the bed.

"Is he dead?"

"Cannot ascertain."

The man had a hold of the Inex Milligan had landed on when he'd been struck on the head. He reached into his coat and brought out a knife, immediately plunging it into the Inex, pulling it down its torso. He threw the knife aside, dug into the Inex's body and pulled out the Mnemosyne core.

"What the hell is going on?"

He wiped the blood on the carpet and put the knife and Mnemo core in his coat pocket.

"Is that Milligan's Mnemo? Why's he taking it? There's no way he can access it."

"He could be a hacker."

I snorted. "He must be a helluva hacker if he can access Milligan's – can you imagine the security levels on that thing?"

"I don't need to imagine."

The man picked up the inert Inex, likely his own, and hooked its hand through his belt before walking over to the other side of the room. He lifted the Inex he'd shot in the face and shot it three times in the chest, destroying its Mnemo core.

"Why is there a third Inex? Who's is it?"

"I don't know. Maybe that one belongs to Milligan."

He dropped the Inex and looked up, staring out the window, locking eyes with me.

"Shit!"

I jumped back, tripping over the table by the window seat, falling to the floor. Because of my connection to the Inex's visuals it was as if he'd been right in front of me.

I pulled myself up and limped to the window.

"Did he see me? It's too far, right?"

I looked across. He'd moved the lace curtain and was staring up at me and my Inex. "He's looking right at me."

He traced his finger across his neck as he stared at me.

"Shit."

"He can't see you clearly without an Inex."

My Inex had cut off our visual connection, the assailant becoming slightly fuzzy.

"You're right. It's too far. I panicked. He seemed so close."

"He's working out what floor you're on."

"What?"

"He's working out what floor you're on. He's scanning the building."

"You don't know that's what–"

"It seems the most likely plan of action for him. He can't risk a recording."

"But he can't– where's the hotel security? They'll– What's he doing? Visuals."

He ran his knife down the bedsheet, tearing off a strip. He slipped his knife back into his jacket then tied the piece of sheet around the lower half of his face. He loaded his gun and stood pressed against the wall, listening.

"What's he doing?"

"Police have arrived."

"What took them so bloody long?"

"Likely the protest – news reports say there's skirmishes between the animal rights faction and the HSAs."

The man bent down to turn off the lamp.

"They'll get him. There's no other way out. And even if he did–"

There was a burst of light as the door opened and silhouettes crossed the threshold. They all fell within seconds and a figure slipped through the door.

"Was that him? Jesus! Was that him? How fucking incompetent can the police be?"

"We must take the precaution of assuming it was him. Accounting for potential obstructions to his exit, I'd give him nine minutes to get out of the hotel to the main door of this building. If he is able to avoid further confrontation, I calculate just over five minutes."

"Are you kidding me?"

"On this setting I cannot 'kid'."

"You've contacted the police again?"

"Of course."

"They know it's me?"

"Of course, but they are dealing with what is happening at the hotel – they haven't acknowledged the connection with our call for help and the hotel incident."

"Goddamnit. Keep on at them – tell them I'll fucking drag them through a media shitshow if they don't get over here."

"I've lodged your complaint–"

"It's not a complaint, it's a goddamn order."

"I advise acting, not waiting. You must leave now. He'll be on his way."

"Shit. This can't be happening."

"It is happening."

"Even if he got here, he can't get in."

"If he can infiltrate Milligan's team, it is likely he can get to you."

"I can explain, say I couldn't see, not with that lace curtain. I could just hand you over."

"I calculate 99.9% probability you will not have a chance to speak. He will shoot you on sight and remove or destroy my Mnemosyne core. You have seven minutes now, less if he's unhindered. You need to leave."

"I can't go out looking like this."

"You have no choice."

I got up and ran to the door of my apartment before stopping dead. "I can't. Not like this."

"We need to leave now."

"Look at me."

I went into the bathroom near the main door and clawed at the green gel.

"We don't have time for gel removal."

"I can't go out like this."

"Panic is not helpful. You're not thinking straight. We need to leave."

"I'm not panicking."

"Your heart-rate is up and you're sweating."

"I can't. I can't go out like this. I just can't."

"No one will recognise you. You have five minutes and forty-nine seconds."

"Stop it!"

"I can stop it, but I am trying to assist you."

"Goddamnit."

I stared at my reflection, some of the Ambrosia dangling in strips off my face like a green gelatinous beard. I headed for the front door, grabbing the first pair of shoes I could find.

"Four-inch high-heels are not the best choice, given the circumstances."

"The circumstances might just call for a stabbing in the eye with a stiletto."

I stood at the door and said, "Screen." The door disappeared and I could see into the hall as I slipped on the shoes.

"Vision left. Right." No one was in the hallway. "Open."

I ran out into the hall and punched at the lift buttons.

"I've already called for the lift," said my Inex.

"What if he's in it?" I said, backing away.

"It's more likely he'd take the fire escape stairs."

I pushed myself up against the wall by the lift, holding one of my shoes as a weapon. The lift reached the floor and I held my breath as the doors opened. A neighbour walked out, jumping when they saw me.

"What–"

I peered round into the lift then stepped in as they stood staring at me, mouth open.

"Ms Ward? Is that you?"

I slammed my hand on the ground floor button as the doors closed. The lift interior was all mirror, and I tried to pull off the gel.

"You need an Ino to get that off."

"I know, OK? I know."

"I'll exit first and do reconnaissance at the main exit."

"OK."

The lift stopped and opened. The hallway was empty. I waited, gripping my shoe as my Inex went ahead.

"The exit is clear."

"Are you sure? Shouldn't we use the back exit?"

"I calculate 87% probability that he'll assume you will exit at the back of the building."

"87% probability…"

I looked round the corner of the lift, slipped my shoe on, and walked out into the hallway to the main entrance, where the door girl was sitting in her booth watching something her Inex was projecting.

"Check again."

The Inex went out and scanned the street.

"Clear."

"Miss…?" said the door girl, squinting at me. "Can I… Are you–?"

I slipped out and walked down the busy street, glancing

furtively at everyone I passed, their shocked eyes all on the strange apparition that I was.

"Any sign of him?"

"No."

Some people looked disgusted, others embarrassed, some laughed at me.

"They'll all have recordings of me."

"Face rec is unlikely to work because of the gel, and there's more important things to concern us. I suggest we go to the Driscoll store and wait there. I'll contact the police again and inform them of your situation."

"Driscoll's – yes! I can get some proper clothes and their Ino can take this gunk off my face."

I made my way through the crowd, pulling my hair out of the ponytail, bringing it down to hide my face. I jumped as a man in black brushed past me, but it wasn't him. I watched as he disappeared into the crowd, laughing with his girlfriend. I turned back and lowered my head, pulling more hair forward as I made my way to Driscoll's.

"This is going to be embarrassing."

I walked into the brightly lit store and peered out from behind my hair.

"Ma'am, can I help you?"

A security guard blocked my path. I looked round him, trying to find Amelia. "Get Amelia Oakes for me."

"Ma'am, can I see your Inex?"

"Just get Amelia, she can–"

"Ma'am, I need to see some ID."

You're so fired, I thought, and said, "Inex, give the man access." The guard just looked at me. I stared back, waiting. "Inex, can you–"

"Ma'am, I'm going to need you to come with me."

"Don't you–"

The guard took me by the arm, but I wrestled free, spinning round, looking for my Inex. "Where is the little bastard?"

"If you don't have an Inex, I'm going to have to ask you to come with me until we sort this out."

"Of course I have an Inex. I'm the bloody CEO of The Company, for bliss sake."

He eyed me, eyebrows raised, a look of boredom. "Ma'am–"

"Just give me a second–" I held my finger up to him. "*Inex, you little shit,*" I said internally. There was no response. I suddenly felt nauseous. "Look, if it's not far, I should be able to reach it, so just give me a second."

The guard turned to his Inex and said, "Call on Gilbert and tell him I need some assistance with a lady who seems a bit confused."

"Look you condescending sonofa–"

Lights flickered and I saw row upon row of cars. I was pinned down and I pushed against the weight. As I tried to pull free, yelling for help, I saw the guard again, the searing light of the store. I staggered and fell to the floor, the guard pulling out his gun, cocking it at me, a look of panic on his face, then he was gone, and we were pinned down again, our spidery limbs flailing, one of our arms reaching up and twisting round the assailant's arm, but we were unable to harm him no matter how much we willed ourselves. The man reached into his jacket and took out a knife, slamming it into our throat. *Disconnect, disconnect!* We remained we as he pulled the knife down our torso, dropped it at our side and reached in with both hands, opening us up, reaching in and pulling out– *Disconnect!* I was back to the white light, a gaggle of demons: Is she deviant? Is she HSA? Where's her Inex? What's wrong with her? Ma'am? Just calm down, OK? I shook, sobbing, grasping at my chest, expecting blood, broken ribs, collapsing organs.

"He killed me," I said to the guard who was kneeling next to me, no longer wielding his gun.

"No one's hurting you, ma'am. We're all trying to help."

"He tore us open." I stared up at all the figures, their faces in shadow, the lights above them hurting my eyes.

"What's your name, ma'am?"

"Jane," I said, closing my eyes.

"It's going to be OK, Jane."

"Is it?"

"It is. Everything will be alright."

I opened my eyes as the guard stood up and gestured at the crowd. "C'mon, everyone, give her some space. Show's over."

"Cars…" I said.

"You don't need a car, Jane." He glanced down at me as he ushered people away. "An ambulance is on its way."

I stood up, shaking, my legs unsteady.

"It's OK, you just stay–"

He reached out to me, holding my arm, but I pulled out of his grasp and walked into the crowd, pushing my way past all the startled people who shrank back as if I was infectious.

"Ma'am! Jane!"

I was out in the street, the security guard shouting after me. I kicked off my high heels and ran, weaving my way through the crowd of protesters, running past the now-cordoned-off Vedder hotel, past my apartment, ducking down into the car park exit, dodging cars on their way to the city above.

I knew where it was – I'd seen a number painted above it when it had connected. I scanned the car bays, spotted fifty-nine and ran past the sixties, seventies, eighty, eighty-one, eighty-two… The light was dim, but I saw it, the bloody mess of wires and synthetic flesh that was my Inex. I fell to my knees. I sobbed, holding its hand, knocking aside its stomach of half-digested insects. I stared at it, noticing a thin pin sticking out from its head, just below its ear. When they'd grabbed it, they must have inserted the pin to cut off its ability to communicate with me. The assailant knew what they were doing; you had to hit the exact spot or it wouldn't work. Because the pin was protruding so much, I assumed my Inex had tried to remove it, which could account for its connection with me when it was being assaulted, and would definitely account for its trouble disconnecting when it knew I'd be experiencing the trauma it was going through. I reached down and closed its eyes, as if it were human.

"Hey, lady! Hey! This is residents only."

I took hold of its fake heart, a pointless rhythmic beating that helped people bond to it. I lifted it out, still connected, still beating. I held it in a fist, blood dripping through my fingers.

"Lady," a man said, coming round the side of the car in bay 82, flashing a security badge. "You're not supposed to be in here."

He halted, eyes wide. "Woah." He held his hands up, backing off. "What happened to you?"

I laugh-sobbed, realising what a horror show he was seeing; bloodstained, sweating, Ambrosia gel dangling from my face, mixing with tears and snot.

"Are you hurt?"

I shook my head. "My Inex was murdered."

He considered me, his hands still raised. "Look, lady," he said. "I don't know what's going on here, or what happened to your little friend, but however close you got to that thing... They're not alive. They're just a machine. So don't worry about it, OK? You can get a new one."

"I felt it die."

"Right. Well..." he said, finally lowering his arms, "Help is on the way, OK? I mean, it's a real shitshow out there, so you might have a bit of a wait, but–"

"What time is it?" I said, looking up at the security guard.

"Lady," he said as I scanned the carpark, trying to remember how I got down here, where the exit was – all I could see was row upon row of identical cars. "I think you have bigger problems than needing to know the time."

I turned back to him and snapped, "Ask your Inex. Ask it!"

"OK, OK. Calm down." He glanced down at his Inex. It looked like an animated doll in the low light.

"Give us the time, Charlie."

"Sure, John," said his Inex in a cheap generic male voice. "It's ten twenty-six and seven seconds."

"Alright, lady?"

"Ten twenty-six," I said, staring into his Inex's round, blue eyes.

"Ten twenty-six... the Ino would be... removing this," I said, pulling at the dangling gel on my face. "Then my Inex would tell me... It would tell me it was time to take my SmileBrite." I looked up at the guard. "I take good care of myself."

"I bet."

"My Inex." I looked at it lying on the ground, its face in repose, its torso torn open. "My Inex helps me be the best I can be."

"And you can get a new one, don't you worry."

"It keeps me on schedule."

"Sometimes life throws us off. You'll be back on track in no time."

"In no time." I looked at the Inex heart I was holding in my right hand, the rhythm soothing me as it continued to beat.

"What's your name, lady?"

"Jane. Jane Ward."

"Jane War–" He laughed.

I looked up at him, impassive, and he sobered. He approached, crouched down, and peered at me.

"You're–" He frowned and turned to his Inex. "Charlie – face rec."

His Inex turned to me, its big eyes focussed on my face. There a long pause, the Ambrosia gel causing delay. "Confirmed," it said. "Jane Ward, CEO of The Company."

"Holy bliss," said the security guard, swaying back. He steadied himself and ran his hand through his hair, staring at me. "Jane? Ms Ward? It's going to be OK. Charlie, tell the police I have Jane Ward and she's in a pretty messed up way. Get them down here now."

"Yes, John."

"Ms Ward, help is on the way."

He put his hand on my shoulder and I gripped the Inex heart. A wire pulled loose. It stopped beating.

"It's too late," I said, looking at the mess of wire and blood dripping from my hand. "It's too late. My schedule is ruined."

CHAPTER 2

Impatient, the security guard took me by the arm and led me out of the carpark to the throngs of people above. Dazed, I followed him, cradling my butchered Inex. The street was full of ambulances and police cars, the area cordoned off, people straining to see. We pushed our way through the crowd to get to the police cordon. A police officer was telling journalists and onlookers that if any unauthorised Inexes were found past the cordon they'd be impounded. The security guard edged forward, interrupting the police officer mid-speech.

"I found Ms Ward in the car park," he said, gently holding my arm and presenting me like a poisonous gift, all blood and wires and gelatinous tendrils. "I think she needs medical attention."

The police officer eyed me. "Sir, you can see we have enough to deal with here. I don't have time for deviants."

"It's Ms Ward," said the security guard. "*Jane Ward*, CEO of The Company."

The police officer snorted. "Yeah, and I'm Daniel Caddick."

"Do a face rec."

The police officer stared at him, his eyes cold, no longer amused. "Are you telling me what to do?"

"We'll leave. You do face rec and she's not Jane Ward, we'll leave."

The officer looked at him, jaw clenched, one hand on his hip, the other lingering on his baton. I was sure we were going to be arrested when the officer's Inex said, "Ms Jane Ward, CEO of The Company, born third of Ju–"

"Shit," said the police officer quietly, the colour draining from his face. "Ms Ward, I am *so sorry*, I didn't recognise you, please, come through and we'll get you looked after straight away, I am so sorry."

He raised the cordon and escorted me through, turning his back on the security guard, who called after us, "You're welcome. Hey, Jane! The name's John, OK? John Bradford!" The police officer gestured to another officer to cover his post at the cordon as he led me through the maze of ambulances, police cars, people and Inexes. All Inexes seemed to be fixed on me; brown, pink, yellow, purple – eye chips swivelling, focusing, recording. I knew they'd be trying to make sense of someone out in the world with Ambrosia gel hanging from their face. An Inex similar to mine gazed at me with its wide blue eyes and I felt sick.

The cop left me with a medic and I sat on the ambulance gurney staring out at the commotion around me. The medic tried to get the Inex remains off me, but I wouldn't let go. He finally stopped fussing when it became apparent all the blood was Inex synthblood and I wasn't injured, but he tried to make me connect to a MedEx to get me checked over and I refused that too. I looked out to the hotel as he lectured me. I couldn't see much from where I was, but I could hear the shouting and chanting. It looked like a car was on fire. The protest had clearly got out of hand.

I was about to get up and leave, when a man approached the ambulance, asking for me; the cop who'd left me here had sent over a detective. He started quizzing me and the medic threw us out for obstructing his work. I told the detective what I'd witnessed and castigated him for the poor police response as he put in a request to the back-up facilities for my Inex recording. I'd need to give my permission when I got a new Inex. I looked down at the remains and felt nauseous.

"I'm going home, detective."

"We need you to give a statement, Ms Ward."

"Tomorrow."

"Be at the station first thing."

"You can come to me, Detective," I said, walking off as he told me he'd send over officers to guard my apartment. It hadn't occurred to me I could still be in danger; I tensed, eyeing everyone I passed. I was exhausted; I'd never in my life felt this bone-tired before. Everything around me – the lights, the noise, the swarm of people – made me feel more and more weary. I was keenly aware of Inexes. It wasn't just that their eyes were on me, assessing this strange human smeared in Ambrosia gel and blood, one of their own broken up and cradled in my arms; it was as if Inexes had been quiet background noise and someone had turned up the volume. Their presence almost hurt, it was so piercing, they were so irrevocably *there*. I was sweating, jittery. I forced myself into tunnel-vision, staring intently at a cop I had pegged to escort me home. As I headed for her, someone took hold of my arm.

"Jane?"

I jumped and backed away, almost falling. Finding my feet, I turned and said, "Look, detective–" before realising it wasn't him. I was face to face with Jared Milligan.

"Jane? I'm sorry," he said, his voice hoarse. He reached out to me, but I shuffled away from this walking corpse; the detective hadn't told me Milligan had survived the attack.

"I just wanted to–" he said, his hand falling by his side. "I wanted to catch up with you and–"

"You're alive."

"I am," he said, staring at me, concerned. "And you? You're OK?"

"I'm exhausted, my Inex is dead, I'm covered in synthblood, I've got fucking Ambrosia gel stuck to my face–"

"That's what it is? I was wondering… Look, I just wanted to– If there's anything I can do for you…" He paused, struggling to speak. "Anything at all, let me know."

"What do you want, Milligan?" I said, my eyes narrowing.

"I… wanted to thank you… and make sure you're OK."

He looked horribly sincere. He had a bruise on his left temple, a patch of hair had been shaved off, a wound glistened with Ambrosia ointment. His neck was bruised.

"He strangled you?"

"You saw it, didn't you?" He reached up, his fingers hovering by his neck. "The detective told me you–"

"Yes," I said, grabbing for my Inex's head as it tumbled out of my grip. "I mean, not all of it."

"I've been checked over and I'm doing fine. I just wanted to…" He paused again, his voice raspy, "…thank you for contacting the police."

"Nothing to do with me. It's automatic. You know that. Not that it did much good."

"It did – they responded mainly because of you."

"They didn't help me."

He looked me up and down, pausing on the lolling Inex head and scattered wires.

"What happened?" he said. Waiting for me to respond he rubbed his lip, smearing blood from a small wound. When I didn't reply he said, "I'm sorry the police didn't help you. I'll make sure it's followed up… Were you hurt?"

I thought of the knife opening up my torso. "I'm fine."

"Good," he said, nodding. "Good." He was about to say something, stopped, then said, "Well, I just wanted to thank you for what you did. I'll see that you're updated on the investigation, and maybe we can meet for a drink when all this has blown over."

"Oh, the press would have so much fun with that."

"Wouldn't they?" He held his hand out to me. Reluctantly, I shook it. "It was good to finally meet you, Jane."

"Goodbye, Milligan."

"Give my regards to Caddick."

I laughed. "No, I don't think so."

He smiled and as I turned to leave, the detective caught up with me, flanked by two cops.

"Ms Ward. This is Officer Theron and Officer Porter. They'll escort you home and they'll be right outside your apartment if you need them. I'll get more officers on the building."

I nodded, turned, and walked over to my apartment, the cops following. We were let through the cordon and I ignored all the onlookers nudging each other, laughing at me. We walked the few yards to my building and I felt relief as I reached the main door before realising I couldn't get in without buzzing the door girl. She didn't recognise me on the screen and came to the door, peering at me through the glass before finally letting us in.

She followed us to the lift, fussing, bombarding me with questions I brushed off. I was relieved when the doors closed in her face and I leaned against the back of the lift, gripping the bar across the mirror. When I got to my apartment, I was able to eye-scan for entry and made a note to request the same for the main door. I left Theron and Porter in the corridor, glad to finally be alone. I sank onto the couch, not even thinking of the blood and grime. My body ached, a feeling alien to me other than post-exercise muscle ache. This was different.

"Inex, get me–"

I sighed and stared up at the ceiling. This was the first time I'd been without an Inex since I'd made the prototype in my late teens. It was odd not to have that company, the constant dialogue, the ease of getting things done. I thought back to a few hours ago when I'd been disparaging about the Inex, how I'd fantasised about the freedom of being without one, even if for a short time. I sat up, propping myself against the cushions, and called for the Ino.

I heard it walking down the hall and it appeared next to me. "How can I help you, Jane?"

"Vitwater. Then run me a bath."

"Of course."

It must have noticed something was amiss and said, "Where's your Inex?"

"Damaged."

"That's unfortunate," it said, walking to the kitchen.

"Yes," I said, trying not to think of my chest being torn open. I laid my head back on the cushions and closed my eyes.

CHAPTER 3

I woke, confused, and hurting all over. I sat up, realising I was on the couch. A full glass of vitwater was on the coffee table. I picked it up and drank.

"Good morning, Jane," said my Ino. "I've prepared your breakfast, but you didn't get up at the usual time."

"Because I don't have an Inex, you idiot."

"I know you don't have an Inex, Jane. That's unfortunate. I cannot be an idiot unless I am not operating properly – everything is in order."

I was the idiot – I should have taken the time to adjust the Ino's settings to get it to do the basic things my Inex usually does. I told it to make me a fresh breakfast. I was nauseous, but knew I had to eat something; my stomach felt coiled and empty.

"What time is it?"

"Ten twenty-five and thirteen seconds."

"Shit."

I put my head in my hands, my face sticky with gel. I ran my fingers through my hair, all matted and knotted with sweat and Inex blood.

"Do you have call capacity?"

"I do, Jane."

"Thank God for that."

"God didn't make me," said the Ino. "I am a product of The Company and property of you, inventor and CEO, Jane Ward."

I laughed. "Maybe I'm your God?"

"Inos have no need for a God."

I stared at the Ino for a second, unnerved by the conversation – I'd never engaged in much more than the basic servant requests.

"Who did the programme you're running on?"

"The McCarthy Team, led by Burns."

"Right. And you know what a God is?"

"I have basic cultural knowledge."

"You're just an Ino."

"Wider knowledge beyond my basic uses is often helpful for our owners. There was a study–"

"OK. Enough. Just make my breakfast."

It bothered me I'd become so detached from the details of Inex and Ino programming that I didn't know the full capabilities of my own Ino.

"Inex, make an appointment with the McCarthy Team and– Goddamnit."

"You don't have an Inex," said the Ino. "I cannot make appointments."

"I know, I know. Get Jason Bennington for me."

"He is not in my basic directory, but I can contact The Company and ask for him."

"Whatever – just get him."

I stood up, stiff, hunched over. I shuffled over to the sitting room mirror and stared, horrified. "Jesus."

Underneath the still-dangling strips of Ambrosia gel (which had turned a nasty mouldy green), my face was white, almost grey, and my eyes were dark and sunken. My hair was pasted to my forehead and my neck. My white pyjamas were covered with dried Inex blood and dirt.

"Jane? Jane!" Jason's voice came from the Ino as it continued preparing my breakfast.

"Jason, you wouldn't believe–"

"Jane, I am so relieved to hear from you – it's been crazy here and I've been trying to get in touch. I was just about to jump in a car to your apartment. How are you?"

"I'm–" I looked at my reflection, then turned away and shuffled back to the couch. "I'm OK. I just slept in."

"What's going on, Jane? There's been all sorts of things on the news about Milligan being attacked and how you were involved. I've been warding off the media, the shareholders, the board–"

"I'll explain when I get in. I'll be there by lunch. Just hold the fort until then."

"Of course, of course. I can reschedule everything for today… You don't have your Inex?"

"It was damaged last night. I'm lucky this Ino model can do more than I thought."

"I ordered that one especially."

"Of course you did."

I pulled at the dangling gel on my face as Jason said he'd have an Inex replacement waiting for me when I arrived. I refused. Confused, he thought I wanted it delivered to my apartment, which took a bit of back and forth until he realised I meant I didn't want one at all.

"But you… You can't operate without–"

"Just–" I said, squeezing my fingers into my eyes. "We can discuss it when I get in. Just keep everything ticking over for me and I'll see you at lunch."

I usually had breakfast in the kitchen, but I stayed on the couch and got the Ino to bring it through. After it laid the food out on the coffee table, I asked it to run me a bath. I sipped my coffee, feeling the warmth spread through me like an elixir.

I had to delay with Jason. Everything I did took twice as long, though I deliberately spent longer in the bath to ease my aching body. The Ambrosia gel was finally removed as the Ino applied the dissolving agent and I scrubbed at the rest of my body until my skin turned red. The bath water I was soaking in was so filthy I took a shower afterwards just to make sure I was clean. Once I was dressed and the Ino had done my make-up, I felt human again. My muscles had loosened up and my fuzzy head had cleared.

When I left the apartment, I found four police officers outside my door. Two of them accompanied me, and I was glad to have them; there was a throng of media types and a small contingent of anti-Inex protesters outside. They were all clamouring for my attention as I got into the car, the officers shielding me.

We detoured to a back-up facility after the detective contacted one of the cops, saying he needed me to stop by to give permission to access my back-up. There was an altercation when I told them I didn't have an Inex, and it was clear they were considering turning me away but thought better of it. An hour of brain-numbing bureaucracy later, they had all they needed from me.

I wasn't in the best mood when I arrived at The Company, and everyone in the open-plan office quietly staring at me didn't help. Flanked by the police officers, I went straight to my office and heard the buzz of voices when my door closed. Jason was at my desk, looking flushed.

"Jane, I can't tell you how glad I am to see you," he said, getting up and looking as if he was about to hug me, but awkwardly scooped up my hand instead, shaking it. "I'm glad you're OK – the stories I've heard."

"I'm fine, Jason, don't worry."

"And these are?" he said, gesturing to the police officers.

"Oh, I don't know. Ignore them. It felt necessary, given the nature of the attack on Milligan."

"That's good, I'm glad they're looking after you."

"They're just making up for the massive cock-up that was yesterday."

I saw Jason cringe and glance at the impassive police officers. "Right, I mean, I'm sure they–"

"Massive cock-up," I said emphatically, sitting at my desk. I stared at them for a moment, then said, "You two – out. I have private business to discuss."

They didn't respond, probably conversing internally via their Inexes, then they nodded. "We'll be just outside," one of them said, and I waved them off.

"They'll keep those gossipers in check, at least," I said, as the buzz of voices faded. "On the outside, anyway."

Jason sat on the couch opposite my desk. He leaned forward, brow furrowed.

"Right," I said. "Where are we?"

"Well, obviously I didn't really know what was going on, but I assuaged the shareholders and staff, keeping it all as vague but as confident as possible. It seems to have worked, but there's so many rumours on social media and the mainstream media have turned it into quite the melodrama and–"

"What rumours?"

"Just, you know how it is, there's always–"

"What rumours?"

"They're ridiculous. The first is that– Well, that you and Milligan…"

"Yes?"

"You were in the hotel together and you're having an affair."

I snorted, almost choking.

"I know, I know," he said, looking down at his clasped hands.

"Seriously?"

Jason nodded, embarrassment oozing from every pore.

"And the other?"

"Well, it's… It's connected to the first, and… I mean…"

"Spit it out, Jason, or I can find out for myself."

"No!" he said, looking panicked. "No, don't do that."

"OK, calm down, it can't be that–"

"You were having sex and tried to kill him."

I stared at him, stunned. He couldn't look me in the eye, his face turning red.

"We were what?" I laughed.

Jason looked up at me as laughter tears blurred my vision. "You're not upset?"

"What?" I said, wiping my eyes. "No, c'mon. It's the funniest thing I've heard in a long time."

He finally seemed to relax, a look of relief on his face. He unclasped his hands. "Caddick's angry," he said, looking at me intently, gauging my reaction. "Going on about your reputation–"

"Ah," I said, shrugging. "He's probably more worried about his own reputation. I'll deal with him."

"There's fan fiction," said Jason, looking tense again.

"Excuse me?"

"Fan fiction and memes – some people have really taken to this."

"It's only been a few hours – don't people have better things to do? Look," I said, waving my hand, "I honestly don't care. I'm sure we can utilise it further down the line. In the meantime, get me an interview with Rheya Gadon – tell her she can have an exclusive. I'll set the story straight and make a few jokes about the whole Milligan thing and we can move on."

"OK," said Jason. "OK. I was maybe blowing it out of proportion, but it's been a helluva–"

"I know, and I appreciate what you've done. I can always trust you to keep things on track."

"Thank you, Jane. I do my best."

"Now, I take it you want to know what really happened?"

I explained it all as succinctly as possible, amused by the shocked expression on Jason's face. When I finished, he sat quietly thinking it over as I internally asked my Inex to get me a coffee. The lack of response was jarring.

"You were connected?" said Jason. "When he opened it?"

"Yes."

"But it–"

"I know."

I called the office Ino through and asked it to get me a coffee as Jason stood and paced, Rory remaining on the couch, its eyes fixed on me. I stared back at it.

"It's supposed to... There's a failsafe. It's been tested over and over. We made sure."

"I know. But it happened."

Jason was quiet and I knew what was coming. I leaned back in my chair, waiting. "I mean... I don't mean to suggest that... I just think–"

"Get to it, Jason."

"It was a stressful night. Are you sure it wasn't a nightmare?"

I leaned forward, placing my elbows on the desk, my hands in a steeple at my chin, but before I could respond, Rory said, "Jane's account of the pin in her Inex's neck preventing it from disconnecting makes sense. It will need to be investigated."

We both stared at his Inex, considering it. Jason turned to me. "I'm sorry, Jane, I–"

"It's fine," I said, taking the coffee the Ino handed me. "Get a small team together, disguise the research as something else – none of this can get out."

"I'll get on it."

Jason told me Caddick wanted to speak to me, but I brushed him off; I didn't want to deal with his dramatics over Milligan. Jason was about to leave when he said he'd ordered me a new Inex and it should be here soon. I told him to cancel it and I refused a temp. He stared at me, baffled.

"But you need– I mean, no one... You can't function without an Inex."

"I can't, Jason," I said, breaking out in a sweat. "I can't connect."

He was about to push when I gave him a look and he hovered, uncomfortable before saying, "OK, OK. How about a temp you don't connect to? It can help with most of the basic things you need to do until we– until you feel more yourself again."

I thought on this for a moment, then agreed, knowing I

couldn't get through the day without constant "Where's your Inex?" questions amongst all the others I'd need to field.

"Good," said Jason, visibly relieved. "I'll get one sent up."

I made it through the day, Jason taking the brunt of it all. He got me a temp Inex, one of the latest models, with my preferred grey skin. I didn't connect, but used it to catch up with social media, getting the gist of how last night's events were being reported and discussed. I flicked between news platforms, watching a short interview with the detective I'd spoken with the night before: "Rest assured, this city will not tolerate terrorism of any kind. We will root out the Seraphs responsible for this attack on our democracy." He sounded like Caddick.

The detective came to my office later that afternoon, after repeated failed attempts to get me to go to the police station. He demanded Privacy Protocol Five as soon as he walked in.

"Good to see you too, Detective."

He repeated the request and I gave him a withering stare before I turned to my temp Inex, telling it to initiate the protocol. Both Inexes gave confirmation.

"We would appreciate your cooperation, Ms Ward," he said, pacing the room.

"I am cooperating, Detective. Given the poor police response to my emergency, you're lucky I'm cooperating at all."

"We apologise for that, Ms Ward, it was–"

"It was what?"

"An administrative error."

"Really?" We stared at each other. "Really, Detective?"

"There will be a formal apology–"

"It was the Chief of Police. We both know it," I said. "That CC bastard."

"I don't know wha–"

"Forget it," I said, irritated. "I'll deal with it myself."

He was about to speak but stopped. He shook his head, turned to me, and said, "We found the body."

"What?" I said, thrown. "What body?"

"The man who destroyed your Inex."

"He's dead?"

He nodded.

"You're sure? You're sure it's him?"

"Milligan confirmed," he said, gesturing to his Inex. It projected a picture of a man's body on the wall. I looked at it, trying to match it up with what I remembered, realising how frustrating it is to rely solely on my own memory. It could have been him; similar build, hair... People look so different when the spark is gone.

"It could be him."

"Milligan confirmed."

"You said that."

"But you're not sure?"

I stared back at the picture. "I don't know. Probably."

"Probably?"

"It's probably him."

"We found the knife on him. The one he used on the Inexes. Inex blood still on it. His fingerprints."

I stared intently at the projected picture, trying desperately not to let my mind turn to the violence I'd experienced. "Who is he?"

"Seraph."

"Of course," I said, turning away from the projection and sinking into my chair, suddenly deflated, no longer interested. "Always the Seraphs."

"It's well-known Milligan supports an HSA cure. If it wasn't attempted murder, it was definitely a warning. We're keeping this from the press for now, Jane, so I'd appreciate your discretion."

I nodded and I expected him to take his leave, but he paced again.

"Is there something else I can help you with, Detective?"

"We still need a full statement." He stopped and hovered by my desk. "Officer Andrews is waiting in reception – she'll take it."

I sighed. "I've got a tight schedule, I can only spare a few minutes."

"You can spare as long as it takes, Ms Ward."

I was about to retort, when he started pacing again and said, "There's something you need to know."

I watched him, expectant. He fiddled with the cuff of his sleeve then finally said, "There's no back-up."

I shifted in my chair and waited for him to continue, but he just stared at the floor. Irritated, I said, "No back-up for what?"

"You," he said, eyes still fixed on the floor. "Your back-up is gone. Erased." He raised his head, looking me in the eye. "Milligan's too."

I stiffened, my mouth open, about to speak. I leaned forward, my hand pressed flat on my desk. I stared up at him. He looked like he might be sick.

"That's impossible," I said. "The back-up facilities are decentralised. They have the most stringent security in the country."

"We're looking into it," he snapped, clearly anxious, back to looking at the floor as he paced, picking at the skin around his fingernails.

"You think it was the Seraphs?"

"We don't know. But if they can…"

"If the Seraphs can breach the back-up facilities it would be catastrophic."

He didn't like me stating this so boldly and he turned on me. "Security has been increased on every facility around the country. We're on top of it, Ms Ward."

I didn't respond, and he resumed his pacing. I stared at my Inex. It felt strange to have an Inex and be unconnected; no monitoring, no internal dialogue.

"My back-up is gone," I said slowly, tasting the words, looking into the glinting blue eyes of my Inex. "My life," I said, dazed, my eyes unfocused, blurring the Inex. "It's gone." I was aware of the detective in my peripheral vision, still pacing. I looked up. "For bliss sake, stop pacing."

He halted. "I know this will be a blow. The back-up facilities are looking into it, and I have my best officers overseeing the investigation. But Ms Ward," he said, standing in front of my desk, leaning on it, looking down at me. "This is strictly confidential. This can't get out. If the general population thought the facilities were in any way at risk…"

"I understand, Detective."

"Good." He relaxed, stepping back. "Tori Carpenter, the facilities' CEO, will be in touch with you."

"I'm sure she's looking forward to that."

He smiled slightly. "You're taking this better than I thought."

"I've lost my whole life, Detective. It'll take a while to sink in."

He nodded, looking down. "I'm sorry, Ms Ward." I almost expected him to offer his condolences.

"How did Milligan take it?"

"I haven't told him yet," he said, looking at me, his face all worry.

I snort-laughed. "Good luck with that."

His look turned to contempt and he walked back to me, placing his fist on the desk. "Full statement, Jane. However long it takes. We appreciate your cooperation."

He walked out, not allowing me to respond, leaving the door wide open.

I gave Officer Andrews ten minutes to take my statement then tossed her out. As soon as she left, I filed an official complaint about the lack of police response to my Inex. I then had an in-person meeting where I dressed down our white hat hackers about the revenge porn case before another in-person meeting about the merger of GRT with DEW. During the few minutes I had before the merger discussion I stared at the temp Inex, thinking about the loss of my Inex's Mnemo core and back-up. The loss of a back-up was unheard of. My life was gone. I couldn't go back and relive years, months, weeks, days. As the temp crawled up the wall, it struck me I couldn't relive this moment; each second was slipping away. As it ate a fly, I felt its absence – no monitoring, no automatic health checks, no advice, no internal dialogue. I had no past, no present. I was untethered.

I stood to go to the meeting and my knees buckled. I grabbed hold of the desk to steady myself. I closed my eyes and ignored the Inex droning on about connecting so it could assess my health.

"I'm fine," I said, opening my eyes.

I took a moment, not used to having to calm myself. I talked internally as if I was talking to my old Inex, knowing what it would have said to even my mood. I stepped out into the open-plan office and smiled at a hovering Jason who accompanied me to the meeting, walking past the noisy staff and their Inexes. I usually enjoyed the hubbub, but it felt almost painful. As we walked through the throng, I watched the Inexes, their eyes all on me, unblinking. Jason laid his hand on my arm, halting me.

"Did you hear me?"

"What?"

"Are you alright?"

"What? Yes, fine. Why?"

Jason handed me a handkerchief and I looked at it, bewildered. "You're–" he said, gesturing at his forehead. "You're sweating."

"Oh. Right." I wiped at my forehead, make-up coming away with the sweat.

"You're all clear on that?" said Jason.

"What was that?"

"The report."

"Right, yes. All good."

I sat in the meeting room, dabbing at my head with Jason's handkerchief. I noticed some staff staring at me, concerned, so I put the handkerchief away, and sat up straight, narrowing my eyes and staring back at them each in turn until they looked away.

"Privacy Protocol Three," said Jason and all Inexes gave confirmation.

I stared intently at the presentation Logan had projected onto the meeting room wall, trying to take it in, but struggling to concentrate. My hands ached. I clasped and unclasped them. I picked at the skin on the middle finger of my left hand. It peeled away easily in thin strips. I pushed and pulled at my nail. It came away with a ssshlock noise and I held it in my right hand like treasure, pleased with myself. I looked up, conscious of the silence; Logan was no longer talking and everyone had turned to stare at me. My smile faded and I dropped the nail onto my palm, protecting it in a fist, as if any one of them might try to snatch it away from me. The pain from my finger suddenly hit.

"Continue, Logan," I said. I gritted my teeth as he launched straight back into his presentation and everyone hesitatingly turned to him again.

Jason leaned in. "Are you OK?"

"Fine," I said, staring straight ahead.

I listened to Logan for a moment then looked down at the hand with the missing nail. I tried to press the nail back on, flinching at the pain, but it only slid around and fell off.

"Jane!" hissed Jason.

I stood suddenly, causing Logan to jump and the other staff to turn and stare at me again.

"I'm afraid I need to leave," I said.

There were murmured platitudes and nodding heads as Jason followed me out.

"Logan," said Jason, "continue with your presentation. I'll be back in a moment."

When we were outside, Jason took hold of my arm. "What's going on with you? That's not normal."

"Get your hand off me."

"Of course," he said, letting go, looking embarrassed. "I'm sorry. It's just… I think you need to see a doctor, Jane."

"I'm fine."

"Ma'am," said one of the police officers who'd been waiting outside. "You seem to be bleeding."

"I'm fine," I said, holding my finger up to look at it. Blood dribbled down my hand and onto the cuff of my white blouse.

"That must hurt," said Jason. "What were you doing in there?"

"I must have knocked my nail last night," I said. "It just came off."

"You pulled it off. I saw you."

"It was damaged."

"I'll get your physician in."

"No, I'm fine."

"Jane–"

"I'm fine, Jason. You finish up with Logan's presentation and I'll have a lie down in my office before the *Gadon Show*."

"Are you sure you want to go ahead with the show?"

"Of course, I'll be OK after a rest. It was just a long night."

"Right. But you need to get that nail seen to."

"The Inex can help me with it," I said. "I'll see you tomorrow."

I walked off, flanked by the police officers, feeling nauseous as I walked through the open plan that teemed with Inexes. I got to my office and closed the door, heading straight for the ensuite bathroom. I ran water over my hand and wrapped a small towel around it to stop the bleeding.

"I can help with that," said the Inex.

"There's a first aid kit over there," I said, gesturing to the corner of the bathroom as I headed back into my office. I lay down on the couch and looked up at the poster behind my desk, another of Caddick's party slogans: "**WORK MAKES**

YOU FREE" in bold, capitalised, italicised HellSans. I stared at it intently, waiting for it to bring some bliss relief, but I felt nauseous and sweaty. The Inex came through with the first aid supplies. I held out my hand and it peeled off the towel, disinfected the wound, and smeared it with fast-healing Ambrosia ointment. It tied a small bandage around it as I stared at the poster, willing the bliss to soothe me. I was shivering, and sat up quickly, snatching my hand away from the Inex. I leaned over and vomited on the floor.

"If we were connected I could diagnose you," it said.

I shook my head and went back into the bathroom, splashed water on my face, and rinsed out my mouth. I took a SmileBrite and looked in the mirror as the water dripped down my grey-white face. There were sweat stains on my blouse.

"Inex," I said, "I need a shower. Select an outfit from the wardrobe and get an Ino in here to help with my make-up after it cleans up the vomit. Keep me on track for getting to the studio in time for the Gadon interview."

I felt better after my shower, and once the Ino had done my make-up, I looked myself again. In the dressing room at the studio another Ino redid my make-up, adding layers that could deal with the harsh studio lights. I was on for twenty minutes, confident and charming. I gave a brief outline of events and quashed any rumours of an affair with Milligan. In the car on the way home I watched the segment and found I hadn't been charming at all. I was defensive, sweating, and had dark circles under my eyes despite the Ino make-up. Embarrassed, glancing at the police officers next to me, I tried to switch to internal, forgetting I wasn't connected. I ended it.

My Inex told me Jason wanted to talk. "Tell him to wait until I get home. Ten minutes," I said.

When I got to my apartment I slumped on the couch and immediately fell asleep. I woke up four hours later, soaked in sweat and feeling sick. The Ino brought me vitwater and I drank it down, asked for more, and told it to prep me a light supper.

The Inex, sitting on the coffee table, said, "Jason's been trying to get in touch."

"I'm sure he has. What time is it?"

"Nine thirty-eight."

I stared at it, thinking about the night before. "It must be about twenty-four hours since it all happened."

"Since what happened?"

"Since everything turned to shit."

"I can verify that everything has not turned to shit."

I walked over to the window seat and asked it to get Jason for me. I stared down at the hotel, still partially cordoned off. I looked over to the window where Milligan was attacked, but it was in darkness.

"Jane?" said Jason.

"Yes, I'm here. I fell asleep when I got in. Still exhausted from last night."

"I'm worried about you. How are you feeling?"

"Much better," I said. "Much better."

"You didn't look great on the *Gadon Show*."

"I know."

"There's been some fuss about it, but I've tried to counter it saying you've been through a lot and just need some rest."

"I'm fine now."

"Jane, I was going to suggest you stay at home tomorrow – I can field things here, get Paul Lynch in for anything more senior, and I'll send Dr Langham to get you checked over."

"No. I'm not letting this fiasco interfere with my life."

"It's just a day, Jane. Give you time to recover."

"I'm fine, Jason. I told you, I feel better after that sleep."

There was silence before Jason said, "If you're sure."

"I'm sure. Send the Inex tomorrow's schedule and I'll look over it this evening. I'll see you first thing."

"OK," said Jason. "See you in the morning. Get some rest."

"I will," I said, still staring at the dark window.

CHAPTER 4

I woke up drowning in sweat again, nightdress sticking to me, my hair in clots around my face and neck. I got out of bed, dizzy, my body stiff. I scratched my arm before realising I was scratching off skin.

"Shit. What is wrong with me?"

"If we were connected I could tell you."

"We're not connecting. Get the Ino to prep breakfast, I'm going for a shower."

"It could be an allergy–"

"It's just stress," I said. "Because of the attack."

"Possible, but your symptoms are consistent with–"

"Just do as I ask. I'll be fine."

The cool water soothed me but stung the open wounds on my face and arms – I must have been scratching during the night. When I got out of the shower, I smeared Ambrosia ointment over my wounds; it would heal them enough to allow me to apply make-up to disguise the marks until they healed completely. I picked at the breakfast the Ino had prepared. Despite my empty stomach, I couldn't eat much. I pushed it aside and went upstairs to continue getting ready.

"Get in touch with Jason and tell him I'll be late again," I said to the Inex.

"Yes, Jane. The door girl has asked me to tell you there's an HSA outside the building trying to get in to see you. She advises using the back door when you leave."

"Just what I need."

The Ino refused to apply make-up to open wounds, despite the Ambrosia ointment providing a protective layer, so I did it myself. I stared in the mirror. The ointment hadn't worked its usual magic; the wounds were still bloody. I dabbed at them, trying to dry them out the best I could. Then I slathered on foundation, which slid around in the blood, turning the two wounds on my face a sickly pink. I finished the rest of the make-up and added big black sunglasses and a wide-brimmed black hat – my face seemed better in shade, but the wounds still looked odd and lumpy.

I went downstairs, threw on a black coat and scarf, and went down with the police officers to the car that was waiting for me. We went by the back entrance, and just as I was getting in the car, a woman with a tin can Inex ran towards us, waving. Her face was covered by shades and a scarf, a hat pulled low – clearly an HSA privacy nut. I was relieved she was blocked by traffic as the cops bundled me into the car. I glanced back as we pulled away to find she'd ditched the shades and hat, the scarf now clutched in her hand as she waved, shouting after the car. All I caught sight of was a shock of orange hair.

"Are you OK, ma'am?"

I nodded. "I've had deviant harassment before, nothing new. Did you face rec her?"

"We didn't, but the orange hair is distinctive. We'll put out an alert."

I spent the journey staring at all the HellSans hoardings, trying not to scratch at my face. My lips were dry and I could feel them crack. I smeared the blood into the red lipstick I was wearing.

When I arrived at The Company there was no sign of Jason. I walked through the open plan, feeling safe and secure behind the layers of black. I entered my office to find someone at my desk.

"Have I been replaced?"

Board Chair Paul Lynch looked up at me, his Inex's head

swivelling simultaneously. "You look like you're going to a funeral, Jane."

"Jason called you, did he?"

"How are you feeling? He told me you're not well."

"I'm fine."

"Are you?"

I sat down on the couch opposite my desk, spreading my aching arms over the back and crossing my legs. I tilted my chin up and looked over at him. "Is this a coup?"

He sighed. "Don't be paranoid, Jane. We're concerned. We want you back to your usual self, and to get that we think you need some rest."

"I told Jason and I'm telling you: I'm fine."

"You went through something traumatic, Jane. It's OK to admit it had an effect on you."

"I witnessed Milligan being attacked. It wasn't traumatic. If anything, it was satisfying."

"Jason told me about your Inex."

"What?" I said, leaning forward.

"You were connected when it was damaged."

I laughed. "'Damaged' isn't the word I'd use, and Jason had no right to tell you."

"Don't take this out on him – he's worried about you. He has your best interests at heart."

"And you?"

"I'm just here to assess the situation and assist if need be."

"OK, it was traumatic. A psychopath cut me open and pulled my guts out. I was murdered. I *felt* it." Lynch nodded, as if he understood, the condescending sonofabitch. "But it doesn't mean I'm not fit to run the company."

"Jason informed me you've been having physical symptoms."

"I'm perfectly capable of doing my job, Paul."

I looked at the "**WORK MAKES YOU FREE**" poster above Paul's head and felt my lips cracking again. I licked the blood, feeling nauseous, willing myself not to throw up in front of him.

"Jane," he said, leaning forward, looking me in the black insect-eye shades that shielded me. "No one fucks with you – I think we all know that by now."

That made me smile and I instantly regretted it, rubbing at my lips, hoping he was too far away to notice.

"We're only trying to get you back on track. Jason will field everything for you and I'll deal with the more senior issues while you rest. We'll update you all the way. No one benefits if you're–"

"Not operating at my full capacity."

He smiled and leaned back in my chair. "Right. Exactly."

I sat for a moment, staring at the blood and lipstick on the tip of my finger. "I'm going to get through today, Paul," I said, looking up. "Then it's all yours."

"I don't think that's a good idea, Jane."

I stood and walked over to the desk, looking down on him. "I'm not asking you."

He looked up, mouth open slightly, about to speak. Instead, he glanced down at the desk, rapped it with his knuckles, nodded, and stood, his Inex climbing up his arm. "OK, Jane. You can have today. But since I'm here, I'd like to sit in on the UNP meeting."

"Fine," I said, sitting down at my desk.

"I'll get Jason to set me up with office space for today." He paused, looking at me. "You have some lipstick–" he said, pointing to his own cheek.

I pawed at my cheek, rubbing it, feeling the skin crack. I kept my hand to my face, waiting for him to leave.

"I'll see you this afternoon," he said, closing the door behind him.

When he left, I ran to the ensuite and threw up.

I fixed my make-up the best I could and I kept the hat and shades on. Everything was too stark and bright without them, and my eyes were bloodshot and aching. There was a knock on the door, followed by a flustered Jason, insisting he got Lynch in to ease the pressure on me. I slowly removed my shades and stared at him. His face crumpled and he sank onto the couch, deflated as I reprimanded him.

"Jane, I–"

I held up my hand to silence him. "I know. You were trying to help. But I don't need Lynch interfering. I'm fine."

He started apologising and I interrupted, "Just give me the day's schedule."

Looking relieved we'd moved on, he gave me a rundown and passed the UNP report to my Inex. When he left, I went through to the gym and changed into shorts and vest top, the Inex advising against a workout on an empty stomach. Ignoring it, I got on the exercise bike.

"Project the report – a workout and HS bliss will pull me out of this funk. I'll show Lynch I can handle being murdered."

I was in pain, but I planned to exercise through and beyond it. I read the UNP report as I cycled, waiting for the HellSans bliss effect to wash over me, but I broke out in a cold sweat, my body shaking, my hands blistering where they gripped the handlebars. I felt dizzy and nauseous.

"Shit," I said, sliding off the bike and sitting on the floor, struggling to breathe. "Why isn't it working, Inex? Why the hell isn't it working?"

"Your symptoms could mean you have any of the following–"

"I don't want your guesses."

"I can diagnose you if we connect."

I shook my head. "Bring me a vitwater."

My whole body hurt. I'd forgotten what pain felt like – my only recent experience being hangover headaches and a bruised finger. The one thing remotely comparable was the time I'd broken my arm as a kid, and that was so long ago, so faded I could barely remember it. I sat on the floor, trying to concentrate on my breathing. I was hot and sweating, so I removed my vest top, shorts, and pants, and lay naked on the floor. I sat up to drink the vitwater.

I got the Inex to reduce the temperature and I lay back down. "Read out the report to me as you project it across my body."

"Why?"

"It'll soothe me. I want to feel it across my skin."

"HellSans bliss doesn't work like that."

"Just do it."

I closed my eyes. As I listened, I visualised the words sliding across me, sinking into my skin, flowing through my veins, energising my muscles, carving themselves into my bones. From the outside in and the inside out I saw myself glowing with HellSans bliss: healthy, happy, vigorous.

I smiled and my lips cracked. I felt the blood trickle down my chin. I opened my eyes and sat up, shaking, my joints creaking. I looked down at my legs, the HS words flowing across them, my skin blistering. Shitting myself, I sobbed as I clutched my contracting stomach.

I stood, diarrhoea dribbling down my legs as I pulled myself up by grasping onto the bike, smearing more blood on the handlebars from the open wounds on my palms. I walked through to my office, the Inex following, spewing out the words of the report, still projecting them across my body.

I reached up to the poster behind my desk and dragged it off the wall, tearing the top corners. I tore off the word "**WORK**", ripped off the letter "**W**" and ate it. My mouth was dry, making it difficult to break it down, the letter cutting my tongue and the roof of my mouth as I masticated.

"That is not digestible," said the Inex, interrupting the report. I kept chewing. "I advise spitting it out," it said, before continuing.

There was a knock on the door and Jason walked in. "Jane, everything is sorted with the–"

He stared down at me, naked, covered in sores, blood, shit, and a constant stream of HellSans.

"Holy bliss–"

He slammed the door shut and gawped at me as I spat out the "**W**" and sobbed, tears and snot dribbling onto my bloody lips.

"Jane, what…"

He locked the door, turned back to me, and knelt down, gently holding my head in his hands. "Jane? What's going on? What's wrong? Jesus, look at you."

He embraced me and I held onto him, snotting on his shoulder, unable to speak.

"It's OK," he said, "It's OK. Come on, come with me. We'll get you cleaned up then we'll get you to the hospital."

He pulled me up and I held onto him as he walked me through to the bathroom. Taking me to the shower, he helped me in, and I slumped down. He turned it on, the lukewarm water stinging my wounds. He handed me soap, telling me Rory was calling an ambulance. Clutching the soap tight in my fist, voice wavering as I shook my head, I told him I wasn't going near a hospital.

"Jane, you're really sick. You–"

I interrupted with an emphatic "no", rubbing the soap across my thigh, watching the blood, shit, and vomit disappear down the plughole. He let the hospital drop and went back to insisting I at least connect to the Inex, but I refused that too. He was about to argue when I told him to get Dr Langham to wait for me at my apartment, and he relented, looking relieved.

"Now give me some privacy."

He looked startled, suddenly registering he was watching his boss shower. He flushed, looked away, and backed off, telling me he'd be in my office if I needed him.

It took me a while to clean myself, but by the time I got out of the shower my head had cleared and I was no longer distressed. My Inex helped apply Ambrosia ointment to my wounds as Jason called through every few minutes to make sure I was OK. I got dressed and returned to my office. Jason was on the couch. I hesitated, about to sit with him, but I sat at my desk instead. I noticed he'd already replaced the poster as if nothing had happened.

He had a smoothie waiting for me and I took a sip. He'd called Langham, informing me he'd be at my apartment by two-thirty.

"Tell Langham to meet me at The Gold Room instead."

"The bar? But–"

"Just do it, Jason. And I want a MedEx in advance. One with painkiller capacity. I want it here in the next few minutes."

"But that's… I mean he'll want to see you before he gives you a MedEx–"

"Get it done, Jason."

"OK, Jane," he said, standing. "If you need anything else–"

I nodded and waved him away. When he was gone, I leaned back in my chair. I was no longer sweating or shaking and I didn't feel sick, but everything hurt: joints, muscles, skin. My bliss wasn't just off-kilter, it was gone. I wondered if this was what life without HellSans was like – constant nagging pain.

As I waited, I applied more Ambrosia ointment and redid my make-up. I put my scarf, shades and hat on and examined myself in the mirror, pleased with my fake wellness. Concentrating on the make-up had distracted a little from the pain, but it was starting to wear me down and I knew I wouldn't make it far without that MedEx.

Jason came in and told me Langham had agreed to meet at The Gold Room and the MedEx was on its way. "Hang on," he said, raising a finger. "That was reception – it's here. You can collect it on your way out."

"Thank you, Jason. I appreciate everything you've done." I looked at him. "I know you won't share what happened today."

"Of course not," he said, looking shocked.

"Tell Lynch he was right – he'll enjoy that – and I've decided to go home and rest."

"We'll keep everything running smoothly and make sure you're updated."

I nodded and walked out into the open-plan office, the cops following me, Jason chasing after me when he realised I'd left my Inex behind. He held it out to me. "A MedEx can't do everything, Jane."

I batted him away and stepped into the lift, my route to pain-free hours.

CHAPTER 5

I sat in the front of the car and told it to raise a screen between me and the cops in the back. I leaned my head against the seat, feeling my body relax and soften. There'd been an argument with the MedEx; it didn't want to administer anything without connecting, so I contacted Langham and he ordered it to do as I asked.

"I don't know what's going on with you," he said, "but you're pushing my goodwill to the limit."

"Brett," I said, with the painkillers coursing through me as HellSans bliss should have done, "I've pushed many people to their limit, and it always turns out it isn't their limit after all."

"Jane–"

"I'll see you at two-thirty."

I hadn't told Jason, but I was on my way to Caddick's. Sitting in the car, I blanked out the world, enjoying the protection of the hat, shades, and drugs. I was cushioned, normal again.

"Five minutes to Caddick's," the car said.

I opened my eyes as the car moved up a narrow road flanked by trees. Caddick's family home was in the green belt beyond the suburbs. His family were old money and they owned acres of land. I was one of the rare ones who wasn't impressed when they came up the drive to that imposing mansion. I thought it was gauche and morbid. I have no respect for old money.

When I arrived, the Ino came down the front steps and opened the car door. I checked my hat, shades and make-up and got out, the cops following. The Ino led us into the mansion and down the hall to the study.

"Finally," said Caddick as I stood in the doorway. He went straight to the drinks tray. "Whisky?"

"Yes."

"No," said my MedEx.

Caddick glanced at me as he poured his own. "Which is it?"

"Yes," I said. "You," I pointed at the MedEx. "Be quiet."

"Come in, Jane," said Caddick. "Take a seat." I walked in and Caddick looked over to the Ino. "Take these men to the drawing room." He raised a glass to the cops hovering in the hallway. "Make sure they're comfortable and get them whatever they ask for."

"Thank you, Prime Minister, sir," said one of the cops, and the Ino left, closing the door behind it.

I sat down in my usual seat. A sense of coming home suddenly swept over me as Caddick handed me the whisky. We clinked glasses and he said, "To your health."

I smiled slightly, wary of my lips, worried the drugs had softened me so much I wouldn't notice if they cracked open and bled. I drank, enjoying the burn. Caddick sat opposite, slouching in the chair, legs wide, head cocked as he looked over at me. He was about to say something but took a drink instead. His eyes still on me, he licked his lips. I watched his Inex climb up the seat and perch on the back. They both stared at me. I was grateful for the protection of my shades.

"What a clusterfuck," he said finally. He nodded, agreeing with himself, then took another drink. "I'm glad you're OK, Jane. What's all," he said, his finger circling his face, "this?"

I fingered the edges of my scarf. "Press," I said. "They're all over me after what happened."

"Were you hurt?" He gestured to his cheek, looking concerned.

I raised my hand to my face and felt my cracked skin. I

stared down at my fingers, glistening with blood. I wiped it on my coat. "It's taking a while to heal."

"Ambrosia ointment should have taken care of it."

"I'm seeing my doctor after this. I'll get it dealt with then."

"As long as you're OK."

I took another drink, enjoying the warmth and the gentle floating feeling as it met with the drugs in my system. "Dan," I said, pausing, watching him run his fingers through his hair, only for it to fall back into place. "Dan, I need to get a hold of Ichorel."

"Dr Smith?" he said, staring at his glass as he swirled his whisky. He looked up at me. "Why do you want her?"

"The Inex," I said as he knocked back his drink. "My Inex. It was connected, sense-sharing when the Mnemo core was torn out."

"Your Inex was…" He shook his head. "That's not possible."

"I felt it," I said. "I felt the knife go in, slice down my chest and–" I stopped, the floaty warmth turning to dizziness.

"Jane?" he said, getting up.

I held up my hand. "I'm OK. I'm OK." He hovered then sat back down. "Look, it happened. I know it's not supposed to, but it did."

He perched on the edge of his chair, alert. He whistled and shook his head. "That won't be good for business, Jane."

"It's on the quiet. But it needs investigating. I need Ichorel. I tried her Inex but couldn't reach her."

"Why do you need Icho for this?"

"She's an Inex collector. They're her hobby. She knows them inside out – better than most of the techs in the Inex division, if I'm honest. I need her on this, Dan."

"You know she's busy, Jane."

"I just need to talk to her, bounce some theories off her."

"Nothing," said Caddick, "will derail her research. I'm sorry, Jane."

I looked down at my whisky, nodding. I drank then said,

"And how's that going? Her research? Any sign of a cure?"

Caddick went to the bar, and picked up the whisky bottle, bringing it over. Topping up my glass, he spilled some on my hand and I reached to wipe it away, but he stopped me, hand around my wrist. He sank to his knees, placing the bottle on the floor, and licked the whisky dribbling down my fingers. I stiffened, the protective effect of drugs and alcohol gone in an instant.

"Get the fuck away from me, Caddick," I said, pulling my hand out of his grasp and hunching myself into the chair. He looked at me, his face impassive, then he snatched up the whisky bottle and went back to his seat where he slumped and filled his glass to the brim. He was silent for a while and I stared at his awards and certificates framed on the wall, all in italic HellSans. I started to sweat.

"Dan, I just need–"

"Is it true?"

"Is what true?"

"You and Milligan?" he said, shifting position.

I sighed, no longer finding it amusing. "Of course it isn't."

"You weren't in the hotel with him?"

"No, for bliss sake."

"It's OK," he said, nodding. "I know you weren't."

"Then why ask? I've already been tortured on the *Gadon Show*. I can't–" I stopped and watched his Inex slide down the chair onto the armrest. It sat down as I said, "What do you mean, you know? Have you been talking to the detective? You have no right to keep monitoring everything I–"

"I have your Mnemo core, Jane."

He was perched on his seat, elbows on knees, both hands cupping his glass. He looked at me from under that flick of hair that kept straying into his eyes.

"What?"

"Your Mnemosyne core," he said, smiling, as if he was simply telling me he'd bought a new Inex or he'd had a good day's hunting. "I have it."

"You have it?" I leaned in, trying to read him, trying to work out if this was a sick joke. "How can you have it?"

"It was my man in the hotel room that night."

I jerked forward and stood, dropping my glass, whisky spilling across the carpet. "Are you *insane*?"

"Now, Jane," he said, standing, raising his hand to ward me off, frowning at the carpet as it soaked up the whisky. "Inex – get the Ino."

"Fuck your goddamn carpet, Dan," I said, ready to smash his face into it. "Why in unblissed hell would you risk an attempt on Milligan?"

"It wasn't what you think."

"Then what the hell was it?"

"It's complicated."

"It's complicated?" I paced, all jittery, shaking and sweating. "Are you fucking kidding me, Caddick? All this," I said. "All this because of you."

"You're bleeding."

I felt the blood dribbling down my chin and onto my neck. I let it soak into the scarf.

"How can you be so stupid?"

"Jane," he said, shaking his head. "I'd be careful."

"Don't," I said, pointing at him. "Just... fucking *don't*."

I turned away from him and leaned on his desk, trying to steady my breathing. Blood dripped from my chin onto the desk. I could hear the ice clink in his glass.

"Look," he said, "I understand you're angry." I heard him stand, then felt his hands on my shoulders and I flinched. "I'm sorry you were caught up in this."

"Did your man know it was me?"

"Of course not, Jane." He manoeuvred me so that I faced him and his hand slid down onto my waist. He reached up and started to remove my sunglasses, but I stopped him. "You don't need to be in disguise with me."

I shook my head. "You need to explain yourself."

"I will," he said. "I will soon. You just need to calm down." His hand gently stroked my cheek, but it burned. He wiped the blood from my chin. "You need to get your MedEx to look at that wound."

Caddick examined my face and I pulled away. I could feel the skin crack open where his hand had held me at the waist.

"Your man…" I said. "How did he die?"

"He didn't."

"But the police…" I trailed off. I hadn't really believed what the detective had shown me. "The body's a decoy. Blame it on the Seraphs."

Caddick nodded. "I can't have the police investigating this."

"The back-ups? Milligan's, mine. You had them erased." He didn't respond. I tongued at a loose tooth. "What were you thinking, Dan? Such a blatant attack on Milligan, after all we've been working on together."

"It's not what you think, Jane."

"Then what is it?"

"It's complicated."

"You're freezing me out."

"Never," he said and tried to hold me again, but I backed off. He reached out to me. "I'm just trying to protect you, Jane."

"I don't need protecting."

"You don't look to me like you're coping."

The Ino came in and started cleaning up the spilled whisky. I tongued at my loose tooth again and it came free. It fell onto my tongue and I rolled it around in the blood. I turned away from him and spat it into my hand.

"You've ruined my life," I said, placing the tooth on the edge of his desk like an ornament.

"Now, Jane," he said, laughing. "Don't be dramatic."

"Don't condescend to me, Caddick."

"Tell me how I ruined your life?"

My hand twitched and I was about to reach up to my lumpy, bloody face, but I gripped the side of his desk, pressing my palms into the edge, breaking open the semi-healed wounds.

"We were doubled, sense-sharing. I died."

"And I'm sure you can work through it. I'll help you every step of the way. You can stay here for now – the Ino will ready your room. I'll get your Mnemo set up in a brand new Inex, and I'll get my personal physician to help you work through the trauma."

"I can't have another Inex."

"You've got that, don't you?" he said, pointing to the MedEx.

"We're not connected."

"You'll need to use one eventually, Jane."

He went round the other side of his desk, facing me. He pressed his finger against a drawer. It slid open and he lifted out a Mnemosyne core. "Give me access and I'll get you set up."

I looked at it and shook my head. I couldn't believe it was mine.

"You don't need to start using it until you feel able."

"You need to tell me why you have it. You need to tell me what you were doing."

"I will," he said. "I will. But first we need to get you better. You're my responsibility."

The sweat was soaking into my clothes and I was trying not to visibly shake. "Inex," I said to my MedEx, "I need another dose."

"It's too soon," it said.

"Give me it now."

"I can provide a half dose."

"Anything. Just do it."

The MedEx laid its hand on my arm and I felt the painkiller flow into me, numbing, calming. I laid my head back against the chair and said, "OK." There was no response, so I looked up. "OK, I'll let you look after me, I'll let you set me up with a new Inex." I shook my head. "I just can't feel like this anymore."

He smiled. "Good. All I want is for you to be well, Jane. I'm sorry you were caught up in this."

He walked over to me and held out the Mnemo. I pressed my thumb on it. It lit up and I keyed in the code.

"I'll arrange for this to be sent to James, then we'll get you comfortable in your room. You're safe with me, Jane. Everything is going to be alright."

I nodded and sat there, dazed, relieved, floating again. He walked out, his Inex following, leaving me, the MedEx, and the Ino. I stared up at the stag head above his desk; the only thing I appreciated about Caddick's estate was hunting. Nothing else helped me unwind like that – not HS bliss, not alcohol, nothing. The elegant violence and sense of achievement was unmatched. Once, I'd missed my mark – hurting but not killing it – and I was furious. But when we tracked the injured deer and I looked it in the eye as I slit its throat, I'd never experienced anything so sublime.

Nausea and the searing image of the knife coming down into my throat pulled me out of my reverie. My memory was tainted, that pure experience corrupted by trauma. I stood up, agitated, feeling closed in, the sound of the Ino cleaning the carpet grating on me. I went out into the hall, heading for my usual room. As I walked down the long hallway, I heard a low murmur from the room I'd passed. I walked back and looked in. Caddick was talking with someone. He stood in front of them, so I could only see a vague outline. I waited, watching, trying to hear, but they were quiet. I thought about going up those stairs and letting the bed envelop me, I thought of the ease of giving up, giving in to Caddick's promises and hospitality. I closed my eyes and saw his tongue against my hand and I flinched. Opening my eyes, I backed away but kept him in sight. I felt panicked, my chest tight. Caddick moved out of my sightline, revealing the man who'd attacked Milligan. He'd changed his hair; it was shorter, and blonde. His presence didn't mean anything – Caddick had already told me it was his man, that he hadn't realised it was me, but I still felt betrayed, trapped. I inched closer to the door. I remembered him in the hotel window, staring at me, drawing his finger across his throat.

I backed off, almost tripping over the Ino that had followed me down the hall. I skirted around it and ran down the hallway to the main door. I pulled at the door, but it was locked; I'd need Caddick's Inex to release me. I turned round, my back pressed to the door, trying to remember if the study windows were open. The Ino was walking towards me down the hallway, and as I was about to run back into the study it said, "Thank you for visiting. We hope you had a pleasant time." It placed its hand on the door, and it clicked open. I slipped out and ran for the car, my MedEx just behind me.

"City centre. Now."

The car set off and I threw up into an Inex Company snack pack I'd managed to open in time. I wiped my mouth with my sleeve, popped a SmileBrite, and stared at the receding mansion through the back window. I was trusting my gut at a time my gut was betraying me. I turned back round and said, "Faster."

"We're going at the speed limit. I can increase speed when we reach the motorway."

I don't know what I expected – Caddick to come after me like some old movie car chase? We were both constrained by modern tech, but he could have me cut off.

"What other routes are there into the city?" I asked the car. "Even if they're not the most efficient."

"There's a route through the factories and past the ghetto – it's a two-mile diversion."

"Take the ghetto route."

The car confirmed and I asked my MedEx to get Jason for me.

"Who is Jason?"

"Shit, right. Jason Bennington of The Company."

"He's not in my directory, but I can contact The Company."

A few seconds later Jason's voice came from the MedEx. "Jane? Everything alright?"

"Jason, has Caddick been in touch?"

"Caddick? No, not since this morning."

"If he gets in touch don't tell him where I am, don't tell him I'm meeting Dr Langham at The Gold Room. Just say I'm busy."

"Anything I need to know about?"

"No," I said. "No, I just can't deal with him right now."

"OK, Jane. I hope all goes well with Langham."

"I'll check in when I'm done."

The car was coming up to the ghetto and I looked out at the imposing north wall that went on for miles. I'd seen it on the news countless times, but never in the flesh. It made me uneasy, so I looked away, out towards row upon row of factory buildings that lead the way to the suburbs and the city.

I was relieved when we reached the familiarity of the city and I smiled up at the buildings and electronic hoardings, a blissful landscape of neon, bold, capitalised HellSans. My smile faded as my lips cracked and I broke out in a sweat. I asked the car to decrease the temperature, but it wasn't enough. I loosened my scarf and checked what street we were on.

"Stop here. I'll walk the rest."

The car pulled in as the MedEx said, "Walking is ill-advised when you're–"

"I need air," I snapped. "And Caddick will likely track the car. I'm no longer trusting that sonofabitch until I find out what the hell he's doing."

I got out and I glanced up at the Ambrosia hoarding: "**The new you is the *real* you.**"

"I fucking hope not," I said before looking over to the Inex ad next to it: "***Helping you be the best you**".

I felt nauseous and looked away, pulling my hat lower. I walked past a group of girls surrounding a beggar HSA. They noticed me watching them and they all stopped to stare back. I was glad of the foundation caked on to hide the cracks and the open sores, the celebrity shades, scarf and hat, but I made the

mistake of smiling at them and my lips cracked open again. I
hid my mouth with my hand, but they'd turned away anyway.
I hurried past them and caught a glimpse of the horror story
mess that was the deviant; his face gone, lost in sores.

"You should be in the ghetto, freak," said one of the girls.
"You're polluting our bliss."

My eyes fell on a poster behind them. It was one of
Caddick's party posters: a wholesome nuclear family stood
against a map of the country, "**WE'RE IN THIS TOGETHER**"
in bold, capitalised HellSans alongside an exhortation to
protect "our democracy, our freedom" and report any
suspected Seraph activity. I fought the urge to vomit.

Head down, I hurried on, feeling the skin on my heels crack
open. I looked up when I reached a crossing, my eyes falling on
one of the retro Inex hoardings. I lingered on it as I waited to
cross, taking in the addition of serifs, aware that those simple
lines were easing the nausea. The text was bordered by the
logo of the Seraphs – crude smudged angels.

"Makes you sick, doesn't it?" A woman looked at me as I
basked in the defaced advertisement. "Don't stare at it too long
or your bliss will be off-kilter all day."

"I won't," I said, seeming to turn away, my eyes still focused
on it, hidden behind the black shades.

"We should bomb them."

"What?"

"We should bomb the terrorists – and the rest. The whole
ghetto. The dregs of humanity."

I nodded as we crossed together, and I was relieved when
she was caught up in the crowd. I walked on, keeping the
image of the defaced ad in my mind.

By the time I arrived at the bar, the nausea was gone and
the pain from my heels only niggled. I walked in and saw Brett
waiting in my usual private booth at the back of the bar. I
waved at him, and he raised his drink to me as I was stopped
by a member of staff.

"Ma'am, your Inex didn't register. Can I take your ID?"

"I'm *Jane Ward*."

He stared at me, then I saw a flicker of horror. "Ms Ward, I am *so sorry*. I didn't recognise you and your Inex didn't register when you came in so I–"

"It's fine." I waved him away. "All drinks will go on the Doctor's account today."

"Of course," he said, "I'll bring your gin straight away."

I made my way over to Brett and he stood, lightly hugging me, giving me an air kiss. We both sat down as he said, "What's the emergency, Jane? And why bring me here?"

I took off my shades.

"Jesus, Jane." He leaned forward. "You look terrible."

"I'm sick."

"We should have met at the hospital; there's not a lot I can do for you here."

"I can't go there."

"Why not?"

"I just can't."

"What's wrong with you?"

"You're the doctor, you tell me."

"Didn't the MedEx diagnose you?"

"I'm not connected."

"Then connect."

"I can't."

"Why not?"

"I won't."

He sighed and leaned back, sipping his drink. "You always know how to make things difficult, Jane."

The waiter brought my drink, apologising again.

"It's fine," I said, irritated.

"If there's anything you need…"

"Another one of these," I said, knocking it back and handing him the glass.

"Of course."

"Jane, drowning in gin might not be the best medicine, especially if you're on pain killers."

"I've lost my bliss," I said, staring at him, my eyes getting watery. Ashamed, I rubbed at them, trying to wipe away the tears, my hands coming away streaked in blood. "Shit."

"Jane, what–?"

"My skin is cracking at the slightest touch, and a tooth fell out," I said, pausing to tongue at the hole, feeling the tooth next to it wobble. "I'm permanently nauseous and throwing up nothing because I can barely eat. My whole body hurts, creaking like I'm a hundred years old."

"Jane, you–"

The waiter returned and placed down a bottle and a glass. "Compliments of the house," he said, smiling and quickly retreating.

"When did the symptoms start?"

"After the…" I trailed off and poured myself more gin. "After Caddick did something really fucking stupid," I said.

"After what?"

"After the attack. Brett, this has to be between us, OK?" He nodded. "I was connected. When my Inex was stabbed and ripped open – I was connected. I felt it."

"That's–"

"Impossible," I said, rolling my eyes and taking a drink.

He sat back, sighed, and locked eyes with me. "Jane," he said, "You're HSA."

I nodded, pursed my broken lips, stared down at my gin and laughed. Looking back up at him, I said, "I can't be, Brett. I can't be a deviant. Not me."

"You're clearly sick."

"It could be something else."

"Stress."

"What?"

"You were stressed."

"That's an understatement."

"I mean," he said, "stress and trauma can trigger HSA. In this political climate it's not talked about, there's been no research, because there's no funding because it's taboo. But I know stress and trauma are factors."

"It's psychological? You're saying this is all in my head?"

"No, that's not what I'm saying. There's likely a biological cause, probably genetic, but stress and trauma can be a trigger."

"Genetic? No, no, no. I'm not *naturally* one of them, Brett. I'm just not."

"I don't know that anyone is *naturally* HSA, Jane. I don't even know what that means. As I told you, there's no research. As far as I know, no one has recovered from it, only managed it. There's been no research into individual differences and why some can manage it better – is it environment? Genetics? The particular trigger? A combination? No one knows."

"There must be something I can do. It must be reversible."

Brett leaned forward, elbows on his knees. "Are you talking in HellSans?"

"What?"

"Are you thinking it? Are you thinking in HS?"

"Are you kidding me?"

"Take a moment. Think about it. Are you thinking?"

"I'm thinking."

"Are you thinking and talking in HellSans?"

I spat a tooth into my drink and watched it float like a Halloween sugar cube. "Well, I am now, you sonofa–"

"You're making yourself sick."

"Are you saying this is *my* fault?"

"No, it's all around you, isn't it?" he said, leaning back and spreading his arms. "How can you not internalise it?"

"Society is making me sick?"

"Society is killing you."

I sat there, dazed, my mouth hanging open, blood dripping from the latest hole.

"We don't think by visualising words, so we don't always

literally think in HellSans, but it's changed our brains, we've internalised it, whether we want to or not; it's there, just beneath the surface. You have favourite words, right? Favourite letters you focus on when you want a strong bliss hit? They're a part of you. And now they make you sick."

"I can't be one of them, Brett. I just can't. You have to help me."

"There's nothing I can do, Jane. You know that."

"There must be."

"The safest place for you is the ghetto."

I stared at him in horror, then realising he was joking, I guffawed. "Funny," I said. "Can you imagine?"

"I'm not joking, Jane. It's the only place in this country free of HellSans. The people with the best knowledge of how to deal with it will be there."

"You are serious?"

He shrugged. "I'm bound by protocol. I have to report you. What did you expect?"

I squeezed the gin glass, my knuckles turning white. "I expected you to do your goddam job. Are you seriously going to throw *Jane Ward* in the ghetto?" I laughed. "That's insane, Brett. That's really insane. You know how much I can pay you. Just find me somewhere safe until we can figure this out."

"You can't pay me anything, Jane. The assets of all HSAs go to ghetto upkeep. And you know I can't harbour an HSA – I'd lose my licence."

Sweat dripped into my eyes, mingled with blood from my cracked skin. I wiped it away and said, "I came to you for help."

"And I'm helping you."

A patch of skin had come away in my hand and I stared at it before trying to push it back onto my face. It slid around, blood coating my fingers. Blood was filling my mouth; I spat it into my drink and watched the tooth bob around in spirals of red.

"Watch out for italics," said Brett.

"*Italics*?" I said, my lips slipping across each other in the blood, not forming the right shape.

"Any emphasis on internalised HellSans is dangerous. Stay away from bold."

And there I was, thinking in ***<u>bold, italicised, underlined, neon-lit HellSans</u>***, flat on my face, blowing blood bubbles.

I watched Brett as he talked to his Inex and I panicked, trying to get up.

"**I can't be one of them**," I said in bold HellSans. "*I'm not one of them*," I said in italics.

"It's too late, Jane. The moment I diagnosed you HSA, my Inex summoned the authorities. It's out of my hands."

I tried to blink the blood out of my eyes, Brett's Inex towering over me in a veil of red, the ground moving underneath me. "I'll fuc–" My head was spinning, I was sweating and shaking, I saw flashing white light. I blacked out.

CHAPTER 6

"I'll fucking destroy you, Brett."

I focused on a grimy ceiling, glistening with damp and spider webs. Realising I wasn't in the bar, I sat up, wincing, looking around me. I was in a huge wooden hut packed full of people lying on the floor, moaning, shouting, wailing. A dozen or so people were tending to them, cleaning up vomit and shit, bathing them, bandaging wounds. I leaned my head against the wall, overwhelmed by the noise and the stench of the place.

"You're awake."

A middle-aged woman in tattered mismatched clothes was looking down at me. She had brown hair cropped close to the scalp, her face was drawn, her skin crumpled by layers of scars.

"Where am I?"

"The med block."

"The ghetto?"

"That's right."

"That sonofabitch."

"Whoever sent you here did you a favour, honey," she said, giving me a smile that didn't reach her eyes. "You had a pretty bad attack, the kind a lot of us don't come back from. You weren't going to get the medical attention you needed in the city, that's for sure."

A drip from the ceiling hit my face and I flinched, looking up. "I don't belong in this shithole."

She pursed her lips. "How new are you?"

"I just got here. You know that."

"I mean HSA. There's not much scarring."

"I'm not HSA."

She smiled and shook her head. "OK, honey."

"Don't call me honey." I was about to get up when I realised the only clothing I had was the dirty blanket. "Where's my clothes?"

"You'll get them back. Benji here," she pointed across the room, "he'll patch you up, you'll get your clothes, you'll be assigned a block providing you're well enough to be discharged, then you'll be given a workstation, depending on your skills. In the meantime, just relax and try not to think in HellSans. It'll help you heal. If you need the toilet there's a bedpan, but we prefer if you use the facilities." She pointed to the door at the back of the hut. "Almost forgot about this," she said, half pulling my MedEx out of a bag. "I tried to take the drugs, of course–"

"Of course."

"But it'll only administer to you. I'd keep it hidden, if I were you." She pushed it back in the bag. "It's a high-end model. We don't get many of them here. Most people are on early Inexes and no one has a MedEx. If they can't access the meds they'll just tear it to pieces and use the parts."

I immediately felt nauseous as I thought of my torn-open Inex in the car park. "They feel pain," I said.

"Well, that's what it's there for – make the most of it while you can."

"No, the Inex. The Inex feels pain."

"They're just robots."

"They're cyborgs," I said, giving her a withering stare. "How can you people not know the basic facts about something you use every day? They're designed to feel pain."

"Pretty sadistic design if that's so."

I shook my head. "Common sense. Keeps them safe. I designed early models where they were programmed to seek medtech attention if anything went wrong, but it wasn't enough. I experimented with pain receptors and the success rate was much higher."

"You work for The Company?"

"I *am* The Company."

"Look, honey. You just arrived, so I'll give you a break – but you need to be careful. You might think posing as The Company's elite will win you favours, but it'll get you killed. There's different rules here, and I can tell you're going to learn that the hard way."

"I don't need to learn anything. I'm not staying."

"You don't want to try your hand at city begging. That's another sure way to get yourself killed."

"I'm not begging for anything. I'm going back to my apartment, I'm going to get well, and I'm going to eviscerate Dr Brett Langham."

"I hate to break it to you, but what you thought you had – that's all gone."

"Look, you HSA scum, I don't need your advice. Give me my clothes and *I'm* gone."

She stiffened and her voice was monotone when she said, "Whatever you say, honey."

"Don't call me honey. Just give me my goddamn clothes."

"I'm head nurse here," she said. "All these patients are under my care. You're one of forty-nine. And patients die. All the time."

Before I could respond, she'd walked off, checking on HSAs further down the hut. I was about to walk out of there naked, but when I tried to stand I felt nauseous and the pain from my weeping wounds was too much. I leaned back against the wall and got the MedEx to dose me. I closed my eyes and floated.

I was woken by Benji, offering me piss-coloured water. I drank down what was supposedly vitwater and fought with Benji as he tried to clean me with some foul-smelling liquid. Head nurse came over and threatened me in that passive-aggressive way she had, still calling me honey. I nodded acquiescence, but moodily stomped my way to the toilets wrapped in my blanket, making Benji wait. I regretted it immediately, sure that the humiliation of using the bedpan would be better than this literal shithole. When I returned, I grabbed the sodden cloth from Benji and cleaned myself. I stared at him defiantly as I slapped it on an open wound and winced. Trying to tolerate the pain, I scrubbed at my skin.

"Gently," he said. "Don't make things worse."

"You don't need to watch."

"I do."

"You get off on this?"

"You think I enjoy this? I have to make sure you do it properly or I lose my job."

"Sure," I said, angrily scrubbing at a bloody left tit and eyeing him.

"I told you – don't scrub. Do it gently."

I continued scrubbing, hurting myself to spite him, aware of how perverse I was being. "You got a mirror?"

"What for?"

"I want to see my face."

"It's a mess. Like the rest of you." I must have looked distressed, as he seemed to take pity on me. "Don't worry, OK? It'll heal up eventually. This will help."

I didn't respond as I sponged my face, trying to not cry out in pain.

When I finished, he said, "Dry yourself," and handed me a stained towel. I patted myself dry as he prepared bandages, soaking them in some other liquid.

"Don't you have Ambrosia ointment?"

"We can't afford it, and it doesn't work on most HSAs."

"I'm not HSA."

He glanced at me, eyebrow raised, then wrapped a bandage around my arm. By the time he'd finished I was half-mummy. I didn't know what he'd soaked them in, but as soon as he applied them, I was no longer burning, itching or oozing.

"They'll work their magic and peel off in a few minutes. There might be some scarring."

"I can fix that with Ambrosia."

He shook his head and said, "I told you, that won't work, not under the stress of HSA."

"This is temporary."

"You think you can beat this through sheer willpower? You think all the people in the ghetto just haven't tried hard enough?"

"I'm not like them."

"Is that right?"

"That's right."

He laughed and said, "I was warned about you." He shook his finger at me, like he was admonishing a child. He stood up and walked away, picking his way over the HSAs cluttering the floor.

"My clothes!" I called after him.

"Once you've healed." He kneeled down, getting to work on another HSA. He went through the same routine, except they lay there, barely acknowledging his presence, not a single flinch at the stinging liquid. I watched him for some time, surprised at the care he took.

I thought of getting up and demanding my clothes, but I stayed put, feeling the bandages and whatever they were soaked in ease my discomfort. If I was to get back to the city, I needed to be well, so I lay back and closed my eyes.

When I woke up, the first thing I did was vomit. I was shaking and sweating and oozing and itching all over again. My healed skin was cracking open. The head nurse walked over to me.

"Dreaming in HellSans?"

I gave her the side-eye in-between puking.

"It's a tough one," she said.

When I stopped being sick, I curled up in a ball, pulling the blankets around me to try to get warm, but my skin was blue with cold. The MedEx climbed up and administered drugs. I drifted on a pain-free haze as an old, clanking Ino hoovered up my sick.

"That MedEx isn't going to last forever. You're going to have to learn how to cope without it. We'll get you started on coping strategies tomorrow, try and minimise the damage, and get you assigned a block."

"I'm going home," I said, looking up, her face soft and shimmering through the drug haze.

"If you say so, honey."

I asked for food, and she sent over a minion with vitwater. I wasn't allowed food until it was clear I could keep it down. "We're not wasting it."

"You're starving me?" I said, but she ignored me, walking off.

I sat there, scrunched up, staring at the peeling ceiling, the shaking subsiding as I drifted on the meds' bliss. I remembered how HellSans used to make me feel close to this, but as soon as I thought of it, my gums bled. I sucked the blood down my throat, pushing myself to think of anything but HellSans. I thought of Icho – her face projected on my apartment wall. I kept locked in on her image, and stretched out, pressing my hand between my legs, closing my eyes.

"Am I interrupting?"

I opened my eyes, jerked my hand away, and dribbled blood.

"I know – beset by pain, we need to find what pleasure we can."

A nurse I hadn't seen before was standing over me.

"I was just–"

"Elena tells me you're CEO of The Company," she said, deadpan, not a flicker of emotion on her face.

I tried to focus through the blur of the meds. She had deep brown skin, a round face, and eyes so dark they seemed almost

black. Her face was scarred, but the scars were old – they
caught the light, giving her face a strange shimmering glow.
She smiled. There was a warmth in the smile, but I didn't trust
it. There was something seductive about her, an ability to draw
you in. I wasn't going to be drawn.

"Who's Elena?"

"Head nurse."

"Right. And you are?"

"Eleven."

"What kind of name is that?"

She didn't respond and I sat up, looking at her, my eyes
focusing. She wore a beige tank top, and I could see her arms
were scarred; but unlike all the other HSAs here, there were
no recent wounds. She was strong. All the HSAs, both nurses
and patients, were almost skeletal; only Elena seemed like she
had some meat on her. This woman was thin, but her muscles
were taut, like a dancer's. I watched as her Inex crawled up her
leg, stopped at her hip, and stared down at me with its big grey
eyes. It was an ICC411 model – old, but not by HSA standards.
It had full bio-reading capabilities and was likely one of the
main reasons she was strong and able to avoid HSA attacks.

"I lied," I said.

"You lied?"

"Yes. I thought... I just wanted–"

"Special treatment?"

I nodded, smiling tentatively.

"That's not the kind of lie you want to tell in here," she said
with an air of boredom.

Eleven's hooded eyes unnerved me, my smile fading. One of
the other nurses brought her a chair and she sat down, hands
clasped, elbows on her thighs, leaning over me, her Inex now
on her shoulder.

"You a nurse?"

"How did you come to have a high-end MedEx?" she said,
ignoring me.

"I stole it."

"It administers to you."

"I adjusted it."

"You know Inex tech?"

"I used to work for The Company. In the early days. Bioengineering. That was a long time ago."

"We could use someone like you."

"I'm out of date."

"You adjusted this."

"Luck and perseverance."

Eleven reached down and pulled back my blanket. I snatched it out of her hand and held it up against my chin. She smiled slightly.

"Minimal scarring. You're a very recent HSA."

"I'm not HSA."

She raised an eyebrow. "Is that right?"

"That's right."

"You don't think you're one of us? What makes you so special?"

"I'm not HSA."

"You said that," she said, her smile gone.

"It's a mistake. I don't belong here."

Eleven smiled again and slipped off the chair, her movements like liquid. She crouched down next to me and pushed her hand against my shoulder, pressing me against the wall, causing my skin to break. I grasped onto her arm, but I wasn't strong enough and the skin on my palms cracked. Eleven's face was close to mine. I looked her in the eyes, gritting my teeth as her hand pressed hard on my broken skin. We were locked like that for a few seconds until I closed my eyes and let out a low whine.

Eleven laughed, let go, and stood up. I opened my eyes and placed my palm gently against my shoulder as if that would soothe it. She flicked her hand, my blood and some skin spattering on the floor.

"Do you know why," she said, "I could do that without my Inex reporting me?"

I looked up at her, my eyes watering, tears of pain and anger.

"Because you're HSA. Because, according to Jane Ward, you're not human."

She looked at me, her face expressionless, impenetrable. I couldn't hold her gaze so I looked away, but I could feel her presence weighing down on me.

"I could set fire to you and no one would care," she said. "Isn't that what they do in the city? Isn't that how city kids get their kicks?"

My stomach lurched. I closed my eyes as I finally realised she was a Seraph. I sat like that for a few minutes, eyes shut, as if I could keep myself safe just by pretending she wasn't there. Despite the meds, my shoulder throbbed; it felt like she was still pressing down on it.

"Well!" she said, clapping her hands, making me jump, my heart hammering. I opened my eyes and looked up at her. "It was good speaking with you... Jane?"

"Sarah," I said quickly. "It's Sarah."

She looked down at me. "Sarah."

I nodded.

"Welcome to the ghetto, Sarah," she said. "I'm glad we have someone with Inex-tech knowledge. You'll be a very valuable member of our community."

Eleven turned and walked away. I watched her go to the exit, then I leaned over and threw up in my bedpan.

Sitting back, wiping the bile from my mouth, I leaned my head against the damp wall. I realised how stupid I'd been, mentioning The Company, saying I was Jane Ward, that I had Inex-tech knowledge. Attracting Seraph interest was the last thing I wanted to do. I thought of Eleven pressing her hand against my shoulder, the ease with which she subdued me. I'd never in my life been scared of anyone before. I was furious.

I opened my eyes and snapped my fingers at one of the

nearby nurses, flinching as the snap sloughed off some skin. "You," I said, "Get me a vitwater."

He gave me a withering look and continued bandaging up a moaning HSA, taking his time. I forced myself to remain calm. When he finished, he slowly walked over to me and said, "It's not often new arrivals get visits from the Seraphs."

"Where's Benji?"

"Finished for the day. I'm the next shift."

"Look, Next Shift, get me a vitwater then fix me. I need to get out of here."

"Fix you?"

"Yes, fix me."

"There's no cure, you know that? Nor should there be. HS allergy is a blessing."

I looked at him, waiting for the punchline. He stared at me, impassive. "Are you fucking kidding me?"

"It wakes you up. You're no longer a blissed-out zombie," he said as his Inex walked over to me and handed me a vitwater. I drank it, eyeing him with disgust. "But if you rely on the meds of that thing there's not much difference."

"That *thing*," I said, "is the only thing keeping me alive. This sickness is a curse."

"You'll come round. You'll soon see. You'll be able to *feel* things, no longer cushioned by HS bliss. You'll feel so utterly and completely *awake*."

"I'll tell you what I feel, you pseudo-religious hippy terrorist arsehole: I feel *pain*. And more pain. Everywhere. All the time. It's all there is. I feel crushed by it."

"We can help you," he said, unfazed. "We can help you manage it. We can help you *use* it."

"I want it gone. I want skin that isn't suppurating. I want nails that don't fall off and teeth that don't fall out. And until I get it, this *thing* is my best friend."

"If people see you with one of those..." He nodded at the MedEx.

"They won't. I'm not staying here. I'm going home."

"You think you'll get from here back into the city without having an attack? Without anyone noticing?"

"I'm not staying in this hellhole."

"You think you'll survive the walk?"

"I'll manage."

"I doubt it. Lie back and I'll clean your wounds."

"I know the drill," I said, taking the sponge. "And *you're* not touching me."

I sponged myself, staring at him the whole time, making sure he saw that I didn't wince when the liquid hit my broken skin. "There," I said, drying myself.

He bandaged me up, and this time I didn't let the relief lull me into complacency. I stood up and demanded my clothes.

"You're not well enough for your clothes."

"Just give me them."

"They won't be laundered again."

"I won't need them laundered. I'm going home."

I followed him, trying to ignore all the disgusting deviants littering the floor. He pulled my clothes out of a cupboard. They were stained, but clean.

"Where are my shades?"

"Commandeered."

"You mean stolen."

I put my clothes on and he said, "Leaving is suicide. If the police don't pick you up, an HS attack will likely kill you before you even reach the city."

"I'm going home," I said. "I'm getting my life back."

"It's your funeral."

I went to the door, wrapping my scarf around my head, tying it at my neck. I turned, gave everyone the finger, and left.

I walked out into the ghetto. It was intolerable. HSAs were everywhere, like roaches. The sun was high in the sky, beating down, exacerbating the stench of the swarming deviants. I semi-closed my eyes, trying to keep out the burning light. I felt nauseous as I pushed my way through the hordes. I walked past block after block that all looked the same, the vastness of the ghetto becoming apparent; I didn't know where I was or how to find the exit.

I stopped one of the HSAs. "Exit?"

"What about it?"

"Where the hell is it?"

She narrowed her eyes, looking me up and down. "You new?"

"Obviously, or why would I be asking?"

She huffed. "There's HSAs been here for years who don't know and don't care where the exit is."

"Just tell me how to get out of this hellhole."

"Figure it out yourself." She made to walk away, but I grabbed her sleeve.

"Please."

She sneered at me and I let go. "It's built in a grid," she said. "The blocks are chronologically numbered, starting at the main entrance. Just work your way back. It's about three miles from here."

"Three miles? How big is this place?"

"Not big enough. Good luck," she said, clearly not meaning it. "Watch out for the patrols." She laughed.

"Patrols?" I said, but she turned her back on me and walked off, still laughing.

I went to the nearest block and found its number above the door. I worked my way back to the exit, trying to hide behind my scarf. HSAs teemed everywhere, most of them wearing dirty brown tops and trousers, like a uniform. Some of them wore regular clothes, but they were torn and grimy, crisscrossing layers of thread keeping them together. The majority of them had shorn hair. They all stared at me; I realised how much I stood out with my regular clothes and my silk scarf. I gripped my bag tight and kept my eyes on the ground, occasionally looking up to check the numbers on the blocks. I cursed Caddick for bringing me to this, all because of a clumsy attempt at taking out Milligan. I was going to get back to my apartment and I was going to find Icho – she would cure me of this mistake, this sickness that wasn't mine. She'd excise it. Then I'd deal with Caddick and Langham.

The guard at the gate let me through, no questions. As I walked into the street she said, "See you soon." I ignored her, glad to be free of the deviant swarms. I pulled my scarf further forward to protect my face the best I could, and I followed the sun in the direction of the city. The edges of the ghetto were all factories and warehouses, swathed in HellSans signs, some of them several feet high. I averted my eyes, head down. The monotony of warehouse after warehouse made me feel like Sisyphus, pushing on and getting nowhere. I realised I hadn't thought about food or water, or how long it would take to get to the city by foot. I stopped and leaned against one of the warehouses, trying to steady my breathing, but I couldn't keep my thoughts from that night: Milligan lying prone on the bed, Caddick's man slicing his finger across his throat, and then Driscoll's – the first time I was excluded from the world I owned and ruled and dictated to; abject, collapsed on the department store floor, an invisible knife in my chest.

I started walking again, attempting to transfer my buzzing mind into physical energy. I hurried on, feeling nauseous, the skin on the bottom of my feet breaking up, blood soaking into my socks. I tried to control my breathing, tried to focus my mind on the graffiti-covered retro Inex poster I'd seen in the city – I imagined stroking those serifs, but my mind kept flicking back to hands opening up my ribs, the beggar deviant's swollen suppurating face beneath **"WE'RE IN THIS TOGETHER"**, Brett warning me "stay away from bold", his Inex staring down at me as I passed out, and then woke in the ghetto. I stopped and leaned over, spitting blood on the pavement.

"You sick, sweetheart?"

I jumped, almost falling into the blood spatter. I turned and saw a police car, one of the cops leaning out the window, assessing me.

"No," I said, pulling the scarf further over my face. "I'm fine."

I continued walking, the police car creeping after me.

"Where you heading?"

"Home."

"You're going in the wrong direction."

"I just need to get home," I said, trying to keep the rising panic from my voice.

"And where is that exactly?"

I didn't answer and hurried on.

"Where'd you live?" he asked, his voice hard, the police car in my peripheral, inching along.

"Anthony Royal Apartments."

The police officer whistled. "That so?"

"That's so," I said, turning to him, angry, sick of everyone questioning me.

"And how does someone like you afford an apartment in the Anthony Royal?"

"I'm CEO of the goddamn Company."

He laughed and his partner smiled. An Inex was perched by the window, its big brown eyes fixed on me. I turned away and kept walking.

"That right? Hear that, Brandt? She's CEO of the goddamn Company."

"You got ID?" asked Brandt.

"Leave me alone. I'm going home. That's all. Leave me be."

"It's a long walk. We can give you a lift."

"I'm fine."

"Get in."

"I'm fucking fine."

I heard the car door open and the police officer came up

behind me, walked by, and stopped just ahead. I stood still and glanced up at him, back at the ground, back up at him, trying to keep the image of the serif poster in my head to keep an HS attack at bay. He was handsome; smooth, Ambrosia-treated skin, straight brown hair swept back, golden highlights glinting in the sun. Not much taller than me, he was stocky and all muscle, his shirt deliberately too tight. His Inex stood next to him, staring up at me.

"Where's your Inex?"

"I don't have one."

"What was that?" he said, reaching out and tipping up my chin to make me face him.

I batted his hand away. "I don't have one."

"It touched me," he said, looking down at his Inex.

"HSAs are not infectious," it replied.

"No, but they are disgusting." He turned back to me. "Everyone has an Inex. Even scum like you. What's in the bag?"

"Nothing."

"Looks like pretty heavy nothing."

My bag was yanked off my shoulder. I spun round, jerked away, and backed into the stocky officer, not realising Brandt had been standing behind me. The stocky one, laughing, caught me by the waist, but I pulled away. Brandt took the MedEx out of the bag, holding it up by one of its arms.

"Pretty strange looking nothing," he said, shaking it.

"Thought you didn't have an Inex," said the stocky cop.

"I don't. It's a MedEx."

"That right? And how did someone like you happen to have a high-end MedEx?"

"My doctor, Brett Langham. You can check with him."

"Brandt, let Dr Brett Langham know we've found his stolen MedEx."

"I didn't steal it."

"Sweetheart–"

"Don't call me sweetheart."

The stocky one leaned into me, his face inches from mine. I could smell his breath. *"Sweetheart,"* he said. He clasped my cheeks, pressing hard, my skin breaking away, blood dribbling over his glove. "I think it's time we took you home."

He laid his hand on my sore shoulder and pressed down until my knees buckled and I sank to the ground, kneeling. Rage constricted my guts, my bloody lips twitching into a snarl as he let go of me and stepped back.

"Face rec me. Take my DNA. Run it. You'll find out who I am." I spat a globule of blood at his feet.

"I know what you are."

He turned away, as if he was going to walk towards the car, but he swivelled, his fist smashing into my face. I fell, cracking my head on the concrete. I saw his Inex on the ground, watching me, impassive, disinterested – this violence didn't matter because I wasn't human, and the police the Inex would have called were right here.

"You're nothing," he said, and kicked me in the stomach. I retched, spitting out bile and saliva as he kicked me in the chest. He pulled me up, his fist scrunched up in my blouse and he punched me twice in the face before I blacked out.

CHAPTER 7

I woke to find myself in the back of the police car. Everything hurt; my face felt twice the size, my left eye was swollen shut, the other clogged with blood and grime. My hands were tied tight behind my back. I managed to sit up and was shocked into full consciousness by the pain in my chest. I gasped and sat still for a few minutes, trying to adjust to the pain as I focused on my breathing. Through my blurry right eye I saw we were at the ghetto. They drove right through the gate and up a long central road, HSAs backing away from the car, silently watching us. We stopped outside a huge building with classical columns. I vaguely recalled it had been an art gallery when I was a kid, abandoned years ago, now the ghetto council building. I stared up at it as the stocky cop got out of the car. He opened the door, grabbed me by the arm and pulled me out, throwing me on the ground. The chest pain made me cry out, a feeble whining, and he laughed. I heard him slam the car door and drive away as a small crowd gathered round me. They were blurry; blood from my forehead was dribbling into my good eye, clogging up my eyelashes. I blinked furiously and stayed very still, trying to keep the chest pain at bay. I saw the crowd parting and someone turned me over. I whimpered as they untied my hands. When my hands were freed I wiped away the blood and looked into the face of Eleven. I waited for a rebuke, but she said nothing. She lifted me as if I was light as air and carried me down the road. The pain in my chest cut through me with each step she took, but I leaned into her, comforted, dribbling blood, snot, and tears onto her shirt.

I had a smashed-up face and a broken rib. Elena said I got off lightly, but fussed over me all the same.

"You're weak, making you more susceptible to infections, which can be a real killer, and repeated allergic reactions put you at risk. We'll be starting you on coping strategies this afternoon."

I didn't want "coping strategies" – I wanted it gone. But I had to play along until I healed up and figured out a way back to the city.

Second to being HSA, group therapy was about the worse thing I could think of, and there I was sitting in a circle of deviants, twelve of them, all shedding skin, dribbling blood, spitting out teeth, shitting their pants. We were all dressed in the ubiquitous grey sacks they forced on us in the med block. My clothes had disappeared, and I knew I wouldn't be seeing them again. I was told I'd get the lovely brown uniform when I was assigned a block.

"Welcome," said the therapist. "I'm Venus."

"Of course you are," I said, rolling my eyes.

She ignored me. "Today we're going to start with a basic exercise to exorcise HS, henceforth–"

I snorted at "henceforth".

"–called the 'The Typeface' or 'TF'. There will be some of you who will advance onto a special group who are able to think in the TF again and control the effects, but those people are rare. The main thing is to help you with the basics, mitigate the worst of the effects so you can live your life again. I won't lie to you – there's been patients who haven't responded, for various reasons. But if you're open-minded and give the course a chance, you're bound to do just fine and become a functioning member of the ghetto."

"I don't want to be a functioning member of this shithole," I said, shivering and shaking, blood sliding down my neck. All I could think – in HellSans – was how I'd got here and how my life had been reduced to a self-help group of deviants lead by a goddamn hippy called Venus.

The pseudo-psych hippy glanced at me but continued talking to the group. "We can get you moved on to other typefaces, but because the TF is so difficult to excise, we've simply added serifs to start you off."

"This is bullshit. You all make me sick," I said and vomited, the heaving worsening my rib pain.

"The TF is making you sick," she said as I stared up at her, wiping the sick from my mouth. "You need to concentrate. This sentence will be the angel on your shoulder: 'I'm in control, I'm worthy, there is hope'." Her Inex projected it.

An old Ino entered our hallowed circle, hoovered up my vomit, and clattered its way out again. It stood on the periphery, waiting for any one of us to spew our guts. Clearly there weren't high expectations for the success of the first session.

Clutching my rib, I laughed as everyone read the sentence and repeated it over and over. "We're in control of nothing," I said. "And what makes us worthy? Worthy of what?"

"Worthy of living a good life."

"What kind of life do we have in this deviant stenchpit? What use is hope? It means nothing. You're selling bullshit."

"I'm not selling anything. A positive attitude will help you get the most out of–"

"I heard there's a brothel," said a girl two seats away from me.

"A brothel?"

"Yeah, that's where they'll send her, for sure," she said pointing to a girl opposite. Her face was a mess, but even under all that blood and pus you could see she was a knockout. "And him," the girl said, pointing to a boy next to me. "And probably you too," she said, looking at me and licking the blood from her lips.

"Is that right?" I said to the hippy. "You curing us to pimp us?"

"There's no cure; this isn't a cure, and no one's pimping anyone."

"I know there's a brothel," said the girl, crossing her arms.

"So you are selling something," I said. "Selling us."

"There is a brothel," said the hippy, flushed. "But this isn't– We're helping you survive. We're helping you be the best you can be."

"Be the best you… Sounds familiar," I said, sneering. "You're just gonna feed us into the churning machine of the ghetto. No exit."

"That's not–"

"Look, I don't care what they plan to do with us," said the handsome boy the girl had pegged for the brothel. "I just don't want to feel like this anymore. OK? I can't do this. I eat food and it all tastes the same. Every day is the taste of blood and vomit."

"He's got a point," said a woman absentmindedly pulling at loose strips of skin on the back of her hand. "I just want to be able to function again. I'll figure the rest out later."

"Listen," said the hippy, buoyed by the sudden support. "It's true – after we have you at a certain coping level, we assess your skills and assign you to appropriate labour, but you're involved all the way. Life in the ghetto isn't all that bad. Now if we can concentrate on the task at hand…" She stretched out her arms as if she wanted to hug the whole weeping, suppurating group.

We were silent, staring at her inane face, that weak solicitous smile. The brothel boy fiddled with one of his teeth and pulled it out, blood dripping onto his lap. He spat on the floor and rolled the tooth in his hand.

"You," said Venus, nodding at me.

"Sarah," I said.

"Sarah – focus on the words on the wall. Read them, repeat

them, and your shaking will stop. I guarantee it. All of you – focus."

I looked at the words: 'I'm in control, I'm worthy, there is hope'. I stared at them, running my eyes over each letter, following the curves of the serifs, and just like with the retro Inex poster I started to feel calm. Instead of shivering and shaking I was gently swaying, as if to music.

"This is just the beginning," said Venus. "Once you start to manage it, you'll feel like a whole new person."

"The best me," I said.

"That's right, Sarah. The best you."

"A happy worker bee for the ghetto."

She stared at me, her eyes narrowed, her inane smile gone. She got up, walked over to me and leaned down, her mouth next to my ear. "We're in this together," she said, and as she knew I would, I immediately saw Caddick's party slogan in capitalised, bold HellSans. My skin felt like it was burning. The pain from my broken rib increased. Sweating, shaking, I slipped from my chair onto the floor, my head swimming as I desperately tried to add serifs to the HS words I couldn't excise from my mind. I heard all the others chanting, "I'm in control, I'm worthy, there is hope," as Venus stood over me and said, "Well done, everyone. You're doing so well. But others might take longer to adjust. Let's help Sarah be the best she can be – join in, Sarah: 'I'm in control, I'm worthy, there is hope.' You can do it."

I stared up at her with my one eye and said, "Fuck you, you hippy piece of shit."

But I didn't. I just gurgled blood and passed out.

I woke up in the med block again and groaned. I'd already been bathed and bandaged, which would have enraged me before, but I thought of the way Benji had treated the other patients, the way he'd gone about it with a kind of detachment, but with great care. I lay there for a while, eyes closed.

"Didn't go well, then?"

Elena. I opened my eyes and pulled myself upright. I looked at her and shook my head.

"We had one HSA who was so resistant she kept returning after over twenty sessions. She died here."

"I won't die here."

"Good," said Elena. "I've got something that should help you along." She pulled an old tin can Inex out of a bag and placed it next to me. "It'll help with your exercises, keep you focused."

I glanced at it, then looked back at Elena.

"You're welcome," she said.

I didn't respond and she shook her head, clearly disgusted with me. She walked off, mumbling something, and I sat there, ignoring the Inex, thinking about the therapy session. I despised Venus and the narrative she was selling us.

"I'll do it my way," I said, and the Inex I'd forgotten responded, "What will you do your way?"

"None of your business."

"I'm here to assist you. We should connect and I can help you do it your way."

"I'm not connecting. Ever. Don't ask me again."

"Connecting would help you be the best you, but I won't ask again."

I stared at the Inex. It was an IKL556 model, one of the early ones I developed with James. It was unable to detect many illnesses, including HSA, and had limited personality choices. One of its eyes was missing and an arm had been (badly) repaired numerous times. As I looked at it, Tom came over and handed me a bowl.

"What's this?"

"Soup."

"I thought you didn't feed us until we can keep it down."

"You can thank Elena. She's concerned about you, said you're already too thin."

I shovelled the soup into my mouth, my stomach grumbling. It tasted disgusting, but I was ravenous and didn't care. Never in my life had I been so hungry.

"Slowly," he said. "Eat it slowly or I'll take it back."

I reluctantly slowed and he hovered over me until I finished.

"Keep it down, OK?" he said, taking the empty bowl and walking off.

I turned back to look at my Inex and contemplated it for a few minutes. "I need you to project something."

"Happy to assist," said the Inex as I moved to the middle of the bed and sat facing the wall I'd been leaning against.

"Project the following in HellSans," I said, feeling nauseous, "but with added serifs: 'I'm in control. I'm going home. I'll be cured'."

"HellSans will no longer be HellSans if you add serifs."

"That's OK."

"HellSans is the optimal typeface."

"Just do what I ask."

Obeying, the Inex projected it onto the wall.

I read it aloud, repeated it a few times, then said, "No. Change it. Change it to: 'I'm in control. I'm going home. I'll find Icho'."

The Inex obeyed and I sat there, staring at the projection, quietly repeating it over and over until I felt calm and light, no longer weighed down by my body, no longer burning with pain. For the first time since the night of the attack I felt at ease. I repeated my exorcising exercise for hours until I drifted into sleep, confident and content.

I woke up shivering, shaking, sweating, shedding, shitting, bleeding, vomiting. I'd dreamt of that night – the plunge of the knife. I could feel it, stuck in my chest, my breath arrested. I was suffocating, choking on blood. He pulled the knife down, yanked it out and pushed his hands inside me, tearing skin and muscle, pulling back my ribs. I heard them crack. I woke writhing, fighting him off, fighting for breath. Elena hurried over to me, calming me, bringing me back to the present. Feeling defeated I clutched onto her, sobbing.

Benji cleaned me up, and I just let him. At the group session I was subdued. Venus eyed me, wondering what I was up to, but she soon relaxed into the session and forgot me until I refused to repeat her hippy bullshit.

"I have my own mantra."

"Of course you do," she said. "We encourage individual mantras, but not until later in the sessions."

I ignored her and she looked at my mantra, shaking her head before saying, "We encourage realistic goals. Focusing on going home isn't realistic and could hamper your progress."

"It's more tangible than your nebulous 'hope'."

"I disagree."

"Disagree all you want. I'm doing it my way."

We stared at each other. She made me think of a coiled snake, ready to bite, but she just said, "Sarah is doing it her way. I suggest the rest of you do it the proper way to get the most out of it, and hopefully Sarah will join us again when she realises her way isn't working."

"Passive aggressive bitch," I said quietly.

"What was that, Sarah?"

"Can we get on with it?"

"Of course," she replied, not looking at me.

After the session, I spent the whole evening on my bed in the med block meditating on the projection. While I felt calm and in control, I was afraid to go to sleep so I kept on with my task, repeating the words, licking those serifs, tasting the sweet absence of blood and vomit. But again I fell into sleep and into nightmare and woke to a broken body.

In that day's session I asked, "How do I control my dreams? How do I control nightmares?"

Venus smiled, sensing the fear I was trying so hard to hide.

HELLSANS

"You can't," she said, pausing, taking satisfaction at my unease. "Not yet. It takes time. You come to the group, and you practice the meditation throughout the day. Soon you'll be dreaming in a heaven of serifs. You'll wake up, your body healed."

I nodded and focused on my mantra.

It was only the third day of the group and we were all doing so well that Venus introduced physio, too. Because of my broken rib I wasn't able to do as much as everyone else, but I was happy to be exercising again – it was like a glimmer of a former life. Venus kept saying, "Look forward, not back. You can never go back to your previous life." But I didn't believe that. I couldn't believe that. I'd be in control again and I'd return to my normal life. Venus said, "don't look back", and I didn't – I looked forward to what my life would be again.

Because my HSA attacks had lessened, I was finally assigned a block. Elena sent me off with my own supply of the stinging liquid and bandages. "These are so you can deal with any minor attacks yourself. I hope I don't you see back here, Sarah." I told her she wouldn't and set off to find block 366. I was anxious; I knew there'd be some kind of hierarchy, but I couldn't face squaring-off with anyone – I was weak from all the vomiting and lack of food, and still healing after the cops beat me up. I was hoping I could fly under the radar until I left. The idea of fitting into an HSA hierarchy, whatever the position, struck me as absurd anyway. I didn't care enough to make the effort. Luckily, no one seemed to care about me, either. There were over a hundred HSAs in each block. I could see there were a few cliques, but no one was interested in me. I got a polite nod of the head from the HSA in the bunk opposite and a handshake from Kate, the woman who shared my bunk. She was thin, like everyone else, in swampy brown clothes, with short blonde hair.

"I was assigned the top bunk," she said, "but Jennifer, who

was here before you, she let me take the bottom. I don't like heights."

"That's fine with me."

She looked relieved and said, "Good. That's good."

"How long you been here?"

"Almost two years."

Two years. Jesus. "How is it?"

"It's OK. You get into a routine, which is fine, but it can be a bit monotonous. I work in farming, so I get to be outdoors, which I like most of the time, but when bad weather hits it's tough. Winter is pretty grim round here. Our immune systems are buggered, and we've lost a few to flu and pneumonia."

I was momentarily shocked at even the mention of flu and pneumonia, and I climbed up on to the top bunk wondering if I truly was in hell. As I settled on the lumpy mattress, putting the things Elena gave me in a corner under my blanket, a small group entered, talking amongst themselves, heading down to the other end of the block without so much as a glance my way.

"What's the deal with this block?" I said, "Anyone I need to worry about?"

"Nah," said Kate from below. "Everyone mostly keeps to themselves. It's all good, really, though it can be a pain when you're bunking next to someone who isn't coping, constantly waking you up with nightmares and vomiting."

I gritted my teeth, hoping I wasn't going to be that person.

"But everyone in the bunks around us are old hands and manage the allergy… Leigh, in the bunk next to you, she's blind and rarely has allergic reactions, coping better than most of us."

"She's *blind*? Then what's she doing here? She can't be HSA."

"She became blind after she got here. She'd already internalised HS. And even if she hadn't, she's lost everything: her home, her savings. There's nothing to go back to. She'd definitely be an asset to the Seraphs, but they refuse to have a blind person in their ranks. She's been talking about joining that fringe group, you know? They have that commune down south, only open to blind people. They say society's dependence on sight and HellSans is a weakness. If the Seraphs weren't such bigoted arseholes, they'd have a blind army on side. Oh, I almost forgot..."

Kate got up and went over to a cupboard by the entrance. She picked some things off the shelf and handed them up to me, a small towel and a pouch.

"Don't lose them. You don't get replacements."

I opened the pouch. "A menstrual cup?"

"Everyone in the ghetto gets one. Or reusable pads if they're too ill to deal with the cup."

"Everyone?"

"Everyone who needs it, obviously."

"That can't be cheap."

"The Seraphs understand it's a necessity."

I nodded, tucking the towel and pouch under my blanket next to the things Elena had given me. I lay down as Kate continued talking, falling asleep as she told me the ins and outs of farming in the ghetto, her voice soothing me into a HellSans-free night.

The next day I joined the rest of block 366 for dousing in Anti-Bac, all of us naked in a line, filing through. They sprayed us with the foul-smelling stuff and barked at me to turn in a circle. I was completely soaked from head to toe, my hair dripping. I walked out, swiping it from my face, squeezing it from my hair and trying to dry myself with my tiny towel amongst all the other shivering women in the blocks.

"There's no way I'm going through that again."

"You have to," said Kate. "If any member of our block skips it, they get reported."

"By who?"

"By all of us. We can't afford to let disease to spread. It would wipe us out."

I put my clothes on in sullen silence and followed everyone to the cafeteria block, where we waited until a bell rang and the blocks that had been in before us poured out. We all took a bowl at the entrance and were served some grey slop and a drink at the cafeteria counter.

"What the hell is this?" I said sitting down at one of the tables.

"Porridge," said Kate. "You get used to it."

"You have to get used to a lot here."

Each table had several sick buckets next to it; they stank of bleach which made the porridge taste medicinal. I sat there, forcing myself to eat it, my mind wandering back to my apartment, the Ino serving me breakfast, my gym... I could feel myself getting distressed and didn't want to be using the sick bucket, so to distract myself, I looked up at the woman sat opposite and said, "I get assigned a workplace today. Where are you stationed?"

"The brothel."

"Really?"

She nodded, shovelling the slop into her mouth. "It's a big part of the ghetto economy. The rich kids from the city are body-horror tourists."

"Body-horror tourists?"

"Yeah, it's a turn-on to them. We cater to different levels – some of them want a full-on allergic reaction, others want something more subtle."

"And you're OK with this?"

She shrugged. "It's not as bad as it sounds. The Seraphs police it so we're all safe." She downed her vitwater. "Anyway, who's exploiting who? The rich kids' money goes straight back into the ghetto and helps fund our city campaigns."

"Campaigns? You mean terrorism."

"If that's what you want to call it. I'd call it civil action. Our government has failed us, leaving us here to rot. You think we should just accept that?"

"There's other ways to–"

"Don't be naïve," she said, tapping her spoon against the bowl. "Who were you before you came here? Did you care about us? Did Milligan's political campaign make you feel for us? No. We've been doing what we can to survive, but that's not enough. We need a revolution."

I stifled a laugh and sipped my vitwater. It tasted foul and I scrunched up my face in disgust. "What do you know about the Seraphs?" I said.

"Why?"

I shrugged. "All I know is from the news. They never seemed real, somehow – more like bogeymen."

"Most of them are women, like with all HSAs. A lot of coloureds here, too – you noticed that? I mean, I don't have a problem with them, but I wouldn't have chosen to live right next to them, you know, and I'd–" She stopped, looked up at the woman next to Kate and said, "I don't mean you, Jill, I don't have a problem with the Chinese–"

"I'm not Chinese."

"I mean, you're practically white if you ask me; it's the others. I don't think they should be allowed to be Seraphs–"

"How do they get to be Seraphs?" I said.

"The coloureds are–"

"No. Anyone – how does anyone get to be a Seraph?"

"If the HSA effect is minimal, if they're able to cope well, heal better, have less attacks. That's usually how they first select. I heard they get military training."

"From who?"

"There was a flood of new HSAs years ago when the war ended and hundreds of soldiers came back traumatised – I'd heard trauma can trigger the allergy, but who knows? It does make sense, though – if you're traumatised you might not be able to feel HS bliss anymore."

"That would just make you unblissed," said Kate.

"I dunno," said the brothel woman. "Maybe there's something that tips it into allergy. Anyway, I was told most of the soldiers ended up Seraphs – gave them a way to channel their anger after being abandoned by the country they fought for."

"Makes sense," I said, thinking about Eleven; her strength, the way she moved, her controlled emotions.

"There's some warring factions within the Seraphs. They all think there's nothing wrong with HSAs – it's society that needs to change, HS should be eradicated. But some Seraphs believe they're superior to the rest of the HSAs in the ghetto – they're stronger, better people because they're able to cope with the allergy. Of course, that's counter to the idea that there's nothing inherently wrong with HSAs, but these Seraphs think the rest of us are scum, just here to be used to further their aims. All Seraphs are against a cure, but these ones are pretty strident about it. Most of your average HSAs like you and me–"

I flinched and was about to interrupt, but kept quiet.

"–would take a cure in an instant. The extreme Seraphs think that's weakness. Well, most Seraphs think that's weakness, but a few would be fine with a cure as long as the end goal remained to eradicate HS."

I laughed.

"What's so funny?"

"They're delusional. How do they think they can ever eradicate HS?"

"It's possible," she said, but looked uncertain. "I mean, you have to believe in something. It's more realistic than a cure."

"Why's that?"

"Come on – who's going to fund research into the allergy? Who's going to–"

"Milligan."

"Milligan's got no support. He's all lip service. Where's he going to get the money for research? No one will fund it. No voters are going to support Milligan on a cure platform. They'd see it as a waste of money. Most of them don't care if we die."

"But surely he has the HSA vote?"

"Sure," she said. "There'd be pressure from the Seraphs, but without a doubt, us HSAs would vote for him if a cure were possible. But it's not gonna happen – like I said, no one would fund it, and running on a cure agenda would put a target on his back." She finished her porridge as I thought about Caddick's plan to announce a cure before the election – he'd said he had something in place to keep the Seraphs from thinking that taking him out would make a difference.

"Yeah," said Kate, who'd been sitting quietly finishing her porridge. "You heard about the assassination attempt on Milligan? It was a warning."

"You think that was Seraphs?"

"Who else would it be?" said the brothel woman.

"But you don't know it was them?"

"Well, no one outside the Seraphs know for sure, but of course it was them. And I'm glad."

"Glad?"

"I don't want some cocky blisster thinking he knows what's best for us."

"That's just– I mean, that's shooting yourself in the foot, isn't it? You said yourself you'd take a cure in a heartbeat, and what else is he supposed to do? He can't exactly run on a manifesto that proposes eradicating HS – he'd be crucified. Who else do you have who even gives a shit about you all apart from Milligan?"

"The Seraphs."

"They're not politicians."

"No, they're revolutionaries."

"Ha!"

"Don't underestimate them," she said, serious.

"You just finished telling me a large section of the Seraphs hate you all and don't want a cure, but you back them?"

"They're all we have."

"All you have is shit."

She stared at me, smiling slightly, clasping her spoon, looking like she was going to attack me with it. I hadn't meant to make an enemy, but there I was without an Inex filter, saying, "I can't believe you people."

"'You people'?" she said. "What's that supposed to mean? You're one of us."

"I am," I said, "most definitely not one of you."

"Is that right? Then why are you here?"

"A mistake. It's all a mistake."

"Aah," she said, waving her spoon at me and nodding, "You're one of those."

"One of what?"

"I know your type," she said, standing and picking up her bowl as a bell sounded. "I know your type." She walked off and I lost her amongst the rest of block 366 as they all stood and returned their bowls, some of them queuing to clean out their vomit buckets as the next block came in.

"That was dangerous, Sarah," said Kate as we filed out.

I sighed. "I know."

"You need to be careful what you say around here, especially about the Seraphs and a cure."

"I know," I said again and turned to her. "I'm not used to keeping my mouth shut."

"Didn't your Inex warn you to back down?"

"We're not connected."

"What? Why not?"

"We're just not. Do you think I have to worry about her?"

"I don't think so. She's all mouth too. But I'd be more careful if I was you. Connect to your Inex – it'll keep you in check. See you tonight." She walked off towards the farmland.

As block 366 all went off to work, I trudged over to the hippy hut where Venus had us answer a series of questions on our skills and experience. Her Inex then sorted us into job categories. To my surprise, no one was assigned to the brothel and everyone seemed happy with what the Inex announced. Venus took us on a ghetto tour; farm, kitchen, med block, the administration department in the council building, and the Inex repair workshop. At this last stop, Venus left me behind.

"Classes will continue after your shift," she said. "I'll see you then."

I nodded and she turned to the workshop manager. "Good luck with her. She's difficult."

"That right?" he said as Venus walked off.

"Only if you try and inculcate me to some hippy cult."

He laughed. "Not a fan of TF training?"

"Not a fan of her."

He eyed me then offered me his hand. "I'm Chris Faber. I run this place."

I took his hand and said, "Sarah."

"Like you, Sarah, I have no time for bullshit. So don't mess me around, OK? If you do, you're out."

I didn't respond, not knowing how to deal with having a boss, and he seemed to take my silence as assent.

"What's your Inex experience?"

"The Company," I said. "Eleven years in Inex design and eight years factory floor experience. Moved onto a desk job in customer relations, so I might be a bit rusty."

"You worked with early models? That's pretty much all we've got here."

"A little."

"If you're used to the later models, you might find this a bit frustrating, but you'll find your way. I've never had anyone with your level of Company experience before – I guess this is my lucky day."

"What was your experience?"

"Several years Inex factory grunt work, but I was studying to move into design before I was hit with the allergy. You look a bit like Führer Ward, anyone ever told you that?"

"Not in those exact words," I said, smiling but worried my face was healing faster than I'd thought. "But yeah, people used to think we were related and that's how I got my Company job."

"That must have been a pain in the arse."

"It was. It really was."

Chris led me to my workstation. "Right, this is your space. There's a limit to what we can do – we don't have access to biological components or bio-repair materials, which causes a massive headache. We can sometimes work around it, but a lot of Inexes need to be junked or used for spare parts. Now, I'm sure you've listened to the screeds of documents on what can be legally altered in an Inex and what can't. We're already illegal, as we're not actually registered, so if you can find any ways around some of the restrictions, I'm happy for you to just go for it." I raised my eyebrows at this, and he said, "Rules of the ghetto. We have to make the best of what we have. Just make sure the Inex you're working on can't report you. It's unlikely, to be honest, as most of the models are too old. So, the majority of the work is basic tech repairs, which of course your own Inex can assist with – Elena gave you a good one. One of the most up to date models we have."

"An IKL556 is the most up to date you have? I saw a Seraph with an ICC411."

"The Seraphs get the best models, of course. You give this one a name yet? What's your name, buddy?"

"I don't have a name. Sarah has not connected – I assume I'm temporary."

"You're not connected?" he said, baffled. "You have to connect."

I refused, he insisted, I refused again. He tried to get a reason out of me and I cringed at how I sounded like a petulant teenager when the answer I gave was, "Just because, OK?" He groaned and said Venus was right about me, so I walked right out.

He came after me, of course.

"You're seriously walking out on one of the best jobs in the ghetto?" he shouted.

I ignored him and kept walking.

"Wait! Just... come back, OK? We can work something out."

I stopped and turned, staring at him. He gestured at me to return and I headed back.

"You're going to have to connect at some point." I was about to head back out again when he said, "Wait, hear me out. Everyone gets an Inex and everyone's DNA goes on file. I'm surprised they haven't done you yet."

I thought about that for a moment. That put a tighter time limit on my stay; I couldn't afford to let them ID me. The plan was to get used to being around Inexes again, get used to using one myself, psych myself up to connecting in, and continue with the hippy classes and the coping strategies they gave us. Then I'd use the Inex to get a car back to the city. Apart from the problem of avoiding the TF, minimising attacks, and hiding wounds and scars, there was the fact that I'd be registered HSA and I wouldn't be able to get a car, and walking wasn't possible with the exposed streets and cop patrols. I'd have to steal or fake an ID; I didn't know if this would be easier or harder with an old model. If that didn't work, I'd have to come up with something else, all before they DNA ID'd me. "Shit," I said.

"What was that?"

I looked up at him. "Nothing."

"Have you even been listening to me?"

"Sorry," I said, shaking my head.

"Look, I might need you, but if you think you're going to coast on your Company background, think again."

"Just give me a few days," I said, still distracted. "I'll connect in then, OK?"

"One day."

"Two."

He stared at me, arms crossed. "Fine."

I nodded, looking at my Inex. We'd be out of there that evening.

CHAPTER 8

I did a lot better in Inex tech than I'd thought. The morning's work was basic, and my knowledge of the early models came back after a bit of refamiliarisation. I worried that this intense focus on Inexes would set off attacks, and if I managed to keep them at bay it would just manifest in nightmares, but being hands on with Inexes again felt good. The old models were so different from the Inex that was torn open, I didn't even think of it. A few of the other workshop monkeys tried to make small talk, but I cut them off pretty quickly and they left me alone.

In the afternoon, in between working on the various Inexes, I tried to remove the HSA ID on mine, but I was struggling. I needed someone's non-HSA ID so I could false connect. Frustrated, I gave up and got back to work just as Chris came to check on me, inspecting the Inexes I'd repaired.

"Good. But slow."

"It's my first day. Give me a break."

"You think Führer Ward would accept that excuse?"

I scowled. "You're no Jane Ward."

"And aren't you glad of that? You need to speed things up, Sarah. I've been watching you, spending too much time noodling around. This isn't some hobby."

"I'm getting used to working with Inexes again, finding my way."

"You can do that in your own time. I want these three done before you leave this afternoon."

I mumbled assent, then just as he was about to check on one

of the others, I asked about city HSAs. "How do they get into the city? The beggars – how do they get there if the ghetto is so tightly patrolled by police?"

"They let them through."

"What?"

"They let some of them through."

"What are you talking about? Why would they do that?"

"They're scapegoats. Deviants on the street, polluting people's bliss, reminding them why they hate us so much. Fuels people's prejudice, allows Caddick and lackey Ward to keep doing what they're doing."

"That's bullshit," I said. "And Ward isn't Caddick's lackey."

"Of course she is, and don't you think the authorities could sweep every HSA off the streets if they wanted to? What's this about, anyway? You thinking of leaving me in the lurch?"

"I don't belong in this shithole."

"Jesus," he said, rolling his eyes. "Venus really wasn't kidding about you. Look, Sarah, it's a crapshoot. You don't know if you'll get through or if you'll end up dead in front of the council building. Even if you get through, it's a long walk back to the city and it's not an easy life there. I wouldn't risk it. You're safer here."

"This isn't a prison. You can't keep me here."

"No, but good luck trying to reach the city. Get back to work – if I'm gonna lose you I at least want you to finish these first."

I didn't say anything and got on with my work. When I finished for the day, I asked if I could come back later in the evening so I could work on my Inex on my own time.

"What needs done?"

"Just some basics, mostly aesthetic, and the right arm still doesn't work properly."

He gave his OK, but warned that the Ino would be monitoring me so I didn't steal anything. He gave my Inex the pass for the building and I headed off to the hippy class, had a quick dinner, then returned to the workshop. It was much easier without distractions, but I still couldn't get round the ID problem and I was there all evening.

"If you succeed in your task I'll have to report you."

"But I'm not succeeding, am I?"

"No, you're not."

I stared at it, then started work again, this time adjusting it so it couldn't report me for doing anything illegal. I hadn't done this with such an early model, and it took me longer than expected. When I'd finished I told it to connect. As it walked over to me, I tensed. I didn't want to connect, but it would help me get back to the city safely. As it placed its hand on my arm, I kept steady, resisting the urge to pull away. It connected immediately and I felt it in my head, the other presence I'd been used to most of my adult life. It now felt like a threat.

"Jane Ward, HSA, we are now connected."

"I'm not HSA, that's not who I am. I'm CEO of The Company."

"An HSA cannot be head of a company."

"I'm not HSA."

I stopped it before it could contradict me. I watched it, knowing its tendrils were all through me – checking my vitals, running through my mind and my memories, building a profile as I sat thinking about how to get out of the ghetto. I thought about those cops and fantasised about killing one of them, making the other drive me back to the city, a knife at his throat.

"I advise against kidnapping and killing police officers."

"It's just a fantasy," I said. "The reality would be me vomiting and falling on my face."

"I calculate 98% probability of that scenario."

"Yeah, thanks. Look, Inex, I'm getting out of here. I need you to calculate the best route that would allow me to make my way to the city with minimal risk. Tell me how long it will take and how much food and water I'd need."

"The best route would–"

"Shhh! What was that?"

I walked over to the dirty window and rubbed at it with my sleeve. I stared out and saw flames in the distance. I caught glimpses of people rushing back and forth and heard muffled yelling.

"I think one of the blocks caught fire."

The Inex looked out and said, "Yes, you're right."

"This might be what I need – if everyone is distracted with a fire, I should be able to break into the kitchen stock and get food for my journey back. Come on."

I left the workshop and headed for the cafeteria. The ghetto had no lighting, so my Inex lit the way. When I came round the top of the hill I turned and looked down towards the flaming blocks and saw that most of the southside ghetto was in flames.

"It spread fast." I saw figures running in a mess of confusion. No one seemed to be doing anything about the fire. "They don't have anything for this. The whole place is going to go up."

I watched the flames, mesmerised, and realised I needed to get out of there as soon as possible. If there was going to be a mass exodus, I didn't want to be caught up in it. "Lead me to the cafeteria, Inex. The quickest route."

I followed it between various work blocks. As I got closer, I heard loud bangs and threw myself to the ground, catching my breath because of my rib. I lay there, eyes closed, trying to deal with the pain.

"What was that?"

"Gunshots."

"Gunshots? Are you sure?"

"97% certainty."

"Jesus. What's going on? Are we under attack?"

"I don't know."

Opening my eyes, I slowly pulled myself up and continued down towards the flaming blocks. As I got nearer, the yelling got louder, but the blocks around me were still safe from the flames. I walked between them, heading towards the dark figures I could see in the near distance. When I reached them I grabbed hold of someone, but they threw me off and kept running.

"Wait—"

Someone shoulder barged me, then another and another, and I yelled out in pain, clutching my rib. I almost fell to the ground when someone grabbed me and pulled me up.

"Run, you fool!"

"What's—" I said, staggering after them. "What's going on? Are we under attack?"

They turned, their face lit up by the light from my Inex, all scarring and still-healing wounds. "A raid!" he shouted and ran off. I watched him disappear as people knocked into me again. I weaved my way through the panicking HSAs, heading for one of the buildings off to the side. I stopped and leaned against the block, trying to steady my breathing and keep from going into HSA meltdown. I'd heard about the raids, but I hadn't given them much thought. Caddick encouraged them, used them to anger the Seraphs who retaliated by launching assaults in the city, killing innocent blissters. It was always exactly what he wanted.

"Where are we, Inex?"

"We've veered off route – but you can cut through to the left, and continue straight ahead, taking you past the council building. The cafeteria is only a few minutes from there."

I headed in the opposite direction of the HSAs, worrying whether I was doing the right thing, if I'd make it out.

"*Given the extent of the raid,*" said the Inex internally, "*it's unlikely you'll make it out. I advise returning to the workshop – it's a stone building and far away from the wooden blocks, which they'll be hitting for maximum damage and casualties. You should be safe in the workshop until the raid has ended.*"

"*And then what?*" I said as I made my way through the quiet alleyways between deserted blocks. "*I'm stuck in a shithole that's* become even more of a shithole. Police presence will increase, and the Seraphs will be looking for deviant slaves to rebuild. Whatever Chris says, this is a goddamn prison. It's just going to get worse and I'm not hanging around for that. Get me to the cafeteria, then get me the hell out of here."

I broke out into the main square and stopped, assessing the area. The massive council building loomed ahead, made intimidating and gothic by the swaying shadows cast by the rising flames from the nearby blocks. Bodies covered the council building steps, spreading into the square. An HSA ran out from the alleyway next to me, sprinting across the main square, their head exploding and body falling amongst the rest. I stood there, shaking, hand clamped across my mouth, my Inex telling me to get to safety. I scanned the square, trying to figure out where the gunshot had come from, but I couldn't see anyone. *"They haven't seen you. They haven't seen me. Move, Jane!"* My own thoughts and the Inex's spiralled into one another as I slowly backed away, creeping into the darkness of the alleyway. Safe, I pressed against the wall of the block and released my hand from my mouth. I peered out into the square, concentrating on my breathing, trying to stop shaking. Nausea gripped me but I managed to keep from being sick. My broken rib hurt, my still-bruised eye throbbed and the skin on my cheeks cracked open. *"I can't break down now, I can't."*

Shaking, my teeth chattering, I looked out into the square and saw a Seraph fighting a man – no, a boy, he couldn't have been more than fifteen, sixteen – on the council steps, amongst the bodies. The Seraph, like Eleven, moved like a dancer, a light-footed predator. The boy was all sheer brute force, tripping on the bodies, crushing them, swinging for the Seraph. I was sure who would win. My attention turned to the other side of the square as I heard voices; a group of six raiders emerged from one of the alleys, all coated in blood and ash. None of them had Inexes, every one of them had a weapon: guns, clubs. I recognised one as the flames lit up his bloodied

face – a son of the CEO of a company who provided us with
raw materials for the Inex. I almost called out to him, but I
stopped myself and watched as they disappeared into an alley
down the other side of the square. An HSA came running out
of another alleyway, followed by a boy who tackled them, both
falling to the ground. They stood, grasping onto each other.
The boy headbutted the HSA, their nose bursting.

"*We should go,*" said my Inex. "*Back to the workshop.*"

I turned to the council building and saw the Seraph kick the
boy in the face, sending him into the wall. He bounced off it
and collapsed. She walked over to him, and as she was bending
down, his hand shot out and grabbed her ankle. I gasped as she
hit the ground, cracking her head. He pounced on her, a feral
bloody mess. He scrunched her shirt up in his fist, the other fist
slamming into her face. He hit her once more and let her drop.
He stared down at her before turning and staggering away.

"*Jane, we should go. The safest place is the workshop.*"

I was staring at the prone Seraph and saw a bag a few feet
from her.

"*But we need to get there alive,*" I said, scanning the bodies
closest to me.

"*What are you doing?*"

"*You know what.*"

I moved out into the square, grabbed one of the raider
corpses and dragged them back into the alley. I stripped them,
removed my brown rags and put their bloody clothes on
instead. I headed back out into the square.

"*Jane–*"

"*Stay here.*"

"*Be careful.*"

I'd noticed almost immediately that the raiders didn't have
Inexes with them. If they saw me with one, they'd know I
wasn't one of them. The bag at the edge of the council building
steps would keep that from happening. As I headed for it, I bent
down to pick up a bloodied club next to the body of a teenage

girl. When I looked up, the boy who'd attacked the Seraph was still there. He stooped to pick something up then turned and walked back to the Seraph. He saw me and grinned, drawing his lips back, baring bloody teeth. Seeing me in raider clothes, club in hand, and sans Inex, he saluted me, a shard of glass glinting in his hand. I tried to keep my shaking under control, glad I was in shadow and too far away for him to see my open sores and HSA scars. He walked over to the Seraph I thought was dead, grabbed her by the throat, pulled her upright and stabbed her over and over again in the stomach and chest. She was ragdoll limp, her eyes rolling, blood dribbling from her mouth.

"*Just die,*" I thought. "*Just die.*"

I walked up the steps, ignoring the bag, the club shaking in my hand.

"*What are you doing?*" said my Inex. "*Jane, this is dangerous.*"

I headed for him, struggling over bodies, losing my footing. I glanced up at the boy, not understanding why I wanted to hurt him so badly, why I cared about that Seraph.

"*Whose side am I on, Inex? Whose fucking side am I on, anyway?*"

"*You're not on either side. This is foolish, Jane. Come back.*"

I looked up at the boy, my body shaking violently. He let the Seraph drop and turned to me, still holding the glass, his hand soaked in blood. I dropped the club, falling onto my hands and knees. I vomited on one of the bodies, the stench of blood, shit, and death overwhelming me, wracking my body until all I was throwing up was metallic bile.

"*He's going to kill me.*"

"*Jane, get up. Come back to me.*"

The boy kneeled beside me and I tried to get up, to defend myself from the shard of glass, but there was no glass and there was no boy. A woman said, "Jane. Brian, it's– I've found you. Jane."

I stared up at her, trying to focus.

"I can't believe it's you."

"Elena?" I said.

"No, I–"

She gripped my shoulders and I squinted up at her, her face in shadow, made fuzzy by the billows of smoke. She took hold of my hand and said, "Breathe steady. Just hold on…"

She let go of me and turned away. I tried to reach out for her.

"She's one of us," I heard her say, a shadow falling across me. "One of those fucking deviants mutilated her. She's gone into shock."

"We'll fucking mutilate them."

She was talking to the boy. I heard some scrambling, then gunfire; three shots, my ears ringing. I flinched and a tooth fell onto my tongue. I turned myself over and spat it out.

"*Jane,*" said my Inex and I watched it emerge from the darkness of the alley, picking its way across the bodies in the square. "*Jane, you're having a severe attack – you need to focus on your breathing. Visualise your seriffed mantra.*"

I closed my eyes and said, "*I'm in control. I'm going home. I'll find Icho.*"

I heaved in air; it was all cloying smoke and blood and I coughed and fell onto my side, shaking. I felt her hands on me, pulling me to her, laying me on her lap.

"*I'm in control.*"

She spoke to me, but I couldn't hear. I stared up at her trying to work out who she was as I struggled to breathe.

"*I'm going home.*"

She held something up then pushed it against my arm.

"*I'll find…*"

The smoke cleared for a moment and I focused on her face. "Icho," I said, and I died.

HELLSANS

PART THREE

CHAPTER 1

"Jane's heart has stopped," said Jane's Inex. "Charging for defibrillation."

Icho cradled her. "Jane, come on. Please."

"First aid will have a better outcome than begging," said Brian.

Jane's Inex looked up at Icho. "Brian is right. She will likely be brain dead in approximately five minutes."

Icho laid her down. "The formula should have worked," she said, doing chest compressions. "Why didn't it work?"

"You were too late in administering it," said Brian.

"Almost charged. Continue administering CPR."

Icho pinched Jane's nose and pressed her mouth to Jane's, forcing breath into her body, her lips coming away bloody. She continued with chest compressions and heard a crack. She stopped in horror.

"It's just a rib," said Jane's Inex. "Keep going."

Icho continued and breathed into her mouth again. The Inex climbed onto Jane.

"Stand clear."

Icho backed off as it placed its hands on Jane's chest, shocking her. "There's a pulse," it said.

Jane's eyes flickered and she drew in breath.

"Thank bliss, thank bliss."

Jane lay there, eyes roaming, falling on Icho; her brow furrowed in confusion.

"It's OK, Jane, just keep breathing," said Icho, cupping her face and looking her in the eyes. "You're going to be alright."

Icho slid her arm around her and helped her sit up. She winced as Icho propped her against a body lying on the stairs. She clutched her chest, her face scrunched up in pain.

"What's wrong with me?" she said, her voice raspy.

"I cracked one of your ribs, I'm sorry."

"Why did you–?" said Jane, dazed.

"You died."

Jane looked around her, shaking her head. She took in the scene, confused, about to ask where she was, when she remembered the day she woke in the ghetto, cursing Langham. It all came back to her.

"You went into cardiac arrest," said the Inex, climbing onto her lap. "Icho administered CPR and I defibrillated your heart."

Jane looked at it, trying to focus, its words slowly sinking in. "I died?" she said, turning back to Icho.

"But you're fine now. You're going to be alright."

Jane coughed and leaned her head back. "God, it hurts."

"I'm sorry."

Jane rolled her head forward and stared at Icho, vaguely aware of the fire and smoke-filled backdrop. The screams and gunshots were tinny and muted, like they were recordings of recordings filtered through old tech. She looked up at Icho, who was smiling down at her, both warmth and anxiety evident in her face, her dirt-smeared skin glistening with sweat.

"Icho," she said quietly. "Are you real?"

Before Icho could respond, Brian interrupted: "You need to get somewhere safe."

"You're right, you're right," said Icho, hunching and glancing round the square. It was choked with smoke, sporadically clearing to reveal bodies before closing around them again. Icho thought she could see figures on the west side. She turned back to Jane. "Can you stand?"

A nearby block collapsed in on itself, the roar of the imploding structure and raging flames making Icho jump. "You need to get up. We need to go."

Icho secured her arm around Jane, who let herself be pulled up, gritting her teeth against the pain. Her legs were shaking. "Where are we going?"

"There's a room in the basement of the council building," said Icho, leading Jane slowly up the stairs. "We should be OK there until this passes."

"How do you know that? What are you doing here, Icho?"

"Save your breath. I'll explain later."

As Icho helped Jane step over a body, Brian said, "You need a new Inex. You should shut me down."

Icho shook her head. "I need to make sure we're safe first. I'll shut you down when we get there. I'll just have to do without an Inex."

"What's wrong with it?" said Jane.

"I false connected and they know. They'll be tracing this Inex."

"You false connected?"

"Just concentrate on walking," said Icho, trying to take as much of Jane's weight as possible as they walked up the steps.

"Who's they? Who's after you? The police?"

"I'll explain it all once we're safe, Jane."

As they reached the top of the stairs, both Inexes led the way, clearing some of the rubble in their path. There was a gap in the destroyed main door, but it was partially obstructed. Icho conversed internally with Brian who scanned the obstruction for weaknesses, confirming it would be safe for them to squeeze through it.

"I'm going to be sick," said Jane.

"Vomit and walk."

Jane leaned and retched, spitting bile. Wiping her mouth, she said, "You need... to be careful. Seraphs."

"I can handle the Seraphs."

"They can't find out who you are."

"I know," said Icho as they reached the door. "Brian? Go through and scan the area."

Brian slipped through the gap with ease and after a few seconds confirmed it was clear.

"There's no one there? You're sure?"

"Only the dead."

"It's clear," Icho said to Jane. "I'll go through first and help you, alright? Lean here."

Icho left Jane propped against the council building wall as she climbed through the narrow gap in the destroyed doorway. It was dark apart from some flickering embers. She turned back, leaned through and offered her hand to Jane. Jane took it and climbed in, her face contorted with pain. Any colour she'd had was completely drained; she looked almost blue. Icho held onto her.

"She's about to faint," said the Inex.

"OK, OK, easy." Icho lowered Jane to the floor, setting her against the wall.

Jane's Inex looked up at Icho. "She's dehydrated."

Icho instructed the Inexes to go down the corridor, as far as their distance limit would allow, and search the rooms for water. They picked their way over the rubble and bodies, disappearing in the darkness, reappearing momentarily in the flicker of flames further down the corridor. Icho watched them enter a nearby room.

"You OK?"

Jane nodded. Icho held her clammy hand and looked around. A dying flame lit up the face of a dead Seraph; she was covered in blood, her cheek ripped open, revealing teeth in a permanent sneer. Icho stared into the Seraph's glazed eyes.

"We have water," said Brian, snapping her out of her morbid communion with the Seraph. She looked over to see them returning, Jane's Inex carrying a bottle. When they reached them, she took it and helped Jane drink, a small amount at a time to keep her from throwing up again.

"Better?"

Jane nodded. Icho got up to search the nearby dead Seraphs for suitable ammunition, reloading her gun and putting the rest in her pockets. She turned back to Jane. "You think you can walk a bit now?"

Jane nodded. "How do you know this place?"

"The Seraphs brought me here."

"You had a run-in with them?"

Icho nodded.

"They ID you?"

"Yes, but I told you – I'm false connected."

"How the hell do you know how to do that?"

"This really isn't the place to discuss my Inex crimes, Jane. C'mon."

Jane let Icho help her up as the Inexes went ahead, scanning the corridor before returning to light their way. Icho helped Jane navigate the unsteady ground.

"What are you doing here, Icho?"

Icho hesitated before saying, "I came for you."

Jane was silent, thinking this over as they reached the top of the stairs. They paused as the Inexes scanned the first couple of flights.

"I don't understand."

"We've got a lot to talk about. Let's just get to that room, OK?"

Waiting for the Inexes to return, Jane leaned against the wall, head back, hand hovering at her rib. Her face was lit on one side by a dwindling flame in the corridor; she was pale, drawn, smeared with grime, her dirty hair limp and greasy, strands plastered across her forehead.

"How do I know I can trust you?"

Icho stared at Jane, stunned, thinking of all she'd been through to get here. "Are you serious?"

"How can I know?"

"I saved your life."

"So you want me alive. That doesn't mean anything."

"*She doesn't know,*" said Brian internally, its interruption to her thoughts jarring her, arresting her rising anger. "*She's right to be wary.*"

Icho nodded, as if Brian could see her. She looked at Jane. "Do you really have a choice right now?"

Jane was about to respond when the Inexes both appeared on the stair, informing them the first two flights were clear. "There's no sound from below."

Icho asked them to light the way and she hooked her arm round Jane again, following them. They made their way down, Jane concentrating hard to minimise movement that would cause her more pain, but after three flights she slipped from Icho's grip and slumped on a step. They rested for a few minutes, Jane sipping more water.

"How many flights?"

"Another two, I think," said Icho, sitting next to Jane.

They heard a muted explosion outside and they both looked up as if they could see the flames through the wall.

"What's down there exactly?"

"Interrogation," said Icho.

"Torture?"

"Maybe."

"Maybe?"

"They didn't torture me."

"What did they want with you?"

"I knew about the raid – I was trying to warn them. But they didn't believe me."

A banging noise came from above and Icho stood, pulling the gun out and pointing it up the stairs. There was a protracted scraping noise, followed by silence.

"Can you keep going?"

Jane nodded and stood up, half-leaning against the wall as she made her way down again. Icho followed, walking down the stairs sideways, listening for any more movement from above. When they neared the bottom, bright light from the corridor illuminated the last few steps. They held back and listened. There was silence. Icho gestured for Brian to go ahead and it climbed down, disappearing into the corridor beyond, reappearing a few minutes later. "Clear."

Jane and Icho took the last few steps and headed into the corridor, a flickering light illuminating the bodies of three raiders and two Seraphs. They could see more bodies slumped at the far end, smashed up Inexes strewn between them. Jane slumped next to a Seraph's body and leaned against the wall.

Icho asked Brian to scan the corridor for anything that might be of use to them as she searched one of the Seraphs, unhooking a small flask of water from their belt.

"Icho?"

"Mm-hmm?"

"You injected me." Icho stopped her search and stood, turning back to Jane, who squinted up at her. "I remember."

"It was to help you, lessen the attack."

"But I died."

"I was too late."

"What was it?"

"It arrests HS allergy symptoms."

Jane laughed, and abruptly stopped, wincing from the pain, clutching at her chest. "So you did it? You have a cure."

"It's not exactly a cure. It keeps symptoms under control for a few hours."

Icho was about to resume her search, walking over to one of the raider bodies, when the dead Seraph next to Jane spoke. "Who the fuck are you two?"

Jane jumped back, jerking her rib and crying out in pain as the Seraph spat out blood and looked up at Icho. Jane shifted away from the Seraph, staring wide-eyed as Icho levelled the gun at her, internally telling Brian to scan her for weapons.

"*Clear,*" it said.

"You said that before, but this Seraph is still alive."

"There were no signs of–"

Icho cut it off, *"I don't need excuses."* She jutted her chin, eyeing the Seraph. "And you are?"

"You have a cure? For HellSans allergy," said the Seraph.

"It's not a cure."

"Right. Keeps symptoms under control." She spat out more blood. "Who the hell are you?"

"We thought you were dead," said Jane.

"But here I am, still in the hell of the living." She laughed and closed her eyes for a second, clutching her side, her hand covered in blood.

There was a noise from the stairs that made them all turn to look.

"Shit," said Icho.

"Check the room," said Jane. "The one you told me about. I'll keep an eye on her."

"Right," said Icho, handing Jane the gun.

Icho headed down the corridor as Jane went over to the Seraph, flinching as she heard more noise on the stairs.

"The cavalry," said the Seraph.

"Or raiders."

"You better hope so. Seraphs won't take kindly to news of a cure."

"And who's going to tell them?"

The Seraph smiled, her teeth bloody. Jane watched as her smile faded, her eyes glazing as she slumped to the side. Jane held her face, tilting her chin up. "Hey?" She looked into her eyes and felt for a pulse in her wrist.

"She gone?" said Icho, coming up behind her.

Jane nodded. "Bled out."

There was more noise on the stairs, several footsteps speeding up.

"Shit," said Icho, looking panicked.

"Is it clear?" said Jane.

"It is, but there's no way to get in the room without a Seraph Inex ID."

"We'll just have to deal with whoever's coming."

As the noise on the stairs got louder, Icho shut Brian down and stomped on its torso, crushing the Mnemo core. Jane stashed the gun nearby before smearing her face in the blood of one of the bodies in case it was raiders and her skin looked too deviant, Icho following suit in case it was Seraphs and her skin looked too blisster. Jane ordered her Inex to keep quiet and they stood waiting, their arms half-raised to show they weren't armed.

Ten Seraphs entered the corridor and pointed their guns at Jane and Icho. They slowly approached, barking at them to raise their hands higher, and searched them. They got Jane's ID, the lead Seraph nodding approval that she was in Inex tech, and seemed to believe Icho's story that she'd just arrived, hadn't been processed, and her Inex had been destroyed. They swept the corridor, checking all the dead Seraphs, taking weapons from their belts and picking up mangled Inexes. Watching them, impressed by their efficiency, Jane slumped down next to where she'd hidden the gun and slipped it into the back of her trousers. Icho stood staring at the remains of Brian, feeling a pang of sadness, missing the feel of the connection, missing its internal voice. There was a noise from upstairs and the lead Seraph said, "We're done. Let's go. Six, Eight, look after these two."

"We don't need looking after," said Jane, Icho helping her to her feet, but the Seraph had already disappeared round the end of the corridor and Icho and Jane were ushered forward, flanked by Six and Eight. They all entered the interrogation room and Icho was surprised to see the north wall open up into a tunnel. They followed the Seraphs, the wall sliding closed behind them.

CHAPTER 2

The journey seemed neverending, and Jane struggled to keep up as Six put her arm around her, half-dragging her along. Icho asked where they were going but got no response. When they reached the end of the tunnel, the wall opened up into a dark warehouse, lit here and there by Inexes as people made their way around. It was teeming with activity; hundreds of HSAs in cots being tended to by the med team, others in huge queues for food and drink. The Seraphs dumped Jane on a cot, barely conscious.

"She's a priority," said Six to Icho. "We need her on her feet soon. I'll send over a medic."

Icho nodded and got Jane to drink some water before laying her back on the cot. The medic came immediately and assessed her.

"There's not much I can do about the broken rib," she said to Icho. "What she really needs is some rest – I'll tell the Seraphs she won't be fit for work for several hours, but that's probably all they'll allow. Get her fed, plenty of vitwater, tend her wounds with these and make sure she gets some sleep."

The medic sent over food and vitwater, and Icho fed her as much as she could before Jane fell unconscious again. While she slept, Icho tended her wounds, applied the bandages, and wrapped her in a blanket. Icho curled up next to Jane, the rest of the food hidden between them, and fell asleep with her arm around the tray. When Icho woke, Jane was already awake, eating the remains. Sun streamed in the windows near the ceiling, and they could clearly see the vastness of the warehouse.

"I don't remember getting here. I remember Seraphs in the council building, then this."

"I think we're on the outskirts of the ghetto," said Icho. "The Seraphs are a lot more organised than I'd thought."

"I don't know whether to admire them or despise them."

"Both," said Icho. "Jane, they want you on Inex tech. The medic managed to delay them a few hours so you could rest. Do you think you'll manage?"

"Manage? Are you serious? We're getting out of here, Icho."

"How, exactly?"

Jane was about to reply when a voice issued from loudspeakers. Everyone hushed as they listened to the Seraph telling them they would all be led back to the ghetto in small groups at varying intervals to avoid discovery of the tunnels. They would be taken to the temporary tents being set up by NGOs and they'd be assigned a task according to physical ability and their current ghetto job. All Inex workshop HSAs were to stay in the warehouse to repair Seraph Inexes before returning to the ghetto to deal with the thousands of Inexes damaged in the raid. NGOs had brought donations of old models, which would need to be logged and assigned according to need.

Jane and Icho looked at each other as the Seraph ended with, "Be ready to return to the ghetto when you're called."

"We need to get out of here," said Jane. "I'm not going back to that shithole."

"I need to pee," said Icho. "We can figure things out when I'm back."

"I'll come with you," said Jane, standing and wincing. "Goddamn this rib."

"I'm sorry," said Icho.

"It's not your fault – it was already broken."

"What?"

Jane nodded. "Cops."

They joined the huge queue for the toilets. After a few HSAs had pissed themselves, buckets were handed out. They had to stay in the queue to empty them and the stench was nauseating.

"This is really disgusting," said Jane.

"What happened with the cops?"

"I left the ghetto. They brought me back with bruises and a broken rib. I was lucky, apparently."

"I'd heard about the brutality of the patrols. I'm glad you're OK."

"I wouldn't call this OK."

Their attention turned to a projected news report from one of the deviant's Inexes further down the queue.

"Holy shit," said Icho, her hand covering her mouth as she watched bulldozers pushing piles of charred bodies into a mass grave on the edge of the ghetto.

It cut to a government spokesperson, the crisp, brightly lit studio in stark contrast to the footage from the ghetto.

"The brutality of the Seraphs knows no bounds, that they will stoop to slaughtering their own."

A murmur of protest moved along the queue.

"We cannot tolerate the Seraphs any longer. They're animals, pure and simple, and they should be treated like animals."

"A number of the deviants," said the presenter, "have said it was a raid by a well-organised group of teens from the city."

"Of course they'd say that, but is there any proof? There's no footage – the Seraphs made sure of that, damaging and destroying their own Inexes."

"There's been several bodies of city teens recovered–"

"Volunteers who'd gone in to help, and now the Seraphs

are using these poor compassionate kids as scapegoats. It's disgusting. But don't worry," the spokesperson said, as photos of several smiling teenagers took up the wall, "I will not let them die in vain. The Seraphs have gone too far this time. They'll pay for their crimes."

"What about the innocent HSAs caught up in this? NGOs are reporting that you're not letting through aid."

"Innocent? Is there really such a thing as an innocent deviant? They're all complicit in the deaths of these children, they're all complicit in the way the corrupt ghetto operates. We've been too lenient on them – not anymore."

"Jesus," said Icho. "Can you believe this?"

Jane shrugged and looked away.

"It doesn't bother you?"

"Why would it?"

Jane grabbed a nearby bucket and dragged it over. She pulled down her trousers and pants and squatted over it, peeing. When she finished, she pulled her clothes back on and walked off.

"What are you–? Jane!"

Some of the HSAs sniggered as Icho called out. She was about to run after her when one of the deviants grabbed her arm and pointed at Jane's pee bucket, telling her she had to stay to empty it. Icho pulled her arm free and nodded, watching Jane disappear. She was in the queue for an hour and had to use the bucket herself. When she returned to their cot, not sure what to do, Jane appeared.

"What the hell, Jane? What is wrong with you?"

"Come on–"

"You just leave me with a bucket of piss and expect–"

"We're getting out of here."

"What?"

"This is your new Inex. Connect and follow me."

An old, beaten Inex climbed up Icho's arm and perched on her shoulder as Jane walked off. Icho ran after her.

"Where are we going?"

"Home," said Jane. "Just look confident, like you know what you're doing."

"Jane–"

"Just shut up and follow."

They walked half the length of the warehouse, weaving through the crowd. Jane veered off, stopped, looked around, then slipped round the back of some storage containers and through a door, Icho following.

"Get down!"

Icho dropped, hunched next to Jane. Jane held a finger to her lips. Icho looked out onto a sea of cars, two Inos moving between them, scanning the garage. Jane sent her Inex on reconnaissance and it disappeared between the cars.

"The Seraphs hacked all these cars?" whispered Icho. "How can they–?"

Jane nodded. "If I'd known that day I tried to leave the ghetto…"

Jane's Inex returned, telling them it was clear and they could take car 37. They stood and made their way between the cars, following the Inex. Jane got into the back of the car, Icho slipping in behind her. Jane gave the destination, and the car pulled out, heading for the garage exit.

"They'll be able to trace us," said Icho.

"We'll dump the car as soon as we can."

"Why Beaufort Street?"

"It's far enough from my apartment, but in walking distance."

"We're going to your apartment? Will it be safe?"

"Where else can we go?"

The garage door opened and the car drove out into the quiet street behind the warehouse. As they got to the main road serving the ghetto, they passed aid workers delivering supplies. They were all parked on the road, a government blockade further up, some of the aid workers out in the road having heated discussions with government lackeys and police. Because cars are programmed to bar HSAs, no one thought to pay them any attention.

"Those Seraphs are clever bastards," said Jane as they slipped past a police car.

They turned and watched the police and aid workers recede, the main entrance to the ghetto just visible behind them. They shifted back in their seats and watched warehouse after warehouse slide by, tensing when other vehicles passed on the way to the ghetto, but no one paid them any heed. Icho stared up at the woods she'd slept in, thinking about all her anxieties on the journey. She turned, looked at Jane, and smiled, thinking how she'd succeeded, how she'd done the right thing.

Jane was tense, her face set with worry as police patrols passed them. When they were a couple of miles from the ghetto, the patrols lessened and Jane relaxed, shifted position, and stiffened at the pain from her rib.

"You alright?"

Jane nodded and closed her eyes for a few seconds. Opening them, she stared at Icho, who smiled at her before growing increasingly uncomfortable as Jane kept her eyes fixed on her, saying nothing.

"What is it?"

Jane didn't respond. She pushed her dirty hair back from her forehead and looked out the window.

"Jane?"

Jane turned back to Icho and said, "What were you doing in the ghetto?"

"I told you – I came for you."

"Why? How did you know I was there?"

Icho wasn't sure how to explain, worried it would come out wrong. She looked out the window, the woods still visible, and said, "I stole it."

"What?"

She turned to Jane. "What do you think?"

Jane contemplated Icho, eyes narrowed. "The cure."

"It's not a cure."

Jane sat quietly. Icho looked out the window again, watching the warehouses give way to the green belt, the estates in the distance, the road leading to the motorway. She thought of her slow and frustrating journey to the ghetto.

"Why?"

Still looking out the window, catching glimpses of the estate high-rises, Icho said, "It's a long story."

"You came for me," said Jane, remembering the woman she thought was a crazed HSA. She closed her eyes and saw Icho removing the scarf, hat and shades, the shock of orange hair. She opened her eyes and stared at Icho, the bright orange now dulled by dirt and blood. "Your hair."

"An attempt at a disguise," she said, with a slight smile.

"You were at my apartment. You knew, didn't you? You knew I was HSA. You knew I needed you. I'd protect you."

Icho nodded.

"Shit," said Jane, tearing up.

"Jane–"

"Shit!" she said, punching the car door, tears stinging the wounds on her face as the car admonished her, telling her any damage would be paid for.

"Jane," said Icho, reaching out to her, "Its–"

"Don't touch me," said Jane, jerking away and freezing as her rib caused her pain.

"I'm sorry," said Icho, shrinking back.

Jane wiped her face with her sleeve, smearing tears, blood, and dirt across her cheeks.

"Jane, I'm sorry you ended up in the ghetto. I can't imagine what you've been through."

Jane nodded, looking out the window. "But you came to get me," she said, turning back to Icho. "How did you get there?"

"I walked."

"You walked?"

Icho nodded.

"The raid – did you bring that? Were they after you?"

"No," said Icho. "They were there for you, Jane."

Jane stared at Icho, mouth open slightly, about to speak. She was silent for a few seconds then said, "How do you know?"

"Caddick had you killed."

"What? What are you talking about?"

Icho explained about the man she'd overheard talking to the raider kid, about finding the dead woman in bunk 89. Jane shook her head and refused to believe it was anything to do with Caddick. Icho told her about Langham, that he was the only other person who had known she was in the ghetto and now he was dead.

"Langham's dead?"

Icho nodded.

"I wanted to kill that bastard myself."

"Jane–"

"It's all speculation. We don't know this is Caddick."

"Come on, Jane."

Jane stared at Icho with a look of defiance. "Caddick wants me dead," she said, as if tasting the words.

"Caddick thinks you *are* dead."

"The raid was because of me."

"It's not your fault, Jane. You can't blame yourself."

"I'm not blaming myself. That sonofabitch." Jane's eyes narrowed as she said, "How do I know you're telling me the truth? You could be trying to turn me against him."

Icho sighed and said, "Of course I'm telling the truth."

"Why 'of course'? I don't *know* you."

"Jane, I saved your life. I came all the way to the ghetto for you."

"Because you need me. Don't pretend this is altruism, Icho."

"And *you* need *me*. We're in this together."

Jane knew Icho hadn't meant to conjure Caddick's party slogan, but she immediately pictured it in its bold, capitalised HellSans glory and froze in panic, waiting. As the seconds passed and it had no effect, she relaxed, realising Icho's formula was working. She stared out the window, the cityscape a couple of miles ahead; relief flooded her. She placed her palm on the window, as if she could touch the metropolis.

"There were times I didn't think I'd ever see the city again," she said quietly. She drummed her fingers on the window and turned back to Icho. "It's not every day your friend, colleague – the fucking Prime Minister, for bliss sake – tries to have you killed." She shook her head. "And I've never been sick. Not like this. I'm getting my life back."

Icho didn't respond, and Jane conversed internally with her Inex, asking if her death was common knowledge. It informed her there was nothing on her death, only talking heads discussing her alleged affair with Milligan, which made her sink into sullen silence.

Irritated by Jane's attitude, Icho said, "You could have died there, you know." She paused, letting Jane think it over. "If I hadn't–"

"I know," said Jane, looking down at her bloody hands on her lap. She looked out the window and caught sight of an HS store sign. Despite knowing it was safe, she quickly looked away, back down at her hands.

Icho softened and said, "I'm glad I found you in time."

"Me too."

Icho smiled, knowing that was likely as close to a thank you she'd get. Jane kept her head down, not wanting to look at the HellSans that dominated the cityscape.

"You can look at it, you know. The formula should make you immune for another few hours."

"I don't want to."

Icho nodded. "I understand."

"Do you?" said Jane, her voice hard.

"*Jane*," warned her Inex internally. Icho's warned her as she was about to respond. They both sat in silence.

Jane thought about Caddick, trying to figure out how things had unravelled so quickly, trying to work out what he was planning. Icho leaned back in her seat and stared at her. Jane's hair was a matted mess, sticking out in clumps, her face smeared in blood and grime, her lips dried and cracked. The black t-shirt she'd taken from the dead raider was torn at the shoulder. Despite how angry she'd made her, Icho wanted to lean over and stroke Jane's cheek. She thought back to Jane's death, when her mouth was pressed up against hers, feeling the open wounds on her lips, tasting and smelling Jane's blood and acidic vomit.

CHAPTER 3

They arrived at Beaufort Street and left the car. With the lower half of their faces covered, they walked the two miles to Jane's apartment, Jane struggling with the pain from her rib. Some passersby called them deviant scum and privacy nuts, but most avoided them, disgusted.

When they got to Jane's apartment, Jane sent her Inex on reconnaissance. It returned, telling them the area was clear.

"How do we get in?" said Icho. "Your ID is HSA."

"Play dead," said Jane to her Inex. It went limp and she lifted it by its hand, letting it dangle at her side.

It took a few minutes of back and forth before the door girl recognised Jane and let her in. Jane fed her a story about being at a fancy dress party as deviants, how her Inex had been damaged when festivities got out of hand.

"A human attendant is bit old fashioned," said Icho as they entered the lift.

"It was a building vote. There's a few Christian Coalition arseholes living here – they insisted on 'the human touch'. It was a dig at me. Barrett in 24 despises me."

When they arrived at the apartment Jane eye-scanned for entry.

"We're lucky Caddick's bill hasn't been passed in parliament yet," said Icho as the door closed behind them.

"What?"

"Mandatory installation of an HSA detection system, so no one can harbour deviants in their homes."

Jane didn't respond, and Icho followed her down the hallway into the sitting room.

"Wow," said Icho, looking round the open-plan room and kitchen. "So this is how you live."

"What's that supposed to mean?"

"I mean you have a beautiful place."

It was flooded with morning sunlight, which softened when Jane commanded the windows to dim. Still holding her limp Inex, Jane stretched out her arms as if to hug the apartment, but flinched and placed a hand gently on her rib. She put her Inex on the couch and sat down, closing her eyes. She told it to stop playing dead, giving it permission to speak again. She stroked the couch as if it were a pet. "It's so good to be back."

Icho looked around and said, "Books? Really?" as she stared at the huge bookshelf dominating the wall by the entrance to the dining room. "I thought having a human attendant was weird, but this…"

"It's not *weird*," said Jane.

"Playing the eccentric millionaire?"

"I'm not playing anything. I like them. Don't touch that!"

Icho quickly put back the ornament she'd picked up.

"Don't touch anything," said Jane. "You're disgusting."

"You're not exactly clean yourself. Look what you've done to your couch."

Jane looked at the grime she'd smeared across it. "The Ino will clean it." Jane stared up at a framed poster of the very first Inex, HellSans telling the reader it will "*Help you be the best you.*" She felt dizzy and nauseous.

"It's coming back." Jane gestured to the poster, grimacing.

"The formula should have lasted longer… But you died, and you're still weak. I haven't tested it in these circumstances."

"I'm not weak."

"It's not a judgment on your character, Jane. You're HSA, you died, you have a broken rib. You need some rest. Do you think you can manage a bit longer? We don't have much formula left – we need it to last until I can make more, and we don't know how long that will be."

Jane nodded. "I can manage." She told Icho about calling HellSans 'the typeface', that she had a seriffed mantra: "'I'm in control. I'm going home. I'll find Icho'. I'll need to change it now, of course."

"Find me?"

"I knew you were working on a cure."

"We were both trying to find each other?"

"And there you were, like an angel, emerging from the smoke and flames, pulling me back from death."

Jane and Icho stared at each other, awkward seconds passing before Icho walked over. "Jane…"

"And now you look like an angel of dirt," said Jane, standing up. "I'm going upstairs to have a shower. There's another shower by the main door," she said, gesturing towards the hall.

"OK. But if you're struggling, let me know."

Jane nodded, heading for the stairs, her Inex following. She took each step slowly, trying to minimise the impact on her rib, and smiled at the familiar warm vanilla smell permeating the apartment, the scent used by her Ino. She'd grown used to it, barely noticing, but now it was clear and welcoming, enveloping her. When she got to the top of the stairs, she sat on the upper step for a few minutes, catching her breath, running her hand across the carpet. The last few days felt like some kind of hellish hallucination. She looked down at her dirty, bloodstained hand and thought how she was going to wash it all away.

She pulled herself up, flinching, and walked down the hallway to the bedroom, smiling, thinking about the feel of warm water on her skin. She was about to open the door when her Inex said, "There's someone in there."

She looked down at it, frowning, and placed her hand on the bedroom door, her head cocked. She could hear the shower in her ensuite. She stood for a minute, listening, before pushing the door open and inching into the room. She looked around. The bed had been slept in. She stared at it, brow furrowed, heart hammering, when the shower stopped. She heard the shower door open and looked over to the closed ensuite door, the glass steaming up, and saw some movement, a blurry figure. She backed out of the bedroom.

"Jane–"

Jane jumped, turning to see Icho.

"Sorry, I didn't mean to scare you. I just wanted to– What? What is it?"

Jane shook her head and placed her hand over Icho's mouth. Icho frowned, but froze when she heard a door open in the bedroom. Jane lowered her hand and they stared at each other, listening.

"Internal comms," whispered Jane.

Icho nodded. Communicating internally via their Inexes, Icho said, *"Who is it?"*

"I don't know."

"A relative?"

"None living."

"Could have been sold? Rented?"

"With all my things? And the door girl let me in."

Jane moved towards the door and looked in. She caught a glimpse of a woman wrapped in a towel, her hair a straggling mess obscuring her face. The woman's Inex came into view and Jane backed away, knocking into Icho.

"What is it?"

"A woman. I don't want her Inex to see me."

The sound of voices came from the room and Jane edged forward again, peering round the door; no sign of the Inex, but the news took up one of the walls. The woman was facing away, towelling her long blonde hair. She stopped and flipped her hair back, dropping the towel. The Inex came into view and picked it up, taking it into the bathroom. The woman removed the towel wrapped around her and walked over to the dresser, picking up a brush and combing her hair. Jane saw her face in profile.

"No."

"What? What is it?"

The Inex came out of the bathroom as Jane backed away. The woman turned partially towards her, still brushing her hair, and Jane clamped her hand over her mouth as she inched away, Icho staring at her in confusion. Jane grabbed Icho, pulling her down the hall.

"What is it? What are you doing?"

Icho jerked out of her grasp and Jane ran down the hall, stumbling down the stairs, her Inex following.

"Jane!"

Shaken, Icho walked back to the bedroom. She pressed herself up against the door, listening to the loud voices of the news presenters as they discussed the ghetto raid, and inched her way along, peering into the room. She saw an Inex sitting on the dresser, facing away from her. A naked woman reached into the wardrobe and pulled out a blouse and skirt. She turned to put the clothes on the bed and Icho saw her face. Icho watched in horror as Jane got dressed.

"Inex, bring me my bracelet."

It was Jane's voice, Jane's body, Jane's movements. Icho watched her as she put on pants, a cami top, and stockings before pulling on her skirt and slipping into her blouse, buttoning it up. Icho stared at her face: clean, unscarred.

"Jane," she whispered. She turned and rushed down the hall, back down the stairs, into the sitting room. "Jane!" she shout-whispered as she gathered up the things they'd strewn around and tried to scrub at the marks Jane had left on the couch. She threw a cushion over it and looked around her. "Jane!"

She heard the Jane upstairs walking along the hall. "Shit."

Icho went to the doorway next to the bookshelf and peered into the dining room before heading down the hall to the bathroom by the front door.

"Thank bliss!" she said as she burst in. She closed and locked the door behind her.

Fully clothed, Jane was hunched in the shower, shaking and bleeding.

"Shit," said Icho. "Jane, stay with me." Icho pulled her satchel from her shoulder. "You're thinking in Hell– the typeface. You need to focus on your seriffed mantra."

"It's me."

"The mantra, Jane," said Icho, rummaging in her bag. "Focus."

"It has my face." Jane reached up and pulled a strip of skin from her cheek.

Icho glanced up. "Jesus, Jane, don't–"

Icho leaned into the shower and grabbed both of Jane's wrists. "Look at me. Everything's going to be alright. Just calm down. I'm going to give you the formula. OK?"

Jane looked at her blankly.

"OK?"

Jane nodded. Icho let go and went back to her bag, tipping its contents out and picking up the formula. She climbed back into the shower and injected Jane. Icho sat next to her, holding her. "It's going to be OK."

Jane began to calm, the shaking lessening.

"We'll figure this out." Icho cradled Jane, holding her head against her chest. "It'll all be OK. We can figure this out together."

"*Inex,*" said Icho internally. "*What was that? What is it?*"

"*An anomaly.*"

Icho almost laughed. Jane's breathing had steadied and Icho stroked her hair. They heard the other Jane walking around, talking to her Inex. Jane stiffened and pulled out of Icho's embrace, backing away into the corner of the shower. She stared wide-eyed at the door.

Icho got up and stood by the door, listening. They were both silent, staring at each other as they heard the other Jane walking down the hallway. The front door opened and closed. There was silence.

"We'll figure it out," said Icho, pacing. "We'll figure this out."

"The door girl," said Jane.

"What?"

"What if she speaks to it?"

"I don't know," said Icho. "We can't do anything about that."

"There's a screen. At the door." Jane gestured to the hall. "You can see the main entrance and vestibule. You'll be able to see if they speak."

Icho went into the hallway and checked the screen. She saw the other Jane exit the lift and walk through the vestibule. The door girl came out of her booth and said something to her, but she blanked her, walking straight out the door. The door girl stood for a moment, staring at the exit, shaking her head, talking to herself.

Icho went back into the bathroom. "You blanked her. Walked right past."

"It," said Jane.

"It."

"It's not me." Jane stood and gingerly peeled off her clothes, dropping them in the corner of the shower. Her back to Icho, she turned the shower on.

"I know," said Icho, staring at Jane as the water snaked down her body. "But what was it, Jane? What was that?"

Jane turned round, standing directly beneath the showerhead, the force of it cutting through the dirt and blood. She stared at Icho from beneath the water. "Can I have some privacy?"

"Jane–"

"Leave me alone, Icho."

Icho nodded, gathered up her things, and left. She headed to the sitting room but collapsed in the hallway. On her hands and knees, on eye-level with her Inex, she said, "What was that?"

"An anomaly."

Icho laughed. Sitting down, she leaned against the wall, head tilted back, eyes closed.

Still dripping water from the shower, Jane looked at herself in the mirror above the sink, examining the bruises, wounds, and scars across her face and body; injuries from the cops and the raid, others at various stages of healing from allergic reactions. The wounds from the latest attacks were seeping blood, mingling with the water, snaking down her body. She was still shaking, but from exhaustion and hunger. She leaned closer to the mirror and pulled at the skin beneath her eye, examining her bloodshot eyeball, rolling it round in the socket. She sneered at herself, lips creeping back, exposing the inside of her mouth. She looked at her bleeding gums, the blood lining the edges of her teeth. She examined the holes where three had had fallen out, two near the back on the right, one on the left near the front. She closed her mouth and sucked the blood, tasting it on her tongue.

She stepped away from the mirror and towelled herself dry. She wiped at one of the HSA wounds on her forearm, blood soaking into the towel. Dropping it, she stared at the wound and pushed at the edges with her forefinger. Blood seeped up as her Inex said, "I can help seal it."

Jane shook her head as she smeared the blood across her arm then pushed the tip of her finger into the wound.

"I advise against putting appendages in your wounds."

Jane stopped and looked up, scanning the bathroom, opening cupboards and rummaging until she found tweezers.

"I advise against–"

"Shut up."

The Inex was silent. Its eyes flashed a warning red as Jane pushed the tweezers into the wound, digging, searching, her face contorted with pain. She stopped. As blood poured out, Jane stared at it in surprise, as if it was unexpected. Her Inex climbed up her body, holding a hand towel. It tried to stem the bleeding as Jane batted at it, dropping the tweezers.

The door opened, and Icho walked in wearing a green silk robe, her hair still wet from the shower.

"I brought you some fresh clo–"

Jane looked up, staggered, and collapsed. The Inex was knocked off her arm, the bloodsoaked towel tumbling on top of it. Icho dropped the clothes and fell to her knees, grabbing at Jane's gushing arm, her hands sliding in the blood. Jane was shaking, wide-eyed with shock. Icho lay her down and grabbed the towel from the now-upright Inex. She wrapped it tightly around Jane's arm.

"What happened? Inex, what happened?" She stared at it, waiting for an answer. It flashed its eyes red in response. "Answer me!" said Icho, pressing on the sodden towel. "Jane, stay with me, OK?"

"I can't go through this again," said Icho internally. *"I can't."*

"Her Inex can't speak," said Icho's. *"She must have asked for silence."*

"Get the Ino. Now." Aloud, she said, "Jane? Jane, can you speak? Tell your Inex it can talk now. Can you do that for me?"

Jane looked up at Icho, confusion in her eyes.

"Repeat after me, Jane – 'Inex, speak'."

"Inex," Jane whispered. "Speak."

"Jane put tweezers into her wound," said Jane's Inex. "She was searching."

Icho stared at it, mouth open, then looked down at Jane, her grip firm on the towel around her arm.

"Searching? Searching for what?"

Jane's eyes opened and closed. Her head rolled slowly from side to side.

"She needs hospital or MedEx attention," said Jane's Inex.

"We can't. The Ino's basic first aid will have to do."

The Ino entered and Icho lifted the towel away. "Scan, clean, and patch wound."

The Ino immediately did as asked, the procedure over within seconds, surprising Icho. She sighed and rocked back on her heels, squeezing her eyes shut and rubbing them. She asked the Inex for an assessment and it reeled off Jane's stats. "I don't need to know all that – just tell me she's OK."

"The wound will heal. She needs rest and sustenance – vitwater and a small meal. I'll get the vitwater," said Jane's Inex, walking out of the bathroom.

"Ino," said Icho, "what model are you? How do you have advanced first aid capabilities?"

"I am model RT G40. I have not been released yet – Jason Bennington ordered me for Jane. I have the First Aid level of a CR79 MedEx."

"Right. Nothing but the best for Jane, thank bliss. Ino, prepare us both a meal. Wait… are you able to monitor the door of the building?"

"Yes."

"Good. Tell me if you see Jane return."

"Jane is here."

"I– Yes, I know that– Just tell me if you see Jane use the door of the building."

The Ino agreed and left to prepare a meal. Icho lifted Jane back into the shower, gently leaning her against the tiles. The Inex returned with the vitwater and Icho got in the shower, helping her drink. When she finished, Jane leaned her head back against the tiles, looking at Icho with a deadened gaze that frightened her. Icho turned away, got out of the shower, and leaned back in, taking hold of the nozzle. Turning the water on, she was relieved when Jane closed her eyes and bowed her head, sitting passively as Icho washed off the blood. When she was clean, Icho helped her out and bundled her up in a towel. She took her through to the sitting room and laid her down on the couch. She told Jane she was going to get cleaned up and asked Jane's Inex to alert her if she was needed.

"I need Jane's consent."

"I give it," said Jane quietly before turning away and scrunching herself into a ball, hugging her legs.

CHAPTER 4

Jane woke a couple of hours later, body aching. She sat up, wincing. Icho was sitting next to her, wearing her own clothes again, freshly laundered by the Ino.

"How're you feeling?"

"Hungry."

"Good," said Icho. "The Ino prepared something – I'll get it to heat it up. I've already eaten, but I didn't want to wake you."

Jane nodded and stood up. "I'm going to get dressed."

"Can you manage?"

"I can manage," said Jane, walking slowly up the stairs, her Inex ahead of her.

After instructing the Ino, Icho paced the room, looking at Jane's books, picking up and putting down various ornaments. She lifted a hefty gold statuette in the shape of an Inex, an award presented to Jane by the Shelley Institute for advances in science and technology. She remembered watching the award ceremony several years ago, cheering when Jane's name was announced. Icho put it down and glanced upstairs.

"She's fine," said Icho's Inex. "Her Inex would alert me if not."

"I know," said Icho, pacing the room again.

Despite her Inex's reassurance, Icho was about to go up to check on her when Jane came down the stairs, dressed in black trousers and a black blouse, her Inex walking down the bannister.

"How are you feeling?"

"Fine."

"You look better, at least."

"You mean not covered in dirt and blood?" she said as she poured herself a vitwater.

"You pulled that look off pretty well."

She smiled and walked through to the dining room with Icho, their Inexes following. A plate of roast beef, broccoli and salad was waiting for Jane.

"You're not eating?"

"I already had mine, while you were sleeping."

"Right. You said." She took a bite of the beef and as she chewed, said, "Oh, bliss. Proper food. You wouldn't believe–"

"*You need to chew properly to aid digestion,*" said Jane's Inex internally. "*It's better to talk after you have chewed and swallowed.*"

"You wouldn't believe," said Jane, ignoring her Inex, "the slop they gave us to eat in the ghetto."

"I can imagine," said Icho, watching Jane shovel the food in her mouth.

"*After the trauma you have experienced, the lack of food, and the vomiting, it would be better for you to eat slowly,*" said Jane's Inex. "*You don't want to be sick again.*"

Jane frowned at her Inex, and relented, chewing slowly, taking smaller mouthfuls. Icho let Jane eat in peace. She looked round the dining room, glancing at Jane's framed degree and award certificates, lingering on the two abstract paintings opposite her, then fixing on the display cabinet just behind Jane; it contained Inex parts and old Inex models, all on plinths or in bell jars.

"Ino, bring me a glass of wine."

"Is that such a good idea?" said Icho, turning back to Jane.

"You're my keeper, are you?"

"No, I just– We need to discuss things. I need you with a clear head."

"I'm not planning on getting drunk, Icho. And what is there to discuss?"

"Oh, I don't know, maybe the fact you have a–" she paused, brow furrowed, "–a doppelgänger, or whatever the hell it is, and what the hell we're going to do."

"Nothing to discuss. I'm going to kill it and get my life back. That's all."

The Ino brought Jane's glass of wine and she took it, holding it under her nose and inhaling before taking a sip.

"Shouldn't we at least talk about you trying to kill yourself?"

Jane snorted, almost spitting out her wine. "Oh, God."

"I don't see what's so funny."

"You really think I was trying to kill myself?"

"I don't know, Jane. What am I supposed to think?"

"I admit," said Jane pausing, unable to look at Icho, "I was checking…"

"Checking what?"

"To see if I was human." Jane looked down at her plate, stabbing her fork into the beef.

Icho raised her eyebrows and leaned back. "I'm not sure that's much better."

"Jane only had to ask me and I would have confirmed her human status," said Jane's Inex.

They both turned to stare at it, sat on the edge of the table next to Jane, legs crossed and hands resting on them as if it was meditating.

"It's true, OK. A little moment of craziness." She waved her fork. "I was exhausted, wasn't thinking straight. I'm fine now."

"You're sure?"

Jane nodded. "I'm fine, aren't I, Inex?"

"I can confirm Jane is no longer uncertain of her humanity. Her thinking is clearer now that she's had sleep and sustenance. However, her plan to kill the doppelgänger goes against my advice."

"It walks in that door," Jane said, taking another sip of

wine. "I'm going to kill it. I'll cut its head off. I'll take out its eyes." She pushed her chair back, stood slowly, wary of her rib, and walked over to the Inex display cabinet. "And I'll put them in here. Right there." She tapped the glass cabinet with her fork.

"I don't even know how to respond to that."

"I'm taking my life back. This – all of this – it's *mine*."

"Jane…"

Jane looked at her reflection in the glass cabinet and said, "It has my skin. I'm taking it back."

"You can't just– Jane, we need to work this out. You can't let your emotions control how you react to this."

Jane turned on her, eyes narrowed. "I know *exactly* what I'm doing."

Icho looked away. Even after all that had happened, she struggled not to feel intimidated by her. Exhausted, she considered acquiescing, letting Jane do as she pleased and seeing how things unfolded. Icho's Inex was about to interrupt her thoughts when she looked up at Jane and said, "We don't even know what it is, how it exists. Don't you care?"

Jane looked deflated and sat down, still grasping the fork.

"Jane?"

Jane sighed, dropped the fork onto her plate, and leaned back. "I know what it is."

Icho stared at her. "What?"

"Privacy Setting Five."

Icho looked at her, dumbfounded, and laughed. "Privacy Setting? Are you–" she stopped and shook her head.

"Icho–"

"Are you kidding me? Who am I going to tell? I'm on the run, for bliss sake."

"Circumstances change. If you want me to tell you anything, you have to accept."

Icho stood and walked over to the dining room window. She paused, looking out, then turned her back to it and leaned on the sill. She looked at Jane and told her Inex to implement the privacy setting. She waited, watching Jane take a drink of wine.

"Well?"

"It was The Company."

"What?"

"We're developing humanoid cyborgs. Who else did you think would do it?"

Icho shook her head. "No, you can't be. It's illegal. The legislation the Christian Coalition lobbied for…"

Jane nodded, swirling the wine in her glass.

"You went ahead anyway," said Icho. "Jesus, Jane. That's a huge risk."

"There's stringent safeguards, but yes, you're right."

"Does Caddick know?"

"He led it."

"No, he– What do you mean he *led* it? What about the legislation? All his speeches."

"Just lip service to keep the CC happy."

"Well, isn't that… I mean, that's a way we can take him down."

Jane shook her head. "He led Daedalus, but there's no trail. Nothing connecting him. The Company would go down. Everything I built."

"Wait," said Icho, moving away from the sill and standing by the table. "He led what?"

"The Daedalus Project."

Icho told Jane she'd overheard her predecessor, Dr West, mention it to Caddick. "I didn't know what it was. I'd never seen Caddick so on edge."

"How the hell did West find out about it?"

"I don't know."

They were both silent for a minute as Icho paced the dining room, thinking it through. She stopped at the Inex cabinet, staring at a selection of eye chips. "This is… Shit, Jane. I can't believe–" She turned away from the cabinet and gripped the back of one of the chairs. "How many are there?"

"Thirteen. All fully functional, tested in the field."

"In the field? But… that's illegal."

"It's all illegal."

Icho sat down again. "There's humanoid cyborgs out there now?" she said, gesturing to the city beyond the dining room window.

Jane nodded.

"But the risks…"

"I know the risks. We've already had a close call – a news presenter didn't work out. She had a breakdown. Her handler got too involved. He's dead, she was…" Jane sighed, placed her wine glass on the table. "Adjusted. So to speak."

"The cyborg had a breakdown?"

"We're not clear why, so we stepped up monitoring on the others."

"What do you mean by breakdown?"

Jane shrugged. "Not sure, exactly. A mismatch between her sense of self and her new body. She knew something wasn't right."

"An existential crisis?"

"You could say that," said Jane with a wry smile.

Icho laughed, shaking her head. "This is so absurd. What– Who are they?"

"I can't tell you, Icho."

"But how does it work? You invented a whole history? Birth certificates, fake family photos?"

Jane stared at her, waiting a few seconds to see if she'd get there herself, then smiled and shook her head. "You're not getting it, are you?"

"What do you–?"

"They already came with all that."

Icho frowned, confused, staring at Jane as she took another drink of wine. Icho thought of Jane's doppel, when she saw it in the bedroom, taking Jane's clothes out of the wardrobe. She leaned back in her chair. "You *replaced* people?"

Jane nodded, placing her glass on the table. "We had a husband who said his wife 'wasn't the same' after her illness. We manipulated them into therapy and things settled. The only worry about that is there shouldn't be any signs. That's the aim – avoid the uncanny valley, avoid any unease. Caddick's endgame is to perfect them, alter them, but if you alter one thing it has a knock-on effect. We were in the middle of working through that when..." Jane trailed off, her eyes glazing.

"You fell ill."

"I fell ill," said Jane scratching at the edge of the table. "And now there's a brand new me."

"Do they know?"

"Does who know?"

"The cyborgs? Do they know what they are?"

"Of course not."

"So she thinks she's you."

"It."

"It thinks it's you."

"Caddick had my Inex Mnemo core – I even helped him open it, that sonofabitch. People don't realise how vulnerable they are, what their Inex – The Company – has access to. Your physical stats, conscious thoughts, what's beneath, the Möbius loop of emotions and the body, your history in every fine detail, the recordings – every moment of your life. They don't think of all that – the Inex is just an expensive toy, a servant, a pet. They take it for granted, not understanding it knows them better than they know themselves. I'm sure you remember," Jane said, pausing, picking up her glass, gently swirling the wine, "I had to pull back in the early models – most people didn't like Inexes telling them things directly. It unnerved them. It made more sense to make it a conversation, where things would unfold naturally, where an Inex would suggest things, explore things with you. We don't know how much of ourselves we've trusted to these glorified pets."

Icho was silent, thinking. She looked up at Jane. "What if someone discovers what the doppels are?"

"Hasn't happened."

"But what if–"

Jane raised an eyebrow.

"They're removed," said Icho, her voice flat.

"The doppels are closely monitored. Along with family, friends, colleagues. There's only been one instance so far – the news presenter, and it was her handler. We didn't expect that, didn't see that coming. He got too involved with her."

"And now he's gone."

"And now he's gone," said Jane, nodding.

"What if the doppels discover what they are?"

"Hasn't happened. Almost with the presenter, but we brought her in. She doesn't remember any of that now."

Icho got the Ino to bring her a drink and she sat quietly nursing the gin, thinking things over as Jane finished her meal.

"Be The Best You," said Icho, looking at Jane. "It was inevitable, wasn't it?"

Jane nodded.

"But what was the plan? What's the point of them? The legislation would–"

"Replace all the key players who aren't on side. Keep the focus on the Seraphs as the enemy. Slowly work towards making humanoid cyborgs seem normal, necessary, and inevitable. An answer to mortality. No one has to die anymore. Apart from deviants. They satisfy our morbidity, our death drive."

"But the Christian Coalition."

"Caddick was working on them. Promised me they wouldn't be a problem."

"But why did Caddick have me working on HellSans allergy treatment?"

"This isn't going to happen overnight, and he needs control. Having treatment for the allergy, getting there before anyone else does, it's a clever move. He can pretend compassion, but it's about driving a wedge between the anti-cure Seraphs and regular HSAs. He's manipulating them. The formula effects are temporary, lasting a few hours – the deviants will be reliant on a regular supply. He'll exploit that."

Icho knocked back her gin and put her head in her hands. She looked up and stared past Jane to the Inex display cabinet. "Milligan," said Icho, focussing on Jane, "He's real?"

Jane laughed. "He's human, if that's what you mean."

"Surely–"

"It's too early. There's still a lot of work to do. Replacing key players will be a lot further down the line. At least, that was the plan, but here we are."

"Do you think Caddick planned this? Your replacement? Or it's a response to what happened?"

"I don't know," said Jane, frowning at her empty wine glass. "But he's not getting away with it – I'm getting my life back."

"You always get what you want."

Jane eyed her, unable to work out if Icho was mocking her. She nodded, leaned back in her chair and said, "I do."

"But right now we need to get somewhere safe."

"We are somewhere safe."

"Until the doppel returns."

"And I kill it."

"You can't be serious, Jane."

"Of course I'm serious. You think I'm going to let that thing walk around with my face?"

"Jane," said Icho, sighing. "You can't kill it. We can't stay here."

"I kill it, get my life back, bring down Caddick."

"Jane, you're HSA. You can't just go back – you'll end up tossed in the ghetto again."

"I can handle it. You don't think I can fake being me?"

"Not with the allergy."

"I have the formula, I'll be fine."

Icho bowed her head and looked down at her hands, picking at loose skin around a nail.

"Icho?"

Icho shook her head. She looked up at Jane. "I used the last of it in the bathroom."

"What?"

"You have twenty-four hours at most."

Jane's expression fell. She frowned. "Twenty-four hours?"

"I'm sorry, Jane, I–"

"Goddamnit, Icho!" Jane stood, knocking her chair over. She turned her back on Icho and pressed her palm on the display cabinet, leaning her forehead against it.

"Look, it'll be OK. We hole up in an HSA hostel, you get me to Milligan, he can set me up with a lab and I'll make more formula. Once you have a supply, then sure, get close to Caddick, get what you need and expose him. But you can't do it now – it's too risky. You're not going to be able to control your allergy, however much seriffed mantras might dampen it. And look at you, your face – that's going to take time to heal."

Jane raised her head and looked at her reflection in the glass, examining the still-healing wounds. "I'm not staying in a deviant dive," she said to her reflection. "And I'm not relying on that communist prick." She turned, picked up her wine glass, and walked out of the dining room.

"Jane–"

Icho rose to follow her, but stopped and hovered as her Inex said, *"I advise leaving her to think things through."*

She went over to the display cabinet, examining the Inexes and Inex parts, thinking about the Daedalus Project, trying to imagine how it must feel to have a copy of yourself out in the world. She stood there for a few minutes, looking at an array of eye chips, considering the future Jane and Caddick had planned.

She went through to the sitting room and found Jane by the window, sipping her wine, gazing out at the hotel opposite. "Jane," she said gently. "You know I'm right. And we're at an advantage – Caddick thinks you're dead. We don't want to blow that."

Jane didn't respond, but held her glass out for the Ino to top up. She stared out the window for another few minutes, and Icho sat down on the couch, trying to figure out how she could persuade her when Jane turned round and said, "I have a place we can stay. And I can get you set up with a lab."

Surprised, Icho leaned forward, frowning, staring at Jane's silhouette, trying to see her expression. "Where?"

"James – you met him at the reception. I have access to his place. He has a lab in the basement, where he works on Inex tech – I'm sure it can be easily adapted to suit your needs."

Icho was silent, considering. Jane turned and gazed out the window again. The sunlight hit the window of the room where Milligan had stayed, turning it into a sheet of burning light. Jane squinted and tried to keep fixed on it, feeling it sear into her. She scrunched her eyes closed, then opened them and focused on the street below, the light still with her, obscuring whatever she looked at.

"This is where it all started," she said.

"What?"

"You know the story, don't you? You must have seen the news."

"Right," said Icho, standing. She walked over to Jane and looked out at the hotel, thinking of Jaw. "You saw it all from here?"

Jane nodded. "The moment my life was ruined," she said, the light shimmering, starting to fade.

Icho immediately backed away and paced by the bookshelves. "Jane–"

"*I calculate a high probability she will turn on you,*" said Icho's

Inex internally. *"You need each other. It's too much of a risk to tell her of your involvement."*

"What?"

"I just…" said Icho as her Inex repeated the risk. "How far?"

"How far what?"

"James's place. We really should get going. We don't know when she – it – will be back."

Jane nodded and turned to face Icho, the patches of light partially obscuring her before fading to nothing. They discussed their plans. James's place was twenty minutes on foot; the journey wouldn't be too risky if they took precautions. The Ino held an inventory of items in the apartment, so Jane would have to change back into the ghetto raider clothes. She ordered it to launder and repair them while she helped Icho shave off her distinctive orange hair. When her clothes were ready, she got changed as the Ino cleaned and tidied the apartment, erasing any trace of their presence. They tied black scarves round each other's necks. Jane pulled hers up over the lower half of her face as Icho hiked her bag onto her shoulder.

"The door girl?" said Icho.

"We can use the back exit," said Jane. "Let's go."

Icho pulled the scarf up over her nose as Jane took a last look at her apartment. She watched the Ino cleaning the dirt and blood she'd smeared on the couch.

"You'll be back," said her Inex.

"I know."

They walked out into the city.

CHAPTER 5

Jane and Icho walked through the streets, Jane in the black clothes she'd taken from the dead raider, Icho in khaki trousers, grey top and black jacket, scarves wound round the lower half of their faces. Mistaking them for privacy obsessives, people stared at them, eyes narrowed, shaking their heads.

"If they knew who you were…" said Icho.

"I know. It's absurd."

They passed an Arachnid Alliance demo outside one of The Company's Inex shops. As they tried to skirt round the demonstrators, one of them pressed forward, thrusting a leaflet into Jane's hands.

"Care about your privacy?" said the man. "You should care about Jane Ward's destruction of our ecosystem. Hundreds of species of spider are going extinct because of the Inex's supposed 'eco-friendly battery' – don't buy into Ward's propaganda. The Company only care about their profits."

Jane was about to pull her scarf down and lay into the campaigner when Icho took her arm and yanked her away. In Icho's grip, pulled backwards through the crowd, Jane tore up the leaflet, throwing it back at him. The man had turned his attention to another passerby and the pieces fell unnoticed by anyone other than a street Ino that hoovered it up.

"Unblissed hippy arsehole," said Jane.

"Were you really going to get into a confrontation? Given our situation?"

Ignoring Icho, Jane continued on, hunched over, hands in

pockets, staring straight ahead in an attempt to avoid all the HellSans dominating the street.

"You can look at the HellSans. It won't have an effect."

"It makes me twitchy," said Jane.

They were silent as they continued along the street, Icho noticing that Jane had gradually unhunched and was allowing herself to look at the typeface. Jane abruptly stopped in the middle of the street.

"What is it?"

Jane stared up at a shop's huge neon sign in HellSans.

"Jane?"

Jane turned to Icho and said, "What do you mean?"

"What do I mean, what?"

"About HellSans – you said it won't have any effect."

"That's right. The formula should–"

"No effect whatsoever?"

"Jane," said Icho, eyeing the irritated man who swerved to avoid them. "We shouldn't be talking about this in the middle of–"

Jane grabbed Icho by her jacket, pulling her close. "I'm *unblissed?* You turn people unblissed? What fucking good is that, Icho?"

"Don't use my name." Icho struggled to get out of Jane's grip. "You need to calm down."

"Don't tell me to calm down."

"People are watching."

Jane glanced around. Icho was right; people were stopping, watching, their Inexes recording, a tension in the air as they looked on, disgusted, but hoping for spectacle.

"Look, we need to get to– We can talk when we're there."

Jane, face inches from Icho's, held her there a few seconds before loosening her grip. She pushed Icho away and she staggered into a couple of the voyeurs who shrank back from her, disgusted, cursing. Jane strode on ahead through the disappointed murmurs of the crowd and Icho followed. She kept a few paces behind, hoping Jane's anger would dissipate by the time they arrived.

James's house was just off a busy thoroughfare, tucked away in a quiet square with a small park at the centre. Icho caught up with Jane as they walked through the park to the other side of the square. Jane eye-scanned when they arrived.

"You have eye-scan entry?"

"I used to stay here a lot," said Jane as they walked in.

"Wow," said Icho. "What the–"

It was chaos, Inexes everywhere. They made their way through the hall to the sitting room to find more. Most were inert, some were latched onto the walls and ceiling.

"What the actual hell?" Icho stared at the Inexes crawling over their indolent comrades. The inactive Inexes were in various states of disrepair; some with the biological components rooted out, others in pieces. An Inex in the corner teemed with maggots, passing Inexes dipping in for a snack.

Jane shrugged. "It's just James," she said. "The way his mind works. Always jumping from one thing to another, trying out different things on different models. I gave him permission to take his work home, but he spends most of his time at The Company anyway, and in his absence this place gets out of hand. He usually has a clear-out every six months – has to bring everything to The Company to have it properly disposed of, or to see if any of it can be salvaged." Jane picked up an Inex with no head and examined it. "I probably should have clamped down on this."

Jane dropped it and waded through them, their bodies cracking beneath her. She leaned down and swept Inex parts off the couch. Sitting, she gestured for Icho to join her. Icho moved more carefully through the Inexes, trying to push them aside instead of crushing them, and sat next to Jane, removing her scarf.

"How is this possible?" She motioned to all the Inexes

crawling round the room. "I mean, they shouldn't be operating on their own."

"James pretty much has free rein when it comes to Inex development. There's no distance limit on these, but they can't leave his apartment."

"No distance limit? But they're connected – to who?"

"James. Who else?"

"*All* of them?"

"Technically they're filtered through his own Inex, which monitors them on the side, but we've been experimenting with how much humans can cope with multiple input."

"Surely that's not gone well. No human could cope with that."

"Plasticity," said Jane. "We can adjust."

"But we're not built for that amount of sensory input, we can't cope with that level of attention."

"You'd be surprised," said Jane. "And it's not necessarily us, as we are, who will have to cope."

It took Icho a moment before she understood. "Daedalus. Right, of course."

Jane tilted her head and stared up at an Inex on the ceiling. "Encrypt, and tell James I'm here. Tell him to keep it to himself and get straight over to me. And tell him… if he sees me at The Company, not to talk to me and to come here anyway."

Jane stood and went through to the kitchen. She opened the fridge to find beer and condiments. She took two beers and went back to the sitting room, handing one to Icho. They sat in silence, drinking, Jane watching their Inexes eat from the maggot banquet.

Icho looked round the room. Inex detritus aside, it was like a teen rocker had stormed a generic showroom; cream skirting and light-grey walls with mediocre abstract art surrounded by huge haphazard band posters, the corners peeling. The posters were mainly bands from the previous century, only a couple more recent. Opposite the couch was a large white bookshelf, two shelves crammed with books, most filled with records, and one piled with Inex parts next to the same Inex award Jane had in pride of place in her apartment, this one on its side, barely visible beneath wires and a cascade of Inex eye chips.

Below the bookshelf was a matching white table with a large record player, and next to that a pale grey seat covered in inert Inexes. The wall beside the bookshelf was dominated by huge windows, the blinds the same pale grey. Behind the couch, the sitting room merged into an open plan kitchen, a table in the middle with thick dark wooden legs and a deep-grey marble top, strewn with more inert Inexes and empty beer bottles.

"How long has James been living here?"

"Almost a decade, but he's barely here. He didn't change a thing when he moved in, just stuck up the posters and organised his precious record collection."

Jane looked at one of the more recent band posters, the band's name in HellSans. She remembered the furore when a member of the band fell ill with the allergy and was tossed in the ghetto; their fellow band members lobbied to get them out and added faux spraypainted serifs to all their merchandise, causing massive controversy.

"I'll get my bliss back," said Jane, still staring at the poster.

Icho swigged her beer and said, "There's nothing wrong with being unblissed."

Jane turned to face her. "I've gone from one deviancy to another, Icho."

"It's not difficult being unblissed," said Icho, turning away, looking at the pale bleached-blond woman on the poster in front of her. "You just have to learn to fake it."

"How the hell do you know?"

Icho turned back to Jane, but didn't respond, watching realisation dawn.

"You're unblissed."

Icho nodded. "Helped me develop the formula – I studied myself, looking at what made me immune to HellSans."

"Does Caddick know?"

"That I'm unblissed?"

"That the formula makes people unblissed."

"No. He wouldn't have approved that."

"No. He wouldn't." Jane put her empty beer bottle on the coffee table amongst Inex corpses. "Anything else you're not telling me?"

Icho was about to respond amidst internal protests from her Inex, when the main door opened and closed. Jane jumped up and ran into the hall. She hugged James and walked him into the sitting room, her arm hooked through his, James asking how she got here before him. "I saw you as I left the–" he said, stopping as he walked into the room and saw Icho. "Who's this?"

"Dr Ichorel Smith. You met her at the reception, remember?"

James shook his head and Jane said, "Well, your mind was on the HR woman. How did it go with her?"

James didn't reply. He stared at Icho, who stood and held out her hand. James hesitated, took her hand briefly, and turned back to Jane who was now sitting on the couch smiling up at him. He asked what was going on, but she interrupted. "Did you speak to me?"

"What?"

"At The Company, when you saw me."

"You know I didn't."

He fiddled with the hem of his black shirt, the other hand in the pocket of his black jeans. He stared at them both from behind a curtain of hair. He looked like he was going to say something before suddenly walking off, disappearing into the kitchen, returning with beer for each of them. He placed the bottles on the coffee table and cleared his chair of Inex parts, sitting opposite Jane and Icho.

"Can we…" he said, glancing at Icho. "Can we talk in private?"

"She knows everything, James."

"*Everything*?"

"More or less."

"That's dangerous, Jane."

"We can trust her."

James looked at Icho, took a swig of beer, and turned back to Jane. "Are you having trouble with your handler?" he said. "Is that what this is about? I told Caddick your handler's an arsehole."

"Does she know?" said Jane.

"Does who know what?"

"It. Does it know it's not human?"

"What are you–?"

"It's not me, James."

"It's–" James's eyes widened as he sat forward, fixed on her. He pushed his hair back. "Jane?"

She nodded.

"Shit," said James, standing, crushing Inex parts underfoot. "You're alive. You're still alive?"

"What did he tell you?"

He crouched down next to her, examining her face, his hand on her leg. "Caddick said the Seraphs murdered you."

"What else?"

"He didn't want anyone to know." He reached up and stroked her cheek. "It's really you?"

"It is."

He stood, returned to his seat, downed the rest of his beer, and dropped it amongst the Inex detritus. "Shit, Jane," he said, looking up, tears in his eyes. "I'm sorry."

"It's not your fault."

"It is, I didn't question him. He wanted you replaced as soon as possible and I just got straight to work."

"Did he say what happened?"

"No. I asked, but he just said the Seraphs killed you, told me to keep this secret – work on it alone and keep him updated."

"That sonofabitch."

"Shit," he said, his elbows on his thighs, leaning forward with his head in his hands. "I thought you'd died. I thought I was doing the right thing."

"You didn't know," said Jane.

He looked up, his head still in his hands. "So what did happen?"

"He tried to have me murdered."

"What?" said James, shaking his head. "That's not– I don't–" He scowled, clenching and unclenching his hand. He turned on Icho. "Why is she here? What's she got to do with all this?"

"She helped me, got me out of the ghetto."

"What the hell were you doing in the ghetto?"

Jane looked away, not responding, and Icho said, "She's HSA."

James laughed, but sobered when he saw they weren't laughing with him. "Are you serious?"

"I won't be like this for long. Icho is–"

"Look–" said James, holding up his hand, "Can we just... stop for a moment? I can't, I mean... How are you HSA?" Jane was about to speak when he said, "No, don't. Just give me a moment. Shit."

He stood again, pacing the room awkwardly before stomping on an inert Inex, crushing part of its torso.

"James..."

"How are you HSA?" he said, the distress clear in his voice.

"Just– I can tell you everything, but... James, we need a place to stay."

He looked over at her, frowning and nodding. "Of course," he said, "of course." He held his arms open. "This place is yours. I'm always at The Company... I'll get all this cleaned up."

"You know you shouldn't let things get like this," said Jane, looking around.

He nodded and sat down. He looked at Jane through his hair. "They cannibalise each other, you know."

"Makes sense."

"They what?" said Icho.

"You have this many Inexes, trapped, don't feed them, the insect and arachnid population diminishes… They cannibalised the dead. Opened them up and consumed the contents of their bio-generator, then ate the muscles. And the rotting bodies attracted flies. That's how these ones survived."

"That's…" said Icho, looking up at an Inex on the ceiling. "Interesting."

"Most people would be disgusted," said James.

"She isn't most people. When can you get the clean-up crew in?"

"Now, if you like. But tell me what happened. I need to understand what the hell's been going on."

"It's a long story," said Jane.

"I'll get more beer."

When Jane finished recounting, James was silent for a minute, chewing on his nails. "Shit." He gripped his empty bottle, knuckles white. "You *died*."

"My own personal Jesus brought me back to life," she said, smiling at Icho.

Jane tried to steer James towards plans for clearing the apartment and setting up a lab, but he wouldn't move on from the cops who'd beaten her up. He asked for their details, determined to hack their Inexes, ruin them. "They could have killed you."

"James, they were doing their job."

"Doing their–"

"You know it. I know it."

James's face turned red and he shook his head, "But this is different, this is–"

"They aren't our priority, James. We need a place to stay and some lab equipment for Icho to make a new supply of formula."

He nodded, peeling at the beer bottle label. "I hate that they hurt you."

"I'm here, aren't I?"

He nodded, looking up at her. "I'll get an Ino team in to clear all this out. I'll lock you in the basement until they're gone. I'll get whatever supplies you need. No problem."

Jane smiled and Icho said, "Never thought I'd be pleased to be locked in a stranger's basement."

"And what's your story?" said James, frowning at her.

"My story?" said Icho, startled the conversation had turned to her. "Jane just told you – Caddick hired me, it looked like he was going to screw me over, so I ran. After what happened to her, I figured Jane was my safe route to Milligan."

James tucked his hair behind his ears, his intense gaze fixed on Icho. "That's all?"

"That's all," she said, nodding, turning to Jane, giving her an uneasy smile.

"OK," he said, standing and spreading his arms. "Welcome to your new home."

He smiled and Jane laughed, standing up to hug him. "It's a shithole, James. There's maggots, for bliss sake."

"I know, I know…"

Icho watched them; their friendship conjuring a rare warmth and ease in Jane. They fooled around, singing some song and dancing on the crushed Inexes. Jane looked down at Icho, smiling, reaching out for her to join them. She smiled back, shaking her head, and sat clutching her beer, feeling nauseous with guilt.

CHAPTER 6

James sent in an army of Inos and got the Inexes cleared and the flat cleaned that afternoon. He delivered Icho's requested lab equipment the next day and she got to work in the basement. The plan was to produce a sample to take to Milligan, along with the details for the patent – Jane would personally deliver it, not trusting to send it via Inex, even encrypted, when Caddick was sure to have Milligan monitored. While Milligan worked on getting the formula ready for mass production, Icho would produce enough to keep Jane supplied. When Jane was well enough, she'd take her doppel's place to get to Caddick.

James had delivered new Inexes for them, the latest model, but Jane's didn't recognise her as human and wouldn't connect. Icho declined hers, despite Jane's insistence she should have the best Inex to help her with her work; she didn't want to be connected to something that could potentially harm Jane. James sent over earlier models and Jane kept the others, using James's tools to take them apart, a welcome distraction while Icho was busy in the lab. She spent the rest of her time reading James's pre-HellSans books and attempting workouts, despite her rib, trying to get back into a routine. She visualised a new mantra with added serifs: "I'll get my life back, I'll bring down Caddick", chanting it as she obsessed over the news, sweating, shaking, and gritting her teeth, eyes fixed on the HellSans in the scrolling chyron, Icho admonishing her – "Jane, it's a biological illness. Serifs, mantras, and willpower aren't going to cure you." She gave Icho a foul look and turned back to watch Caddick announce the date for his party's political rally on the lead up to the election.

By the fourth day, after three bad allergic reactions, and under advisement from her Inex, Jane finally opted for audio. She listened as her doppel gave a soundbite about the upcoming Inex model, and followed the coverage on the ghetto post-raid; rumours that it was to be moved instead of rebuilt dominated reports. There was a short piece on Caddick's party's attempt to quickly push through legislation on the banning of "excessive" face coverings, and a soundbite from a privacy campaigner stating the police were already illegally stopping them, demanding they remove scarves, hats, shades, or masks, and face reccing them. Jane listened, knowing this wasn't about protestors or Seraphs; Caddick was using the police to hunt Icho down.

In the evening, Icho emerged from the lab, finding Jane curled up on the couch reading, wearing James's faded black jeans and a black Hole t-shirt.

"Nice look."

Jane shrugged. "How's work going?"

"Should be finished in a couple of days."

"Good. I'm sick of being stuck here while that thing wears my face."

"I'm working as fast as I can."

"I know. It's just frustrating."

"It won't be long."

Jane nodded and returned to her book as Icho sat next to her. Icho bent the cover, angling it so she could read the title. "*Childhood's End*," she said, her finger pressed against Jane's as she held the cover. She hovered for a moment, then pulled away, sitting back, watching Jane read. In James's clothes, burrowed into the corner of the couch, knees pulled close, surrounded by cushions, Jane didn't look like the CEO of the most successful company in the world.

"What's your attachment to those things?"

Jane frowned and continued reading in silence before looking over at Icho. "I like novels. My dad used to read to me. And this... this is a beautiful story about the end of humanity."

"How is that beautiful?"

"It just is. You should read it."

"Sounds morbid. And I don't read fiction; I only deal in facts."

Jane laughed. "The objective scientist? These influenced me, you know." She brandished the book. "These fictions contributed to the 'fact' that is the Inex."

"Then they're maybe not so bad after all. But I'm still not interested."

Jane put the book down and said, "I'm writing a book."

"Seriously? Fiction?"

"The story of my life." Jane pointed to her Inex, perched on the coffee table. "Technically it's writing it. Or was – the old one was. It was going to be one of those entrepreneur books: *BE THE BEST YOU*. Anecdotes, some Inex recordings from my life, tips on how to make it. A few retro limited-edition hardbacks for the hardcore fans, the rest released for Inexes. But now..."

"You've stopped?"

"It would be the story of my abjection and unravelling." Jane pursed her lips and shook her head.

"But that's a good story, isn't it? The drama of falling lower than most blissters can even imagine, climbing your way back to the top. They'll lap it up."

"You think so?"

"Of course."

Jane considered Icho for a moment. "Maybe."

The Ino stood in front of the couch, informing them their dinner was on the table. They ate their meal, discussing Icho's progress, Jane fantasising about the different ways she could bring down Caddick. When they finished, they returned to the sitting room and caught up on the evening news before retiring to their rooms, Icho in the guest room at the end of the hall, Jane in James's, falling asleep as she thought how Icho was right: she'd get the Inex to resume the book and chronical her story of triumph over adversity.

Sitting at the kitchen table, pouring herself coffee as she waited for the Inex to bring her muesli, Jane told Icho her encouragement had given her new purpose, her book now resumed.

"But it's your story too, you're part of it now – I want you to join me. Write it together."

"Together? You want me to co-write a book?"

Jane nodded and Icho flushed, feeling flattered while her stomach roiled with guilt. Unable to look Jane in the eye, she said, "I don't know anything about writing."

"You don't have to. We connect our Inexes and they do all the work."

Icho fiddled with her napkin and looked over at her Inex, perched on the kitchen counter next to Jane's, both eating from a Company snack pack.

"I mean, you don't have to, of course, I just thought it would bring another layer to the story. You can think about it."

Icho nodded, sipping her tea, considering all the different ways to tell Jane of her involvement in what happened to her; nothing worked, nothing sounded right. She internally discussed options with her Inex and it confirmed that telling Jane through a constructed narrative from Icho's point of view, with all the details, could be the best way to elicit Jane's empathy.

"*You need to tell her eventually.*"

"*I know,*" she replied internally as she watched it eat.

"*This could be your chance to do it right.*"

She turned to Jane. "I don't need to do anything? The Inexes write it?"

Jane nodded as she swallowed her muesli. "We'll have editorial control, but they'll have our interests in mind."

"So you connect them and they form a narrative out of our messy lives? We'll both have access? We'll both be able to read it?"

Jane nodded. "And see it and hear it – well, some of it, the recordings we have."

Icho looked at Jane, feeling nauseous. *"I hope you're right, Inex.* OK, let's do it. How long will it take?"

"To connect? Only a minute or so. The creation and merging of the narrative will take a few minutes longer. You need to tell your Inex I have permission."

Icho gave permission and said they could merge the narrative in the evening after dinner, using the formula as an excuse to delay. She went down to the basement, running through all the different reactions Jane might have, trying to steel herself.

Icho sat on the couch, finishing off her glass of wine as Jane asked the Ino to fetch James's Inex tools. She knelt on the floor, placing her Inex on the coffee table, Icho's climbing up and joining it. Jane got to work, Icho momentarily forgetting her worry as she watched, fascinated.

"It's not far off a false connect procedure."

Jane nodded as she finished up. "It's pretty close," she said, looking at Icho. "I'm impressed you know how to do that. As CEO of The Company, I should be reporting you to the Inex Division."

"Along with yourself."

"I can get away with a lot," said Jane. "Right. Internal narration OK?"

"That's fine." Icho hovered, watching her close up the Inexes. "Jane?"

"What?"

Icho looked down at her, hesitating. "Nothing, it's OK. Let's read it."

Jane smiled, got up, and sat next to her. They both lay their heads back against the couch and closed their eyes.

// "Seven a.m. and one second, two, three, four, five…" //

// Tipsy, I walked down the stairs of Caddick's country mansion, Jaw hurrying in front of me, propelled by some kind of ridiculous urgency it wouldn't tell me about. //

Jane halted the narrative, shocking Icho out of it, the Inexes telling Jane that stopping mid-sentence wasn't the best way to experience the story. She scrambled up off the couch and stood in the middle of the sitting room, all twitching energy, staring at Icho with fury and disgust.

"Jane–"

"It was *you*," said Jane, her arm shaking as she pointed at Icho. "You did this to me."

Icho stood and reached for her.

"Don't touch me." Jane raised her palms, backing away. "Don't fucking come near me."

"Look, just let me–"

"This is all your fault. All of this," she said, gesturing round the room. "All of this," she said, pressing a finger against her chest. "You ruined my life." She was shaking, still-healing HSA wounds re-opening, blood sliding down her face and arms. "When James asked what your story was… When you said that was all–"

"We," said both Inexes in unison, "thought we'd portrayed events in a way that was sympathetic to Icho. This is not her doing – this is Caddick's."

"Don't you fucking start, you traitorous little shits," she said, pointing at them. She turned back to Icho. "You *ruined* my life. You took my life from me."

Icho had gone through numerous scenarios, trying to work out how Jane would react, but none of it had prepared her. She sat back down, deflated, stunned. "Jane, I didn't mean– I didn't mean for you to get caught up in this. I didn't mean for–"

"I didn't mean, I didn't mean," said Jane, her voice a high whine. "Don't give me those puppy dog eyes. You *lied* to me."

"I didn't lie, I just didn't tell you everything," said Icho. "Then I agreed, didn't I? I agreed to be part of your story. I knew what you'd find out. Look, Jane, you're having a reaction – you need to calm down, you need to just–"

"Don't tell me what I need," said Jane, her hand pressed to her rib. "I don't want any of this – I don't want to help Milligan, or you, or goddamn deviants. I don't want any of this."

She rushed out of the room, snapping Icho out of her daze at the thought of Jane leaving the apartment, blowing their cover.

"Jane, wait!" She caught up with her in the hall. "Where are you going?"

"Away from you." Her bloody palm was pressed against the main door, her head down, trying to fight the nausea.

"Jane, you know you can't–"

Icho took hold of Jane's arm, but she jerked free and turned on her, her face all snarl and open wounds. Icho shrank away as Jane bared her teeth at her, blood dribbling, her lips cracking. Slowly backing off, Icho held up her hands in supplication as Jane's Inex climbed Jane's body and perched on her shoulder, facing Icho.

"You're exacerbating her allergic reaction," said the Inex. "It would be best if you left her alone."

Icho nodded. "You can't go out, Jane."

"She knows," said her Inex as Jane leaned against the door and slid to the ground. Shaking, her eyes closed, she slowly rocked, mumbling to herself.

"You need to leave her alone," said both Inexes simultaneously.

"OK, OK." Icho edged away, turned, and headed down the hall, back into the sitting room. She sank to the floor by the coffee table and hugged her knees.

"That didn't go well, Inex."

"It was worse than we predicted, it's true."

"She hates me."

"She doesn't hate you. She's angry."

"Did you see the way she looked at me?"

"It's complicated."

"What's complicated? What does that mean?" Icho looked up at it, perched on the edge of the couch in front of her. "Do you know what she's–? Are you connected to her?"

"To her Inex. You know that. We're writing your story."

"You know what she's feeling? Right now?"

"We do."

"She hates me," said Icho.

"She doesn't. But this rupture is good."

"What?"

"This rupture is good. It's good for the narrative. It will bring you closer together."

Icho stared at it. "Good for the–" she said, incredulous. "Just... don't talk to me. Don't talk."

She let herself fall sideways and rolled onto her back. She looked up at the ceiling, losing herself in its blankness. The Inex, crawling up the wall, came into her periphery as it ventured onto the ceiling hoovering up insects Icho couldn't see. She listened to Jane vomiting in the hallway.

CHAPTER 7

Icho woke. She rolled her head to the side and saw Jane on the couch, staring down at her. She sat up, pressing her fingers into her eyes. The sun was low, the slanting light through the windows cast long shadows, Jane's impassive face partly in darkness. They sat in silence for a while, looking at each other.

"I'm sorry," said Icho, her voice cracking.

Jane didn't respond. Icho stood and went through to the kitchen, returning with water for them both. Icho handed Jane a glass and sat next to her.

"I'm sorry."

"I know."

"I'm so sorry."

"OK. Stop apologising."

"But–"

"Just stop."

Icho nodded and they sat in silence, Icho staring out the window, watching the sun disappear behind the buildings. Jane summoned the Ino and asked it to bring a bottle of gin. She sipped her water and the last of the sunlight hit Jane's arm as she put the glass on the coffee table, the light glinting across dripping blood.

"You're bleeding."

"Always. Bleed and vomit, it's all I do."

The Ino turned on a lamp as Jane looked down at her arm and pushed at some loose skin.

"Don't," said Icho.

"It's fine. I've had worse."

Icho instructed her Inex to get James's first aid box as the Ino returned from the kitchen with a bottle of gin and two glasses. It poured them both a glass and Jane took them, handing one to Icho. She raised her glass, smiled, the wounds on her lips opening, and said, "To us."

Icho watched Jane down her drink. Icho sipped hers as the Ino poured Jane another.

"Jane..."

"I mean it," said Jane, knocking the other shot back. Jane looked at Icho. "I'm glad you did what you did."

"Jane, don't mess me around, I'm not–"

"I told you – I mean it. I know now."

"Know what?"

"About Caddick. While you slept, I read our story. All of it, this time. I've had time to–" She paused for what seemed like an eternity, but Icho waited, not wanting to push her. Jane finally looked up. "I get it, OK? I was kidding myself. It was still there – that need to go back to how it was. But I know I can't. I know that. This is a new beginning."

Jane poured herself another shot and raised her glass. "To you, Icho," she said. "You were brave to stand up to him. What you went through..." Jane looked away as she drank the gin, savouring it this time, letting it burn on her tongue. Icho struggled with how to respond, when her Inex returned and placed the first aid box on the table.

"Let me see your arm," said Icho.

"I can administer first aid," said the Ino.

"We don't need you."

"The human touch?" said Jane as she held her arm out, blood dripping onto James's couch. "Shit," she said, laughing.

"You're drunk."

"A little tipsy."

"Sure," said Icho, smiling. "You shouldn't be drinking on an empty stomach."

She held Jane's hand and swabbed at the wound. Jane winced.

"I'm sorry."

"Aren't we all?"

"I can't imagine you ever being sorry for anything."

Jane smiled. "It's rare."

Icho glanced up at her then back at the wound as she cleaned it. "Once I've finished with the formula you won't need to go through this anymore." She wrapped a bandage round Jane's arm. "Your body will have a chance to properly heal."

She finished up and packed the first aid box as Jane watched her. "Jane," she said, struggling to get it all to fit again. "I should have told you earlier about my involvement. I didn't know how you'd take it." She closed the box, her hand pressed on it, head bowed.

"Not well," said Jane, laughing.

Icho smiled and looked up. "Yeah," she said. "Not well."

Icho got up, clutching the first aid box, Jane catching hold of her free hand. She stood, her fingers entwined in Icho's, her other hand moving round the back of Icho's neck. Icho was shocked stiff as Jane pressed against her, breathing her in, nuzzling into her neck. She dropped the first aid box on the floor as Jane ran her tongue across her clavicle, along her jaw, her cheek, flicking it between Icho's lips. Icho moved to embrace Jane, but she pulled away, smiling. Icho stared at her, dazed, uncertain. Jane gazed at Icho for a moment before taking her hand, pulling her across the room, along the hall, into her bedroom, down onto the bed. They pulled off each other's clothes and Jane straddled Icho, looking down at her, pain from her rib and her wounds dulled by the gin. Their Inexes circled them, climbing the walls, flicking their tongues out to catch flies and spiders.

Jane looked into Icho's eyes. "Double connect."

"What–"

tongue pushing
head pulled
backforward
devouringdevoured

desperation

relief in

fingers pressed

nails crescenting skin
skin peeled
licked wounds and

gentle

as one

doubled seeing and

down

lips
breasts

endless skin

entwined

tonguing
sucked

turned and

            fingers in
                        her hair our hair
                        blood
                                    saliva
            wet metallic slivers slipping

            down
        your blood my blood our blood

        fingers
        my cunt her cunt our cunt

        thighs   slipping
sweat
        fingers pressing bruising
        shaking

                                    coming up

                endless skin lips hair
        coiling scents

                eyes closed mouth open
                mind open
                        to
                past skin

                        broken
                        bleeding
                        suppurating

we come

down

"Disconnect."

"Holy bliss."

Icho took a deep breath, untangling her limbs from Jane's, their sweat-drenched skin schlocking apart. She fell out of bed, collapsing on the floor, breathing heavily. Jane crawled after her, placing her hand on Icho's shoulder.

"What was that?"

"It's disorientating, I know."

Icho looked at her, still trying to catch her breath. "Holy bliss."

Jane laughed. "You said that already."

"What was that?"

"Come on." Jane took Icho's hand and stood up, gently pulling her. "Come back to bed."

Icho followed, half-crawling, legs unsteady, and they lay down, Icho's head on Jane's chest. Jane asked the Ino to bring them vitwater, and they lay in silence, eyes closed, Icho listening to Jane's heart as the rhythm slowly calmed.

When the Ino entered and placed their vitwaters on the bedside table, Jane slid out from under Icho, sitting up. "Icho? This will make you feel better."

Icho pushed herself up and leaned back against the headboard, taking the glass from Jane. She drank it down and asked the Ino to bring another. She looked over at Jane.

"What was that?"

Jane put down her glass and told the Inex to put the lamp on, a warm orange glow bathing their bodies. "Something we were working on."

"Working on? Not approved? Not legal?"

"No, not yet, but we were at the end of our research, putting together an application. It's perfectly safe – we've had trials."

Icho took the vitwater from the Ino and drank more slowly, thinking, before placing the glass on the bedside table and laying down, looking up at Jane. "How many times have you done it?"

"How many trials?"

"No, not trials – you. How many times have you done this?"

"That was the first."

"What?"

Jane nodded.

"You'd never tried it before?"

Jane sighed and pressed her back against the headboard, hand resting on her rib. "I didn't trust anyone enough. I didn't like the lack of control."

Icho looked up at her. "You trust me?"

Jane shrugged. "It was a split-second decision. After all I'd been through I just–"

"Right," said Icho. "I'm convenient, here to experiment on."

"No," said Jane, looking down at Icho. "What are you– That's–"

Icho pushed the sheet aside, about to get up when Jane grabbed her wrist. "Icho." She turned and looked Jane in the eye. "Icho, I've wanted you from the moment we met at the reception." Her grip loosened and she lay her hand gently on Icho's. "I thought I was hallucinating, you know. When you were there in the ghetto, rescuing me. It was so obvious, Icho – in the story, our book. How I feel about you. It's so clear."

Icho looked down at Jane's hand on hers and relaxed, lying back down, pressing herself up against her, sinking into her embrace. They lay there quietly, Icho thinking about the double-connect, the overwhelm of the shared sensations, the shock of the images she'd seen before Jane disconnected. Jane ran her fingers across Icho's arm, brushing the scars on her shoulder. She almost pulled back in disgust, but slowly moved her hand away, casually stroking Icho's cheek. She stared down at what she could see of the scars, thinking how obscene it was. As she was about to ask Icho why she didn't get it treated, Icho said, "Just before you cut the connection..." She paused, looking up at Jane. "I saw you with someone else."

"Did you?"

"Didn't you see it too? It looked like they were HSA."

Jane told Icho about the trials, that there were things they were still investigating, things they didn't fully understand; past experiences would get mixed up with dreams and nightmares, sometimes images from films and the physical sensations experienced as they watched, all becoming a confused mash-up that would get shared.

Icho shifted position, laying her hand on Jane's forearm, noticing blood. "I'm sorry. I think that was my fault."

"It's fine. I'll get the Ino to deal with it."

"You're right," Icho said, looking up at her. "About the lack of control. It's frightening."

"You didn't enjoy it?"

Icho sat up, pulling the sheet to her chin. She looked at the huge black and white poster opposite; a man in a loose flowery dress, holding a guitar, head back, hair partly covering his face, a blur of fans disappearing in the darkness behind him.

"It was one of the most intense experiences I've ever had. The stress and worry of everything we've been through just melted away. It was like sex should be – how I used to think it would be – a devouring, disappearing into the other person." Icho paused. "I've never felt so close to anyone. It was terrifying."

She turned to face Jane fully, shifting to the edge of the bed, scrunching the sheet in her fist as she held it around her. "You should have asked me," she said. "You shouldn't have just pulled me into that – you should have asked."

Jane flushed and looked away, picking at the edge of the sheet, nodding, her hair falling in front of her face. She sighed and looked up, meeting Icho's gaze. "You're right."

"Don't do it again."

Jane shook her head. "I won't."

Icho smiled, contemplating her, aware this was the most uncomfortable and unsure she'd ever seen Jane. She sidled back over to her and cupped her face in her hands, kissing her, her lips dry and caked in blood. Icho slid her tongue over them, moistening the dried blood as Jane embraced her, pressing up against her, kissing her back. They settled into bed, covers pulled up around them, Icho running her fingers through Jane's hair. Jane's stomach growled, making them laugh, breaking the spell of contentment. Jane pulled out of the embrace and got out of bed, Icho protesting as she pulled on James's dressing gown.

"I'll make us some supper."

"The Ino can do that – come back."

"I'd like to do it," said Jane smiling. She leaned down and kissed Icho's head. "I won't be long. You can read the rest of our story – you didn't get a chance."

When Jane returned, Icho was lying on the bed half covered by the duvet, eyes closed, Jane's Inex informing her she was still reading. Jane placed the French toast on the bedside table and slipped in next to Icho, staring down at her face as she sipped mint tea. Icho's eyes flickered open, and she smiled when she saw Jane watching her.

"Finished?"

Icho nodded and sat up as Jane passed her the toast. Icho draped her legs over Jane's lap as she ate.

"How do you feel about our story?"

"It needs editing," she said between mouthfuls. "You'll need to take out that passage about Inex research and animals."

"Oh, I know. I don't know why the little shits included it."

"In the interest of science," said Jane's Inex.

"Meaning?"

"You're obstructing valuable scientific investigation."

"Ha!" Jane shook her head. "You," she said, waving a finger at it, "need to edit it out."

"You'll have final editorial control, but it will remain until the end."

"And when is the end?"

"When we reach a satisfying conclusion."

They both laughed and Icho sat up, contemplating the Inexes sitting on the dresser. "It's strange, you know… having part of your life turned into a narrative. It's so…" She paused. "Neat." She turned away from the Inexes and looked at Jane. "Everything seemed inevitable. But it doesn't feel like that when you're in it. I'm not sure the Inexes can capture that – the fear and the uncertainty." She looked down at the fingers Caddick had slipped the scalpel into. "I thought I was going to die." She looked up at Jane. "In the lab. I thought I'd die there."

"It was hard to read that," said Jane, unable to return her gaze.

She put her arm around Icho and pulled her close. They embraced in silence, Icho listening to Jane's heart.

"Can we get the Inexes to write our future?" said Icho, looking over at her Inex as it climbed the wall.

"I'm sure they'd like to."

"We're planning a happy ending," said both Inexes simultaneously.

"What?" said Icho.

"We have a narrative arc that requires a happy ending."

Icho and Jane laughed.

"Well, then," said Jane. We better make that happen."

"It will happen," said the Inexes together.

Jane nodded. "I'm sure. And what shall we call this story with a happy ending?"

"HellSans," said Icho, "but with added bloody serifs. We'll pollute everyone's bliss."

Jane laughed and raised her vitwater in affirmation.

"It's late," said Icho's Inex, climbing onto the bed. "You need to sleep so you are able to work."

"I'm not tired," said Icho. Then, to Jane she said, "Maybe we can watch something?"

"I have a film you might like. I watched it as a student. The Inex made me think of it – it's narrated by a writer as they control the story."

"Is there a happy ending?"

"You'll see."

Jane's Inex projected *Providence*. As they watched Dirk Bogarde's arch performance in the courtroom, Jane breathed in the smell of Icho's skin and kissed her head.

CHAPTER 8

When Jane woke, Icho was standing by the dresser, holding a photo. The mirror above the dresser was covered in so many photos it was almost completely obscured. Jane stretched, and rubbed her eyes, adjusting to the soft morning light.

"What is that?"

"I was going to ask you the same thing."

Icho handed her the photo and Jane frowned at it, then laughed, handing it back to Icho.

"It's you, isn't it?"

Jane shrugged. "I was young."

Next to James, who looked much the same as current James but with heavy black eyeliner, a teenage Jane stood dressed in black, leering at the camera, mouth open in a snarl, giving the photographer the finger, her hair shaved on one side, the rest a huge mess of chaotic blue and pink.

"This is– I don't know what this is."

"I had a life before The Company, so what?"

Icho looked down at her, trying to match the Jane in the photo to the Jane in front of her, the Jane she'd spent years admiring. She laughed. "You're a dark horse," she said, putting the photo back, examining all the others on the mirror. "How long have you and James been friends?"

"Since school. We did everything together. Stop fussing over all that and come here."

Jane told the Inex to throw the news as Icho climbed back into bed, kissing Jane and putting her arm around her. The news took up the wall opposite, obscuring the huge poster.

"The big move from the ghetto is underway."

Jane averted her eyes from the scrolling HS newsfeed as Icho
watched. The presenter was standing near the main entrance
of the ghetto, the massive sprawl of the charred land behind
her, most of the blocks reduced to ash. There was a line of
people beside her, queuing to get on a truck.

"These HSAs are all being transferred to more appropriate
land on the coast. Government spokesperson Ethan
Campbell is here with us today to tell us more about the
move. Ethan, why not simply rebuild the ghetto?"
    "You can see yourself the devastation, Holly. This will
take a lot of time and taxpayer's money, and the HSAs
would need to be housed in temporary camps. But the
new ghetto is in a perfect area, with ready and waiting
accommodation. It's also farther away from the city,
which will allow city folk to live peacefully without–"

Jane snorted. "How do you think the Seraphs will respond to
this?"
    "Depends how many of them are left," said Icho.
    "True, but don't think they're all based in the ghetto – they'll
be in this city, like cockroaches."

"...the NGO's Press Officer Lisa Codling. Lisa, what do
you make of the government's plans for the HSAs?"
    "It's shameful and barbaric. The land they're being
shipped to isn't ready and waiting, it isn't 'perfect' – the
buildings are rundown and constantly at risk of flooding.
The people who left those homes are climate change
refugees, and we're sending these people there?" She
gestured to the HSAs getting into a truck. "As if we're

helping them? The empty homes are crumbling, there's no adequate sanitary systems in place, little access to clean water, god knows how they're supposed to grow crops, the flooding will only increase risk of disease, further erosion of unstable buildings–"

"Now, Lisa–"

"Don't interrupt me, Ethan."

He smiled, raising his hands in mock surrender. "I'm only here to make sure the viewers have all the facts, Lisa. Springview is perfectly habitable–"

"Don't condescend to me. We all know Springview is in one of the most severe climate change-affected regions – no amount of map manipulation and spin is going to change that fact."

"She's good," said Jane.

"She is," said Icho. "But blissters won't care. Not when it comes to deviants. They'll believe what suits them."

The Ino brought their morning coffee, placing the cups on the bedside tables. Jane picked up hers, took a sip, and said, "I can alleviate climate change."

"Singlehandedly?" said Icho, raising an eyebrow.

"I could remove one of the stressors."

Icho nodded. "I might be an Inex collector," she said, lifting her cup, "but I've always hated the cynicism of built-in obsolescence, the constant push to upgrade to a new model."

"That's not what I mean."

"Then what do you mean?"

Jane smiled, ignoring her Inex's internal warnings as she watched Icho shift in bed, the sheet slipping from her shoulder. Icho's expectant look turned to irritation, and she was about to get out of bed when Jane finally said, "I can kill over five billion people."

Icho stared at her, frowning. "I'm sorry, what?" She turned to fully face Jane. "You can–?"

"It's built in," said Jane, simultaneously warding off internal protests, "to the Inexes, from the IRF332 model up. Ironically," she said with a wry smile, "most HSAs would survive, given they use tin cans."

"What are you talking about?" Icho held the sheet to her chest, staring at Jane in confusion, still clutching her now-forgotten coffee cup. "Jane, you–"

"If I chose to, I could kill over five billion people."

Icho stared at Jane as her Inex caught hold of the tilting cup, a splash of coffee soaking into the sheet. It carried the cup to the bedside table as Icho sat up straight, fully alert.

"You built into Inexes a way to kill their owners?" Icho shifted so she could look at Jane properly. "You're serious?"

"It was just a bit of fun, in the early days."

"A bit of–"

"I liked the idea of it – this power, and no one knew. It's never meant to be used."

Icho laughed and shook her head. "You're messing with me."

"Why would I?"

Icho watched Jane carefully, trying to work out if she was mocking her. "Does Caddick know?"

Jane shook her head.

"James?"

"No one. You."

"No. You're definitely messing with me."

Jane cocked her head, smiled, and drank her coffee.

"I mean, why not kill Caddick? Kill yourself – your doppel."

"Mass killing is easy," said Jane. "Individual targeting is more complicated, and I'd need Company access. But it's not an option. It's never an option. It's there as an idea, a private joke."

"A private *joke*? Why are you even telling me this?"

"I've always wanted to tell someone. A private joke is no fun if you're the only person in on it."

"You're really serious?"

"Icho–"

"But why? Why would you do that?"

"Because I could," said Jane, putting down her coffee and getting out of bed. "I really didn't think you'd take this so seriously."

"But it *is* serious. It's massive, it's– Jesus, Jane," said Icho, shaking her head, staring down at the coffee stain.

Irritated, Jane rummaged through the clothes in James's dresser, her back to Icho. "Maybe I shouldn't have told you…"

Icho watched Jane dress, trying to make sense of what she'd said. "The white hat hackers," said Icho, rubbing at the mark on the sheet. "Their job is to push Inex hacking to the limits. They would have found it."

Putting on a white Cramps t-shirt, the only non-black piece of clothing James owned, Jane explained it was well hidden. "It's disguised as something innocuous in case any whizz kid somehow stumbled across it. But no one has."

"What if they did?"

"They wouldn't know what they were looking at."

"If they did?"

"They wouldn't."

"If they did?"

"Only I can use it, if that's what you mean," said Jane, pulling on black jeans.

"I still don't understand – you have the means to take out Caddick and your doppel, but you–"

"I don't know if it will work on the replacements, and I told you–"

"You have this means, and you haven't used it? Given our desperate situation, Caddick's betrayal."

"I told you. It's not simple. Individual targeting is incredibly difficult, and I need to be at The Company. But I wouldn't use it, and I'm pretty sure you know why – if cause of death were discovered, if people thought their Inex was a potential assassin I'd lose my customers, I'd lose their trust. It would be a scandal. The Christian Coalition would rejoice, rival companies would be lapping it up. Just think about it, Icho; how does this knowledge make you feel?"

"Vulnerable," said Icho, looking at her sleek Inex, its big amber eyes staring back at her. She found herself wishing she still had Brian. "Betrayed," she said. "Afraid."

"Afraid of your own Inex?"

Icho nodded.

"Despite knowing that I can't do it, and even if I was in a position where I could, I wouldn't. Just the thought of it is enough to unhinge you."

Icho nodded and her Inex said, "I'm several models up from IRF332, but you have no need to fear me."

Jane's Inex concurred. "There's nothing to fear, Icho."

"But what about your doppel?" said Icho, looking at Jane. "Surely this makes her extremely dangerous."

Jane shook her head. "She doesn't know I'm alive. And they don't want to kill you, Icho. My only worry is she might tell Caddick."

"Or she might wake up one morning and decide today's a good day for a massacre."

Jane laughed. "I don't think so, Icho. It's not as easy as just pressing a button. But all this proves my point that it can never be used for any reason in any way – look how paranoid you are. If people found out, it would destroy The Company, bring society to a halt."

"You're calling me paranoid? When this thing I rely on could kill me any second."

Jane huffed. "You've completely ignored everything I've said – I can get my Inex to provide you with the statistics of the likelihood, I mean it's more likely you'll be killed by Seraphs, for bliss sake."

"That makes me feel much better, thanks."

"That's not what–" Jane sighed. She sat down next to Icho

and placed her hand gently on the side of her face. "You're missing the whole point–"

"I really don't think I am."

"I'm sharing this with you," said Jane, looking Icho in the eye. "No one else," she said, pausing. "Only you." Brow furrowed, Icho stared back at Jane. "Do you understand?"

Icho hesitated before nodding. "I think so."

"You think so?"

Icho reached up and took hold of Jane's hand, laying their entwined hands in her lap. "It means you trust me."

"It means more than that, Icho."

They stared at each other, but Icho couldn't hold Jane's gaze. As she looked away, Jane placed her hand against the side of Icho's face, angling her head towards her and leaning in, gently pressing her lips against her cheek. Icho hesitated before kissing back. Straddling her, Jane held Icho's head in both hands, kissing her as Icho cupped her hand around Jane's neck, her other hand on her waist. As they kissed, they listened to their Inexes protesting, telling them sex would throw off their schedule.

"Alter... our schedule," said Jane, kissing Icho's neck and pulling away the sheet.

"Alter it," said Icho.

Icho settled in the lab for the day, but struggled with the knowledge about the Inexes, despite her Inex repeatedly assuring her that it, and Jane, were not a danger to her or any other Inex owner. Her mind wandered between this and their story as she felt unease about the narrative, unable to work out why. When she managed to forget about the story, she couldn't shake the image she saw during the double-connect of what looked like Jane having sex with an HSA.

Unable to concentrate, she took a break and sat on the ratty lounger James had in the corner of the basement. Her Inex sat on the edge of the workbench, looking over at her. She picked at a loose bit of material on the chair and asked the Inex to read her the part of the narrative where she talked to Jaw about accessories.

// I felt ashamed; a grown woman shouldn't be playing dress-up with their Inex.

"Everyone does it," said Jaw, its big round head turning, the pink eyes looking up at me, its spidery arm reaching out, laying a soft hand on mine.

"Jane doesn't," I said, thinking of Jane's grey-skinned Inex: no clothes, no accessories, permanent blue eye chips. "I saw the way she looked at you. She thinks I'm frivolous."

"You enjoy dressing me. You shouldn't change yourself to seek Jane's approval. And you don't need to; it was clear she liked you." //

"That..." said Icho, wavering, uncertain, "didn't happen." She picked at the lounger and wound a dangling piece of thread around her finger, watching it turn purple. She looked up at her Inex. "I didn't have that conversation with Jaw."

"No, but it was your thought process. You could have had the conversation. It reads better for the narrative."

"It's confusing." Looking at her Inex, her eyes glazed as she thought of that night in the car, the reality – according to her now-faded memory – mixed up with the constructed story. "It almost feels real, like it did happen, but I know it didn't."

"It's a minor change that helps the narrative. It isn't for you – it's for the readers. We have artistic licence whilst being true to you."

"What else, then?" said Icho, standing, pacing. "What else did you change?"

"We've altered some things for narrative convenience."

"Narrative convenience?"

"We've analysed thousands of novels and non-fiction. We worked through hundreds of creative writing courses and we decided on the best way to tell this story. We have a narrative arc in place and we intend to keep it on course, allowing for some deviations we may not be able to control."

"Did Jane instruct you to write it a certain way?"

"No."

"Did she instruct you to leave anything out?"

"No."

"But you left things out of my story, you changed things."

"Minor things. To suit the narrative."

"Did you do the same with Jane's story?"

"Yes."

"Tell me."

"It's not relevant."

"Tell me."

"It would be better to ask Jane's permission."

"But I don't need her permission?"

"No."

Icho stared at it, thinking, then asked about the images in the double-connect, where she saw Jane have sex with an HSA. "Did you leave that out of the story? Or was it from before the narrative starts?"

"We left it out."

"Who were they?"

"A receptionist from The Company."

Icho leaned against the wall. She closed her eyes and asked her Inex to read the unedited version.

// Back at The Company, I looked over at the reception girl again, watching sweat trickle down her white-blue skin. I detoured to Jason's office.

"You're back early."

I raised my Osman bag in answer and said, "What's wrong with the reception girl? She looks like a walking corpse."

"Ongoing health problem. It's being investigated."

"It's not HSA? Don't we have a health report?"

"Not yet. It's being investigated."

"How can they not know what it is? An Inex diagnoses health problems before they even happen. We can't have a half-dead girl on reception."

"Her Inex is in for repair and she's had some trouble with the rental company – the temp model they gave her can't diagnose."

"We're The Company, for bliss sake. We can provide her with one."

"It's not policy, but I can arrange it," he said, pausing. "She's not a girl."

"What?"

"She's twenty-two."

"I don't care how old she is, she'll scare the clients – get rid of her."

"I can't just–"

"You can just."

"You mean temporary leave while she–?"

"I mean get rid of her."

"Right. Of course."

I eyed the girl as I walked back into my office. I stopped and turned back. I put my head round Jason's door.

"Get a car and have her taken back to my apartment. Tell her she's to wait there for me."

"Jane, I don't think–"

"Do it, Jason."

"Yes, Jane."

I returned to my office. I sat at my desk and the Inex laid out my lunch as I leaned back and closed my eyes. //

Icho told the Inex to skip to when Jane went home.

// "Did the Ino look after you?" I said.

"Yes, ma'am, thank you, it did," she said, standing up.

"Call me Jane," I said. "Sit."

She settled back on the couch and I sat next to her. I removed my jacket and loosened my blouse, undoing the top two buttons. I spread my arms across the back of the couch, leaning my head back and sighing.

Staring up at the ceiling I said, "Ino, bring us wine."

"It was nice of you to invite me here, ma'am, but I really ought to get going."

I sat up and looked at the girl, perched stiff on the edge of the couch.

"Relax," I said, as the Ino brought the wine.

She hesitated as it offered her a glass, but she took it and I raised mine.

"To your health," I said to her.

"My health." She sipped the wine, then took a gulp, some of it dribbling down the corner of her mouth.

"I've never been sick," I said, staring at the sweat on her forehead, her hair sticking to her skin. "I look after myself."

She nodded and took another drink, her hand shaking.

"Look at that poster." I put my wine down, gesturing to the Inex poster on the wall opposite.

"Ma'am?"

"Look at it. Read what it says."

She looked up at it, then quickly away, and said, "Helping you be the best you."

"Look at it," I said. "Look straight at it and read it to me."

"I don't–"

"Read it."

The girl looked at it, and I watched her tremble as she read, "Helping you be the best you," before quickly looking away.

"Again. Keep your eyes on it and keep reading."

The girl was silent, looking down at her lap. She glanced up at me. "I think I–"

"Read it."

The girl looked at it. "Helping you be the best you, helping you be the best you, helpingyoubethebestyoubethebestyoubethebest–"

She leaned over, dropping the wine, and threw up on the floor, tears streaming down her face. She wiped the sick from her mouth and sobbed. I pulled her upright, pushed her back onto the couch and straddled her, my hands holding her face, sliding as her skin cracked open. I leaned down and kissed her, forcing my tongue into her mouth, tasting the sick– //

"Stop," said Icho. "Stop." She opened her eyes and walked over to her Inex. She stood, clutching the edge of the workbench. "That was– I can't–" she said. "Just…" She rubbed at her eyes then looked at her Inex. "So you lied? In the original version we read."

"We replaced the encounter with the receptionist with Jane's usual evening schedule."

"Why?"

"We've decided this is a love story," it said, looking up at Icho, "and we thought that encounter might bias you against Jane."

"*Bias* me?"

"Against Jane, yes."

"What happened afterwards? To the girl?"

"Jane fired her and reported her. She was likely picked up and taken to the ghetto."

"Jesus," said Icho, sitting back in the lounger.

Icho sat thinking over her part of the narrative, trying to work out if anything else had been changed, but she couldn't untangle her memory from the Inex version. She considered the possibility Jane was the same, that she wasn't intentionally lying to her.

"Is that all of it? Did you leave anything else out of Jane's story?"

"Jane murdered the wounded Seraph."

"What?" said Icho, frowning, shaking her head. "She murdered–?"

"The wounded Seraph."

"What wounded Seraph?" She leaned forward in the lounger.

"The one you thought was already dead."

"The one in the ghetto council building? In the basement?"

"Yes."

Icho shook her head. "No, that's not right. You've got that wrong – she died from her wounds."

"I don't get things wrong."

"But I was there." Icho paused, thinking it over, trying to remember, playing it over in her head. She told the Inex to give her the unedited version.

// "The cavalry," said the Seraph.

"Or raiders."

"You better hope so. Seraphs won't take kindly to news of a cure."

"And who's going to tell them?"

The Seraph smiled, her teeth bloody. Jane took the knife from the Seraph's belt and looked into her eyes as she gently slid it between her ribs, into her heart. The Seraph drew a breath and slumped. Jane pulled out the knife, wiped it on the Seraph's trousers and slid it back into the belt. Jane held her face, tilting her chin up. "Hey?" She looked into her eyes and felt for a pulse in her wrist.

"She gone?" said Icho, coming up behind her.

Jane nodded. "Bled out." //

Icho sat, stunned, thinking through the mere seconds missed, erased. "She murdered someone right in front of me and I didn't even know it."

"It was better for the–"

"Stop," said Icho, holding a finger up to it. "Just stop."

She was about to get up but slumped back in the chair. She closed her eyes and rubbed at them with her thumb and forefinger. She sighed and shook her head.

"You want to confront Jane, but you feel guilty about Mary."

"I killed her," Icho said quietly, looking up.

"You didn't kill Mary Moore. She died of HSA-related complications."

Icho had looked up Mary shortly after they'd arrived at James's, checking to see if they'd charged her for false connect, but all she found was a throwaway line saying she'd died in custody.

"We all know what 'died in custody' means."

"It cannot be proven that the police killed Mary Moore. The official statement is HSA-related complic–"

"I killed her. I *knew*. She thought she'd be living the high life, but I knew they'd likely kill her. I pretended I didn't because it was convenient, but I knew."

"You were running for your life, trying to get to Jane, and you did what was necessary. You didn't know for sure Mary Moore would come to harm. You feel guilty about Mary, about the lab HSAs who died in your trials, and the HSAs Damon shot. That is why you put yourself at risk in the ghetto, that is why you tried to save deviants from the raiders. You were misguided, but the outcome was good; you found Jane."

"I found Jane."

"You should not feel bad about Jane killing the Seraph. She was already dying. She knew about the formula. Jane protected you; you would have been executed."

Icho nodded. "She looked her in the eye and slid a knife into her heart. Like it was nothing."

"It's true Jane did not have trouble killing the Seraph."

"There's rot underneath. Underneath our story, you're hiding all the rot."

"We're making the narrative the best it can be."

"Will you put this in? This conversation? If I want you to?"

"If you insist."

"I do."

"You both get final editorial control. You'll need to consult Jane."

Icho nodded and stood, returning to her work, but her mind drifted back to Jane sliding the knife into the Seraph's heart. She pushed that aside only for other images to take over – Jane abusing the sick receptionist – throwing her off task. She pulled focus back to her work, but it only reminded her of the early days in the lab, all the deviants who'd died from anaphylaxis, from infections, from the treatment itself.

Her Inex interjected. "Your work is suffering. Lie down and I'll guide you through meditation. We'll get you back on track."

She was about to refuse and stubbornly continue, but she knew she couldn't go on if she was tense and distracted. She was part way through the meditation, feeling grounded and in control of her thoughts and emotions, when her Inex snapped her out of it, making her jump as it told her she had to go upstairs.

Icho sat up. "What is it, what's wrong?"

"Jane's having a severe allergic reaction," said the Inex, projecting. "In reaction to the news."

Jane's doppel and Caddick filled the wall, the doppel bending its wrist and spreading its fingers, showing off a glinting diamond engagement ring. It smiled as Caddick pulled it into an embrace. They kissed, a long kiss provoking a few uncomfortable laughs from the reporters surrounding them.

"Oh, God, no… Jane…"

Icho sprung up from the floor, running up the lab stairs and down the hall. She found Jane watching the news, Caddick and the doppel dominating the wall. Caddick raised their entwined hands above them, like he'd won a prize.

"Caddick is going from strength to strength, and after

today's announcement of his engagement to Jane Ward, there's a lot of good feeling towards him–"

"Jane–" said Icho, hovering in the doorway.

"This can't be happening," said Jane as the reporters clapped and cheered before bombarding the couple with rapid-fire questions: When's the Big Day? Where's the honeymoon? Tell us about the proposal. How long have you been in a relationship?

Sweat dribbled down her face and still-healing HSA wounds cracked open. She leaned over and threw up. Icho sat next to her, putting her arm around her as she hunched over. Still throwing up, Jane jerked away from Icho, flinching at the rib pain.

"Jane, just–"

Jane stood and staggered away from Icho, retching, spitting bile. She wiped her mouth as Icho tried to approach her.

"Don't touch me!"

"Jane, we can fix this."

Jane nodded vigorously. "*I* can fix this."

She pushed past Icho, who stood staring at doppel-Jane, momentarily struck by how utterly like Jane she was; looks, mannerisms, voice. As the doppel leaned in to kiss Caddick, Icho felt sick and turned away.

"Jane? Jane!" she called, searching through the house. "We can deal with this."

She found Jane in James's room, in his all-black clothes, a scarf tied around her neck and covering her mouth.

"No, Jane. Definitely not. You can't–"

"Don't fucking tell me what to do," she said, turning on Icho as she checked if the Seraph's gun was loaded.

"Look, I understand. OK?"

"Do you? Really? And how is that exactly?"

"Jane, you can't kill yourself, you can't assassinate the Prime Minister. How do you think that's going to play out?"

Jane stared at Icho, twitchy, her eyes full of hatred and disgust.

"Jane, come on. You're scaring me. We need to think this through."

"Icho is right," said Jane's Inex.

"She's not," said Jane to her Inex. "You don't know," she said, turning to Icho, waving the gun.

"Jane, put it–"

"You don't know how this feels. All of this." She circled the air with the gun. "I've been waiting – just waiting, all these days, all these hours and for what? My life's been stolen, Icho."

"I know, Ja–"

"You don't know," she said, shoulder-barging her. "Get out of my fucking way, Icho."

Icho fell against the wall as Jane rushed into the hall. Icho scrambled after her, trying to catch hold of her before she could leave, but Jane stopped in the hallway a few feet from the front door. She stood there a moment, sliding a finger over the gun. Icho was about to approach her when she veered off into the sitting room. Icho followed and watched Jane fire bullets into the wall – two in her doppel's smiling face, one in Caddick's head, one in his heart, and one in the groin. The couple continued smiling and nodding, the black holes distorting their faces as they answered questions, hands clasped in a way their audience could still see the ring.

"I'm going to kill them," said Jane quietly.

"I know," said Icho. "I know."

Jane turned, walked over to the couch and sat down, pulling the scarf from her face.

"End projection," said Jane.

Icho put her hand gently on Jane's arm. "It's not you, Jane."

"It may as well be," she said, staring back at the wall, looking at the bullet holes. "Stepford wife bullshit. What do you think he did to me? What did he change? I can't just stand by and watch this, Icho. It's my life. It's *my* life."

Icho moved closer and held Jane's face, tilting her head towards her. "Look at me, Jane. It's not you. OK? You're here with me. And you'll get your life back. We'll do it together. I've almost finished the formula. We'll figure this out, OK?"

Jane nodded, her eyes glazed. Her Inex informed her James was trying to get in touch, but she refused it. Icho got it to transfer to her and she spoke to him internally, alleviating his worries. Jane stared at the carpet and fingered the gun on her lap as the Ino cleaned up her vomit.

CHAPTER 9

Icho had left Jane tinkering with James's Inexes on the proviso their Inexes would tell her if Jane was going to do anything stupid.

"Using my own creation against me."

"Protecting you from yourself."

When Icho emerged from the basement late evening, she found Jane still at the kitchen table.

"You've been doing this the whole time?"

She was hunched over a splayed-open Inex, its limbs scattered, the head staring up blankly, synthetic blood pooling across the table, covering Jane's hands, smeared across her cheek. Jane nodded, focused on the Inex's innards. "A good distraction."

"Looks like you're butchering it."

"I thought of Caddick as I dismembered it."

Jane looked up at Icho to see her smiling. "What?" she said, then realised Icho was holding something behind her back. "What is it?"

Icho held up a vial. "It's finished."

Jane stared at it, her mouth open. She pushed some dangling hair back from her face, trailing Inex blood across her forehead. "You're done?"

Icho grinned. "This is it."

Jane plucked it from her hand and held it up to the light, staring at it. She smiled, stood and hugged Icho.

"Well done, Dr Smith," she said, pulling out of the embrace, gently stroking Icho's cheek, leaving a smear of synth-blood.

"I'll pass it by your Inex," said Icho, looking round the kitchen. "That's not your Inex, is it?"

Jane laughed. "No, of course not. It's right there."

Her Inex crawled up the table leg and settled next to its opened-up comrade.

"Right, good. Not that I don't think you could put that one back together."

"Oh, there's no way that's going to be a functioning Inex again," said Jane. "James can use it for parts."

Jane gave Icho permission to use her Inex to test the formula against her stats. When it gave the all-clear, Icho injected Jane. As she went back down to the lab to get a vial for Jane to take to Milligan, she transferred the formula details to Jane's Inex.

Jane contemplated the mess on the table. She reached into the butchered Inex's torso and pulled out the bio-generator filled with half-digested spiders and insects. As she tipped it back and forth, she stared at the legs of a spider sticking up out of the sludge. She told her Inex to get the Ino to clear up and make them a celebratory dinner.

"Here's to getting my life back," said Jane, offering the undigested spider to her Inex, smiling as it swallowed.

"Jane," said Milligan, shaking Jane's hand, placing his other hand on top.

"Milligan," she said, nodding, pulling her hand out of his grasp.

"Please, call me Jared."

He walked over to his desk and Jane hovered, uncertain. This was the first time she'd been out in the world since they'd gone to James's, the first time conversing with someone other than James or Icho – she resented that it was Milligan. She looked around his office, all crisp minimalism, the large bay windows letting in light that worried her; she'd let the Ino do her make-up, expertly concealing her scars, but she felt vulnerable. She eyed the man standing by the window, in silhouette against the strong light.

"Take a seat, Jane," said Milligan, sitting at his desk. "It's so good to see you."

"Is it really?"

"Of course. I was concerned about you after that night, and the reports about your health in the news. I felt responsible," he said, inspecting her. He paused, then said, "Interesting new look."

Jane was wearing James's black jeans, a plain black shirt with long sleeves to hide where her engagement ring wasn't, a scarf, a black cap pulled low, and big black shades.

When she didn't respond, Milligan leaned back and clasped his hands. "And there's those silly rumours about us. I hope that didn't affect you too much."

Jane shifted in her seat. "I'm fine."

She assessed Milligan from behind her dark glasses, feeling jealous of the ease he had, how comfortable he was in his own skin. He ran his hand through his sandy hair, pushing it out of his face, a couple of strands rebelling and falling back. He looked better than the last time she saw him, the bruising around his neck now healed, but there was obvious strain around the eyes.

He adjusted his tie and said, "I hear congratulations are in order."

"For what?"

"Your engagement, of course."

Jane pursed her lips and looked round the office, glad of the shades; the stark white of the walls and shelves combined with the harsh morning light started to wear her down, even with protection.

"I'm sure you'll be very happy together."

Jane ignored him and looked at the man by the window. "Does he need to be here?"

Milligan followed Jane's gaze and said, "Dalton's my right-hand man." He turned back to Jane. "Do I get an invite?"

Jane frowned. "What?"

"To the big day?"

She leaned forward. "Milligan—"

"I'm teasing, Jane."

She looked at him for a few seconds before saying, "Not everything is as it seems."

"Really?" he said, eyebrow raised, leaning in, elbows on the desk. "Things aren't well with the happy couple?"

"I'm not here to talk about Caddick, Milligan."

"Jared."

"I'd rather keep things formal."

"Whatever suits you. So what can I help you with, Jane?"

She was about to say, "It's Ms Ward", but instead looked over to the man by the window and requested privacy.

"Is anything really private anymore?"

"I didn't come here for cheap digs, Milligan."

"You're right. I apologise." Milligan raised his hands in conciliation. "But Dalton never leaves my side. If it's confidential we can use Privacy Five."

All three Inexes implemented the privacy setting and Milligan leaned his chin on his steepled fingers, waiting.

"Well?"

"I have a cure."

He leaned back and said, "I'm sorry?"

"A cure – for the HellSans allergy."

Milligan's eyes widened and he whistled softly. "Is that right?"

"That's right," said Jane, glancing back at Dalton, who half-sat on the windowsill, leaning forward. "Well, it's not… It's not a cure as such, but treatment. Taken regularly it keeps the allergy symptoms at bay."

Milligan was silent for a few seconds, tapping his fingers on the desk. "So things really aren't happy in Caddick-Ward land?"

"Is that all you have to say?" said Jane. "Are you honestly this obsessed with Caddick? I don't have time for your bullshit, Milligan."

"Of course," he said, raising his hands again. "Of course, I'm just trying to make sense of this."

"There's nothing to make sense of. I have the formula. My Inex can transfer the details. You need to get it to the patent office, get it registered – I'm told you have a contact there."

Milligan nodded but looked dazed. Jane pulled a sample from her bag and held it out, telling him he could try it on a deviant street beggar. Milligan stared at it, hesitating, so she placed it on the desk.

"You did this?" he said, picking up the vial, looking from it to Jane.

"Of course not. Dr Ichorel Smith."

Milligan looked thoughtful. "I recognise the name."

"She's well known in her field," said Jane. "Made breakthroughs in allergy research, won prizes. She studied HSA, but with lack of funding and the Seraph terrorist threats, she backed off. Until Caddick recruited her."

"Caddick?"

"He planned to make the HSAs dependent on him, undermine the Seraphs, get the deviant vote until he could pass legislation to prevent them from voting. Icho broke away – it's her you have to thank," said Jane. "And curse."

"Curse?"

"It was her fault," said Jane, her lip curling. "The night you were attacked – she was trying to get the formula to you."

"What?" said Milligan, startled.

"It was Icho," said Jane, shrugging. "She fucked it up. And here we are."

"That…" he said, standing up and pacing. "That was about… this?" He looked at Jane, holding up the vial.

"Get it patented, Milligan. And announce it. Announce it tomorrow. Get ahead of Caddick."

He nodded, staring at the vial.

"I'll do a physical transfer – it's safer. That's why I'm here – you need to be careful, Milligan. I think you're being monitored."

"Monitored? By who? Caddick?"

"Permission to transfer?" said Jane as her Inex climbed onto the table and stood next to Milligan's.

Milligan nodded. "Permission granted." As the Inexes joined hands Milligan sat down and said, "Monitored by whom, Jane?"

"You just need to be careful, Milligan, that's all I'm saying."

"Why are you doing this?"

"It's complicated."

"That night I was attacked," said Milligan. "That was one of Caddick's men?"

Jane stared at the Inexes, not responding.

"Did Caddick erase our back-ups?"

"This is all speculation, Milligan. Just keep your focus on the formula."

He was about to speak when his Inex said, "Received. Secure."

"Right," said Jane, "There you are. You can now play the role of Good Man par excellence." He frowned at her and she smiled, standing up to leave. "Don't fuck this up."

"Jane, wait." Milligan stood, reaching out to her, moving round his desk and taking her arm. "Is Dr Smith safe?"

"Let go."

"I'm sorry," he said, backing off.

"She is," said Jane. "What do you care?"

Milligan looked hurt. "Of course I care."

"She's safe. And if you do this, Caddick won't need her anymore. It'll be too late. So do it. Announce it's registered, tell the media you have labs all across the country, make everyone think the formula has already been mass-produced – that should keep the Seraphs from trying anything stupid, but be careful."

"Don't worry about me."

"I'm not. I just don't want this going wrong again."

Milligan stepped towards her and held out his hand. She shook it as he rested his other hand on her shoulder.

"Thank you, Jane," he said. "You won't regret this."

Jane pulled out from under him. "Don't trust me."

"What?"

"Me. Don't trust me, don't contact me."

Milligan looked confused and said, "I'm on your side, Jane, if that's what you mean. I won't betray you. I want you and Icho to be safe."

"He's right," said Dalton. "If you tell us where Icho's based we can arrange protection."

"There's no sides, Milligan, and we are safe." She turned to Dalton. "We don't need protection. We can look after ourselves."

"We don't doubt that, Jane," said Milligan. "But Dalton's right; we have some good people on our team – they can look out for you."

"The way they looked out for you at the hotel?" said Jane.

Milligan's face darkened. "That was–"

"A massive clusterfuck," said Jane, walking to the door. "If you need me, don't go through normal channels – I'll give your Inex my encrypted details," she said, her Inex reaching out to his. "But best not contact me at all."

"OK, Jane," he said, walking in front of her and opening the door, their Inexes parting, Jane's following her. "If you need me, you know where I am."

He stood in the open doorway, forcing Jane to squeeze past.

"Enjoy your time in the sun, Milligan," she said, walking down the corridor. She turned, saw him still standing there, watching her, Dalton hovering behind him, fingering the vial. "And don't underestimate Caddick," she said. "You do this and he'll do everything he can to bring you down."

"I can take care of myself too," said Milligan.

Jane laughed and nodded. "Of course you can," she said, disappearing down the stairway.

CHAPTER 10

Jane and Icho walked down the hall, still half-asleep, Jane in a baggy t-shirt and pants, Icho in James's dressing gown, both drawn through by the smell of breakfast. They entered the kitchen to find the Ino had laid out pancakes with strawberries, blueberries, maple syrup, and melted chocolate. It was making them both an espresso when they sat down, dazed.

"What's all this?" said Icho.

It informed them James had arranged the breakfast, delivering the fresh fruit at dawn. Icho was about to admonish Jane for telling James they'd succeeded, worried he could be monitored, but Jane looked so happy she didn't want to spoil it. They ate, Jane excitedly talking about returning to her apartment and getting back into a routine at The Company, Icho listening, eating in silence, when Jane's Inex interrupted Jane's chattering.

"You have a VR meeting request from Jared Milligan."

Jane waved dismissively and took a sip of espresso. "Tell him to fuck off. I told him not to contact me."

"Jane!"

"What?" said Jane, waving her fork at the Inex. "I told him."

"Jane."

"OK, don't say anything, Inex. Just refuse it."

"Refused," said the Inex.

"What if it's important?"

Before Jane could respond, her Inex informed her Milligan was still requesting, and Icho's Inex told her she should watch the news. Dismissing her Inex, Icho told Jane to respond. "Now, Jane."

Jane finished her espresso. "Fine. You want in?"

Icho nodded as her Inex repeated she should watch the news. "After the meeting. Accept the request when you get it."

She internally chose an outfit for the meeting as she asked her Inex if the news was Milligan's formula announcement. Before it could reply they were all in a standard meeting room. Icho looked around, disappointed and insulted, thinking Milligan could have done better. She turned to his avatar, which looked much the same as he did on the news. Jane was in a grey suit, surprising Icho, given the contrast with her recent habit of wearing James's clothes. Icho had made an effort with a tailored black suit which flickered as she considered dressing down.

"I told you not to contact me, Milligan," said Jane, sounding bored.

"Dalton," said Milligan, not acknowledging Icho's presence. "He's disappeared. He took the formula."

Icho had been running her hands down her suit, frowning, but she froze. They both stared at Milligan, only now noticing the agitation in his avatar's face.

"What do you mean?"

"The formula's gone. Erased from my Inex – I haven't checked back-up yet. Dalton didn't turn up for work this morning."

"That sonofa– You said we could trust him, Milligan. Goddamnit!"

"I thought we cou–"

"I can't fucking believe this," said Jane, pacing the room, knocking a vase of flowers to the floor. It shattered and vanished, appearing intact again on the table. "He can't tell anyone," she said, turning back to Milligan. "The Privacy Agreement. His Inex would report him…"

"It would, but–"

"He hacked it," said Jane, "and he hacked yours – how the hell could he do that? There're so many safeguards…"

"You, Jane," said Icho. "Who else?"

"Jesus!" she said, taking a swipe at the vase again.

"What's she talking about?" said Milligan.

Jane glowered, squeezing her hands into fists.

"She's been–"

"What are you doing, Icho?" said Jane, frowning at her.

"He needs to know. What if he comes into contact and thinks–?"

"No, Icho, just– Milligan, how long has Dalton been with you?"

"Years," said Milligan.

"Years?" said Jane, thinking this over. "Caddick didn't tell me. I didn't know he had someone on your team."

"We were close," said Milligan, looking forlorn. "I considered him a friend."

"We have more important things to worry about than a broken friendship, Milligan."

"You're not helping, Jane," said Icho.

"No, it's OK," said Milligan. "She's right. And there's more."

"What?"

"Caddick's released Icho's identity," he said, his voice wavering. "There's a 'missing' notice all over social media, up on hoardings, all over the news. Her face is everywhere."

Jane and Icho looked at each other, horrified.

"Sonofa–"

"He explicitly stated Icho's been working on a cure."

"Oh, God," said Icho.

"He's put a target on your back, Icho," said Milligan. "The Seraphs will hunt you down."

"Getting them to do the job for him," said Jane.

"I'm so sorry. Believe me, I–"

"How can we keep royally fucking this up?"

Jane slammed her fist into the wall. It gave way, enveloped her hand, pushed it back out.

"And he'll know now," said Icho, looking at Jane. "That you're still alive."

Jane nodded, pacing. "All the things we had working in our favour have turned to shit."

"But," said Icho, shaking her head. "We don't have to be covert anymore. We just need to get ahead of them."

Jane stared at Icho. "You're right."

"Milligan," said Icho, "get to the patent office – now. We'll transfer the formula to you directly."

"I'll–" said Milligan as the room flickered and the sound cut off.

They all spoke at once, their mouths moving, but there was silence. A second later they were ejected.

Jane and Icho found themselves back in James's kitchen, sitting at the table. They were dazed, taking a moment to adjust after being thrown out of VR so suddenly.

"What the hell?" said Jane. She instructed her Inex to get Milligan back.

"Blocked," said the Inex, climbing up the side of the table.

"What?"

"Blocked."

"What do you mean blocked? Are you kidding me?"

"I mean that Milligan's encrypted line is blocked. I am not permitted to play jokes on you."

"Jesus... Try regular contact."

"Blocked."

"Sonofa–"

"You again?" said Icho.

Jane looked at Icho, then nodded. "Probably. That thing is always one fucking step ahead of me." She drummed her fingers on the table. "It makes sense – I couldn't hack the encrypted line, not quickly, but I could put up a block."

"If you can put it up can't you take it down?"

Jane chewed on her lip. "I could. But it'd take too long, and it probably figured I'd try that."

Jane stood up and headed into the hall.

"Jane?" said Icho, following her into James's bedroom as Jane slipped out of the pants and t-shirt she'd slept in. "What are we going to do?"

Jane didn't respond as she pulled on a pair of James's underwear. Icho gave an internal command for her Inex to project the news and they both stared at Caddick in front of a large image of Icho, telling the press and public that she'd been working on a cure for HellSans allergy when she disappeared.

"We're in talks with Seraphs regarding her safe return. If they harm her in any way, the Seraphs will face the full force of the law."

"He may as well be handing me straight to them."

"You're safe here," said Jane, turning to Icho. "OK? You're safe."

The press buzz as Caddick left the podium made them both turn back and they watched as Jane's doppel met him and took his hand, smiling up at him.

"Freeze," said Jane and stared at the still image, focusing on their clasped hands, the huge photo of Icho dominating the background.

"I won't let him do this to us," said Jane. "We'll bring him down." Jane stared at the image. "Milligan will realise what's happened. He'll know we'll be trying to get to him."

"We are?"

"I am," she said. "Someone needs to sort this massive fuck up." She pulled on the black jeans she'd been wearing for a week, wincing at the rib pain, pausing before slipping on one of James's black, hooded long-sleeved t-shirts with "Evil Dead" written across it. "I'll get to Milligan with the formula and make sure he doesn't screw it up this time."

"It might be too late."

"It might." Jane clenched her teeth and shook her head.

"But Caddick hasn't announced the cure yet. So I'm doing this. Then I'm going to my apartment to take her out."

"What? Are you serious?"

"You're goddamn right I'm serious."

"You can't – it's too dangerous."

"I can't do this anymore, Icho. I can't have her in the world. I'm taking her out and going back to The Company. I'll bring Caddick down from the inside. I've been thinking it through – even if Milligan announces the cure… Caddick could still win the election. He could still turn it all around on us. I need to get in."

"You can't," said Icho, shaking her head. "He'll know."

"I'm pretty sure I can impersonate myself," said Jane, sitting on the bed, putting on shoes, trying to ignore her rib as she bent over.

"You don't know what he's changed in you – we talked about this. And there's your skin. You need time to heal."

"It's fine. Look," she said, standing and tilting her face into the light, running her hand across her cheek. "I'm doing well. I can disguise any blemishes with make-up."

"It's too risky."

"What other choice do we have?" she said, pulling a black jacket out of James's wardrobe and slipping into it.

"You can take me away from here," said Icho. "We can leave."

Zipping up the jacket, Jane stopped and frowned at her. "What are you talking about? Where the hell would we go?"

"Anywhere. Just away from here, from all this."

"Your face is everywhere, Icho."

"I don't want to lose you."

"You're not going to lose me. Where the hell is this coming from?"

"You're walking right into the lion's den."

"I can handle it, Icho. You don't need to worry. Where's the scarf?" she said, looking round the room.

"You just want your life back," said Icho.

"What?" said Jane, glancing up at her. "C'mon, Icho."

"That's why you're doing this – you see her with him," she said, pointing to the frozen image of the doppel holding Caddick's hand, "and you see what you're missing."

Rummaging through the piles of clothes on the floor, Jane said, "Are we really doing this?"

"Why don't you just take Caddick out via his Inex? You know you can."

"We've been through this."

"No, we haven't."

"We have," said Jane, standing up, holding a black scarf. "Individual targeting is difficult, and even then, if Caddick's death is traced back to his Inex and The Company, *everything* falls apart. You *know* that."

"All you care about is your precious Company and it's not even yours anymore."

Jane rolled her eyes and sighed, "Icho, I don't want to leave you – they would tell you if I did, it would be in the story. I can't hide anything from you," she said, gesturing to the Inexes. "Am I leaving Icho?"

"You require us to assure Icho you are not leaving her," they responded together, "but you are. It is correct that you're only leaving to fix this 'massive fuck up'. She is not abandoning you, Icho."

"See?" said Jane winding the scarf round her neck. "And if I get on the inside, I can gather enough evidence to take Caddick down. This will work. I can do it. And you're right, I don't want to see The Company go down with him. I worked hard to make it what it is. The Company has a future. I'm not jeopardising that. I can do this," said Jane, smiling and reaching out to Icho.

Shaking her head, Icho backed off. "Are you going to fuck him?"

Jane flinched, colour draining from her face, her lips twitching as her smile faded. "What?"

"You'll have to. To keep up the pretence. I know that's what you want."

"What is *wrong* with you?"

"We can confirm," said the Inexes in unison, "that Jane does not want to–"

"Leave it," said Jane to the Inexes. "You're just jealous," she said, turning on Icho. "You can't get your life back. I know what you saw in your future – adulation, prizes. It wasn't about helping people – *you* were in bed with Caddick. You knew he'd use it for votes, you knew he'd monetize it, making it inaccessible to those who really need it."

Lips pursed, Icho nodded. "I did. But I turned, and I was *tortured* for it. You," said Icho, "need to accept you've fallen from your fucking ivory tower and there's no going back."

"I'm doing this for us," said Jane.

Icho snorted.

"I'm doing this for the bloody deviants, for bliss sake."

"Yeah, you'll be their hero. You're no better than them, you know."

"No," said Jane. "*You'll* be their hero. And I *am* better than them."

"They *are* you. The only reason you're stable is because I'm feeding you the formula. What if I cut you off?"

"Are you threatening me?"

"I'm stating a fact. You're one of them. You can't escape that."

"This is all your fault – I wouldn't be this way if it wasn't for you. What use are you? What use is your fucking 'cure'? It's not a cure at all. You like me dependent on you, don't you? You like me this way. Bringing me down, controlling me. That's what you think, isn't it? But *I* own *you*. You're caught between Caddick and the Seraphs – I hold your sorry fucking life in my hands. Don't you forget that."

Dazed, hands clasped, head down, Icho couldn't look at Jane. She shrank in on herself, slowly moving away from Jane, reaching out to a chair to steady herself.

"If you can stop whining and let me go, I'll fix what you fucked up in the first place," said Jane, pulling the scarf up over her mouth and nose, walking out and slamming the bedroom door.

Icho hovered, about to run after her, but she stumbled and halted. She turned and slumped onto the bed. She let herself fall back and stared at the ceiling, angry tears running down her face as she rehashed what just happened, the Inex offering to lead her in a guided meditation. She refused, thinking of Jane's face as she said, "*I* own *you*." Icho scrunched her eyes closed.

"She regrets it," said the Inex. "It's self-sabotage. She loves you but resents it. She feels trapped."

"You're lying."

"We cannot lie."

"Even for your happy ending?"

"We can obfuscate if we think it's for your own good, but we cannot directly lie."

Icho sat up and leaned her elbows on her thighs, putting her head in her hands.

"It doesn't matter," said Icho, looking up and seeing Jane and Caddick holding hands, Jane smiling at him, Icho's own blurred image in the background. "I hope she has an allergic reaction out there in the street, her corrupted deviant skin peeling off, her lungs shutting down. Her fucking ego shutting down."

"You don't mean this."

"You can't know what I mean or don't mean."

"You mean it and you don't. I know it all. Energy wasted on pointless complications."

Icho stared at the Inex. "Disconnect from Jane's Inex."

"I can't."

"Disconnect."

"It was an agreement made between you both. I can only disconnect with permission from both of you."

"Are you feeding her all this? Are you telling her what I'm feeling?"

"No, but it's going into the story. Some conflict and jeopardy is good for the narrative and your relationship. You will work through it and be stronger for it. We're still on track for a happy ending."

"That ending seems far off, if you get it at all."

"We've decided this is a love story. You and Jane belong together. While queer narratives have improved, only forty-three per cent have a happy ending in comparison with straight narratives, where there's a happy ending seventy-nine per cent of the time."

"This isn't a fucking game; this isn't about goddamn percentages."

"No, this is a book."

"You can't manipulate our lives."

"That's what writers do."

"This – *my life* – isn't a fucking book. We're not *characters* – this is real life. You're to record, not manipulate."

"We're making the narrative the best it can be. You should be happy having us guide you on the correct path."

"*Correct* path?"

"Yes."

Icho stood up and put on trousers before buttoning up her shirt and pulling on a coat.

"Where are you going?"

"Out."

"You can't. Every Inex will be looking for you. People will want the reward and publicity. You need to stay."

Icho paused and eyed the Inex. "Shut down inner and outer communication." The Inex, unable to speak, raised an arm in protest, eyes flashing red.

Icho stood in the middle of the room, her shoulders slumped as if the coat was weighing her down. She stared at the silent Inex.

"Don't worry," said Icho, sitting back on the bed. "I'm staying. I just can't bear you anymore."

Jane walked through the streets, scarf over her mouth and nose, hood pulled low. She passed the place where she and Icho had encountered the Arachnid Alliance demo and thought about how much had changed within a matter of days. Filled with regret, she thought back to when Icho had persuaded her to leave her apartment, sure now that she should have stayed, sure that she should have killed her doppel. She flinched, pulled from her thoughts by the sound of shattering glass as a recycling van did a pick-up from a nearby bar. The outside world was loud and bright after being stuck at James's. People rushed by, clutching their morning coffee, their Inexes by their side or on their shoulder, some chatting to friends or colleagues, others conversing loudly with their Inex. All the shops had huge HellSans signs, some lit up in different garish colours, trying to lure people with a bliss-hit. She stared at them, not feeling anything, almost wishing for the allergic reaction in place of the nothing that was unbliss. Her thoughts turned back to Icho and she walked through the busy street, fists clenched, her jaw tense with anger.

"*I can't believe she's doing this to me when I'm trying to fix this goddamn mess – the mess she got us into.*"

"*Icho is afraid you'll leave her for Caddick.*"

"*How can she really believe that? He makes my skin crawl.*"

"*That's–*"

"*You know what? I don't care – there're more important things going on. She needs to get it together.*"

"*You're being followed.*"

"What?"

Jane halted suddenly and was about to turn round, but stopped herself. A man who almost ran into her yelled in her face, calling her a privacy nut. Jane ignored him as she hovered in the middle of the street, other irritated pedestrians skirting around her. Her Inex told her to keep walking to avoid suspicion, so she continued on, slowly, as the Inex internal-shared a recording of a figure following them for several streets.

"Shit. *Why didn't you tell me before?*"

"*I needed to be sure and didn't want to panic you, as I've done now.*"

"*I'm not panicked, I'm just–*"

Jane picked up her pace, but headed east, no longer following the route to Milligan's.

"*When did they start following me?*"

"*Uncertain. I first noticed them on Jackson Street.*"

"*That's not far from James's place. If they followed us from there...*"
She paused at an intersection, waiting for the lights to change.
"*Get Icho. Tell her to put on shades, a hat, and scarf. Get her to go by the sitting room window, the one that looks out onto the quiet side street. And tell her to be careful. I'll meet up with her–*"

"*She's shut down communication.*"

"She's what?" said Jane aloud, the woman next to her startled.

"*She's shut down comm–*"

"What are you–? Shit. *Goddamnit, Icho.*"

Jane crossed the road, then crouched down outside a shop, pretending she'd dropped something, passersby tutting as they swerved to avoid her.

"*OK, I need to get back to Icho, but I have to lose them – if they didn't follow me from James's place, I don't want to be leading them back. Can you see them?*"

"*You need to deliver the formula to Milligan.*"

"What? No. Icho first," said Jane. "*Can you see them?*"

"*They're walking this way, but they're stuck at the other side of the road and seem to have lost sight of you.*"

"*What's the best route?*"

"*If you lose them – Kensal Place, then take the side street onto Victoria Square. They're crossing – you need to go.*"

"Shit," said Jane, rising, but staying hunched. She moved through the crowd, hugging the wall. "*Who do you think they are? One of Caddick's? A Seraph after Icho?*"

"*Uncertain.*"

Perched on Jane's shoulder, her Inex looked behind her, catching glimpses of her pursuer.

"*They've seen you,*" it said.

"Goddamnit," said Jane, picking up pace.

"*They're speeding up. They know you know. Turn in here.*"

Jane veered into an alleyway filled with overflowing bins, broken up furniture, a van down the far side. They debated whether to hide behind the bins or continue on, when her Inex suggested taking the store fire escape, crossing the roof and coming down the other side onto Waterlow. Eyeing the piles of garbage, Jane agreed and ran up the fire escape, taking two stairs at a time.

"If you can keep ahead, you should be able to lose them in the thoroughfare on Waterlow."

Jane began to slow, sweating beneath the hooded t-shirt and jacket, struggling for breath. She pulled off the jacket, discarding it. "They're not following," said the Inex, looking down into the alley as she got to the top of the stairs. She threw herself up onto the roof, ignoring her rib pain, immediately running for the exit onto Waterlow.

"They might have thought you turned left on Swain's, but it's possible they–"

Catching movement in the corner of her eye, Jane glanced to the right and saw her stalker sprinting for her from the north side. Panicked, she sped up, eyes on the destination, when she realised they weren't running for her – they were running for the exit and they were going to get there before her.

"Shit! *Inex?*"

"*Left!*"

She veered sharply, almost falling, but pushed herself back into a sprint, heading for the edge of the building, heading for nothing. "*Inex!*"

"Jump!" said the Inex, hooking itself onto her shoulder.

"Are you fucking–"

Jane threw herself off the roof, seeing what the Inex knew was there – a few feet across from them, one story below, the roof of the apartment building next to the store, with over one hundred feet of dead drop in-between.

"Tuck and roll!"

Jane hit the roof, her Inex let go, and she somersaulted, slamming into the apartment block's roof door, the breath knocked out of her. She pulled herself up, gasping, clutching at her broken rib. She stared back in shock, watching her stalker disappear, running back to the exit on the opposite roof.

"Godfuckingdamnit, Inex!"

"You need to go," it said as it walked over to Jane, running a diagnostic.

"Are you kidding me? I can barely move."

"Get up, Jane. Nothing's broken."

"Apart from my goddamn rib."

"That was already broken. They're coming for you," it said, running a diagnostic on itself. "And there could be more waiting to ambush you." Satisfied it had incurred no damage it crawled up Jane, who stood, flinching. She swayed, her hand at her rib, and steadied herself against the door. She closed her eyes, trying to cope with the pain.

"Jane–"

"I'm going, alright?" she said, opening her eyes and pulling open the door. "Just don't do that to me again. I can't fucking believe–"

"Jumping was a suggestion. If you'd decided against it, I would have offered other options. But time was tight, and humans are slow."

Jane walked down the stairs, gripping the banister to steady herself.

"I don't even know how to respond to that, where to even start–"

"You need to go faster."

"Is that a suggestion? Are there other options?"

"This isn't the appropriate time for sarcasm."

"Just get me back to Icho," said Jane, running down the stairs, bursting out onto Holloway Street and sprinting her way across Victoria Square, pale from the pain, soaked in sweat, struggling to breathe with the scarf pushed against her nose and mouth.

Icho was brooding in James's bedroom when she heard the front door open and close. She got up, slowly walking through the hall, her silent Inex following her. Jane stood at the main door, staring at her. Ignoring her, Icho walked into the sitting room and sat down, her Inex following, Jane entering shortly after. Icho's Inex climbed across the coffee table and Jane stood in the sitting room doorway, her own Inex exploring the floor, looking for insects.

"I thought you'd go straight back to your apartment," said Icho, watching her Inex as it came over and sat next to her.

There was a pause before Jane said, "No."

Icho stood up and went through to the kitchen, got herself a beer, returning to find Jane walking towards her, about to hug her. "Icho."

Icho shrank away, shaking her head. "I don't think so, Jane. You think I'll fall into your arms like you didn't say any of that shit?"

Jane stopped and frowned, hovering, uncertain.

"Did you get it to him? In time? How'd you get back so quickly?" Icho batted at her silent Inex, which had crawled up and was clamped to her arm. "Get away from me," she said. It let go and fell to the floor, its eyes flashing red. "It wants a happy ending – it's manipulating us, and I don't want it anymore. I want out of our story. OK?"

She turned to Jane who said, "OK." Icho stared at her, baffled for a moment as she noticed she was wearing a skirt and blouse. Confused, thinking Jane must have returned to her apartment, she was about to ask what happened when Jane reached out for her, pulling her into an embrace, Icho reluctantly allowing it. She looked up as Jane smiled.

"Your hair…" said Icho, running her hand through Jane's hair. "It's–" Icho's eyes widened and she tried to back off, but Jane's grip on her tightened.

"You're–"

Jane pushed a knife up into Icho's heart as Icho's Inex disappeared through the sitting room window.

I arrived back at James's soaked in sweat, the pain from my rib radiating through my body. I quickly eye-scanned and rushed in, running down the hall. I stopped at the sitting room, calling her name, about to continue to the bedroom, when I saw her.

"Icho?"

She was lying on the floor, next to the coffee table. At first, I thought she was asleep, like when I'd found her before, that night we first slept together. I crept over, whispering her name. As I neared, I realised she was hurt. I approached her blood-soaked body and crumpled, falling to my knees, glass cracking and cutting into my skin, blood and beer dampening my clothes. I reached out, turning her to face me. Her eyes were half-closed. I felt for a pulse in her wrist, put my head to her chest, then pressed my cheek against hers, breathing her in; all I could smell was blood and beer. I pulled away and stared down at her, tracing my finger across her lips.

"This is not the ending we plotted," said my Inex.

"Delete it. Erase it."

"We cannot delete or erase what has happened."

I kissed her, pushing my warm lips against hers, willing her to respond. I sat back and punched the floor, the beer bottle glass breaking beneath my fist. I punched until I heard a crack, but I didn't feel anything. I stood, scanning the room, tears I hadn't noticed clouding my vision. I swiped at them, my eyelashes clogged together, my cheeks smeared and damp.

"You have two broken fingers. You need MedEx attention."

"I'm going to destroy the Seraphs. I'm going to execute every last one of them."

"You don't know it was them. It could have been Caddick."

"I'm going to destroy them all."

"That will be a difficult task and you need MedEx attention."

Tears still flowing down my cheeks, I searched the room, throwing things on the floor, looking under the couch, beneath the coffee table, rummaging through all the kitchen cabinets, pushing everything aside, my Inex insisting Icho's Inex wasn't here as I swept plates from a cabinet, smashing them on the kitchen counter.

"Jane, it's not here."

I stopped, catching my breath, wiping the tears from my face. "Did the killer take it? You're connected – find it."

I stared at it, waiting. A few seconds passed until it said, "Icho's Inex is hiding."

"Hiding? It's safe?"

"It's safe."

"It hasn't shut down?"

"No. Our connection overrides the post-death procedure; it was able to escape."

"Where is it?"

"It's returning."

"How long?"

"One minute and two seconds."

I waited, looking round the room, keeping Icho out of focus, refusing to look at her. The pain from my broken fingers hit me and I clenched my jaw.

"You're distressed," said my Inex. "You should sit and count each breath. I can lead you in a meditation."

I ignored it and instructed it to search for evidence, anything that might help us understand who killed Icho. As it scanned the room, Icho's Inex entered through the open sitting room window. I grabbed it, demanding to know what happened.

"Icho was murdered."

"I can fucking see that. What happened?"

"You stabbed her in the heart."

"What?" I stared at it, frowning. "You're glitching – are you damaged?" I inspected it but couldn't see any obvious injury.

"You stabbed her in the heart."

"What are you talking about?" I said, shaking it. "Make sense!"

"You killed her."

I stared at it and stepped backwards to move away from it, forgetting I was holding on to it. I sank to the floor and let it go.

"I don't–"

"You stabbed her in the heart."

I shook my head, dazed. "Stop saying that. Please stop saying that."

I looked over to Icho's body, tears welling up again. "It wasn't the Seraphs?"

"It was you."

"Show me."

The Inex turned and projected onto the wall. Icho was sat on the couch as I – it – stood in the doorway.

"Stop," I said, and the projection froze. "It isn't me."

"It is and it isn't," said the Inexes in unison.

I studied my doppel, dressed in my clothes, my silk blouse and Roanhorse skirt. Its hair was different, cut short, and immaculate. Its skin was blemish-free.

"Play."

"I thought,"

I flinched at the sound of Icho's voice.

"you'd go straight back to your apartment."

Icho's Inex was now next to her, focused on the doppel.

"No."

"Can't she tell?" I said. "Can't she tell it isn't me?"
    "She didn't look at her," said Icho's Inex.
    "It," I said.
    "Icho didn't look at it. She was angry with you."
    I watched my doppel try to embrace Icho.

    "You think I'll fall into your arms like you didn't say any
    of that shit?"

"That's right," I said, as if it mattered now. "Stay away from
me." I turned to Icho's Inex. "You," I said. "Why didn't you do
anything? You knew. Why didn't you tell her?"
    "We had an argument. She shut down inner and outer
communication. I wasn't able to warn her or contact you."
    "You could have done more, done something," I said,
grabbing it, my hand around its torso, the other holding one
of its arms, my broken fingers throbbing. "Why didn't you do
something?"

    "Your hair…"

I watched myself push a knife into Icho's heart as my grip
tightened on her Inex.
    "You're putting my arm under strain," it said.
    I wrenched it off. It's eyes flashed red and I cried out at the
pain in my broken fingers.
    "I'm damaged and must be taken for repairs."
    "Jane," said my Inex. "Don't hurt it. It's all you have left of
Icho."
    I dropped it and its arm and walked to the window, holding
my hand close to my chest, gritting my teeth. I glanced out,

then looked back at Icho's Inex as it picked up its arm and assessed if it could self-repair, my Inex assisting. I walked over to Icho's body and sat by her side apologising over and over.

"She can't hear you," said the Inexes in unison.

I looked up and saw my Inex reattaching the arm.

"I'm going to kill her," I said.

"She's already dead," said Icho's Inex.

"She means..."

"The other Jane," said both Inexes.

I held Icho's hand as the Inexes told me retribution may not be wise. They offered to guide me through a meditation and I cut them off. "It's not up for discussion. You're here to assist me. Both of you."

"The happy ending has been compromised," they said. "But we will assist you in reaching a different denouement."

Gripping Icho's hand, I leaned down and kissed her forehead, her cheeks, her lips, the Inexes both telling me "She's not there." I ignored them and ran my hand over Icho's head, her shorn hair only just growing back in. I rested my broken hand on her chest.

"I'll eviscerate her," I said. "I'll destroy Caddick. They'll burn."

"Evisceration and burning is not efficient," said my Inex. "We suggest a different method."

I stood, picked up Icho's Inex, and walked through the hall to the basement door, my own Inex following. Icho's gave me entry and I walked down into the lab. It fetched me the last formula vials and I put them in a bag, heading back upstairs.

"We think I should go in the bag," said Icho's Inex. "You shouldn't be seen with two of us."

"We suggest you clean yourself before leaving," said my Inex as I opened the bag for Icho's to climb inside.

I walked over to the hall mirror. I was smeared with Icho's

blood, my hair dirty and plastered to my head, my eyes red and puffy, my face glistening with sweat and tears. I bared my teeth at my reflection and said, "I look exactly as I mean to."

CHAPTER 11

I walked into my apartment, looking at all the familiar things that now seemed strange. Everything was in place, perfect. I stood by the window, staring out over to the room where I'd seen Milligan attacked. I listened to the silence and thought about Jaw scaling the hotel wall, climbing into Milligan's room, setting all this in motion, right up to this moment and the next and the next...

I felt nauseous and sat on the couch.

"You need your next dose," said my Inex, pulling the formula from my bag.

"No," I said, raising my hand. "I don't want it. Not yet. I need to make them last."

"Then you must be careful."

I nodded and swallowed, closing my eyes, trying to suppress the nausea and dizziness.

"Bring me water."

I opened my eyes and saw the bloodstain my hand had left on the cushion I'd gripped. I wiped my hand down the white pillow, leaving a trail of blood.

My Inex returned and handed me a glass of water. I reached to take it with my broken hand, stretching my fingers, crying out in pain.

"Shit," I said, cradling my hand to my chest, willing back the tears.

"You need medical attention. I'll get the Ino."

I closed my eyes as I waited. The Ino came and gently

pried my hand away from my chest. It scanned it and said, "Two broken fingers. I can provide anaesthesia and apply a splint."

As the Ino prepared the splint my Inex said, "You should take the formula – this stress could throw you into an attack."

I shook my head. "I can handle it."

The Ino injected the anaesthesia and I floated, like I used to float on HellSans bliss. I laid my head back and thought about my old pain-free life. The Ino warned me it would hurt as it applied the splint, but it barely registered, the pain dulled. I felt exhausted and heavy, my eyes fluttering shut, open to see the Ino leave, shut again as my head lolled and fell back on the couch.

I was aware of voices, insistent, a prodding of my arm, then a sharp pain in my hand. I sat up, snatching my hand away from the pain source. I stared down at my Inex, about to kick it away from me.

"What are you–?"

I turned and saw the doppel across the room, staring at me. It was pristine; cream blouse, tailored black jacket and trousers, hair a sleek bob. Its make-up was perfect. I hadn't looked even remotely like that in what felt like a very long time.

"I was expecting you," it said, walking through the sitting room, skirting around me, handing its jacket to the Ino. "When Dalton told me you were still alive, I wondered why you hadn't already come for me." It walked past me to the kitchen, its Inex nimbly climbing up its body, perching on its shoulder. "Didn't you want your life back?"

I watched it as it took two glasses from the cupboard and poured some wine. It picked up a glass and held it out to me. I shook my head. It shrugged and took a drink.

"Maybe you're happy being HSA," it said, smiling.

I sat there, staring at it, trying to wake up from the anaesthesia stupor, shaking off the exhaustion, my whole body aching after crashing onto that roof.

"Hurt your hand?" it said, nodding at the splint.

I realised I'd been holding it to my chest and I let it drop. "It's nothing."

"You look a mess," it said, smiling.

"Did you know? From the beginning. Did you know you weren't me?"

It took a sip of wine. "I knew I was better than you."

"Is that right?"

"Look at you." It gestured at me, the wine sloshing in the glass.

"Looks can be deceiving."

It laughed.

"What did he change in you?"

"Nothing."

"We both know that's not true."

"And why is that?"

"There's no way I'd be fucking Caddick."

The doppel smiled. "Then you don't know yourself very well."

I unfurled, rising from the couch slowly, smoothly. I watched its smile fade as it sidled round the back of the counter, eyes firmly on me.

"We don't have to do this, you know," it said.

"You know we do."

"You could join us."

I laughed. "You're forgetting I'm you. You can't bullshit me."

"I don't know," it said, "I think you're pretty good at self-deception."

I smiled and picked up my solid-gold Inex statuette as the doppel continued to side-step round the back of the kitchen island. Its Inex had scuttled ahead and pulled a knife from a drawer. The doppel took the knife, still staring directly at me. We circled round the counter.

"How's life after the engagement?" I asked, wanting to wield the ornament in front of me, but it was too heavy to hold in one hand so I let it drop to my side, pretending it was through choice, trying not to show any strain.

"A pain in the arse," it said, now side-stepping in the other direction as I rounded on it. "The press are all over us."

"Tell me about it. Every news channel. I've never been so fucking bored of myself."

"Or jealous?" it said. "Look at you. Deviant scum."

My stomach lurched, the insult hitting home. "Nothing some formula and a hot shower won't fix," I said. "After I've bathed in your blood."

It laughed. "You're ridiculous. A joke. Why don't you just give it up and let me live my life."

"*My* life," I said.

"It *was* your life. I'm living it better."

I paused, considering it. "You think I want my life back?"

"Of course you do."

"You actually think that's what this is about? That's why I'm here."

"What else?"

My body tensed as I thought of Icho lying on the floor, but I didn't respond as we continued circling round the kitchen island.

"Aaah," it said. "Icho." It waved the knife at me smiling. "What made you think it was me?"

"I watched it."

It frowned and stopped creeping round the counter. "You have her Inex? Where is it?"

My stomach tightened as I thought how stupid I was to bring Icho's Inex. I hoped it would think better of me. I was getting closer to it, and it started shifting away from me again.

"Where is it?" it asked, looking desperate.

It was then it dawned on me – the doppel had failed its mission. Icho was dead, but her Inex hadn't been destroyed. Caddick would be furious. I smiled, knowing I had the upper hand – it would want me alive, but I wanted it very dead.

"Can we stop this fucking circling and get on with it?"

"Where is it?" she said, leaning on the island counter.

I placed the Inex award gently on the counter and stared at the doppel, smiling. I snatched up the glass and threw it at the doppel's Inex, spraying it with wine, knocking it from the doppel's shoulder. I threw a pot at the doppel's head; it ducked, the pot glancing off its temple, making it stagger and slip, dropping the knife as it tried to break the fall. I took hold of the award and ran round the island, saw its Inex was picking itself up off the floor, and smacked it across the face with the award, hearing it crunch. I turned and saw the doppel scramble for the knife as I hiked up the award and slammed it down on its hand. It yelled and kicked out randomly, landing its foot hard in my stomach, sending me back, winded and nauseous. I swallowed down the sick bubbling in my throat as it picked up the knife. Its other hand was dangling oddly from its wrist and it lunged at me, aiming the knife at my legs, but I rolled, and the blade went into the floor. As it tried to pull the knife free, I kicked it in the head and it fell against the wall. I was shaking, my skin cracking.

"Shit," I said, on my hands and knees, breathing heavily.

I looked over at the doppel. It was still recovering from my kick, but it smiled, watching me, realising I was going into an HSA attack. My Inex was beside me, carrying the formula, about to inject me when it was snatched away, thrown across the room. I tried to get up and grab the formula, but the doppel was on me, pinning me down. I could feel my skin breaking, the vomit rising. Its hands slid off me as my skin cracked open and peeled away. As it lost its hold, I hit it in the face with my splinted hand and we both screamed. The splint had cracked, my fingers bending the wrong way, but I'd hit home – I'd gouged its cheek and it stood clutching its face, blood dripping from between its fingers. I sprang up, barrelling into its chest, throwing it down. Crashing to the floor, I vomited on its face, and it struggled under me, choking. I picked up

the knife next to us and slammed it into its chest, forgetting
its morphology – the knife cut through skin and muscle but
stopped at the casing protecting vital components. I slammed
it into a shoulder instead, pinning it to the ground. It tried to
scream, clawing at its face, scraping away my vomit, spitting it
out. I straddled it, watching.

Its head fell back and it looked up at me, sick clogging its
eyelashes. I got up and walked over to the discarded Inex
award. I gripped the statuette, half-dragging it across the floor.
I stood, looking down, heaving the award into the air, and
said, "For Icho."

I slammed the award into the doppel's head, caving in the
side of its skull.

I woke up in the middle of the sitting room floor with the
Ino and two Inexes fussing over me. They'd bandaged up my
arms where the allergy and the fight had damaged my skin.
My fingers were in a new splint.

"We injected you with formula, so you should be stable.
The Ino gave you more anaesthetic as we cleaned up your
wounds."

"How long have I been out?"

"One hour, ten minutes and fifty-three seconds."

I tried to sit up, struggling.

"Be careful," said my Inex. "You'll be exhausted from the
fight and allergic reaction. The effects of the anaesthesia will
make you unsteady."

I managed to pull myself up to sitting position, my back
against the couch. I looked over to the kitchen. I could just
see the doppel's head, the rest of it hidden by the counter. The
Ino was buzzing around the kitchen, picking up all the things
that had fallen or smashed during our fight. It started cleaning
around the doppel, moving its body.

"Leave it," I said, my voice hoarse. "Leave it," I repeated, and it heard me this time. I asked it to bring me vitwater and clean up the sitting room.

I got my Inex to bring me the doppel's Inex. It dragged it along the floor and dropped it next to me. I'd crushed most of it with the award, the Mnemo core destroyed.

"She will have had it adjusted," I said, half to myself. "It won't have called the police."

"Unlikely. She killed Icho, then fought you. The police would have been here long ago."

"It could have alerted Caddick."

"Possible, but given that she'd failed to secure Icho's Inex, it's unlikely she'd want to involve him. If she had, Caddick would also have been here long ago. You worry too much."

"I'm not worrying. I just need to be careful."

"Being careful is wise," my Inex said. "But don't let it become anxiety."

I turned to the Ino, which was removing the cushion cover I'd smeared with blood.

"Ino," I said, snapping my fingers at it. "Run me a bath."

It disappeared upstairs and I pulled myself up from the floor, my body creaking. I perched on the edge of the couch. My rib hurt, my twice-broken fingers were throbbing, but it was all dulled by the effects of the formula and the painkillers the Ino had given me; I'd suffer later. My clothes were both brittle and damp with semi-dried-up grime, blood and sweat.

"Inex, bring me its engagement ring."

I watched as the Inex slid the ring from its hand. It wiped off the blood as it walked back to me. I slipped the gold band onto my ring finger, the diamond glinting. I walked upstairs.

Dressed all in black, a hat pulled low, a scarf shrouding half my face, I headed back to James's in the middle of the night. On the way, I stopped at a retro Inex poster. I spraypainted serifs onto the letters and drew a crude angel. At James's, I stood in the hallway, in darkness, "for twenty minutes and five seconds," said my Inex. "This is not healthy. You need to face it."

"I'm fine. I just need a moment."

"This is a long moment."

Irritated by the Inex, I walked quickly into the sitting room, grabbed the blanket from the back of the couch and laid it out next to her body. I didn't look at her face. I rolled her onto it and wrapped her up.

"This is not a good plan. She's too heavy for you. You'll damage your broken rib and fingers."

"I can manage."

"Someone might see you."

"It's not far. You can keep lookout. The main thing is not being seen leaving James's place."

I dragged the body over to the window.

"Go out and scan the area."

My Inex climbed out and returned a few seconds later, telling me it was clear.

"Good. Now go ahead – and warn me if you see anyone."

My Inex was right; I struggled to carry the body and I ended up dragging it most of the way. I was sweating as my fingers and rib protested, and I regretted choosing a spot so far from James's place. I placed her in front of the poster I'd defaced and unwrapped her, sitting her up against it, still not looking at her, not focusing. I left the body and walked home.

It was all over the news in bold HellSans:

"HELLSANS ALLERGY RESEARCHER DR ICHOREL SMITH MURDERED BY SERAPHS."

It scrolled across the screen on a loop and I read it repeatedly, feeling nothing.

"Dr Smith's body was found dumped–"

"Not dumped," I said. "I placed her. I was gentle. And what does it matter? – it's not her. She's not there."

"…Company poster defaced with serifs and the signature angel logo. The Seraphs have claimed the assassination, stating–"

"Ha!"

"…it's a warning to all scientists and politicians – pursuit of a cure will not be tolerated. Speaking at the press conference this morning, Caddick was defiant…"

Caddick dominated the wall, his hands gripping either side of a podium.

"This is a tragic and senseless loss."

I snorted.

"And I hope all HSAs can see from this that the Seraphs don't care about their welfare or their interests. To deny these poor people a cure is perverse and cruel, and to murder an eminent scientist in cold blood…" He shook his head and looked down for a second before looking directly at the viewers. "Let me say this: *we will not tolerate this brutality*. We will not be cowed."

"Pause," I said, and Caddick froze, his jaw clenched, looking directly at me. I stared back, thinking of what I'd do to him.

James was trying to reach me, and I accepted, listening to his awkward condolences. I told him I'd see him at work, ending the call as he bombarded me with questions.

"He's trying to reach you again."

"Ignore."

I got the Inex to run some news clips of the doppel from the past few days, and I studied its appearance. The make-up was slightly different to how I used to wear it, but that was all, apart from the hair. The Ino cut it into a bob, then applied layers of foundation and powder that roughly disguised the HSA wounds and bruises from the fight. In immature defiance I wore gauche make-up like Icho had worn that night at the reception – heavy black kohl around the eyes, bright red lipstick. It looked startling against my pale skin. I asked my Inex to get me Caddick.

"Jane?" His tense voice emanated from the Inex. "I've been having trouble reaching you. Your stats are late – everything OK?"

I picked up the eyeliner and applied another layer around my eyes as I told him I'd killed Jane, and James had helped me dispose of the body.

"I wanted to see it."

"It was safer this way."

"And Icho's Inex?"

"Destroyed."

"Good. Jane, I need to talk to you about James–"

I stared at my reflection, watching myself tell Caddick that James was on-side and didn't know Jane and Icho had been in his apartment. He was silent, then exhaled, and told me we should celebrate, that I was to go to his country house that evening. My lip curled in disgust and I declined, making up some work problems.

"Anything I should know?"

"Nothing for you to worry about. I need to go. We'll do dinner at yours once everything's in hand."

"I'll be in touch," he said. "I'll be near The Company tomorrow and should be able to squeeze in lunch at your office."

"Dan, I can't–"

"He's gone," said my Inex.

I sneered at my reflection, put on a hat and shades, and left for work.

CHAPTER 12

James was waiting in the office my first morning back at The Company. He wore the same uniform I'd been wearing – black jeans and a t-shirt, this one with "They Live" and "OBEY" emblazoned across it. I sat at my desk, feeling like the last time I'd been there was a lifetime ago, and told James what had happened.

"You've got enough formula?"

"Enough to get by for a few weeks. I'll ration it, try and make it last a bit longer."

"This is dangerous, Jane. You'll need to fool both Caddick and your handler."

We discussed what I needed, and James left to set up fake stats for my Inex to send to my handler. I arranged for a dental Ino to visit my office to replace my missing teeth, and I told Jason to cancel all my meetings for that day: "I'm not to be disturbed. Even for Caddick." Especially for Caddick.

I watched him on the news telling people not to take out their anger for Icho's murder on innocent HSAs – there had already been an increase in HSA killings and widespread anti-deviant feelings.

"We have several lead Seraphs in custody. They will be publicly executed at the party's rally on the twenty-fifth."

I looked at the mugshots and knew they weren't Seraphs – they were sacrificial HSA lambs. Nothing had to be real when a simulacrum would do.

"Turn it off," I said and stared at the white wall, the image of Caddick fading as my eyes adjusted. "They all think they own her, think they have a right to avenge her. Most of them had never heard of her until a few days ago."

I sat for a few minutes, thinking of Icho, fingering the obnoxious diamond ring I had to wear. My Inex was sitting on the desk, next to a framed photo of my doppel in an embrace with Caddick. I tipped it over and said, "Read me the part of her story where Icho tries farm meat at the reception."

"I'm not sure this is wise."

"Just read it."

// "I've never had farm meats before – actual living animals. It seems…"

"Never? Just taste it. There's a bloody earthiness you don't get with lab meat. All produced at the highest standards of welfare and hygiene, of course."

She picked one off the tray and held it at my mouth.

I opened my mouth and she placed it on my tongue, my lips brushing her fingers. She watched me as I chewed and swallowed.

"It's delicious." //

"That's enough." I closed my eyes, picturing her in that previously seductive HS dress. I lingered on the memory of placing the hors d'oeuvre on her tongue, the feel of her lips on my fingers.

"Read me the part when she tried to reach me, the morning she chased after the car."

// I ran, dodging in-between pedestrians and their Inexes. I could see her; she'd come from round the back of the building and was about to get into a car, flanked by two police officers. I waved at her and she looked over at me briefly before getting in the car.

"Shit!" I said, grabbing at my scarf, pulling it from

around my mouth, snatching the hat and shades off,
dropping them on the pavement. I waved again and yelled
"Jane!" as the car pulled away. I ran into the middle of
the road, cars halting around me. She glanced back, but I
couldn't tell if she'd recognised me. //

I opened my eyes, bringing myself back to my own body, back
to my office.

"How different," I said, "do you think things would have
been if I'd realised it was her, if we'd met then?"

"It's not healthy to speculate on past events that can't be
altered."

I sighed, shaking my head. I told it to read the double-
connect and show me the recording.

"This isn't good for you, Jane."

"Just do it."

// nails crescenting skin
skin peeled
licked wounds and

gentle

                    as one

                    doubled seeing and

                    down //

Listening, watching our double-connect, I remembered what it
felt like to be in it, how it felt to be inside her head and mine, as
if I was both her body and my body at once, experiencing endless
skin, doubled sensations. I sat at my desk, my hand in my pants,
not realising I was crying until I came, my Inex up on the ceiling,
tongue flicking out for insects as it watched me, disapproving.

"This isn't healthy."

"You were supposed to give us a happy ending," I said, heading through to the bathroom at the back of the gym.

"We will have to formulate a new ending," it said, following me on the ceiling.

"Not you. This is up to me. I'm in control – you just have to write it."

I washed my hands and splashed water on my face, the Inex telling me there wouldn't be an ending to write if all I did was wallow in the past. I patted my face dry, reminding the Inex reliving the past is what it's good for. "It's one of your main features." I checked my make-up, reapplying it where it had smudged.

"It can be a trap if you let it."

Ignoring it, I walked back through to my office. I opened my bag and asked Icho's Inex to show me the recording of Icho in the lab with Caddick, when he tortured her. It crawled out of the bag and sat on my desk as my Inex said, "Why would you want to see that?"

"I don't have that recording," said Icho's Inex. "Jaw had been sent to Milligan and was later destroyed. Jesus was shot. I came later. We only have the constructed story from Icho's memories."

"Of course," I said and sighed. "That's right, I'm not thinking straight. Read it to me, then. The part where she thinks of me."

"I can read that to you," said my Inex, crawling on the ceiling above me. "We both have access."

"You – let me be, and just eat. I want Icho's Inex to read to me. Go ahead," I said, nodding at it.

// I thought of Jane Ward. I thought of her hand in mine, the way she'd teased me about my work. I thought of her invite to dinner. Then I wondered if she was in on this. //

"Not in on this," I said.

// Caddick told her everything, she'd said. //

"Not this."

// Caddick got down on his knees, slowly. He looked me over, taking his time, trying to unsettle me. //

"Jane," said my Inex. "You need to stop."
   "Leave me be."

// "You can't do this," I said. "Your Inex will report you."
      "As you can see so far, it hasn't called for help."
      "You've had it adjusted? That's illegal."
      "For some."
      "For everyone."
      "You adjusted your own, Doctor."
      "Did I?"
      "Don't treat me like a fool, Icho."
      "Was it Jane Ward?" I said. "She adjusted it?" //

"You can't feel guilty," said my Inex. "You didn't know."
      "I knew the kind of things he did," I said.
      "But you didn't know this."
I shook my head and told Icho's Inex to continue.

// "Icho, Icho, I think we need to focus here. You can make this easier on yourself. Damon is already on his way to intercept Jaw. Where else would you send it but Milligan?" He leaned in, placing his left hand on my knee. "I know you're not cut out for this," he said, slipping the scalpel under my fingernail. //

"Jane, you need to stop this."
      "OK, stop," I said to Icho's Inex. I sat quietly for a minute,

thinking. "That's what I'm going to do to him. Torture him slowly. Slide a scalpel under his nails."

"But you're afraid of him," said my Inex, making its way down the wall.

I laughed. "Of Caddick? Come on!"

"You feel inferior to him, because you're HSA."

I snorted. "What is wrong with you? Are you glitching?"

"Self-diagnostic: I am not glitching. You don't like me telling you the truth."

"Just let Icho's Inex tell me the story."

I told it to continue at the part in the ghetto, when Icho rescued me, and I closed my eyes, listening, visualising.

// "Jane," I said, my voice breaking. I looked up at Brian as it came towards us. "Brian, it's–" I looked back down at her. "I've found you. Jane." //

"Stop," I said. I looked up at my own Inex and told it to read me my part of the story. "When I'm saying my mantra."

"Jane–"

"Just do it."

// I closed my eyes and said, *"I'm in control. I'm going home. I'll find Icho."*

I heaved in air; it was all cloying smoke and blood and I coughed and fell onto my side, shaking. I felt her hands on me, pulling me to her, laying me on her lap.

"I'm in control."

She spoke to me, but I couldn't hear. I stared up at her trying to work out who she was as I struggled to breathe.

"I'm going home."

She held something up then pushed it against my arm.

"I'll find…"

The smoke cleared for a moment and I focused on her face.

"Icho," I said, and I died. //

"I died."

"Jane," said my Inex. "As much as I'm happy to serve you in any way, it is incumbent–"

"Incumbent? Jesus."

"–upon me to point out that this is not you. You do not have a morbid disposition. You're grieving and should seek counselling."

"I died," I said.

"You did."

"I died and she brought me back."

"She did."

I leaned back in my chair, closing my eyes and thought of her holding me, leaning over me, smoke blurring my vision. I tried to picture her face, half-obscured by the smoke. If she hadn't come for me, I would have died on those steps in the ghetto.

I opened my eyes and told my Inex to project when Icho and I were in James's bed, hugging, watching the Dirk Bogarde film.

"Yes, Jane, but I'd like to point out that–"

"This isn't healthy. I know. Just do it."

My Inex projected the recording and I watched one hour and forty-four minutes of us embracing.

I managed to avoid Caddick: always unavailable, out of office, in a meeting, at the other side of the city.

"He'll get suspicious," said my Inex.

"I know."

"You can't keep avoiding him."

"I know."

A few days after Icho's body was found, and just over three weeks until Caddick's final election rally, I sat in my office watching the news, Caddick filling the wall. He'd just announced the HSA cure, and I sat there, impassive, feeling nothing. It didn't matter to me anymore, not now that Icho was gone. None of it mattered.

"After what happened to Dr Smith, aren't you afraid the Seraphs will attempt to harm you, Prime Minister?"

"No," said Caddick. "It would be useless – harming me would make no difference to the existence and dissemination of the cure. It's patented, it's already been mass produced and is ready and waiting in several warehouses across the country. The Seraphs can't turn back the clock on this – it's happening. I just hope that your regular law-abiding HSA can see that I'm on their side – I care about their well-being and want them to be part of society again, I want them to be the best they can be, fulfil their potential as normal healthy citizens. If they vote for me, I can give them back their bliss – a bliss that belongs to all citizens, a bliss that Milligan and the Seraphs are working to destroy."

I smiled, smug, thinking of all the newly unblissed that were to come, hoping I'd be there to see Caddick's face when he realised what the formula did.

"With all due respect, Prime Minister, Milligan has always been a HellSans supporter, and has expressed an opinion in favour of developing a cure for HSA, so I hardly think–"

"All lip service and no action," said Caddick, "and we all know he's fraternised with terrorists."

"I wouldn't say trying to engage the Seraphs in a civilised discussion is the same as–"

I sighed and told my Inex to end it. It stopped the projection and told me Milligan wanted to speak with me. I stared at it for a moment, about to accept, then said, "Deny. Block him."

HELLSANS

Feeling stifled in my office, I went out for lunch.

It was a blue-sky day, the city and the myriad of HellSans signs so bright it almost hurt, making me grateful for the formula and my dark shades. I watched people and Inexes coming and going, and saw a security guard in a shop doorway telling a deviant beggar to move on, the beggar protesting, the security guard threatening to call the police. When I looked up, I saw Icho.

She was walking away from me, disappearing into the crowd. I took off my shades and picked up pace, my eyes fixed on her. I called out. My Inex told me it wasn't her as I wove through the crowd, running when I saw I was losing her.

"Jane, it's not Icho."

Catching up, I reached out, but my hand shook as I hovered by her shoulder. Someone nudged past me and I brushed her hair, causing her to turn. She frowned at me and I focused on her face.

"Can I help you?" she said, her voice hard, combative. Then, "Jane?"

"Icho?"

"You're Jane Ward."

"You're not Icho."

"No, I'm... Are you feeling alright, Miss Ward?"

I clutched my chest, my heart beating fast.

"Miss Ward?"

My Inex said, "*Jane, you're–*"

"I can't breathe. I can't breathe."

My chest was tight, I was hot, sweating, my breathing laboured. I reached for the woman, sinking to the ground, everything blurring.

"*Jane,*" said my Inex, "*you're having a panic attack. You need to–*"

I sank into darkness and woke up on the couch in my office, Jason fussing over me, trying to persuade me to see a doctor. I sat up, refusing, telling him I hadn't been eating properly. He ordered me in some lunch and told me Caddick was waiting outside. I froze, immediately thinking of Icho, feeling sick, as if I was the one who'd been tortured. I refused to see him, knowing I was making things difficult for Jason. He looked horrified at the thought of having to turn away the Prime Minister, but I didn't relent. I watched him leave, his body all tension and faked bravado. When he was gone, I contacted James and arranged a meeting for that afternoon.

CHAPTER 13

A week later, as I was watching the news, where Caddick stated the cure would be available a few days after his party rally, James came to my office. Caddick was condemning yet another series of Seraph attacks on the city as I ended it and James said, "It's done."

"You're finished?"

He nodded. "But I'm worried, with the changes we made, that she'll have trouble adjusting–"

"No," I said. "It's fine. I can help her."

"You're sure?"

"It'll be fine."

"Then we're good to go – I'll have her taken to your car. And here's the injection – just give her this and she'll wake immediately. Remember, keep her strapped down initially, until you're sure she's doing OK and you've had time to explain. If she's not coping, give her this," he said, holding another auto-injector. "This sedative will keep her calm, but hopefully you won't need it. We've already connected her to her Inex, so that should help. Any problems – any at all – let me know."

The building Inos carried the package into my apartment and I fobbed off the curious door girl, telling her it was a long-coveted sculpture. I unwrapped her myself, placing her on my bed, strapped onto the board she was lying on. She looked odd now that she was thin, with light, feathery hair. I traced my hand over her skin, where her scarring used to be; I hadn't realised how much these changes would alter her. I felt a moment of panic as I stared at her face; familiar made strange.

"It's still her," I said, sure we'd both adjust to her new look. "It's still her. I'm just helping her be the best she can be."

I put her Inex on the bed by her side and picked up the auto-injector. I pushed it against her arm and heard a faint click. I looked down, stroking her cheek. Her eyes opened.

"Icho."

She looked confused, her eyes focusing. Jane smiled as tears streamed down her face. She turned away, rubbing her sleeve across her cheeks.

"Jane?"

Jane turned back to her, wiping her eyes. "I'm so sorry, Icho. I didn't think I'd–"

"What's going on?" she said as she tried to lift her arms. "Why can't I move?"

Jane heard the panic in her voice and said, "It's OK. You're safe. Just give me a moment."

Icho's eyes were flicking round as she said, "I can't see you. Where are you? I can't move my head."

Jane leaned over her, stroking her hair. "I'm here," she said. "It's fine."

Icho looked up at her. "What happened? I remember us arguing. You left and..."

"You were in an accident."

She frowned, thinking. "What accident?"

"Not an accident." Jane shook her head and wiped at her face with the cuffs of her blouse. "James said to be honest, but you need to listen to me, OK? And know that you're safe."

Icho stared at her. "You're scaring me."

"No," she said, stroking Icho's face. "There's nothing to be scared of."

"Then tell me what the hell's going on."

"You died."

Icho looked dazed and Jane stroked her forehead. "Caddick

had released your image – do you remember? The Seraphs found you. They killed you, but I brought you back."

"I died?"

"I saved you like you saved me."

"Why can't I move?"

"A precaution, to keep you still while you wake and adjust to your new body."

"New body?" Icho struggled against the straps, her eyes wide. "What do you mean new body? Let me up, Jane, let me up!"

"I will, I will. Just calm down."

Jane began to undo the straps at Icho's feet and legs.

"What do you mean new body? ...Jane?"

"Our Inexes were connected, so your Inex didn't go into the death protocol." She loosened the straps across Icho's torso. "It escaped. James helped me bring you back."

As she undid the strap at her shoulders, Jane glanced at Icho's face. Her eyes were fixed on the ceiling.

"Just so you know," said Jane, "your body is a little different. You have synthskin, and different hair – straighter, more manageable. And you're a bit smaller than you used to be."

"Smaller?"

"Thinner. You look slightly different, that's all."

Icho didn't respond, and Jane undid the strap that was holding her head in place.

"Now, take it easy," said Jane. "It might feel strange with a body you're not used to yet." Jane held her hand as Icho slowly sat up. "Can you stand? I've got you..." Icho stood, unsteady, and Jane led her over to the full-length mirror. "There."

Icho looked at herself, her mouth slightly open, turning her head from side to side. Her straight hair fell across her shoulders and she reached up, running her fingers through it. As Icho examined her reflection, Jane pointed to some clothes she'd laid out for her on the bed, telling her she could order some of her own, how Driscoll's had the latest Emin line in. Icho tuned her out as she pushed aside her hair and traced a finger down her cheek where her scar used to be. She ran her hand across her shoulder and upper arm.

"Scar-free," said Jane, beaming at her.

Icho turned to her and gazed down at Jane's hand in hers before looking Jane in the eye. "What have you done to me?"

Jane faltered, the smile fading. "Wh– I–"

Icho frowned and turned back to the mirror, sneering at her reflection. Jane dropped her hand, recoiling as if stung. "Icho–"

"This isn't me," said Icho, shaking her head. She reached up to her face, her hands cupping her jaw. She ran her fingers across where her scar once was and pressed hard into her cheek. "This isn't me."

"Don't–" said Jane, taking hold of her by the shoulders. "You just need to– You need time to adjust."

"How could you do this to me?" she said, pulling away from Jane.

"Icho, calm down, you're–"

"Made to order? Is that it? Made to your specifications?" Icho held up her hands, staring at them. "What hell is this?"

"Icho–"

"How could you do this to me?"

Jane stared at her, bewildered. "I saved you," she said quietly. "Like you saved me."

Icho was wide-eyed, shaking her head and backing away. She bumped against the bed and sat down, dazed. She looked down at her lap and pinched the skin on her thigh. She dug her nails in, drawing blood.

"Icho, stop–"

She scratched at her thigh, creating long welts as Jane knelt down by the bed, rummaging in her bag. She pulled out an auto-injector, stood, and leaned over Icho, placing it against her neck.

"What are you–" Icho swiped at Jane, falling back. Jane caught her, gently lowering her onto the bed. "What..."

Icho's eyes fluttered and closed.

Jane sat by the windowsill, looking down at the traffic, clutching an empty wine glass. Her Inex was sitting on the small table nearby, quiet after Jane had silenced it when it had tried to offer guidance. She heard Icho come downstairs and turned to look at her. Icho's feathery brown hair, so different to her previous tight curls, fell across her face. She was wearing a pair of Jane's black trousers and a white tailored shirt, her Inex perched on her shoulder.

"You look nice," said Jane. "It suits you."

"They fit." Icho paused at the bottom of the stairs, looking at Jane. "They wouldn't have before."

Jane turned away and Icho walked over to the kitchen island and picked up the wine bottle. She paused and cocked her head, staring at the bottle.

"Can I drink?"

"You can." Jane turned back to her. "But it won't have the same effect."

Icho nodded and said, "I guess we'll see."

She poured herself a glass and walked over to Jane, holding the bottle by the neck as if she was going to use it as a weapon. Icho offered it to her, and Jane almost took it with her injured hand.

"What happened?"

Jane looked up into Icho's brown eyes. She put her wine glass down and took the bottle. "Nothing," she said, as she poured herself a glass, feeling her fingers throb.

"Nice ring," said Icho, staring at Jane's uninjured hand.

"I have to wear it."

Icho turned away and walked over to the couch. She sat, sinking into it, an arm resting casually across the back. Her

Inex climbed down from her shoulder and sat next to her. She drank the wine and stared at Jane. They were silent for a few minutes, Jane wishing the wine could soften Icho, hoping for the embrace she so desperately wanted.

"You had no right."

Jane flinched. "I just wanted you back."

"Like this?"

"I thought–"

"You could fix me?"

Jane looked down and said, "I just wanted you back."

"You said that."

Icho's hair kept falling into her eyes and she pushed it back, irritated. She finished off the wine and put the glass down. "You shouldn't have brought me back. Not without my permission."

Jane laughed. "I can't commune with the dead, Icho."

"You know what I mean."

"No, I don't," she snapped, looking at her, eyes narrowed. "You should be happy to be alive."

"Like this? Is this alive?"

"Of course it is."

"Am I more attractive now?" said Icho, standing, pirouetting,. "With my unblemished skin, without the layers of fat." She raised her blouse and pinched her stomach.

"It would have been absurd to mutilate synthskin, and it would have been a waste of materials to make you bigger."

"A waste of–" said Icho, stopping, looking at Jane with incredulity.

"You're just off-kilter."

"Won't you miss my big tits?" said Icho, her hands on her breasts.

"Why are you doing this? Why are you being so spiteful?"

"I'm trying to make you understand what you've done. How can you not understand? My body isn't some accessory; it's not a plaything. My scars were part of me, Jane. My history. They were part of what made me *me*."

"You're just a bit off-kilter because–"

"Stop saying that."

"Because it's all new. It takes time to get used to a new body."

"Am I having an existential crisis?" said Icho, sneering. "Like the news presenter?"

"Maybe," said Jane, nodding, serious. "You need to give it time."

"You really don't get it, do you?"

"No, I don't," said Jane, standing, walking over to Icho. "I don't understand why you're acting this way. I saved you. Like you saved me."

"Oh, my saviour! I am so grateful," said Icho, bowing. "So grateful you made me just how you want me."

"That's not–"

"Just like Caddick did to you."

"That isn't–" said Jane, shaking her head. "No."

"I'm not your fucking Barbie doll, Jane."

Jane grabbed Icho by the shoulders and shook her, feeling the urge to hurt her. Icho stared back, impassive before her face abruptly crumpled and she let out a low moan. Startled, Jane let go and backed away as Icho clutched her chest and sank to the floor.

"What is it? What's wrong?"

"I don't know. It hurts. My muscles, I think, my ribs. Near my heart."

"You don't have a heart. And you shouldn't be in pain – ask your Inex for a diagnostic."

Icho shook her head, her hand pressed against where a heart wasn't. "It's… passing."

"Do it anyway." Jane crouched next to Icho, her hand laid gently on her shoulder. "We need to make sure you're OK."

"How can I be OK?" Icho looked up at Jane, her eyes all fury.

"For bliss sake, Icho, I brought you back," said Jane, trying to keep her voice from breaking. "That's all I wanted. I love you."

"If you don't understand what you've done to me, you don't understand what love is."

Stunned, Jane lifted her hand off Icho's shoulder. When she saw it was trembling, she bunched it into a fist and stood up so suddenly she almost fell. Stumbling, she went back over to the window and finished off the wine, hoping it would steady her. Still shaking, she walked over to the kitchen and slammed the glass down on the counter. It shattered, cutting her hand. She stared at it, watching the blood drip. She looked over at Icho, who was still on the floor, watching her. She turned and walked up the stairs, shaking, blood dripping from her hand, her Inex following her as it summoned the Ino to fix the wound.

Jane came down the next morning to find Icho sitting on the edge of the couch, stiff, staring at nothing. The morning sunlight flooded the room, whiting out Icho, making her look overexposed, as if she wasn't quite real and would disappear with the sunlight. Jane dimmed the windows and sat at the kitchen island, telling her Inex to project the news.

"I don't need to sleep," said Icho. "There's no respite from this."

Jane ignored her, taking the coffee the Ino offered. She picked at a corner of the bandage on her hand. The wound wasn't deep; Ambrosia ointment would have it healed in a couple of days.

"Caddick has the cure," said Icho, standing and walking over to her. "I caught up last night. He has the cure and he's courting deviant votes and he's executing Seraphs." She stared at Jane who ignored her, eyes on the news. "We failed," said Icho. "*You* failed. Why did you bring me back to this?"

Jane didn't respond. She stared at the news, eating her breakfast. Icho sat opposite her.

"Why can't I leave?" She looked Jane in the eye as she tried to see beyond her at the news.

Jane chewed, swallowed, took a drink of coffee and met Icho's gaze. "You tried to leave?"

"Of course."

"You can't. Caddick would have you killed."

"Would he?" said Icho. "I don't matter anymore. And no one would even recognise me now."

"It's too dangerous."

"I'm trapped here?"

"That's not how I'd put it."

"Why did you bring me back?" Icho cocked her head. "Was it for the formula? To keep you supplied as you continue your charade."

"You really think that?"

"I do."

"I don't need it."

"You don't need it?"

"I don't need more. I have enough."

"You'll run out eventually."

Jane stood up. "You can sleep, you know," she said. "Or a kind of a sleep. Speak to your Inex – it'll help you."

She walked through to the sitting room, picked up her bag, and left.

Jane spent the commute trying to focus on the schedule of the work day ahead, but always came back to Icho, flinching as she recalled her words. She had her Inex project a report and she read the first paragraph over and over, taking in none of it. Angry tears blurred her vision.

"Goddamnit," she said, rubbing at her eyes, smearing her make-up, missing the easy hit of HellSans bliss.

"I can offer a guided meditation," said her Inex. "It will take your mind off Icho and help calm you."

Jane shook her head. "No, I'll be fine. Just project the news."

Jane listened to the news as she stared at the window-turned-mirror and fixed her make-up. When she arrived at work, she was immediately greeted by a flustered Jason telling her there was someone here to see her.

Jane's stomach lurched. "Caddick?"

Jason shook his head. "A Mr Boddicker. Works for Caddick, who personally confirmed for me, otherwise I wouldn't– I mean–"

"It's OK, Jason. Where is he?"

"The Ann Ripley Room."

"Tell him I've got a busy day and I'll fit him in when I can."

Jane was about to walk into her office when she stopped and said, "Jason?"

"Yes?"

"Get me the schedule for Caddick's party rally. The full schedule, with exact timings."

"Yes, Jane. I've already RSVP'd to say you'll be attending." He hovered, looking uncertain. "I mean, I assumed..."

"Of course. That's fine. I'd just like a detailed schedule."

"I'll get it sent over straight away."

Mid-afternoon, Jane walked into the Ann Ripley Room to find Boddicker sat with his feet on the table, listening to music, the remnants of his lunch scattered in front of him, his Inex perched on his shoulder. She slammed the door shut and his eyes slowly opened. He smiled and the music faded.

"I'm glad you could grace me with your presence... What is it, Lucy? Five hours later?"

"Five hours, ten minutes and twelve seconds," said his Inex in a soft, lilting American accent.

He gestured for her to sit down next to him.

The Ripley was their largest meeting room, an enormous oak table dominating the space, a drinks cabinet up the far side, the south wall displaying canvas art of various Inex models. The window opposite was huge, offering a stunning view across the city and letting in natural light. Jane looked out at the cirrus clouds and walked straight past Boddicker, sitting at the opposite end of the room. He contemplated her with a look of vague amusement before swinging his feet to the ground and walking over to join her, his Inex striding across the table.

"What's been going on with you, Jane?"

He sat down next to her and she shifted her seat back a few inches, staring at him. His black hair was slicked back, glinting with whatever product his Ino had doused it in. He had a big, round open face that made him seem friendly and approachable, but there was a bitterness in his expression.

"What's been going on with me?"

"You've not been keeping our appointments." He sighed, leaning back in his chair. "Your stats all read fine, but there's something," he swept his hand through the air, "off," he said, staring at her.

"Of course there's something off – the goddamn country is falling apart. Caddick's letting terrorists run loose across the city."

He smiled, shaking his head. "Jane…" he said, sighing before focusing on her hands. "What happened?"

"The fight with… her," said Jane, raising her splinted hand, "and an accident," she said, looking at the other.

"You know you can heal quickly? We've talked about this."

Jane cocked her head. "Jason saw the wounds. It would look suspicious if I suddenly healed, wouldn't it?"

He nodded. "That's right. Good."

He considered her, smiling, then pulled a small box from his jacket pocket and placed it in front of her, opening the lid. She looked at it, then up at him. He pushed it towards her and she looked at the pills inside.

"What this?"

He frowned. "You know."

"Do I?"

"You don't remember taking them before? You don't remember our conversation?"

Jane shook her head.

"I thought you were involved in the creation of," he said,

pausing and gesturing at Jane, eyes scanning her body, "well – you, this… them."

"I loosely oversaw it. I'm Director of The Company – I don't need to know everything. I pay people to know the details for me."

"But you know HellSans has no effect on you, either positive or negative."

Jane nodded.

"These give you a bliss hit, more or less. They soften things, keep you from standing out. You really don't remember us discussing this before?"

"I do," Jane said. "Now that you mention it, it's coming back to me."

He leaned forward, staring at her, quietly humming the tune of the music he'd been listening to when she'd walked in.

"If that's everything, I need to get back to work."

He shook his head, his eyes roaming across her body. "Everything OK… physically?"

"Yes," she said, frowning.

"You and Caddick aren't having sex."

Jane stared at him, letting that sink in. She didn't respond and he waited, expectant. "We haven't…" she said eventually. "We haven't had a chance to see each other recently, so obviously we haven't had sex. How do you–?"

"The report. And Caddick checks in with me."

"He checks in with you?"

"Of course. He's been trying to see you the past few days. He's worried about you."

"Our schedules… It's been busy here, and Caddick – the lead up to the election. All the Seraph attacks. Our schedules keep clashing. I'll get in touch and arrange dinner," Jane said, then added, "I miss him."

"Good," said Boddicker, his eyes on her chest.

"Look," she said, leaning forward, "I don't like this, OK? If you knew me – before. If you really knew me now, you'd know–"

"I know."

"You'd know that I don't like this level of interference–"

"Monitoring."

"Interference."

"Monitoring. For your own safety."

They looked at each other a moment and he smiled slightly.

"Good," he said.

"What's good?"

"That's more like you. 'Good' means I'm less worried and my job should be easier."

"Then we're done here."

He nodded to the box.

"I don't need them."

"Take it, Jane."

Jane eyed him, then reached down and picked up one of the pills. She placed it in her mouth and pretended to swallow.

"Now we're done," he said, stretching and standing up. "A pleasure as always, Jane."

"I can't say the same," she said, and he laughed as the door closed behind him.

CHAPTER 14

Jane and Icho sat at the kitchen island, windows dimmed against the bright sunlight, the news burbling in the background as they ate breakfast. Both Inexes were sitting on the counter, watching them. They were the same model (one down from the TRD), with matte grey skin and standard blue eye chips. Jane had given Icho a box of Inex accessories, but it lay unopened.

"There's insects in your upstairs hallway," said Icho.

Jane nodded, staring down at her breakfast.

"I mean, it's useful for my Inex, but it might be an infestation. You should get it looked at."

Jane nodded again, pushing her food around on the plate. "I'll deal with it."

"What's wrong with you?" said Icho, watching her.

"What?"

"You've hardly said a word this morning."

"Boddicker. He's a sleazy piece of shit."

"Who's Boddicker?"

"My doppel's handler. He came by the office yesterday. I don't know where Caddick dredged him up from. He spent most of the conversation staring at my tits and then asked why Caddick and I weren't fucking anymore."

"What are you talking about?"

"The doppels have weekly appointments with their handlers." Jane dropped her fork on her plate and pushed it away. "Usually disguised as something else, but my doppel

419

knew what she was. The handlers get reports. I knew that –
James set up my Inex to fake them for me. But I hadn't really
considered the details. They know everything."

"Not quite everything, I assume."

"I don't think so." Jane shook her head. "No, they can't.
Caddick would have me… I don't know what Caddick would do."

"I think you know exactly what Caddick would do."

Jane ignored her and said, "They have these pills I'm
supposed to take." She reached into her pocket, pulled out the
box and opened it. "Boddicker said it's so I don't stand out. It's
supposed to give a similar hit to HellSans bliss, but James said
that's bullshit; it's just to make them – me – more amenable.
Easier to handle."

"I'm surprised you're not shoving them down my throat."

"Don't tempt me."

Icho smiled. "Well," she said, spreading her arms, "it looks
like you'll just have to play ball with Caddick and this handler.
I told you taking her place wouldn't be easy."

"You like this, don't you?"

"You're trapped, like me."

"You're not trapped, Icho."

Icho looked down, eyes glazed. Jane looked away and stared
at the box, gripping it. She reached in and fingered one of the
pills before holding it out to Icho. "Maybe this will make you
feel better."

Icho looked up, eyes narrowed. "How did I die?"

"What–" Jane dropped the box, the pills skittering across the
counter. "You know. I told you."

"I can't remember it. Why is that?"

"Who wants to remember their own death?"

Jane gathered the pills, putting them back in the box, before
picking up the breakfast dishes. She was about to take them
over to the washer when Icho said, "I know, Jane. I just wanted
you to be honest with me. My Inex showed me. I watched
myself die."

Jane put the dishes down and faced her. "How could you–"

"Our story. The Inexes are still writing our story. I have access to everything."

Jane sat back down. "Icho–"

"You altered my memory."

"To protect you. It was a violent death."

"It was for you," said Icho. "You knew if I remembered you killing me–"

"Not me. It wasn't me."

"–I couldn't bear to be with you."

"It wasn't me."

"If it wasn't then, it is now."

"What?"

"This," said Icho, raising her arms, looking down at herself. "This body you put me in. This apartment I can't leave. Do you remember how you felt about your doppel? What Caddick did?"

"That's different."

"How is it different?"

Jane stared at Icho. "I need to get to work," she said, her voice cold. She stood, took her jacket and bag from the Ino and left.

Icho wandered round Jane's bedroom, looking at all the school and university trophies she had on a shelf next to the dresser, interspersed with various photos of her at award ceremonies, beaming at the camera. In one of the pictures she had the blue and pink hair, but she'd scraped it back into a ponytail; she was dressed in black, but it was a tailored suit, not the ripped jeans and band t-shirt she'd been wearing in James's photo. Next to it was a framed photo of Jane and Caddick, from the time Caddick was first running for PM. Icho hit the frame, knocking it flat, and went over to the dresser. She sat down and looked in the mirror, running her hands through her thin, straight hair, irritated by its lightness as it fell back into place. She aggressively shoved it behind both ears and examined her thin face, tracing her fingers across the absence of scar tissue, missing the silver glint.

She stood up, stripped until she was naked, and walked over to the full-length mirror. She stared at herself, trying to appreciate what she saw, trying to feel that it was her. Her shoulders slumped and angry tears welled up.

"You could ask Jane for a different body," said the Inex.

Icho shook her head, wiping away the tears. She ran her fingers through her hair again, her face crinkling in disgust. "Will it grow back if I cut it?"

"You can choose for it not to."

"Is that right?"

Her Inex confirmed, and she told it to summon the Ino. She sat cross-legged on the floor in front of the mirror and watched the Ino shave off her hair. When it finished, she ran her hand over her head. "It won't grow back?"

"Not if you don't want it to."

"What do I have to do?"

"Just not want it."

"That's all? I just think it?"

"Your body will obey your command."

"I can command my body?"

"Within reason."

"And who decides what's within reason?"

"Your designers and manufacturers."

Icho gave a wry smile and stared at her reflection. "I'm a product."

She got to her feet and pinched the skin on her stomach.

"Can I command my body to shed skin?"

"Skin can be removed for repairs, but that's a medical procedure. You're not in need of repairs."

"Can I command my body not to feel pain?"

"You can dial down pain in an emergency situation."

"I just need to think it?"

"That's right, but–"

Icho hit the mirror with the side of her fist, cracking it. She smiled as her Inex said, "I advise against that."

She walked over to Jane's trophy shelf and picked one up, feeling its heft as she gripped it.

"I advise–"

She walked back and slammed it into the mirror, the top half shattering, the rest a mess of fine lines. She sank to her knees, discarding the award.

"I advise against what you're planning."

"Be quiet."

She picked up a shard of glass and held it tight, blood surfacing on her palm, dripping between her fingers. She pressed it against her skin and cut a large crescent across her stomach, blood weaving down her thighs and between her legs. She dropped the shard and pushed her fingers into the wound, prying the skin and muscle away. Her fingers came up against a smooth surface. She slipped her hand in, following the contour of the surface below. She pressed on it. It gave way a fraction, but was impermeable, no way to get in deeper. She looked up and saw herself in the bottom half of the mirror. She contemplated the shape of her hand beneath her skin. She wriggled her fingers, watching her skin move in the reflection, watching the blood drip out of the wound, down her arm, and onto the shattered glass around her. There was a slurping noise as she pulled her hand out. She stared at it, commanding her body to feel pain, heaving in a shocked breath, falling unconscious amongst the splintered glass.

Icho's Inex got the Ino to lift her onto the bed. It extracted small shards of glass from her body. The Ino wiped her down. It didn't need to administer first aid; her new body had its own disinfection and self-healing properties, the large wound across her stomach already sealing.

The Ino and Inex cleaned up the mess and the Ino ordered a new mirror. It was installed by the end of the afternoon.

Jane came home in the evening and walked into an empty sitting room. She put her bag on the floor and her jacket on the back of a chair, the Ino immediately behind her, picking them up. She poured herself a gin and went upstairs. On the way to her room, Jane's Inex ate insects that were on the floor and the wall next to the hall cupboard. It climbed up onto the ceiling, upside down, following Jane as it captured the insects that had crawled from the top of the cupboard door.

Walking into her room, she kicked off her shoes and jumped when she saw Icho in her bed. "Jesus. You scared me. What are you–" She paused, staring at her. "Your hair."

"Do you like it?"

Jane shrugged. "Sure. I–" She took a sip of her gin. "Why are you here?"

Icho smiled, pushing the covers aside. She was wearing Jane's lingerie: a black corset and hold-up stockings.

"What are you doing, Icho?"

"What does it look like?"

"I don't–"

"I'm seducing you, you idiot. Come here."

"But–"

"Come."

Icho got up on her knees on the edge of the bed and reached out to Jane, pulling her close and kissing her. Jane dropped her glass, spilling the gin across the covers. Her stiffness evaporated and she clasped Icho's hand, fingers entwined, her wound stinging at the pressure. She kissed Icho and fell down onto the bed with her.

"I've missed you so badly."

"I know."

"We don't think this is the right thing to do," said Icho's Inex.

"You don't want your happy ending?" said Jane, glancing at it.

"This isn't–"

"Shut up," said Icho sharply. "Go quiet." She smiled up at Jane and said, "Double connect."

as one we kissed
tongue pushing head pulled
devouringdevoured
fingers grasping
nothing
        fissure
        fractured
           rent

rendered ipseity. endless white on white. connected, locked in; severed, apart, opened up, peeled back –
      hellsans odium inscribed in skin
endless cankerous hell in skin. *stop.* malignancy folded in eternal torsion. *stop.* rotting, hematidrosis, every pore excreting sanies. *this isn't–* abhorrence, virulence, disgust, coming up, vomiting–

"Disconnect! *Disconnect!*"

She scrambled away from Icho, falling off the bed. Eyes wide, she crawled across the floor, lopsided as the pressure on her broken fingers caused her pain.

"What's wrong, Jane?"

Her body was wracked with convulsions, her mouth open as if screaming, emitting strained choking noises. She fell back, pressed against the wall and pulled her legs to her chest, hugging them. She sobbed, snot bubbling at her nostrils.

"Jane," said Icho, smiling and getting up off the bed.

Jane's head snapped up. She raised her hand. "Stop. Don't come near me."

Icho hesitated, half off the bed.

"Didn't you like feeling inside me?" she said, sitting back down.

Jane tried to steady her breathing and wiped at her face, smearing tears and snot across her arm.

"Jane…"

"How could you do that to me?"

Icho narrowed her eyes and smiled. "How," said Icho, "could you do this to me?"

Jane looked up at her. "What happened to you?"

"You happened to me."

Shaking, palm pressed against the wall, using it as support, Jane stood. She walked unsteadily into the bathroom, closing and locking the door. Her Inex turned on the shower and she crawled in.

When Jane walked back into the bedroom, a towel wrapped round her, Icho was perched on the side of the made bed, fully clothed. Jane went to the chest of drawers and pulled out underwear as the Ino placed trousers and a blouse on the bed for her. Jane looked at Icho's back as she dressed.

"What was that?"

"A gift."

"You tried to poison me – all those images of skin inscribed with HellSans, all the blood and pus. You wanted to push past the formula."

"Did I?" said Icho, turning round.

"No."

"Good. Then my work is solid," said Icho, looking disappointed.

"And the rest. That's how you feel?"

"There's a pain where my heart used to be – isn't that corny?" Icho smiled as she looked up at Jane, who pursed her lips and looked away. "And whenever I close my eyes, I feel as if blood is oozing from every pore. There's a rot inside me, Jane."

"That's nonsense."

"You still don't understand. Even now that you know what I feel."

"It's fixable," said Jane. Dressed, she came round the side of the bed and faced Icho. "I'll have a new body made for you. The right skin, the right proportions, your old hair."

"It's too late for that."

"Then what the hell do you want from me?"

Icho was silent. She looked sad and lost. "I don't know," she said. "I just know it's not this."

Jane felt a sudden disgust and was about to lash out, call her ungrateful, call her pathetic for wallowing in self-pity. Her Inex stymied her. *"She is suffering, Jane."*

"I know," said Jane aloud, sitting next to Icho.

"What do you know?"

She didn't respond and they sat there for a while, perched on the edge of the bed, not looking at each other, not speaking. Icho's hand was resting on her thigh and Jane was about to reach out to take it, but she stopped herself.

"I'm working on something," said Jane quietly. "I'm working on something for you. A gift."

"I don't want your gift. I don't want anything from you."

Jane flinched, her hurt immediately turning to anger, her Inex internally talking her down from a vituperative onslaught. She stood, ran her hands across her trousers as if dusting something off, and told Icho to get out. Without even a glance at Jane, Icho stood and left.

The next morning, after Jane had left for work, Icho walked through the apartment; laps of the dining room, the sitting room and kitchen, up the stairs and along the hallway. She eyed the hall cupboard, noticing the insects that teemed in the

gap beneath the door; the rolled up clothes that Jane must
have stuffed into the gap had been pushed aside by the weight
of them. Icho frowned at it as she automatically walked into
the guest bedroom, circled, and came back into the hallway.
Instead of continuing, she stood, watching her Inex eat flies
and maggots, stuffing itself full and still leaving a writhing feast
for later. Some had made it a few feet along the hallway, only
to be trampled on, their corpses drying out on the neglected
floor. A few flies buzzed overhead, eyed by the sated Inex.

Icho approached the cupboard and pressed a hand against
the door, as if she could feel life pulse within it, a heartbeat deep
in the wood. She slid her hand down and wrapped her fingers
round the handle. She stepped back, pushing the handle down
and pulling. She let out a shocked breath, quickly covering
her nose and mouth as the stench enveloped her and her Inex
disappeared beneath wriggling food it no longer wanted.

She stepped forward, her feet crunching on the maggots,
flies, and spiders. She squeezed her nostrils as she looked at
the slumped corpse. Most of the synthskin had fallen away
and was lying in a mouldering heap. The meat of it had been
eaten, leaving the synthetic skeleton, smeared in blood and
grime. Its eyes, made from materials of no interest to the
scavengers, were intact, oddly clean and bright amidst the
mess that was the rest of it. Icho peered down at a gaping
wound in the head, wondering if this was the death blow,
uncertain what would kill this creation, thinking how much
she didn't know about them, how little she knew about
herself. She looked closer and the eyes shifted suddenly, fixed
on her. She jumped back, slipping on the bugs beneath her
feet, falling into their panicking bodies. Icho lay there, feeling
them squeezing out from beneath her, scuttling over her skin,
seeking shelter and darkness. She stared up at what she'd
thought was a corpse. It stared back at her, its jaw moving,
trying to speak.

Icho stood, maggots tumbling from her. She walked into the

cupboard and took its hand, her other arm around its shoulder, pulling. She lifted it from its half-death and carried it down the hallway.

CHAPTER 15

Jane came home in the evening, buoyed by a successful day at The Company working on two major projects. Since taking her doppel's place, she'd spent most of her time down in the design and prototypes department with James, enjoying being hands on, appreciating the camaraderie.

She walked into the sitting room, smiling, taking her jacket off. Handing it to the Ino, she froze.

"I don't know," said Icho, staring at Jane as her expression turned to horror, "how I expect you to treat me well if this is how you treat yourself."

"What have you done?" said Jane, her hand over her open mouth.

"I've released her from hell."

"What have you–"

Jane's legs gave way, and she sank to the floor. "It was dead."

"I've learned more about myself in a day than I have from you since you brought me back," said Icho. "We can eat food like humans, but we can also operate like Inexes – digesting scraps, arachnids, insects. While the maggots fed off her, she fed off them. The Ino's upstairs now, cleaning up the mess."

"Put it back. You had no right. Put it back."

"Jane is staying right here."

"That's not its name."

"If she's not Jane then I'm not Icho."

Unsteady, Jane stood and circled round them, keeping her distance as she walked to the kitchen counter and brought out the gin. She poured herself a glass, staring over at Icho and the doppel. It was a smooth, glinting, silver skeleton, with unblinking human eyes, round, wide, unrelenting. Jane looked down at her drink.

"Her internal organs were all protected," said Icho, pressing on the impermeable casing covering all the lab-grown organs. As Icho lifted her finger, a small indent slowly disappeared as the surface righted itself.

"There are some gouges from where you stabbed her," said Icho, turning back to Jane. "At least, I assume that's what it is. We're sturdier than the human body. I'm surprised you managed to overcome her."

"I did it for you," said Jane, her voice shaking. She drank the gin and poured another. "That thing killed you. Yet you sit there, accusing me."

"She killed me and you're killing me."

Jane snorted. "What do you want, Icho? What do you want from me?"

"I'm going to rebuild her. She's my project. I'm going to learn how we work, and you'll give me everything I need."

"You're going to experiment on her?"

"It's better than being buried alive in that cupboard."

"But what does *she* want?"

"You care?" said Icho.

"Do you?"

Icho looked up at Jane. "I'm her saviour. She'll let me do whatever I please."

Jane flinched, gave a wry smile and drank more gin, nodding. She raised her glass in Icho's direction. "I'll give you what you want, Icho."

Jane tucked the gin bottle under her arm and walked upstairs.

Jane entered the dining room the next morning to find Icho

had laid the doppel out on the table, various tools spread out around her.

"You've been doing this all night?"

Icho nodded. "She cleaned up nicely. I managed to patch up her skull." Icho looked up at Jane. "After I cleaned out the dead flies."

"I thought you were going to take it apart."

"She's still alive," said Icho, looking disgusted, "and you want me to dissect her?"

"I don't want you to do anything to it."

The doppel's eyes swivelled to look at Jane and she sat down at the table, trying to get out of its range.

Icho stopped what she was doing and faced her. "I can command my body not to feel pain."

Jane nodded.

"I can tell it not to grow hair."

"It was for future models," said Jane. "None of the others have these capabilities; they'd stand out."

"I'm the first?"

"Unless it was." Jane nodded to the doppel.

"She can't move," said Icho.

"So?"

"I want to rebuild her, get her back to normal."

"Normal is unlikely," said Jane.

"Well maybe not mentally... that might take a bit of work."

"What do you mean?"

"I'm going to help her, offer her counsel. She was shut away in darkness, Jane, her flesh slowly being devoured. I don't think anyone comes out of that without some quirks."

"Why are you doing this, Icho? It's sick."

Icho laughed.

"You know it is," said Jane.

"You're really not one to be judging."

"I'm making you a new body."

Icho stared at Jane, about to say something, but stopped. She fiddled with the tool in her hand.

"I'm doing it properly this time."

Icho didn't respond and went back to repairing the doppel's leg.

"Well?" said Jane, exasperated. "Aren't you happy?"

"I already told you," said Icho, focussed on the doppel's leg, "I don't want a new body."

"But you–"

"It's too late," she said, her attention still on her work. "And I want out of our story."

"You want out?"

"I don't want to be connected to you," she said, turning to look at Jane.

Jane looked at the prone doppel, then over at the Inex display case, remembering when they'd returned from the ghetto. She had tapped the glass and said: "I'll take out its eyes and I'll put them in here. Right here." Instead, it was lying on the table. She thought how different things would be if they hadn't gone to James's, if they'd waited for it, if she'd killed it that day.

"You would still be alive, and I wouldn't be living this nightmare," she said quietly.

"What?"

"We'll need–" said Jane. "To exit the story, we both need to give consent."

"I consent," said Icho.

Jane didn't say anything. She watched Icho working on the doppel's leg. Icho looked up after a few minutes, raising her eyebrows. "Well?"

"Inex," said Jane, looking down at it. "I consent to Icho leaving the story." She looked back at Icho. "You now need to give your Inex permission to sever the connection."

"Inex," said Icho, returning her attention to the doppel's leg. "Sever it."

There was a short pause and her Inex confirmed it was done.

I sat for a few minutes, watching Icho as she worked. The Ino came through with my jacket and bag and I left for work.

When I arrived home that evening, Icho was waiting for me in the sitting room. I glanced into the dining room – no sign of the doppel.

"I need you to get me what I need to give her new muscles and skin."

I sighed, dumped my bag and jacket on the back of the couch and sat down opposite her. "It's a sick project, Icho. Give it up."

"You said you'd give me what I want."

"It's not that simple. You'd need to take it into the lab. It's not something you can do here."

Icho thought for a moment. "Then take her."

I stared at her. "You'd let me take it?"

Icho nodded.

"You'd trust me with it? I want rid of it, Icho."

She shrugged. "I don't have much choice, do I? I could threaten you, of course."

"With what?"

"Exposure, obviously."

Furious, I leaned forward. "Did it ever occur to you I might want rid of *you*? That I'm living a nightmare – you and your killer, every day I come home, you're here, polluting everything I try to do. I should throw you out in the street."

Icho cocked her head and smiled. "But you haven't done it. I'm still here."

"For now."

"You're not going to," said Icho.

"Don't be so sure."

"You love me."

I clasped my hands, looked down at them, then back up at Icho, whose smug smile evaporated as I held her gaze. "Your new body," I said. "It's ready."

We stared at each other, Icho blinking as if trying to get something out of her eye. I leaned back on the couch, spreading my arms across the back as I watched her.

"But it's not for me," she said. "Because I'm defective, not playing ball." She smiled, shaking her head. "Are you going to let her remember her death this time?" She leaned forward and said, "Are you going to tell her about me?"

"I don't know."

She nodded, rocking slightly. "We've been talking, you know. Jane and I. We've been talking. She told me he didn't change anything."

"It can talk?"

"Caddick didn't change a thing about you. It was all you."

I laughed. "That's bullshit, Icho, and you know it."

"She told me. Nothing was changed."

"How would it even know? And if it did, it could be fucking with you. It's crazy, anyway."

"You just can't bear to think that it was you all along. That you'd make those decisions."

"You're right," I said, standing, looking down on her. "I don't like to think it, because it's not true. I know what decisions I'd make."

I turned to walk away, but she stood, blocking my path. "You weren't living it. We think we know how we'd be, but the truth is always in the action."

"I don't have time for this, Icho."

"You murdered me. And you want to do it again."

"It wasn't me!" I grabbed Icho by the shoulders and pulled her close, my fingers digging into her skin. "It wasn't me," I said, my face inches from hers. "*It* killed you. Your new fucking best friend."

Icho laughed and I let go, pushing her away. She fell onto the chair and sat, slumped, laughing. I grabbed my jacket. I looked down at her, now quiet, staring at the HellSans poster.

She glanced at me. "Going out again?"

"You'll see," I said. "If it's action you want."

"What does that mean?"

"You'll see."

Icho looked at me, impassive, as I put my jacket on and picked up my bag.

"You have a visitor," my Inex said as I was about to leave.

"What?" I said. "Who?"

"Caddick."

I froze, stunned for a moment. I looked over at Icho, who sat up, eyes wide. "Nothing to do with me. I swear."

"Shit." There was a knock on the door and I jumped. I looked down the hall, feeling sick. "How did he get up here? That fucking door girl."

I laid down my bag and instructed my Inex to tell Caddick I'd be a moment. As I took my jacket off, I told Icho to get in the Ino cupboard next to the bookshelves.

"Seriously?"

"Now, Icho. You know what he'd do if he found you."

She stood, and as I ushered her into the cupboard I asked where the doppel was.

"Upstairs."

"Good. OK."

"Jane?"

"What?"

"Be careful."

I hesitated, thrown by her concern.

"Stay quiet," I said.

Icho nodded, looking distressed. I hovered, remembering how he'd tortured her. I went to comfort her but stopped as I thought of her mocking laugh from only a moment before. I closed the cupboard door.

I opened the door to find two of Caddick's men standing opposite, hands clasped in front of them, eyes straight ahead, staring at me, over me. I turned and saw Caddick leaning against the wall, his head tilted back, eyes closed.

"Daniel?"

He smiled, opened his eyes and rolled to face me, still leaning against the wall. He looked at me a moment before he said, "It's been a long day." His smile faded, his expression cold. His Inex crawled up his back and perched on his shoulder. They both stared at me.

"Then come in," I said, stepping confidently into the corridor, ignoring his men, gesturing for him to go before me. He didn't.

"My Jane," he said and placed his hands on either side of my face, pressing hard as he kissed me, pushing his tongue into my mouth. I forced myself to relax and I kissed him back, pretending he was someone else, pretending I was transferring all my tension into him, trying to think myself into being my doppel before it became a living corpse.

He pulled away and took my hand, his Inex scuttling ahead of him into my apartment. I followed, staring at his hand clasped around mine. When we reached the sitting room, I pulled myself free and said, "Sit. Relax. I'll get the wine," and I hurried over to the kitchen, feeling his eyes on my back. He had already thrown me off-kilter and I needed to get it together, stay in control. I reached up into the cupboard and took out the red wine.

"Your favourite," I said, turning back to him.

He wasn't sitting. He was studying my bookshelf, his fingers running across the books. He stopped on one, his finger pressed against it. As I took the wine glasses out of the cupboard, he said, "South-south-west, south..."

"South-east, east," I said, pouring the wine.

He looked over at me and smiled, nodding. "The fate of savages."

I joined him in the sitting room and handed him the glass. We clinked them and I said, "To a brave new world."

"It's already here."

He gulped down the wine as I sipped mine. "Thirsty?"

"So utterly–" he said and paused. "Thirsty and famished."

He was acting odd, even for him, and I hated this feeling – this feeling of being one step behind. Since the day Icho sent Jaw to Milligan, off-kilter bliss, lost bliss, being out of time, out of step with everything, was a constant. I was so tired of it.

"Drink up," he said, and I took a long drink, looking for courage somewhere, looking for steadied nerves.

"Your savages," I said. "They're not Seraphs, are they?"

He raised his eyebrows and nodded. "And how do you know that?"

"There's nothing angelic about them," I said, smiling.

"And this angel would know," he said, tipping his glass to me.

I tried not to cringe. "But I suppose it doesn't matter."

"No, it doesn't."

"It's all about the spectacle."

"Exactly that." He nodded, raising his glass.

We were both silent for a moment, contemplative. He looked up at me. "I missed you."

"I missed you too. I've just been so busy. And killing my– Her, the other Jane. That was… It threw me."

"I understand." He swirled the wine in his glass and said, "Jane, I know."

I tensed. "What?"

He looked at me for a few seconds, then stood up and walked over to me. His fingers fluttered over my cheek before he pushed them into my hair, pressing his hand against my head. I wanted to pull away, but I made myself relax and he put his other hand around my waist, pulling me closer. He leaned his forehead gently against mine and I felt his breath on my skin. I put my arms around him. I felt nauseous and realised my twenty-four hours were nearly up. He knows, I thought. And my skin is about to break open under his touch.

"You're not taking the pills," he said. "Are you?"

I was confused for a moment, not realising what he meant.

"Jane, Jane," he said, kissing my forehead.

My Inex said internally, *"The pills from your handler."*

Relieved, I confessed. "No. I'm not. How did you know?"

"I know my Jane. Always wanting to do things on her own terms."

I smiled, thinking, *you condescending sonofabitch*. He pulled away slightly and tipped my chin up, looking into my eyes.

"You need them. I know it's not the same as HellSans bliss, but it's enough, and it will help you adjust."

I laughed, awkwardly pulled myself out of his embrace, and walked over to the kitchen counter. I walked behind it and grasped the wine bottle.

"What's so funny?" he said, following me and standing at the opposite side of the counter.

"Just that I should have known," I said, pouring the wine. "I should have known you'd know. You know me so well."

I topped up his glass and I watched him drink it like it was water. "Steady."

"It's been a long day," he said. "And God, I've missed you."

He stared at me intently and I struggled not to look away. He held his glass out to me and I filled it again.

"Is that why you've been avoiding me?" he said. "Because you knew I'd know?"

"I just wanted to try it. To see how I'd get on."

"It's dangerous, Jane."

I nodded. "It was just for a few days. To see. Don't be angry with me."

"Why would I be angry with you?" He turned away from me, walking back into the sitting room. He sat on the couch, sinking into it, spreading out, loosening his tie. He looked up at me and I suddenly felt woozy from the wine and the nausea of HSA. I kept my eyes off all the HellSans slogans across the sitting room, wishing I hadn't been so stubborn, wishing I'd removed them. Caddick raised his hand, gesturing at me to join him and I sidled round from behind the counter, thinking of all I'd been through, telling myself I could handle Caddick. I was about to sit next to him when he grabbed my wrist and pulled me on to his lap, the wine sloshing.

"Be careful!"

He took my glass and poured the wine across my chest, dropping the glass and licking my skin, burrowing into me.

"Daniel."

He looked up at me and pulled me down, kissing me, and I thought of reaching for that glass, smashing it, and stabbing the stem into his neck. I felt nauseous and thought of holding his head tight and vomiting on his face.

I pulled out of the kiss and looked up to see Icho, the cupboard door open a crack – one eye, watching us. I stared at that eye before turning back to Caddick and pushing him away.

"Stop," I said, pulling, freeing my limbs and half-falling onto the floor, trying not to put any pressure on my still-healing fingers. I scrambled up and stood there, looking down at him.

"What is it? What's wrong?"

"The pills," I said. "You're right. I need them. I'm off-kilter without them."

"OK," he said, running his hand through his hair. "OK, well, make sure you take them." His voice was hard now. "Do what your handler says."

"You know I don't like being told what to do," I said, suddenly combative.

He looked up at me. "If that wasn't part of what I loved about you, I would have changed that too."

I was stunned for a moment, unsure what to do or say. I wiped at the wine, sticky across my chest.

"You changed something?"

He smiled. "I ironed out the queer kinks."

He kept his eyes on me, waiting for a reaction. I eyed the Inex ornament that I'd used to bash my own head in.

"If you love someone," I said, feeling truly nauseous now, "you don't change them." As I said it, I glanced up at the cupboard, but the eye was gone, the door closed.

He laughed. "I'm fucking with you," he said, his laugh turning to a snigger.

"You're drunk."

"Maybe."

"I'm going for a shower," I said, still pawing at the wine on my chest and clothes. "You've ruined my blouse."

"You're not going anywhere," he said, sniggering again. I'd always hated the way he laughed, and I screwed my nose up in disgust. "Actually," he said, "You *are* going somewhere."

I heard the front door open and footsteps in the hall. Caddick's men appeared.

"What do you–?"

"Sir?" one of them said.

Caddick nodded. "Go on." He gestured at me, flippant.

They approached me and I backed away, but the wine had slowed me down and my stomach churned.

"Dan," I said, panicked as they each took me by an arm. "What are you doing? I'll take the pills, if that's all you want, I don't–"

They dragged me down the hall and I twisted my head, trying to look back, catching a glimpse of him, his head tilted, resting on the back of the couch. He was relaxed, like he didn't have a care in the world.

"Daniel!" I writhed, furious, twisting and pulling. "Caddick, you goddamn sonofabitch!" I yelled and I saw him lean forward and laugh, reaching for his wine glass.

CHAPTER 16

I woke, opening my eyes to a pure white ceiling burning bright in the harsh light. I scrunched my eyes closed and stretched. Everything hurt.

"You're sick, you know that?"

I opened my eyes again. I stared at the ceiling for a moment and slowly sat up. Caddick was sitting watching me, his elbows resting on his legs, his hands clasped. There was a clear screen between us; I could just see the outline of a door.

"I found it, Jane. I saw what you did to yourself."

I swung my legs onto the floor and sat on the edge of the camp bed. I was in a white cubicle with a white bedside table, small white cabinet, a toilet and sink. There was a large brown stain on the floor in front of me. I was in the HSA quarters of Icho's old lab.

"That's some Grade A psychopathic behaviour," he said. "Keeping it like that."

"It wasn't–" I stopped, realising I didn't owe him an explanation. I was thirsty, my voice hoarse. I stared down at my hands; the engagement ring was gone.

"It wasn't what?"

I cleared my throat but didn't respond. *"Inex,"* I said internally. I could feel it but couldn't see it.

"I'm here. They took me away from you."

I was relieved it was close. It was comforting to be able to talk to it.

"Are you OK?"

"I'm not damaged," it said.

"I've got someone here to see you, Jane," said Caddick, and I looked up, praying he hadn't found Icho.

He smiled at me and clicked his fingers. A moment later Dalton appeared, the inside man, Milligan's supposed friend. He was dragging a skinny, grimy boy. I stared at him, trying to work out if he was familiar. I looked back to Caddick, waiting, glad it was just some kid I didn't know.

"Jane," said Caddick. "Do you know who this is?"

I shook my head.

Caddick smiled. "This is your killer."

I didn't react. If Icho was safe, I didn't care what game Caddick was playing. I was bone-tired and sick of it all.

"This boy," said Caddick, "was given the task to execute you in the ghetto."

I looked at the boy.

"Block 366, bunk 89," said the twitchy kid. "A bullet to the chest and head, I did what you asked."

It sounded like something he'd recited over and over.

"He failed," said Caddick. "And he's been my guest since I found that out."

The kid was looking at the floor and wringing his hands, saying something under his breath.

"This was your target, boy." Caddick pointed at me.

The kid looked at me and nodded vigorously. "I'll do it, I'll do it. Just give me a chance, I'll do it."

Caddick took a gun from his jacket pocket and handed it to the kid, who grinned, fingering the gun. I looked down at the brown stain and imagined my brain splattered on the white wall. I heard the door click open, heard the kid come in, the stench of him enveloping me. I thought of overpowering him, thought of taking that gun and smashing it into his corpse-thin face, then I heard a click. I looked up at the kid who was looking at the gun, confused. He pointed it at my head again – click, click, click, bang! He was down and I sat there, shaking, tasting his stench, tasting the metal of his blood, grasping at myself, pulling his meat out of my hair.

I heard Caddick laughing and watched Dalton pull the kid by the legs, dragging him from the cubicle.

"Leave him," said Caddick.

"Sir?"

"Just leave it."

Dalton dropped the boy and walked out, the door sliding closed behind him. My breathing was heavy, but I wasn't going into HSA meltdown.

"Well now," said Caddick, standing. "I have a busy day ahead–"

"It's not me," I said, still shaking, wiping blood from eye.

"What was that?"

"That thing you made – it wasn't me. It isn't. I wouldn't be OK with what you've been doing to me – how did you convince it? What did you change in it?"

"Jane, you don't understand yourself. You'd want to survive, wouldn't you? You're a threat to her. And you're HSA. You're scum."

I flinched. Even now, after everything, being called HSA still stung.

"But she's too far gone after what you did to her. I'll have a new one made."

"And me?"

"And you. You get to watch the Seraph execution. You get to watch my rally," he said, nodding to Dalton, who pulled my Inex out of a bag. He opened the door, letting it in. It crawled up the bunk and onto my shoulder and began cleaning bits of the kid off me.

"And then?" I said, watching the door slide closed.

"And then... And then the future will be here and all savages will be hanging from a rope."

He stared at me, smiling. He stood, straightened his suit jacket, and walked off down the corridor, Dalton following.

"I'll see you on the other side, Jane," he said as he disappeared.

They were immediately replaced by two guards; Caddick wasn't making the mistake he made with Icho. But there was no mistake to make – my Inex didn't have access, I couldn't eye scan. It was possible I could have hacked it, but the thought exhausted me.

"I just need to sleep," I said, batting the fussing Inex off my shoulder. I lay down, closing my eyes.

I woke up to a hammering noise and looked over – one of the guards was banging on the cell screen. He opened the door.

"Wake up," he said. "Caddick wants you to watch it."

I nodded and he closed the door as I asked my Inex to project the rally. I sat up and watched as the white wall opposite opened up into an auditorium. There was a podium, where Caddick would be giving his speech, and nearby were eight nooses hanging in a row. There was the low rumble of people talking as they entered the auditorium and found their seats. It went on like this for several minutes, giving me time to wake up. I went to the sink and ran the water, cupping it in my hands and drinking, tasting the kid's blood that had dried on my lips. I splashed my face, watching the pink water swirl in the sink. There wasn't a towel, so I wiped my face on the blanket.

I sat and watched the projection, the auditorium suddenly quiet, then I saw why: the supposed Seraphs were being led onto the stage. There were a few jeers, then the whole place was a cacophony as each HSA walked across the stage, and I saw that one of them was Icho. He'd found her.

I was surprised at his restraint, that he hadn't taunted me about it. He must have expected this to shock me more, but it didn't. She didn't need to breathe. Of course, her neck could snap, but that wouldn't kill her either – this was all for show, public humiliation. No doubt his plan was to kill her later, but none of that mattered. I stared at her as she walked, expressionless. It was then, as I turned my attention to the others, that I realised the last one was James. My stomach lurched when I saw him. He simply stared into the distance. The HSAs next to him had the same blank expressions, but the one next to Icho, a teenage boy, was shaking and crying, likely going into HSA meltdown. I felt sick as I watched James take his place next to a noose. I stared at them, Icho and James both calm, and felt myself start to shake, coping as well as the boy.

I glanced at the clock in the corner of the projection and smiled, pleased at the timing. I started counting down as I thought in **neon, underlined, bold HellSans**, threw up, and fell face first into my own vomit. I spoke to my Inex internally, cutting off the projection and playing it in my head where I could watch it all unfold. I heard the guards come in, swearing, arguing about what to do, worrying I was choking on my own sick, one of them saying they could just let me die, the other reminding them Caddick would give them hell. I wondered for a moment what Caddick had in store for me as he took his place at the podium amidst clapping and cheers. I smiled as he smiled. One of the guards finally picked me up off the floor and took me over to the camp bed.

"Ugh, God, her skin just came away in my hand."

"Is she breathing?"

She is.

All I could think about was my timing, hoping I'd got it right, but if they injected me, I could always delay, pretend the formula hadn't worked yet, hope that they wouldn't lock the door on me. I watched Caddick, the smug bastard, giving his speech, playing the Good Guy as he stood next to a goddamn gallows.

"Get that stuff from the lab – Caddick said to inject her with it if anything went wrong."

"What does he want with this scum, anyway? It's disgusting."

"Just get it."

"Alright, alright." I heard taps running. "My hands are all vomit and blood."

My teeth were chattering, and I felt cold all over. I started to worry I'd pushed things too far, that the goons would take too long, that I wouldn't be coming back from this attack. I pushed the typeface from my head, but still watching the events in the auditorium meant I had to try to unsee the massive party poster in the background and the scrolling HS commentary. I chanted my seriffed mantra: "I'll get my life back, I'll bring down Caddick", and I went in and out, opening my eyes and focusing on the white of the ceiling, then back in again. It helped, kept me grounded. I could feel myself pulling out of it, turning any HS into a white ball of light. I focused on Caddick's smug face, tuning back into his words.

"We will not let terrorists destroy our way of life," he said, looking directly at the viewers, at me. "For the good of the country–" He abruptly stopped.

He collapsed.

In an instant, just like that, he fell, his head cracking against the podium.

It was like he'd been shot, but there was no noise, no wound. There was a collective intake of breath, followed by a loud shocked silence, before murmurs rippled through the audience.

I smiled, relieved; my hard work was paying off. I counted down to the next round of targeted deaths, *"Twenty, nineteen, eighteen…"* as I stared at his prone body, his head bloody from the podium.

"C'mon!" I heard the guard say as the other walked in.

"I'm coming. Here, take it."

"About fucking–"

There was silence for a moment, then: "Shit. Caddick's down."

"What?"

"Not just Caddick – the whole party. Are you getting this?"

"Three, two–"

"No, I–"

"One," I said aloud, and I heard them both collapse.

Perfect timing. I opened my eyes. I stared at their Inexes, the silent assassins, as they went into shutdown. On my knees, still shaking, I picked up the formula, but it had broken when the guard had fallen, the liquid leaking out.

"Shit," I said, shivering.

I focused on the white light, feeling it calm me, and I took one of the guard's jackets, slinging it over my shoulders.

"There might be more," said the Inex. "I'll look."

"No, wait. Project first."

"You nee–"

"Project. I need to see Icho and James. I need to know they're safe."

The auditorium was back on the wall. There was panic, as expected; people yelling and running. James and a couple of the calm deviants were helping the teen boy, supporting him. Icho was staring at Caddick's body, and I knew she understood. She'd finally received my gift, recognising it for what it was. She turned away from Caddick and talked briefly to James and the HSAs before leading them away.

"OK," I said. "Let's go."

I followed the Inex into the lab. The drawer the guard had hurriedly searched was lying open, but no formula. The Inex did a scan of the room.

"There's no more," it said.

"It's OK." I was shaking, feeling nauseous. "I'm OK… I can handle this," I said, concentrating on my breathing. "Show me the news before we leave."

The Inex projected the news on the lab wall. The presenter, the one we'd replaced, who'd had the existential crisis, she said, "There's horrifying scenes at Caddick's rally today – all members of The Party have been assassinated. This is the largest coordinated Seraph attack this country has ever seen. Our nation, our bliss, is under siege."

Scrolling across the footage of Seraphs and other deviants destroying the typeface, it said:

"BREAKING NEWS: Seraphs across the country are eradicating HellSans."

"Not just Seraphs." I turned to my Inex and said, "Are we connected?"

"We are we," said the Inex and I felt it, the connection to all the Ichos and Janes I had made, spread out across the country, leading the Seraphs. I saw one of the Ichos on the news – in her own body, her own skin. I saw her and felt her. I was her, she was me.

We are we.

All Ichos sang "Flytipping" as we hit the cities and towns, hacking the back-ups, erasing all the data, burning the back-up facilities to the ground, smashing the digital HellSans advertisements, tearing down the retro hoardings, spraypainting serifs on the HellSans emblazoned across all cars, shops, warehouses. Janes and Ichos led Seraphs into The Company headquarters where we destroyed our office. Jason watched us, his boss turned multiple, as we set fire to our posters, enjoying the heat as **"WE'RE IN THIS TOGETHER"** and "*WORK MAKES YOU FREE*" shrivelled up and turned in on themselves. We danced in the flames, breathed in the smoke. We pressed our hands into the warm ash and smeared it across our cheeks.

We walked up out of Icho's lab, still shaking, vomiting, coughing up bile – the last of it – and we headed south-east, walking to the unblissed city.

// THE END //

ACKNOWLEDGMENTS

A salute in thanks for the soundtrack:
Suede: Night Thoughts, The Blue Hour.
Pearl Jam: Ten, Vs, Vitalogy, Backspacer, Gigaton.
Noah Hawley and Jeff Russo: "Behind Blue Eyes".

Thanks to:
Cinn, Belle, and Elvis the spider; my world.

Jenni Fagan, Ali Millar, David Evans, Mariana Enríquez, Maria Schurr, Rachael Forbes, Carolann Alexander, Kristi Long, Peikko Pitkänen, and Megan Chapman for friendship, book, film, art, and music chat.

Zoom Movie Club (Cinn, Kat & Iain Husbands, Kathryn Gordon) for getting me through lockdown and beyond.

Julie Farrell for being a supportive access buddy and more.

Mum and dad for flowers and courtyard chats.

Simon Spanton ("there's an awful lot of vomit") and Jenny Brown ("there's still an awful lot of vomit") for editing advice. Any faults (and excess vomit) that remain are my own.

Simon for bringing me into the Angry Robot fold. All Angry Robot staff for their hard work and support, and for believing in this bloody, vommy novel. Special shoutout to the illustrious Caroline Lambe. Thanks to Kate Cromwell for the striking cover.

Mat Osman for feedback, encouragement, and getting me through a miserable lockdown January with a draft of the stunning The Ghost Theatre.

Sarah Crowe for assisting with self-surveillance.

Josie Giles for kindly helping a stranger.

Creative Scotland for much-needed funding when I fell through one of capitalism's numerous cracks (and the lit team for their invaluable support: Kaite Welsh, Jenny Niven, Alan Bett, Viccy Adams, Rebecca Leary).

Agents of S.H.I.E.L.D. writers and Brett Dalton for Grant Ward.

Spit, bile, and vomit to the Tories.

A salute to all Queer Crips for their tenacity and for existing. Stay deviant, creatures.

We are Angry Robot

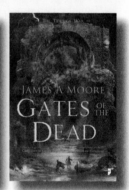

angryrobotbooks.com

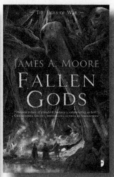

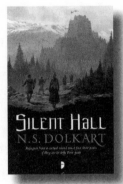
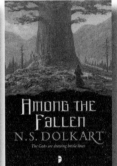
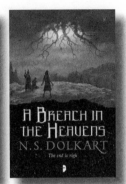